Times are changing: railways are being built across the land, bringing new freedom and possibilities. Jessie tastes that freedom when she meets an ambitious young navvy, newly arrived in Yorkshire. The attraction between them is overwhelming. And Jared Wilde is determined to make Jessie his wife.

The primitive, colourful shanty towns that spring up around the railway works are nothing like the safe world Jessie once knew. But in spite of the hardness of life there, she find happiness was Jared. Until another navvy becomes determined to destroy their future together . . .

Jessie

Anna Jacobs

CORONET BOOKS
Hodder & Stoughton

First published in Great Britain in 1998 by Hodder and Stoughton
First published in paperback in 2000 by Hodder and Stoughton
A division of Hodder Headline

A Coronet Paperback

8

A CIP catalogue record for this title is available
from the British Library

ISBN 978 0 340 69299 8

Printed and bound by CPI Group
(UK) Ltd, Croydon, CR0 4YY

Hodder and Stoughton
A division of Hodder Headline
338 Euston Road
London NW1 3BH

To Janet Woods
Only fellow writers and good friends understand
this addiction called writing – and you're both of those!

CONTACTING ANNA JACOBS

Anna is always delighted to hear from readers and can be contacted:

BY MAIL

PO Box 628
Mandurah
Western Australia 6210

If you'd like a reply, please enclose a self-addressed envelope – stamped from inside Australia or with an international reply coupon from outside Australia.

VIA THE INTERNET

Anna Jacobs now has her own web domain, with details of her books and excerpts to read. She'd love to have you visit at http://www.annajacobs.com

She can also be contacted by e-mail on
anna@annajacobs.com

If you'd like to receive e-mail news about Anna and her books (once every few weeks only) you are cordially invited to join her announcements list. Your e-mail address will not be passed on to any-one. E-mail Anna and ask to be put on the list, or there is a link from her web page.

Prologue

❦

South Yorkshire: 1817–18

'*A*gnes Helliwell, I would never, ever have thought it of you!' the housekeeper raged, glaring at her head maidservant. She was so disappointed, she could barely prevent herself from shaking the younger woman. But that wouldn't help now.

Tears were flowing down Agnes's face. She was bitterly ashamed of her condition and had lain awake night after night worrying, fretting, weeping, wondering how to tell Frank. And now the housekeeper had heard her being sick in the mornings and had guessed. Her cheeks flamed and she could not meet Mrs Prudhom's eyes.

'Who is the father, Agnes?'

The word came out as a whisper. 'Frank.'

'*Our Frank?* The new footman?'

Agnes could only nod.

Martha Prudhom's lips tightened. She had told Squire Butterfield that she didn't trust Frank Burton, but he hadn't listened to her. He always believed the best of people. And the mistress was too ill to concern herself with such things. Not long to live, if the housekeeper was any judge, and then the two little girls would be without a mother and the kind, but impractical squire without a wife. She looked at the maid and sighed again. It was no use going on at the girl now. You couldn't mend a broken egg. 'Is he going to marry you?'

'I – he doesn't know yet.'

There was silence. Then: 'Well, we had better tell him, had we not?'

Agnes could not stop the tears. She didn't want to see Frank's love change to hatred. Men resented being trapped into marriage. Everyone knew that. She was not the sort of woman to weep easily, but lately she had cried at the slightest provocation. Seeing the housekeeper waiting for an answer, she confessed breathlessly, 'I c-can't do it.'

Be practical, Martha told herself. It was all she could do now to help the maid who had been with them since she was twelve; the lass she had thought the world of, who could turn her hand to anything: helping Cook or serving tea to the mistress and her friends. 'Then I'll do it for you. Go and sit in the still room and do not come out until I send for you.'

But in the end it was the master who told Frank, for Martha had grave doubts about whether the fellow would stand by Agnes. And she was proved right, too, for the master had to force him to do his duty.

While this was going on, Agnes sat in the still room, tears drying on her face, dreaming of Frank Burton. He was the most handsome man she had ever seen: tall, with chestnut hair and bright green eyes that twinkled at you on the slightest provocation. And so charming! He could persuade a fish to fly, Frank could. Or a sensible woman of one and twenty to lose her head and heart, not to mention her virginity.

When he'd come to work at Butterfield Priory last year, he had singled out Agnes for attention – well, she knew she was quite pretty but it had never seemed to matter until now – and, oh! he made her feel like a queen sometimes. No one else had ever made her feel like that.

She jerked to her feet as the housekeeper came in, her heart thudding in her chest, her eyes searching Mrs Prudhom's face.

'Well, it's all arranged, you foolish girl. Frank will marry you as soon as it can be arranged. The master has decided that you may stay on here until the wedding – though there must be no more carrying on in this house, thank you very much. The first banns can be called on Sunday. But after you're married, you'll both have to leave, find yourselves a cottage in the village and other work.'

Martha would have kept Frank on and let Agnes work at a day rate for a while longer, but the squire had told the mistress what had happened and *she* was insisting they both leave. And he could deny her nothing. Patience Butterfield had a narrow view of her Christian duty and had given poor Charles little joy in the marriage, but he was a loyal soul.

Agnes sighed in relief. 'Thank you, Mrs Prudhom. I'm that grateful to you.'

Frank was less grateful to his employer and seriously contemplated running away rather than getting wed, something he had carefully avoided until now. 'The old cow,' he grumbled, as he and Agnes sat outside on a bench, strictly supervised by Mrs Prudhom who kept peering out of the window. 'She might have let you work till it started showing, at least. We're going to be damned short of money, even with what you've got saved.'

Agnes shivered. She knew about being short of money. When her father and younger brother died of a fever, the family had gone hungry for months. She had felt so lucky to be taken on at the big house. Her ailing mother and her new baby sister had been sent into the poor house, and she had never seen them again. Mrs Prudhom said her mother had simply faded away and died, and that her sister had been 'found a good home'. But although Agnes had begged to be told where Mary was, the Poor Law Guardians had refused and nothing more had been heard of her little sister since. Better that way, the parson had said firmly, and Mrs Butterfield, who had been very much in charge of household matters before she fell ill, had told the young Agnes to stop being a nuisance or she would be sent to the poor house herself.

She shook off the sad memories and slipped her arm through Frank's. 'What are we going to do, love? How are we going to live?'

He shrugged. 'Damned if I know.' But he eyed her with approval. There would be compensations to being married, at least. He would enjoy having a warm female body that was his whenever he wanted it, without all that coaxing and fussing around. And it would be good to have a son.

Agnes swallowed. She had expected more of him. But when

he turned the full warmth of his smile upon her, her anger was forgotten, as always.

'We'll work something out. And then,' he winked at her, 'we'll be able to have a bit of fun whenever we want. No sneaking into linen rooms or haylofts.'

She couldn't think why she felt so disappointed in his response.

In the end, with time ticking past all too quickly and no job or cottage found, she took her worries to the housekeeper and Martha Prudhom consulted the squire again. The outcome was that a tumbledown cottage on the edge of the estate was repaired and a few simple pieces of furniture provided. 'Though if it had been up to me, that lazy young rascal would have got nothing,' Charles Butterfield grumbled to the housekeeper. 'And don't you say a word of this to my wife.'

'No, sir. Of course not. But Agnes has been a good worker until now, exceptional in fact. She's earned a bit of help from us.'

Later, Martha Prudhom had a word with the innkeeper's wife, which resulted in the former footman being taken on to serve in the bar. Not that Frank was grateful for that, either, and what Agnes had ever seen in him, the housekeeper could not understand. There was trouble ahead for that poor lass, no doubt about it. Leopards didn't change their spots just for a few words spoken in church.

Frank and Agnes were married in the village church, with Martha Prudhom and Bill, the other footman, standing as witnesses. For a few weeks things went well enough. Agnes had enough money saved to tide them over and they could purchase the rest of what they needed gradually. Frank had nothing saved, which puzzled her a bit, but he got huffy when she asked him what had happened to his wages and said it was coming to a poor pass if a man couldn't help his family, so she let the matter drop. But she was a bit mystified about the family bit, because he'd said there was no one he wanted to tell about his marriage, no one he was close to, and that he'd never got on with his dad anyway.

When they went home to the cottage after the wedding, Frank looked round and pulled a face. 'It isn't very comfortable, is it?'

4

'It's ours and it's clean, at least. You can take the chair. I'm happy with a stool.'

He didn't sit down, just winked at her. 'Nothin' to stop us enjoyin' ourselves now, is there?'

She was startled. 'In the daytime?'

'Any time.' He pulled her to him and started fumbling with her skirt.

It was over so quickly that she felt like weeping. Maybe it was her condition, but it had never been so – so unsatisfactory before. She turned to Frank and found him asleep, a smile on his face. She lay back and tried to relax, but it felt wrong to be in bed while it was still light, so she got up and went outside to dig the garden. It would soon be time to put in a few things and the gardener had promised her some seeds and cuttings.

For the next few weeks, Frank was insatiable and enjoyed their nightly encounters enormously – far more than Agnes did, though it had been exciting before. 'There are some compensations for bein' married,' he said once or twice. But he didn't tell her he loved her. He hadn't said it once since the wedding. He also enjoyed her cooking and proved to have a huge appetite for food, but he didn't thank her for preparing the meals, either.

She found some casual work scrubbing and doing rough cleaning. She would stand cradling her belly sometimes and wonder that a child could change your life so greatly. She dreamed of having a daughter and felt quite sure it would be a girl. Mary, she'd call her, after the lost sister. A nice simple name. She'd always liked it.

The first time Frank gambled away his wages with some friends who drank at the inn, Agnes could not believe her ears. He came home late and confessed his sin at once, so contrite that she forgave him. But she went hungry that week for the first time since she was a child and wept over the lost money when she was alone. They hadn't managed to buy anything else for the cottage since they got married, either, for somehow the money was spent every week. And it was precious little anyway. It didn't even occur to her at first that he was keeping some back for himself.

Frank didn't go hungry, of course, because Mrs Varley at the inn had grown rather fond of him and slipped him the odd leftover from the kitchens. In fact, Frank was putting on weight, while his wife was losing it, except round the belly. He didn't like her swelling body at all and had made tears come into her eyes once or twice by comparing her to a cow in calf.

One evening of that hungry week, he brought home some stale bread and Agnes fell on it with such ravenous hunger that she was ashamed afterwards, for she had eaten it like a wild animal, cramming it into her mouth and gulping it down, while he watched her and chuckled.

She was to be ashamed about many other things before her child was born.

As the months passed, Agnes could not help growing bitter that she had fallen so low. This led to quarrels, for Frank now didn't hide the fact that he kept back part of his earnings, or that he wasted the money on ale and other frivolities.

But it was when she found out he was seeing another woman that Agnes truly tasted the dregs of hopelessness. She wept herself to sleep, then refused to weep again, growing stony-faced and no longer stopping to chat to other women in the tiny village.

'Eh, marriage don't suit her,' they said to one another. 'She's got all gaunt an' pursy-mouthed.'

'Poor lass. Things'll get worse before they get better, with that drunken fool to husband.'

'If they ever do get better,' another sighed. Frank was leading their own husbands astray as well, and the married women of the village no longer considered him charming.

Agnes's child was born on a Sunday morning in September, with the church bells pealing out across the meadows and the autumn sun shining down upon the little cottage. Frank came into the loft bedroom afterwards to look at his daughter. While Agnes was marvelling at the tiny hands and feet, and thinking how pretty the baby was, he just stared down and frowned.

'I'd hoped for a boy.'

'Oh, but she's lovely. And I wanted a girl.'

'You women always do.'

She bent her head and kissed the child to hide her tears.

'We'll call her Jessica,' he decided. 'It's always been my favourite name.'

'We'll call her Mary. Jessica's too fancy for such as us. She's the child of servants not the gentry.'

He leaned over the bed and poked his face almost into hers. 'If we don't call her Jessica, I'm off. And then she'll be nobody's child.'

She stared up at him, suddenly vulnerable. 'What do you mean, off?'

'I'll leave.' He gestured round, scornful and scowling. 'Think this is any sort of life for a fellow like me, what's been a footman in big houses in London?'

'You should have stayed there, then.'

'Aye, I should that.'

'You were the one who courted me,' Agnes whispered through dry lips. 'Persuaded me. I'd never even done it before. It's your fault as much as mine.' More, if truth be told.

'To my regret.' Frank glared down at her. 'The least you can do, now you've trapped me, is to let me give the child a name I favour.'

She closed her eyes and let the tears trickle out of them without making any attempt to wipe them away. 'Jessica Mary, then.'

'Good. But we'll call her Jessica.'

Only when the door had slammed behind him, did she open her eyes and stare down at the child breathing softly and peacefully beside her. 'I shall not have any other children,' she told her daughter, 'and I'll see that you do better than me in life, that you don't waste yourself on a fine face with nothing behind it! You might have a,' her voice faltered as she remembered Frank's cruel words, 'a *nobody* for a father, but you'll have a mother who loves you and I'll find some way to look after you properly.'

But that promise was to prove hard to keep. For the next few months, Agnes survived mainly on what she earned from her scrubbing or what she had grown in her little garden during the summer, potatoes and cabbages mostly. The gardener had showed her how to preserve them in mounds of earth. He gave her vegetables, too, from time to time, the mis-shaped and half-rotten ones, and she was glad of them.

Jessie, as the child soon grew to be called, since her father had now totally lost interest in her, was a good baby, content to lie in her wicker cradle while her mother worked. But what Agnes was going to do as the child got older and started toddling around, she didn't know. In fact, thoughts of the future filled her with blind terror, though she hid that behind a stony expression.

When the squire's wife died, just after Christmas, the villagers were treated to a good meal of bread and ham and cheese in her memory. But the unaccustomed rich food made Agnes vomit and then she wept bitter tears to think that she had wasted it all. She should have slipped some into her apron pocket for later and just taken a bite or two.

Frank did not get home until late and by then she had pulled the ladder up into the loft with her and the baby. 'You're not coming into my bed,' she shouted down at him. 'We can't feed this child properly, let alone another.'

'I've got rights!' he roared, swaying on his feet. 'I'm your husband.'

'An' you'll have to claim them by force,' she retorted. 'I'm not bringing another child into the world when you're such a bad provider.'

He snorted and turned to the makeshift mattress on the floor of the downstairs room. 'Well, who wants to bed a broom pole like you? You 'aven't got a curve to your name since you had that child.'

'It's for lack of food that I've grown thin.' Her former hearty appetite had vanished, thank goodness, and she could manage on very little nowadays. 'Because *you* drink up all the money you earn!'

A gentle snore showed her yet again how little he cared.

One cold February night, Frank didn't come home at all. Agnes was not surprised that he was late, but as the hours passed, she began to worry. He'd never stayed out all night before. He'd got another woman somewhere, she knew he had, for he had stopped pestering her. And anyway, she had smelled the slut on his skin: sweat and lavender and a sort of mustiness. But she wouldn't let herself care about that, for she wasn't going to let him touch her ever again. Not willingly, anyway. And if that meant his taking other women, so be it. At least her belly wouldn't swell again and she'd be able to take advantage of what scrubbing work there was.

In the morning, when two men carried Frank's semi-conscious body home, she could only stare at them in shock.

'Found him sleeping in t'ditch,' Tam Appleyard said. 'Funny sort of bed, that!'

His friend chortled. They had decided not to tell Mrs Burton which ditch, because it was certainly not on his way home from the village, but they both knew where old Frank had been that night, the randy old goat, because he'd been boasting of it before he left the inn.

Frank seemed only half-conscious and muttered something about being cold.

She got out the straw mattress she had just put away and thumped it on the floor in front of the fire. 'Lie him down, then,' she snapped, shaking out a blanket. 'He'll likely have taken a chill.'

When she was left alone with him, however, she frowned, for he was breathing stertorously.

'Cold,' he muttered. 'So c-cold.' But when she laid a hand on his forehead it was burning hot.

Those were the last coherent words he spoke to her. By evening, he was in a high fever and she had to send for the doctor. Then, when he came, she had to confess that she had no money to pay him with, which didn't encourage him to return.

The fever went straight to Frank's chest, which might be broad and manly but had always succumbed easily to colds and chills. In two days, he was gone. And Agnes could only sit by the bed and whisper, 'Thank goodness. Oh, thank goodness.' She hadn't wanted him dead, but it released her from a tie which she knew would have brought her even lower as time passed, for he was that sort of man.

Martha Prudhom was the only other person, apart from a couple of Frank's drinking cronies, to attend the brief pauper's funeral provided by the parish. Afterwards, the friends went off for a drink and the housekeeper lingered beside the grave, where

Agnes was staring with blind concentration at the earth being piled into it by the gravedigger.

'What are you going to do now, lass?'

Agnes blinked and turned round. 'I don't know, Mrs Prudhom. But I'm never, ever going to get married again, that's for sure.' She blinked and eased the baby into a more comfortable position against her shoulder. Eh, she had not meant to show her bitterness to anyone.

But Mrs Prudhom just nodded. 'Very wise.' She hesitated, then said, 'I may be able to help you.'

Agnes swallowed hard, but could not speak.

'Come inside the inn and we'll have a pot of mulled ale. It's freezing out here.'

'I'm not going in there, letting *her* serve me.' She knew that Mrs Varley had been one of Frank's conquests, for he'd boasted of it to her.

Martha looked at her. So the poor lass knew about that, then, and likely about the others. Well, Frank Burton had made little attempt to conceal his philanderings. 'We'll go back to your place, then.'

The two women walked through the small grey-stone village and stopped for a moment at the cottage gate.

'I haven't any money for rent. It won't be my cottage for long.' Agnes stared down at the child she was carrying. 'But I'm not going into the poor house. I'm not. I'd rather beg in the streets and sleep under hedges. My mother died in the poor house and they sent my sister away from me. I'm not losing Jessie. I might as well kill us both quickly now as let us die in there.'

'The squire won't throw you out of that cottage, you silly girl. You know he won't. So we'll have none of that sort of talk.'

But Agnes made no sign that she had even heard.

Inside, Martha Prudhom stared round in disbelief. The one room was clean - painfully, immaculately clean. But there was not a bite of food in the house, not one single bite. Nor anything to drink other than well water. 'I'll go and get some food from the house,' she said gruffly. She had not realised how bad things were, had been too engrossed in nursing her late mistress and then, after the inevitable happened, in comforting the squire and the two motherless girls. But why hadn't Agnes come to her for help?

When she returned with a well-filled basket, Agnes was sitting rocking the baby and just stared up at her visitor like someone who had lost her wits.

Martha had to make a cup of tea, put it into Agnes's hands and guide it to her mouth. She had to urge her young friend to eat some bread and butter. But as the warmth of the drink and the wonderful feeling of food in her belly got through to Agnes, she listened to what the housekeeper had to tell her with rapt attention.

'I've had a letter from a cousin of mine, who's been working for a parson in a village over beyond Leeds. She's getting married – at her age! – and wonders if I know anyone who could take her place. She thinks a lot of her employer. Says he's a gentleman in every way. I could write and suggest you, Agnes.'

There was no reply.

'Agnes?'

Her voice was toneless, hopeless. 'He won't want someone with a child. And I'm not leaving my Jessie with anyone else. She's all I've got.' She would never let Frank's taunt come true. Jessie wasn't nobody's child. She was Agnes's. And one day, she was going to make something of herself, unlike her mother.

'He might let you keep her. I could write and ask, if you're interested?'

For the first time, a trickle of hope ran through Agnes. 'I'd work my fingers to the bone for him if he did.'

'I know that, Agnes. You're the best worker I've ever seen.'

Agnes stared at her, then shook her head, as if she dared not even hope.

'Now, while we're waiting, you and that child need to eat, so you can come and help me clean out our attics. I've been meaning to do that for years. And now the mistress has gone, there'll be no one to complain of the noise. Five shillings a week and all meals found. Eh, lass, don't take on so.'

For Agnes was weeping, great gulping sobs of relief.

A week later, Martha puffed her way up to the third-floor attics.

'There you are, love.' She looked around in satisfaction. 'And making a good job of it, too, as I knew you would.'

The baby cooed from the drawer Agnes had sat her in, and waved the bone teething ring she had been chewing on.

Martha studied them both. A bonny baby, big for her age, with her father's hair. She looked at Agnes. Once, the girl had been well built and rosy, too. Now she was painfully thin. But she was still clean and so was the child. The housekeeper knew how much effort that took in a cottage where every drop of water had to be carried in from the well.

'Mr Marley has written to say that he is prepared to consider you,' she said, brandishing a piece of paper. 'I've given you a good recommendation and explained a little of the circumstances. He doesn't object to a child, so long as it's kept quiet. Jessie can share your bedroom and there's a dame school in the village which she can attend later.'

The room seemed to swoop and spin around Agnes and for the first time in her life, she slid to the floor in a faint.

'Men!' snorted the older woman, who had had her own disappointments in life. 'We'd be better off without them.' But then she thought of the squire and her fierce expression softened into a smile. Well, at least there was one man whom she could respect, a man who was gentle and kind, though he tried to hide it behind his outward bluster. She put a cushion under Agnes's head and patted her hand until she came to.

While all this was happening, the baby chewed placidly on the bone ring and mumbled to herself. She was a bright-eyed little thing, forward for her age, already sitting up well.

Later that day, as Agnes began to sort out her things and pack them in the wicker trunk Mrs Prudhom had given her, she smiled for the first time in months. Then she looked at her daughter and nodded. 'I'll make sure you do better than me in life. No man shall ever make you as unhappy as your father made me.'

Three days later, as the stage coach took her east towards Leeds, where she would be met by a gig and taken on to the village of Hettonby, Agnes stared out of the window and refused to be drawn into conversation with the other passengers. She was glad to be leaving all the shame behind her. I shan't go back to Mellersley, she decided. Never. Mrs Prudhom said I could spend my holidays at Butterfield Priory, but I won't do that. I don't want to be beholden to anyone ever again.

When she arrived at Hettonby, grim with determination to do so well that her new employer would keep her on, Parson Marley at first wondered if he had made a mistake in employing such a dour woman. Until he tasted her apple pie and her rich beef stew. Until he found his linen perfectly ironed, his house sparkling with cleanliness. Until he realised that she wasn't a gossipy sort of woman and would leave him in peace to get on with his studies and parish duties.

And the child was no trouble. A happy little thing, with an intelligent look in her eyes. Yes, all was right with John Marley's world.

All was right with Agnes Burton's world, too. And she would make very sure that it stayed all right this time.

1

Hettonby: 1825–29

*T*wo old women stood at the door of Granny Todd's cottage and watched the child go skipping across the green, on her own as usual and the last to leave the little dame school because she had been helping put the other children's knitting away.

'That Jessie Burton never seems to get as dirty as the rest,' the visitor commented.

The little girl's starched pinafore did indeed look relatively clean and fresh over her dark blue dress, even after a day's wear. But her russet hair tossed defiantly behind her like a banner in the wind, and her bonnet was swinging from one hand in a way that would have earned her a slap from her mother.

'Well, she may be a tidy little soul, but she's going to be a real handful, that one is!' Granny Todd nodded her head wisely.

'Jessie Burton? But she seems such a nice lass,' protested her neighbour.

'Nice, aye. Nice enough for anyone, she is. Clever, too. But obstinate with it. She'll go her own way in life. You can see it in her eyes. Those eyes'll never stay quietly at home in a cottage. Destined for a life of adventure, that child is, you mark my words!'

'Well, I never!' The neighbour stared down the lane with renewed interest. Granny Todd had taught generations of the poorer children from Hettonby their letters and she had an uncanny knack of predicting the future of her charges.

The parsonage lay at the narrow end of the green, next to the red-sandstone church built long ago by the Garthorpe family, who used to live in the old house beyond the village before it crumbled in on itself. The bones of the last Garthorpes were mouldering quietly away under a fretted stone monument at the side of the churchyard and the living of that same church now lay in the gift of Lord Morrisham, a latecomer to the nobility, whose father had first made a fortune in the India trade, then purchased himself a title. After that, he took up an option on some land near Great Sutton and built a huge mansion, which he passed on to his only son. This generation of Morrishams worshipped in the smaller and more modern church there, whose living was also in their gift, but Clarence Morrisham still liked to keep an eye on what was happening in the other two villages on his estate.

When Jessie got home from school, she went round to the back entrance of the parsonage and entered by the kitchen, where her mother gave her a glass of milk and a scone, and asked as usual, 'How did your day go?'

The child pulled a face. 'We didn't do much reading. Granny wanted the knitting finished.'

Agnes's lips pulled into a tight, angry line. She didn't send Jessie to school to learn how to knit, or just to be kept out of mischief, either. She sent her there to be educated. Her frown deepened at the next question, which she had not been expecting.

'Mother – what was my father like?' Jessie knew he was dead but very little else, and although she had asked her mother about him several times, she had learned very little. But still, every now and then, something drove her to ask again.

'He was a fool,' declared Agnes, shaking her duster out of the back door with unnecessary vigour.

'You always say that. Why was he a fool? Why won't you talk about him? At least tell me what he looked like!'

'He was tall, with broad shoulders.' Agnes sniffed. 'A fine figure of a man, folk always said. That's why he was a footman. They like their footmen to look good, the gentry do. He had hair the same colour as yours, like a ripe chestnut, but you've got my eyes. Blue. His were green.'

She looked blindly into the kitchen fire for a moment, then decided to reveal a little more. Jessie had asked about Frank a few times now and the child had to learn what life was really like. She had to grow up sensible. 'He was a bad provider, your father was, and sometimes we went hungry. When I complained about him spending what little we did have on ale, he used to hit me.'

Jessie's mouth wobbled and tears filled her eyes. She knew about men who beat their wives. There were one or two in the village and they were not well thought of. She didn't like to think of her own father behaving like them.

Agnes Burton patted her daughter's hand, a rare gesture, for she was not a demonstrative woman. She found she could not, after all, tell her daughter everything. 'And that's all I'm going to say about your father. Go and cut me some rhubarb for tea.'

In that same year, with Jessie coming up for nine, Agnes Burton saw her opportunity to do something about getting her daughter a proper education and seized it with both hands.

'Did you hear what His Lordship's doing now?' Granny Todd asked her one day at the market.

Agnes shook her head, but lingered to listen to the gossip, for once.

'He's to build two new schools. One here in Hettonby and another over in Great Sutton.'

'You don't seem upset about that?' Agnes commented, feeling the breast of a chicken tied to one leg of a stall and slapping its pecking beak away from her hand.

'Bless you, no! Them schools are only for the children of farmers and tradespeople. They won't affect *my* little scholars.'

Founding schools was the fashionable thing to do, now that the government was beginning to take an interest in education, Agnes Burton knew, for she read all the parson's newspapers once he'd finished with them. It was her treat of an evening when the day's work was done. Lord Morrisham would no doubt enjoy feeling philanthropic. That was fashionable, too. 'Are the schools for both girls and boys, or just boys?' she asked, trying to sound casual.

'Both,' Granny chortled. 'Though they're to sit on different sides of the room. I heard tell His Lordship thinks everyone should learn their letters. He won't let his housekeeper take on a maid at the Hall 'less she can read an' write.'

Agnes felt a brief spurt of nostalgia. Mrs Prudhom had taught her to read and write properly, saying if a maid wanted to get on, she needed such skills. The former housekeeper was Mrs Butterfield now, of course, for she had married the squire a year after his wife died. But Martha was not too proud to write to her old maid a long newsy letter every Christmas, always with an invitation to spend a week at Butterfield Priory come the summer – an invitation that Agnes inevitably turned down. There was no going back. You made your bed and you lay in it without complaining. But you did better for your children, if you could.

Granny was still talking. 'And the schools are to have proper schoolmasters, too, though folks'll have to pay for their children to attend. He don't believe in giving things away for nothing, His Lordship don't.'

Agnes seized the chicken by its legs, nodded to the stallkeeper and waited until the neck had been wrung, a job she detested. Then she said goodbye to Granny and walked briskly home, feeling full of energy. A new school in Hettonby. Yes, she saw her chance now.

She approached her employer that very evening about getting a place in the school for Jessie.

'Ah. Yes. Well.' John Marley stared at his housekeeper in dismay. He knew that His Lordship's new school was not intended for the offspring of servants. 'Um – is she old enough?' he asked, cautiously feeling his way. The only time he really saw the child who lived under his roof was when she accompanied her mother to church every Sunday morning or played out in the back garden with her dolls, and he thought her a neat, well-behaved little thing.

'Oh, yes, sir. She's definitely old enough. She turns nine in September.'

'Oh, well . . .' He sought desperately for a tactful way to put Agnes off. 'His Lordship was thinking more of catering for the children of – of farmers and – and people who can afford to pay for proper schooling.'

'How much will it cost?'

'A guinea a term.'

'I can afford that for a year or two. I've got a bit of money put by for my Jessie's education.'

'Oh.' Another silence for a while, then, 'But isn't – doesn't she go to Granny Todd's school already?'

'Yes, sir. And has learned all that Mrs Todd can teach her.' Which was leading to mischief from Jessie and complaints from Granny lately.

'I see.' But even a man as gentle and easy-going as John Marley could not help being aware that the farming classes were as rigid in their belief in knowing your place as Lord Morrisham himself. They would not take kindly to a servant's brat going to the same school as their own children. He hummed and hawed a bit. 'Well, I'll have to think about it and – and consult His Lordship. It is his school, after all.'

Sensing an excuse in the offing, Agnes staked all her precious security on a desperate gamble. 'In that case, sir,' her voice was as quiet and respectful as ever, but steely in its determination, 'if she can't attend, I'm afraid I shall have to give notice and ask you to start looking for a new housekeeper.'

Mr Marley's face fell visibly. It was a minute before he could speak, so horrified was he at the prospect. 'But – but I thought you were happy here! You've been with me a long time now.'

'Yes, sir. I'm very happy in my job. But I've been worrying for a while about how I can get some proper schooling for my Jessie. Granny Todd does her best, but she's not a real teacher, is she? I'm afraid I shall have to look for a position in a town, somewhere my Jessie can attend a proper school. I don't want to leave you, sir. I've been very happy here. But there you are. I have to think of the child's future. She must get a good education.'

The parson looked at her face, the tight strong lines of it, read the determination in every inch of her lean body, and knew he was beaten. 'Now, don't be so hasty, Agnes! I haven't said it's impossible, just that I wasn't sure. I'll speak to His Lordship myself about your daughter – the very next time I see him. I shall be going over for a game of chess soon, I dare say.' When His Lordship had nothing better to do and wanted an hour filling. For John Marley was the only person who dared win against him, and knew that his patron cherished a secret desire to best him. Well, let him if he could. John wasn't going to pretend or cheat. In anything.

When the door had closed behind Agnes, he sat lost in thought. She had not asked any other favour of him in all the years she had worked for him. She was never ill and did not even take time off, as she was entitled to do, because she said she had no family left to visit in Yorkshire and would rather stay and see things done properly at the parsonage than spend her money traipsing around the countryside. She did take a day off to go to Leeds market every now and then, and that was all. Every Christmas, though, she got a letter from Yorkshire, on fine cream notepaper, so there must be someone left from her family. But she never talked about them. And John did not feel he had the right to ask her.

She was, he decided that night over a piece of tangy apple pie smothered in fluffy cream, a wonderful cook and housekeeper. The best he had ever had. And he did not want to lose her. He rang for a second piece of pie and murmured a compliment when it was brought. As he slid the last spoonful into his mouth, he came to the conclusion that he would help Agnes get proper schooling for her daughter. That was a laudable ambition, surely? But he would interview the child himself before putting the matter to His Lordship. It didn't hurt to be well prepared when you had an argument to win.

Jessie was summoned to the study the next afternoon – a great matter, this. 'But *why* does Parson want to see me?' she asked as her mother ruthlessly dragged a brush through her hair and plaited it so tightly that her daughter's eyes watered.

'It's about His Lordship's school. You do want to go to a proper school, don't you?' Agnes retied the bow on the frilled Sunday pinafore, before turning Jessie round to face her. 'You know how you like reading and writing and doing your sums.'

'I've read all Granny Todd's books,' Jessie agreed wistfully.

'Well, if you go to His Lordship's school, you'll be able to read lots more books,' Agnes promised recklessly. 'And no more knitting.'

Jessie's eyes lit up.

'Now, off with you and mind your manners.'

The child went along to the front of the house and knocked on the door of the parson's comfortable study, entering quietly when a voice called, 'Come!' As usual, the place smelled of leather and books and pipe smoke. She loved the smell there and often helped her mother dust the study before Parson got up.

'Mother said you wanted to see me, sir.' She clasped her hands behind her as she waited for him to speak. Her mother said that was the tidy thing to do with your hands when someone grown-up was speaking to you.

John Marley stared across his desk. She was tall for her age, but even so, she was dwarfed by the massively comfortable furnishings of his study. He had never, now he came to think of it, interviewed the child before without her mother being present. He studied the vivid face, immediately captivated by a pair of sparkling blue eyes, fringed by long dark lashes. Hair of a burnished russet colour haloed the face, highlighted by golden glints where the sunlight touched it. Already stray curls had escaped from Agnes's ruthless plaiting, as they always escaped their bonds, do what she might.

If Mr Marley studied the child gravely, she returned his stare just as gravely, for her mother was not there to poke a bony finger in her side and hiss a reminder about good manners.

'Well, Jessie. So you'd like to go to a proper school, would you?'

'Oh yes, sir, please, sir!'

'Why?'

Head on one side, she thought over her answer. 'Well, you can learn to read properly at a real school, can't you, sir? All the long words. Granny Todd doesn't know the long words. I can make some of them out, but the others puzzle me. I don't know how to say them and I don't know what they mean.' She spoke clearly, with her mother's accent, learned long ago at the big house, not the flatter vowels of the villagers.

'I've read all Granny's books,' she added wistfully. 'Lots of times.'

'Have you, indeed?'

21

'Yes, sir. They're very easy. And besides . . .' Jessie hesitated and peeped up at him through her lashes.

'Yes, go on. Besides . . .'

'Well, your books here,' she gestured round at them, 'I help my mother to dust them sometimes – for a treat, you know – and they're so beautiful that they must surely be full of wonderful things.'

He was totally won over. Any young child who appreciated the beauty of his beloved books and the value of learning deserved a decent education.

No, Lord Morrisham must agree to take the child, for John would, he realised in surprise, miss Agnes herself as much as he would miss her services. He enjoyed her astringent wit as she commented on the less capable of his parishioners, he appreciated the gentle reminders about some duty or other when he was lost in his books, and he relished the occasional shrewd comment on national affairs from her reading of his newspapers. Nobody's fool, his housekeeper. He'd never find anyone half as good to replace her, and he didn't intend to try.

The very next day, John Marley hired the gig from The Crown and drove over to the Hall. It was the day Lord Morrisham dealt with estate matters and he was usually free by mid-afternoon.

When the request was put to him, His Lordship didn't mince his words. 'Dammit, man, you know this school isn't intended for servants' brats!'

'Jessie is an exceptional child. Extremely intelligent.'

'I don't care how intelligent she is. What will the other parents think about such as her attending my new school?'

John Marley wavered, thought once again of his housekeeper and summoned up all his courage. He had defied His Lordship once or twice before, in his own quiet way, for Lord Morrisham occasionally made a decision which might injure John Marley's flock in Hettonby and he couldn't allow that. 'If the school is to be closed to such a specially deserving case, then I don't think I shall be able to spare the time to teach in it, after all, Your Lordship, for it is obviously not truly concerned with the propagation of learning.'

Clarence stiffened in outrage, made a loud huffing noise that usually brought folk into line, then stared at his parson in puzzlement when Marley's expression did not change. Not like the fellow to bestir himself over a servant's brat. Could she be his own by-blow? No. He did a quick calculation, then dismissed that idea. For a start, the man hadn't got it in him. Too much of a Holy Joe. And anyway, the housekeeper was from near Rotherham, not from round here, and had brought the brat with her. Lord Morrisham remembered her arrival distinctly, for he had advised against hiring a woman with a child and was somewhat annoyed that the parson hadn't heeded him.

'Bit of a rum thing to ask,' he complained when the silence continued.

'All good schools have special scholarships for worthy cases, m'lord, and always have had, since medieval times.'

'Since medieval times, eh?' His Lordship hummed and hawed a bit, to save face, then gave in. He was satisfied enough with his parson and hated change – unless he instigated it.

John returned home glowing with triumph and rang at once for his housekeeper. 'I have arranged for Jessie to attend the school, which will be held in the church hall until a proper school house can be built.'

Agnes murmured a thank you and clasped her hands together to hide their sudden shaking. She had been dreading leaving the parsonage, absolutely dreading it. 'And how much will the fees be, sir?'

'Nothing!' The parson could not hold back a chuckle.

'I can pay!' Her voice was sharp. She had vowed never to accept charity again as long as she was able to stand upright on her own feet.

'You won't have to pay. His Lordship has set up a special scholarship, open to any promising child, to be awarded at my discretion, and *it* pays the fees. Jessie is to be the first recipient.' He beamed at her.

Actually, he and His Lordship had decided over a bottle of port and one of their games of chess that this method of allowing Jessie into the school would give the least offence to the parents of the other pupils, and would also best demonstrate His

Lordship's generosity. A few judicious repetitions of the term 'benefactor' had helped matters considerably.

Agnes stared at her employer, opened her mouth, then shut it again without speaking. Frugality warred with pride, and frugality naturally won. If she did not have to pay fees, there would be even more money to save for Jessie's future, not to mention her own old age. 'Thank you, sir. We're both extremely grateful to you. More grateful than I can say.'

'Aha! But there's more.' He beamed at her. 'The scholarship pays for any books that are needed as well.'

Her voice was sharp. 'I could have afforded them!'

'You won't have to. I am impressed by your daughter, my dear Agnes, and shall make it my business to keep a close eye on her progress from now on.'

After that he did indeed begin to take an avuncular interest in the child, or at least, in her scholastic achievements, which was all he really cared about. And he did not lose his paragon of a housekeeper, which was even more important to a plump, comfort-loving man.

2

Sutton Hall: 1829–34

*W*hen Jessie walked across the village green to the church hall on the first day the new school was open, she was smiling and eager, confident in her new dress and pinafore, looking forward to making friends, for her mother would never let her play out on the village green with the other children.

Rosie Plumworthy was waiting for her by the gate. 'You can just go home again, Jessie Burton. We don't want your sort in our school,' she announced, black eyes shining like two ripe sloes in her plump face and one arm stretched out to bar the way.

Jessie stopped dead in her tracks, shock at this unexpected attack making her mouth drop open.

'Just look at you, gaping like an idiot. Perhaps you *are* the village idiot.' Rosie preened herself as the two girls behind her laughed sycophantically. 'Trot off home, stupid! If you can find your way back, that is. We don't want you here.'

Jessie knew how important it was for her to go to school, for her mother had told her so again and again. 'I'm coming to school,' she announced, and took another step forward.

Rosie scowled and stretched out her other arm. 'Oh, no, you're not. We're not having you.'

Jessie took the initiative, shoving her tormentor backwards as hard as she could and taking her completely by surprise. 'His Lordship himself gave me a place here.' She poked a shocked Rosie in the chest, making her take another involuntary step backwards. 'So get out of my way.' Although she was a year younger, she was as tall as the other girl and at the moment, her expression was fierce, giving her an uncanny resemblance to her mother.

Rosie stood her ground, but she was beginning to feel worried. 'I won't.' No other girl in the district had ever stood up to her.

'I'm not afraid of you, Rosie Plumworthy, or anyone else.' Jessie glared at the cronies and they took a hasty step backwards.

Glancing sideways, Rosie found her supporters no longer ranged beside her and after another exchange of scowls, decided not to risk a fight on her own. 'Hah! You're not worth bothering with. But you'll be sorry. See if you're not.' Turning her back on Jessie, she sauntered away. Her friends followed close on her heels, one glancing nervously over her shoulder several times as she went.

A group of older boys, who had been standing a few yards away, watching with great interest, turned their backs and began to talk and laugh loudly. No one in the church yard was even looking at Jessie now.

She went to stand near the door to the hall. No one made any move to speak to her, so she held up her head, clasped her shaking hands in front of her and prayed for the school bell to ring. It seemed a long wait. And even the few children she knew kept away from her. But she wasn't going to cry. She was not.

When the schoolmaster summoned them inside, she breathed a sigh of relief. Here she felt safer, free from further persecution.

'Take your places, children.'

After some pushing and shoving, which made the school-master tut and say, 'Now, children, there are places for all!' Jessie found herself sitting alone on a bench right at the rear. And she stayed there alone all morning.

At noon she went home to eat, but her mother, in the middle of a washday and too busy to talk, just plonked a plate down in front of her. Jessie chewed her food slowly, wishing she did not have to go back to school. She delayed as long as she could, until her mother told her to get out of the house, do, and arrived just before the proud new monitor rang the school bell. There was a group of lads blocking the gate, presenting a united wall of backs, and they knew very well she was there, but they didn't move until the master summoned them inside.

Agnes was unsympathetic when she found Jessie sobbing her heart out in the bedroom that first evening. 'Whatever's wrong with you, child?'

'No one at school will s-speak to me. They say I'm just a servant's brat.'

'Oh, is that all?'

Jessie hiccupped to a halt, unable to believe that her mother could take this disaster so lightly. 'I'm not going back there.'

'Oh, yes, you are! It's your only chance of decent schooling and you're not throwing it away on a whim.'

'But-'

'Look,' Agnes tried to find words to soften it, but couldn't, so just said baldly, 'the world's like that, and folk like you and me can't do anything about it. *What can't be cured must be endured.* That's all we can do sometimes - endure.'

'But they - they - '

'You go to that school to learn your lessons, not to play with the other children, make no mistake about that, Jessie Burton. What does it matter if you don't make friends, as long as you learn to read and write properly and to do your sums?' Having learned to live without friends herself, Agnes could not understand why Jessie was taking on so.

'But - '

'I mean it, miss. You'll go to that school and you'll work hard. Let alone I want you to have a good education, Mr Marley stuck up to Lord Morrisham to get you in, and we're not letting him down.'

After that, the child did her crying quietly before her mother came up to join her. She would lie in the small narrow bed that stood across the foot of her mother's in the attic bedroom they shared and allow a few tears to trickle down her face, not enough to make her eyes red, but enough to ease the hurt a little.

And afterwards, she would curl up and dream. Bed became a place of refuge. There, no one could hurt her. There, she could look forward to better times, to making friends, and - as she grew older - to meeting boys and finding a husband and having a family of her own. For she hated being an only child. However much they fought among themselves, the brothers and sisters she knew always stuck up for one another against the rest of the world. And she envied them that.

Gradually, the overt hostility stopped – from everyone except Rosie Plumworthy, anyway – but for most of the three years Jessie spent in the school, she remained the outsider. Even kindly Mr Snelling could not help being aware of how the others treated his brightest pupil, but he knew that if he intervened openly, he would only make things more difficult for her.

Jenny Peakes, the daughter of the new village shopkeeper, arrived at school during the second year and was placed next to Jessie. She defied Rosie enough to talk to the girl who shared the double desk with her and never played nasty tricks, but she did not risk defying the whole school community, and outside in the yard played always with the others, leaving Jessie standing or skipping on her own in one corner.

The boys were fairly indifferent to all this, for they sat always on the left side of the hall, and later the new schoolroom, and they played out in their own half of the yard.

So Jessie learned to keep her feelings to herself, to ignore Rosie (because she found that this response infuriated the other girl more than any other) and to get on with her work – which was always excellent.

And when Mr Snelling gave her extra lessons with the older boys in the keeping of accounts, because she was ahead of the other girls in arithmetic, or let her copy poetry from his own books in handwriting practice, she was grateful to be kept busy, for the others sometimes seemed so slow and she did get bored at times.

The Sunday before Jessie turned twelve, her mother sat her down for a serious talk. 'You'll not be going to school any more after this week.'

Jessie gasped and clutched at the edge of the table. 'Why not? I haven't done anything wrong, have I?'

'Not that I know of.' Agnes raised one eyebrow in mute inquiry.

Jessie shook her head in equally mute denial. 'But if there's nothing wrong, why can't I keep going to school?'

'Because you'll be turning twelve. It's time for you to start earning your own living.'

'I won't go and work in Mrs Plumworthy's dairy! I won't!'

It was Agnes's turn to be startled. 'Who said anything about Mrs Plumworthy's dairy, for heaven's sake?'

Jessie's eyes were bright with tears. 'But that's the only place that's going in Hettonby.'

'You're not going to work in the village. You're going into service over at the Hall. Parson has arranged for us to see the housekeeper about it. She's looking for another maid. I told Mr Snelling when I saw him at church last Sunday and he knows you won't be at school tomorrow.'

Jessie stared. 'You didn't say anything to me.'

'Not till it was all arranged, no. Why should I? But I'm saying something now, aren't I?' Agnes waited, a frown gathering on her brow. 'Well, aren't you pleased?'

'I don't know. I - I hadn't thought of such a thing.'

'No. That schoolmaster has been putting too many fancy ideas into your head.'

Donald Snelling was a gifted teacher of the Three Rs, but as he had a passion for poetry, he had also tried to pass that on to his scholars. Agnes could see no use in fiddling about with rhymes. She had gone down to the school the previous year and told him roundly that he should be teaching her daughter to keep accounts, not recite useless verses. Amused by her vehemence, he had done just that. Though he had continued to teach her poetry as well.

'Well? Say something,' Agnes prompted when the silence dragged on and her daughter kept staring down at her pinafore. 'You knew you'd have to find a place one day.'

Jessie nodded. Yes, she'd known that. But 'one day' had always seemed so far away. And although she was the tallest girl in the school now, she didn't feel grown up, not grown up enough to leave home and go to work, anyway. A quiver of apprehension shivered through her belly. She had never lived anywhere but at the parsonage.

'Mrs Coxleigh, the housekeeper, said she'd consider you. If

you're suitable – and I'll make sure you are – you can start next quarter as a junior housemaid.'

The words were out before she realised it. 'But I don't want to become a housemaid.'

'*What did you say?*'

Jessie clapped a hand to her mouth and waited for a slap, but it didn't come. She peeped sideways at her mother and winced at the stormy expression on her face. 'I – I don't want to go away from you, Mother. I don't want to leave Hettonby.'

Agnes wasn't having any of that nonsense. 'You always knew you'd have to go away from here when you started work.'

Jessie began to weep and tried to cling to her mother.

Agnes pushed her off and glared at her, more touched by this display of affection than she dared admit, but just as determined not to let emotion stop her doing the best she could for her daughter. 'I never heard such nonsense in all my life! Or such ingratitude.'

'Please, Mother – '

'Not another word from you, miss. And if you so much as hint at this to Mr Marley, I'll spank your bare backside till you can't sit down, old as you are!'

From then on, Jessie hardly dared open her mouth. Her mother never made idle threats.

Taking a rare half-day off, Agnes rode over to Great Sutton with her daughter on the carrier's cart to allow Mrs Coxleigh to inspect the applicant.

As they came out of the woods and breasted a small rise, Sam Lubb let the horses slow down to an amble and pointed a grubby finger. 'There it is! Sutton Hall.'

Jessie gasped. It was far bigger than she had expected, a long sprawling building, larger even than the church in Hettonby, built of cream-coloured stone, not the reddish sandstone of the church, with a grey slate roof.

'His Lordship's father had the middle bit built,' Sam informed them. 'Then His Lordship added them two side bits. That's why the middle's darker.' He chuckled. 'It's got a bit dirty after all these years.'

The house seemed to the bewildered girl to have hundreds of twinkling windows and dozens of smoking chimneys. The sheer size of it completely overawed her and she didn't say a word from the minute it came into view.

Sam dropped them off at the end of the drive and they had a half-mile walk just to get to the house. Once there, they went round the side, as the parson had told them to, past the entrance to a very busy stableyard and on to the rear entrance, which servants and those delivering goods used.

Agnes pulled the bell and the door was opened by a fresh-faced young maid, who showed them into a passage between the servants' hall and the kitchens, and left them to sit on a hard wooden bench awaiting the housekeeper's pleasure.

Jessie sat gaping open-mouthed at the bustle around her until her mother gave her a nudge. 'Close your mouth and stop looking so gormless!'

But she could not stop staring, even if she did it more discreetly from then on. There were people coming and going all the time. Dozens of people, it seemed. She had not realised the Hall would be so huge!

To one side they had a clear view of the largest kitchen Jessie had ever seen. A girl was chopping vegetables at one table, mountains of vegetables, surely enough to feed the whole of Hettonby. Another table held a large haunch of beef and the plucked carcasses of several chickens. A woman was stirring something in a pan and an older woman was talking to a man with muddy trousers. The girl chopping vegetables looked up and winked at Jessie in a friendly way.

Perhaps, she thought, with the first stirrings of hope, perhaps it would not be so bad to work here, after all. Perhaps she would even be able to make a friend or two.

A few minutes later the maid who had answered the door came back to show them to the housekeeper's room. Agnes took all this in her stride, but Jessie, following her mother along what seemed like miles of corridors, felt very nervous. How would she ever find her way around such a large house? How dark the wood panelling on the walls was and how thick the carpets! And why were the curtains drawn in so many of the rooms they passed? She edged closer to her mother.

Agnes gave her a poke with one bony finger. 'Just watch where you're walking, our Jessie. You're treading on my hem.'

'Sorry.' It came out as a whisper.

The maid knocked on a panelled wooden door which stood ajar and poked her head round it. 'Mrs Burton and her daughter to see you, Mrs Coxleigh.'

'Show them in.'

Jessie followed her mother inside a room that was even larger than Parson's study. By now, she was terrified at the prospect of being sent to this place all on her own – but she was even more terrified of what her mother would say if she did anything wrong.

Behind a highly polished desk sat a thin lady with steel-grey hair, dressed in rustling black silks with an elaborate lace cap and apron. She was studying them openly. Jessie wriggled under that scrutiny, feeling as if all her faults were instantly obvious to the lady, who had made no attempt to stand up or to shake hands with her mother, as grown-ups usually did.

'I am Mrs Coxleigh, housekeeper to Lord Morrisham. Please sit down.' No one ever boasted of serving Lady Morrisham. Her Ladyship was a faded nonentity, exhausted by years of childbearing and as terrified of her loud, red-faced husband as the servants were.

Mrs Coxleigh might have been a queen giving an audience to her lowly subjects. 'Thank you for accompanying your daughter, Mrs Burton. We do like to meet the families of our girls.' She did not wait for a response, but turned to the child. 'You are Jessica Mary Burton and you are twelve years old, I believe?'

'Yes, ma'am. But please, ma'am, they call me Jessie.'

'Much more suitable for a servant,' approved Mrs Coxleigh. 'One of His Lordship's own cousins is called Lady Jessica. We couldn't have a servant of the same name. It wouldn't be fitting.' Another stare skewered Jessie to the spot. 'And are you a good girl?'

Seeing that the lady was waiting for a reply and that her mother was frowning at her, Jessie managed, 'I – I think so, ma'am.'

'I believe you can read and write?'

'Yes, ma'am.'

32

'She's had three years in His Lordship's own school,' put in Agnes. 'He gave her a special scholarship to go there. She's a very good scholar.'

Mrs Coxleigh nodded. 'I don't usually take girls from Hettonby. Until now, they have lacked proper schooling. But Parson Marley has spoken very highly of both you and your daughter, and of course His Lordship's school has made a big difference to standards locally.' She nodded to herself, approving the severe clothes and obvious cleanliness of the mother. The daughter looked nice and healthy. She had a fresh complexion and was a sturdy girl, promising to be tall and strong when she grew older. Mrs Coxleigh did not like small, slender maids. They could not cope with the heavy lifting.

'I shall give your daughter a quarter's trial, Mrs Burton.'

Jessie sighed in relief and her mother allowed herself a quick, tight smile.

'The wages are three pounds a year, payable quarterly, for the first two years. If you give satisfaction, Jessie, your wages will be increased after that. Lord Morrisham can be a very generous employer to those who serve him well. Though he will tolerate no slackness, mind! You will work hard, but you will have one full Sunday and one half Sunday off each month. Is all that clear?'

'Yes, ma'am.' The words came out as a whisper, but that too pleased the housekeeper.

'Very well, then. You may start next month, on the first Monday.' She turned back to Agnes. 'Your daughter will need an outfit.'

'Of course. That is understood.'

'We supply the aprons ourselves, but she will require three print dresses for summer, three dark woollen dresses for winter, four changes of underwear – we insist on personal cleanliness and the laundry maids wash for the staff every fortnight – and four pairs of black knitted stockings. A plain bonnet to wear to church, mobcaps for work and a good, warm cloak. Three nightgowns with high necks and long sleeves. A pair of stout leather shoes and two pairs of soft leather slippers for indoors. I have the list here.'

She looked challengingly at Mrs Burton as she handed it over, but Agnes nodded calmly. She knew perfectly well that the cost of the outfit was a kind of entrance fee to service in the big houses. Long ago, Mrs Prudhom had taken her in without an outfit, but that was rare generosity. She was quite prepared to provide twice what Mrs Coxleigh had asked for, if necessary, for her daughter's sake. For what other reason had she been saving her money?

On the way back to Hettonby, Jessie was very quiet, but her mother didn't notice that at first because she was delighted to have got her daughter into a place with such good prospects.

'If you play your cards right,' she said for the umpteenth time, 'you may have a chance to go for lady's maid when you're older, and everyone knows that's one of the best jobs of all. Ladies' maids get lots of perks – their mistress's old clothes, the chance to travel, more time off – oh, it's a good life, right enough!' She sighed with as much pleasure as if she were getting the chance herself and became lost for a few minutes in dreams of her daughter's wonderful, secure future.

Jessie sat silently beside her. A rabbit had just bobbed out from behind a tree and there was a thrush singing in the woods. She wished she could get down from the cart and run alongside it, wished she could go and explore these woods, which were much bigger than those near Hettonby. But most of all, she wished she weren't going to work at the Hall. It was so big and dark, and she didn't know anyone there. Her mouth drooped at the corners as the cart rumbled along, and her shoulders were hunched despondently. But for once, Agnes, flushed with triumph at achieving a lifetime's ambition, did not notice.

During the next few weeks, Jessie did not attend school, but helped her mother to sew the things for her outfit. On the evening before she left, Mr Marley presented her with a handsome, leather-bound Bible of her very own, the possession of which seemed to set the seal on her new, grown-up status as a wage earner. Mr Snelling called to give her a volume of Shakespeare's sonnets and express the hope that she wouldn't quite forget what he had taught her over the years.

Her mother clicked her tongue impatiently at the impracticality of the schoolmaster's gift and presented her daughter with a leather purse containing nine shiny silver shillings, one sixpenny piece, a threepenny bit and three pennies.

This was the most money Jessie had ever possessed in her whole life and she flung her arms round her mother. 'Oh, thank you!'

'This is just in case you need anything before you get your first wages next quarter day and it's to be paid back over the next two and a half years at a shilling a quarter, mind.'

Jessie, feeling quite rich at the prospect of earning three whole pounds a year, nodded happily as she fingered this largesse. She would feel better with money behind her, more grown up. And the girl in the kitchen had looked friendly. Perhaps it wouldn't be so bad at the Hall after all.

The following day the carrier again drove her over to Great Sutton, but this time she did not have the support of her mother and her heart was fluttering with nervousness beneath her new cloak of scratchy brown wool. Sam Lubb arrived at the parsonage very early and heaved her shiny new tin trunk up on the back of his cart in a careless way that made her want to protest. It had her initials painted on it and a stout lock, the key to which hung round her neck on a piece of ribbon, bumping against her flat chest as she walked. The trunk was another gift from her mother and had been sent for all the way to Leeds.

She was to arrive at eight o'clock sharp and to report to the housekeeper, who would then hand her over to the head housemaid for training.

Jessie felt quite sick with apprehension by the time the cart drew up at the rear of the Hall, but after Sam Lubb and a footman had panted inside with the trunk and dumped it in the back hallway, it was an hour before anyone there had time to attend to her. They just left her sitting on the same hard wooden bench as before in the passageway near the kitchen, and she grew more nervous by the minute.

When the summons to the housekeeper's room did eventually come, she followed the maid, a different one this time, older than the others, and bobbed a curtsey to Mrs Coxleigh, as the other woman did. Her tin trunk was standing in front of the desk and she wondered why it had been brought here.

A rough hand shook her shoulder. 'Pay attention, girl! Mrs Coxleigh has spoken to you twice.'

Jessie blushed. 'I'm sorry.' She answered all the questions put to her, though she couldn't see what business some of them were to anyone else but herself.

'Open your trunk now.'

Jessie gaped at Mrs Coxleigh.

'Are you deaf, girl? Open your trunk. I haven't got all day.'

Jessie did as she was ordered and then watched in deep resentment as the housekeeper and her assistant pulled out and inspected every item in it. She did not dare protest, but she felt angry. It was *her* trunk, *her* things. They had no right to go through them.

'I'm glad to see that you have your own Bible, but I'm surprised you feel the need for poetry.' Mrs Coxleigh weighed the handsomely bound volume in her hand, but finally returned it to Jessie. 'You are not to waste your time reading this, except on your day off.'

Two footmen were then rung for to carry her trunk up to the long attic bedroom which she would share with five other maidservants.

Jessie turned to follow them but Vera, the chief housemaid, grabbed hold of her arm. 'Mrs Coxleigh hasn't finished with you yet.'

The next few minutes left Jessie scarlet with embarrassment and stifled outrage. It was the custom at the Hall, as at most large houses, to inspect the persons of all new servants for head lice and fleas. No exceptions were made and regular checks were carried out. The search was made by Vera under the gimlet eyes of the housekeeper and was very thorough.

Jessie buttoned up her clothes again afterwards with tears in her eyes, her face red with shame. No one, not even her mother, had seen her naked body for years. But she did not dare protest because she knew her mother would kill her if she offended Mrs Coxleigh or did anything to put her new job at risk.

That night and for many nights afterwards, Jessie wept herself to sleep in the narrow, lumpy bed which she was to call her own for several years to come. And right from the start, she hated working at the Hall, hated it with a passion as she alternately sweated in the large overheated rooms where the family lived or shivered in the draughty corridors and servants' quarters. She was resentful of the sneering footmen, and hurt by the tricks the other housemaids played upon the young newcomer. But most of all she missed being outdoors, as she had known she would.

Her mother was proud and happy that she was working at the Hall, but Jessie knew, even during her first bewildering year, that she could not spend her life doing this. There was nothing she could do about it until she grew up, however, nothing except endure. The words were graven on her heart now, she was sure: *What can't be cured must be endured.* Sometimes, on bad days, she recited them under her breath like a litany.

3

Blackholm: 1832

*R*eginald Stafford died of an apoplexy while berating the
stable lad for some imagined carelessness. Typically, he died with
a look of anger on his face, and although they laid him out with
great care, they could not erase that look.

When the lad came running to fetch her, his daughter Elinor
walked slowly across to the stables. It was a trick, it must be,
another of his stupid hurtful pranks. But there was his still body
lying waiting for her. She checked very carefully, afraid to believe
that her father was indeed gone, then she let out a great sigh of
relief. 'Yes, he's dead. Carry him up to his room, please.'

She followed them and once they had laid the body down,
asked them to leave. Then she searched his pockets. If she didn't
do it, someone else might. When she found a fat roll of banknotes,
anger surged through her. 'Oh!' Kitchen bills left unpaid and *he*
walked round with this. She tucked the money into the pocket
hanging on a tape under her full skirt, then went to pen a hasty
note to her brother, Simon, fumbling through her father's untidy
desk for the sealing wax.

That finished, she turned to ring for the housekeeper and let
out an exclamation of surprise as she found her hovering behind
her.

'Are you all right, miss?' Mrs Blount asked.

Elinor realised with some satisfaction that there would be no
one for the woman to report her findings to now, but decided

that she would wait until Simon returned before dismissing her. 'I'm perfectly well, Mrs Blount. I'm just writing to tell my brother what's happened. You may return to your duties.'

'It's a right shame, and the master only fifty-three.'

Elinor merely inclined her head. She could not voice any words of regret for she had hated her father, hated the way he treated them, particularly her, hated even the sight of his red face and knowing eyes. Of course, she had not dared show her feelings when he was alive and she had no intention of parading them in front of others now. 'I'll just walk down to the receiving office with my letter.'

'I can send t'stable lad.'

'No need. I feel like some fresh air.' And she didn't want Mrs Blount prying open the letter. 'But you can send for Mrs Peggins to lay him out.'

The housekeeper watched her go, then rifled hurriedly through her master's pockets. 'Bitch!' she said when she didn't find the money she knew he'd been carrying, the roll he always peeled a note from when she'd pleased him particularly. She went down to the basement to grumble to the cook about her young mistress. 'Hasn't wept once, she hasn't.'

'Well, would you?'

'He was her *father*.'

'Poor sort of father he's been.'

'Poor sort of children he were landed with.'

'Oh, you *would* take his side! Well, you'll have to look for another place for yourself now, won't you? You're not liked by them as'll inherit this one.' She spoke with some satisfaction, for she, too, disliked the housekeeper.

Fanny Blount smiled. She might not need to work at all. He had promised to do something for her in his will, promised faithfully.

Simon Stafford read his sister's letter in his rooms at Oxford, where he was studying subjects that interested him not the slightest because his father had threatened to disown him if he didn't carry on the family tradition and attend that university. He was betrayed into one exclamation of, 'Oh, thank God!' and a great shuddering sigh of relief, but had himself under control again as he went to obtain permission to return home.

He travelled up to London, where he took the mail coach north to Halifax, arriving late at night. The next day he took a slower coach to Hebden Bridge, then a cab out to the tiny hamlet of Blackholm. By the time he arrived, he felt exhausted, but for the first time in years he was not filled with dread as he approached the sprawling house on the edge of the moors which had been in his family for well over a century. He frowned at it. How dingy it looked! A great square, three stories high, of uncompromising stone, weathered and darkened by years of winter winds and storms. Why had his father not had the ivy cut back and the woodwork painted before the winter? And some of the slates on the roof were cracked. Last year he'd noticed that the servants had to set buckets in the attic to catch the drips when it rained, but his father seemed to care only for the horses and stables.

In spite of its imperfections, Simon beamed at the house as the carriage drew up, for he loved every dilapidated corner of it. He would look after things better now that it was his. And he wouldn't be returning to Oxford, either. After he had set everything in order here, he would train as an engineer as he'd always wanted to.

Elinor met him at the door and they embraced warmly. She was the elder by five years, but they were very close. How could they not be? Their mother had died when Simon was ten and Elinor had brought him up, protecting him when she could from their father, who had always been a figure of terror to them both. 'Oh, I'm so glad you're home!' She hugged him again.

Mrs Blount was already hovering at the end of the hall, listening. Seeing their eyes upon her, she came forward in the rustling black silks that were far too fine for her situation. She let her fingers trail against the skirt as she walked. The master had bought this outfit for her when she complained of feeling dowdy. He had given her quite a few things in gratitude for her services, for she had known how to please him. His children were too stupid. And they were weak. *He* had been strong. A fine figure of a man. 'Would you like to see your father, Mr Simon?' she asked in a soft voice, ignoring Elinor completely.

His reply was curt and he was already turning away from her

as he said, 'No, thank you. But I'd appreciate some tea, if you could tell Cook?'

Upstairs, in his sister's small parlour, Simon sat on the couch with his arm round Elinor's thin shoulders. 'How exactly did he die?'

'As you might expect. In a fit of rage at the poor stable lad.'

He made a disgusted sound. 'Well, I shan't miss him, nor shall I pretend to be grief-stricken.'

'It feels so strange,' she said wonderingly. 'No one shouting. No crashes and bangs from the library. And I've banished his dogs to the stables.'

'Ugly brutes – just like him. We'll get another dog and you can train it properly.' He knew his sister's love of animals. 'There'll be just you and me from now on, Elinor. And as soon as the funeral's over, we'll get rid of *her*.'

'Do you suppose he's left her anything?'

'I hope not.'

But they both feared he might have.

'Still,' he consoled, 'we'll be able to do as we please from now on.'

'I can't remember ever feeling so happy. Or so free.'

'Nor can I.'

Their quiet joy was spoiled that very afternoon, even before the funeral. A note was brought round to the heir from the lawyer, suggesting a plain funeral and as little expenditure as possible, given the circumstances. Simon showed it at once to his sister.

She turned pale. There was only one interpretation you could place on this. 'He *can't* have spent everything, surely?' But his desk had been full of unpaid bills.

There was silence, then Simon shook his head. 'Who knows what he did with the money? *He* never seemed short, anyway. But whatever else, we'll still have the house.'

'I've no objection at all to a small, plain funeral. He doesn't deserve any better.'

Looking at her face, at the hatred she didn't attempt to conceal when only he was there, Simon wondered yet again what she had had to put up with while he was away, first at school, then at university. She had always refused to discuss it, saying: *Least said, soonest mended*. But he knew how unhappy she had been.

'Is there anything you need to tell me, love?'

Elinor didn't meet his eyes. 'Nothing.' Then, almost as if she couldn't hold back the words, she added, 'But there's a lot to forget.'

When they drove back from church after the quiet funeral the following afternoon, Hoskins, the lawyer, came with them but no one else had been invited – which had caused some talk in the district.

Mrs Blount, still angry at being refused permission to attend the funeral with the other mourners, instead of sitting at the back of the church with the servants, was already waiting in the hall. 'Is the will to be read in the library?'

Simon looked at her in amazement. 'What concern is that of yours?'

She ignored him and turned to the lawyer. 'Am I not mentioned in it? The master promised he would leave me something.'

'No servant is mentioned. It's a very simple will and concerns only his children.'

The sound of her indrawn breath echoed round the hall.

'Please come into the library, Mr Hoskins,' Elinor said in her quiet voice.

All three ignored the housekeeper, who was left standing there alone, fists clenched by her sides. When the door had closed upon them, she looked round furtively and tiptoed into the parlour. 'It's only fair I be paid for my trouble,' she muttered, fingering the trinkets and trying to work out which would not be missed for a day or two and which of those were the more valuable.

In the library, after some hemming and hawing, Mr Hoskins spread out a piece of paper and tapped it with a plump forefinger. 'The will leaves everything to you, Mr Stafford, and nothing to your sister – '

'That's typical of him,' Simon muttered, and turned to Elinor. 'But don't worry – I'll look after you. I'll always look after you.'

The lawyer cleared his throat to get their attention. 'I'm afraid . . .' he hesitated, then rushed on to get it over '. . . there won't be much left to inherit.'

They both froze and sat staring at him, the resemblance between them very strong at that moment. They favoured their mother, tall and thin, with mousy hair, aquiline noses and long elegant limbs, rather than their burly father with his tree-trunk legs and short neck.

Simon felt Elinor's hand reach out to grasp his. 'I don't quite understand?'

The lawyer sighed. He had been dreading this moment. 'Your father's been overspending for years, living like a lord and investing unwisely. Always against my advice, I do assure you. Your mother's money was spent even before she died, and since then he's been juggling things. I'm amazed he lasted this long without bankruptcy. And – ' another sigh – 'I'm afraid the creditors will be down on you soon.'

Simon felt bitterness churn within him. Typical of his father! And not a word to either of them, let alone any attempt to economise. He could see only one ray of hope. 'But my sister's annuity – that's still secured to her, at least?'

'The first annuity is, the one from her godmother. He found a way to circumvent the second one that your mother asked in her will should be set up.' He bowed to Elinor. 'You'll have an income of about two hundred pounds a year, my dear, but that's all. And – ' best get all the bad news out in the open ' – it's my guess that you'll have to sell this house and all its contents to pay off his debts.'

When the lawyer had gone, they went to sit in the front parlour, for the library had always been *his* room.

'I can't believe it,' Elinor said at last. 'Even he – ' She left the sentence unfinished.

'At least *you* will have something.'

'We'll share whatever is left. We've always shared things.'

Simon shook his head. 'No, I'll not sponge off you. I'll find a way of earning my own living. And it won't be all bad. I can become an engineer, as I've always wanted.'

'I thought there were indentures to pay?'

They both sat thinking, then he looked at her. 'We need to salvage something, if we can. Why should we pay *his* debts? Do you still have Mother's jewellery?'

She nodded. She hadn't used it much, for the pieces were old, ugly and not worth a great deal. Besides, she did not like to draw attention to her thinness and plainness.

'When did you last wear any of it?'

She frowned, trying to remember. 'About two years ago, I think. We haven't been invited out much lately. I had wondered why – but I just thought Father had offended people. He often did.'

'He's probably in debt to half our neighbours.' Simon took a deep breath. 'I think we shall have to lie about the jewellery, Elinor, say he took it from you a while ago to sell. Can you do that?'

'Oh, yes.' She could do anything to help her beloved brother.

'I'll go back to Oxford to get my things and lodge the jewellery in a bank in London on the way. Can you manage here while I'm away – stave off any creditors?'

'Of course.' If she could manage to live with a man like Reginald Stafford, she could manage anything else.

He sighed. 'I had hoped to buy you some pretty dresses, let you enjoy yourself for a change and – '

'Find me a suitor?' she quizzed.

'Why not? You'd make a wonderful wife and mother.'

'No. I have no desire to marry. No desire whatsoever.'

Her tone was so flat and uncompromising that he was startled. 'Still dreaming of Paul?'

'I'm not so foolish. He'll have long forgotten me. But I saw how Father treated Mother, saw too how the law allowed it. I don't intend to put myself into any man's power.'

He stared at her. She looked ten years older than her twenty-three years, faded and wan. 'I'll make it up to you,' he promised, 'somehow.'

'It's over now. Whatever happens – *whatever!* – can only be an improvement for me.'

After another silence, he said, 'Let's pay *her* off now and tell her to leave at once.'

'What a wonderful idea! Let me do it.' Elinor went to tug at the bell pull and frowned at a small table full of nick-nacks. Something was missing. Had the parlourmaid broken an ornament? When the housekeeper arrived, she said in her usual quiet tone, 'Ah, Mrs Blount. We find that we no longer need your services. Could you pack your things and be out of the house within the hour, please? I'll have your money ready for you.'

The housekeeper gaped at them and tried to sound indignant, though in fact she would be only too glad to get away quickly now. 'You can't mean it! I've been here for four years.'

Elinor's hand on Simon's arm stopped him from intervening. 'Oh, but I do mean it. You were my father's creature and did well from him. Now that he's gone, I no longer wish to share a house with you. Nor shall I give you any references.' She looked at her little fob watch. 'One hour.'

'*He* promised he'd leave me something. You ought to do as he wished.' It was worth a try.

'Well, he didn't leave you anything and I have no intention of giving you any extra money.'

Simon took a step forward to stand slightly in front of his sister. 'Is there anything else, Mrs Blount?'

She slammed out of the room and ran up the stairs.

When the sound of her footsteps had faded away, he asked, 'What about Cook?'

'I'll keep her on for the time being.'

'And the other maids?'

'I'll put them on notice, but I'll ask Thirza to stay with me. She and I know one another's ways and she has no family left.' Elinor gave him a wry smile. 'I shan't be sorry to leave this house, actually, though I know you love it. I have nothing but unhappy memories of it since Mother died.' Though at least when Mrs Blount came to them, *that horror* had stopped. 'Leave the household arrangements to me, Simon dear.' She walked slowly across the room to stand by the mantelpiece. Again, something seemed to be wrong and it took her a minute to realise what. She walked round the room, checking, before she voiced her suspicions.

'Simon – some of the ornaments are missing.'

They stared at one another, then he looked upstairs. 'I wonder – '

'What?'

'If dear Blount is trying to take anything with her?'

Elinor frowned, then nodded slowly. 'I do believe she might be. I'd better go and oversee her packing.'

'I'll come with you.'

An hour later, as a loudly protesting Fanny Blount was driven away by the stable lad in the pony trap, Simon looked at Elinor's white face. 'Are you all right?'

'Yes. I'm only glad we caught her.'

He lifted her hand to his lips. 'You're a wonderful woman, my dear. Do you have any money left at all?'

'Oh, yes.' She put one finger to her lips and led the way upstairs to what had been the schoolroom and later her own private sitting-room. She locked the door behind them and went to fumble in her box of painting materials for the roll of banknotes. 'He had this on him when he died. I searched his pockets, and when I found it – well, I thought I was entitled, so I took it and hid it where *she* wouldn't think to pry. Do you need some money, love?'

'No. I think you and I resemble our mother. I've never spent all my allowance, not even when I was at school – though I didn't tell *him* that. He seemed to think I'd want to live *en prince*. I, too, have a little money set aside.'

'Good. Shall you stay on at Oxford to finish the year, at least?'

'No. I've had more than enough of Latin and Greek. I'll just go back and get my things, then we'll decide together what to do, where to live.' Simon gave a wry smile. 'There's nothing to stop me becoming an engineer now. But I want to see you settled first. I had thought to set the estate in order before I undertook any training, but if we have to sell it, the main priority will be finding you somewhere to live.'

He left the same evening, catching the night mail to London, with the jewels hidden in his luggage.

Back in Yorkshire, Elinor had another visit from Mr Hoskins to tell her that more debts had come to light and that the bailiff would be sending a man to stay on the premises and check that they didn't try to take anything away. She went to her room to sit staring out across her beloved moors and after some thought, sent away all the maids except Thirza and dull Clara. When they had gone, she went round the house in one of Cook's voluminous aprons, selecting very carefully the small items which had some value and tucking them in her pockets. She smiled as she replaced them with one or two showy pieces which had caught Mrs Blount's fancy, but which were worthless.

With Thirza's help, she smuggled her haul out of the house a few pieces at a time in shopping baskets and the two women hid them in the old half-ruined shepherd's hut on the edge of the moors.

'They'll be all right, miss,' the maid said cheerfully. 'No one ever comes here. Folk think it's haunted.'

Elinor hugged the other woman suddenly. Thirza was ten years older and Elinor didn't know how she would have managed without her these past few years. Only Thirza knew how bad things had been, the unmentionable way her father had treated her until Mrs Blount arrived on the scene. Sometimes only the fact that Thirza slept in her room had kept *him* away. Sometimes, when he was very drunk, even that hadn't made any difference and Thirza had had to run for her own safety.

When Simon returned to the small grey-stone village a week later, he found a sign at the gate of his home advertising a GRAND AUCTION OF HOUSE AND CONTENTS. He tried to tell himself that he didn't care about losing it, but he did. He loved the place, loved every stone, every crooked roof tile. He was humiliated by the knowledge that his father owed money to so many of their neighbours and it hurt him that Elinor should be made homeless. She didn't deserve to be poor, any more than she had deserved for her father to drive away her one suitor, the only man she had ever loved.

Inside the house, he was surprised to discover a burly man stationed in the hall. 'Who are you?'

'Bailiff's man, sir. Here to see nothing's taken away.'

'Damn you, do you think we're thieves?'

'Don't think anything, sir, just do my duty.'

In the library, Simon found Elinor closeted with a neighbour who turned out to be another creditor. She was explaining calmly what they were doing and how the lawyer was supervising things through the bailiff and his men, who were in attendance day and night. Simon stopped to listen and did not interrupt. By the end of the conversation, the neighbour was apologising to Elinor for having to treat her like this.

Simon could not have handled the man half as well as she was doing. Again, she was surprising him.

Five weeks later, they both stood by the front door of the house they no longer owned as the last of their possessions, including the things they had salvaged the previous night from the ruined hut, were carried out to the waiting drays. Nothing of value was left now, as far as anyone knew. They were taking with them some pieces of furniture for Elinor's new home, mainly pieces which were of no real value to anyone else, but one of them, Elinor's own writing desk, had been purchased for her by Thirza's cousin at the auction. All the money that the open sale had raised had gone to pay the creditors, and even then, some of them had not received their full due.

Simon stole a glance at his sister. She was dry-eyed, composed. He was the one unable to hide his sadness.

'Come on, Simon. Let's go now.' Her hand was gentle on his arm.

'I shall never come back to Blackholm. Never!' He drew a deep shuddering breath, then helped her into the carriage where the maid was already seated. 'I'm glad you're not going to be living nearby.' He turned to the maid. 'And I'm glad you're staying with my sister, Thirza. I don't know what we'd have done without you and I'd like to thank you for all your help so far.'

Thirza wriggled uncomfortably. 'Eeh, I'd not desert her now, Mr Simon.'

'Look after her for me.'

Elinor tapped him on the hand. 'Stop talking about me as if I'm not here, you two. I can look after myself.'

'Shall you be all right in Halifax?' he asked as they jolted away.

'Yes, of course. I have enough furniture and linen left from the house to set myself up. I'll be very comfortable.'

'I wish you'd taken a better house than that one.'

'I can't afford the rent of anything better.'

He scowled down at his feet.

'Cheer up. Thirza and I will do very well for ourselves.' She smiled across at her maid, who bobbed her head in acknowledgment, the tightly drawn back hair and knobbly bun emphasising her skinniness, but her eyes warm with affection as she looked at her mistress.

Later, as they waited at the inn where she would be spending the night, for him to catch the stage coach to London, he was still worrying. 'I should have waited an extra day to see that everything goes all right for you.'

'I'm old enough to manage. And Mr Dentinby wants you to start at once.'

She watched bleakly out of the window as the coach rattled away along the dark, rain-swept street. She hadn't told him how she was dreading living in Halifax, away from the moors, away from the one or two acquaintances she valued, cut off from all she had ever known. And she wouldn't tell him, either. Only Thirza knew her secrets. And Thirza wouldn't tell anyone.

4

Sutton Hall: 1834–36

The years at Sutton Hall taught Jessie many hard lessons, principally that it was just as important to stand up for herself in the new adult world as it had been in the old world of children. If she didn't, no one else would, that was certain.

Strangely enough, the first couple of years there were the best, in spite of her homesickness, because of her friendship with Sally Norton, a kindly housemaid who was responsible for training the new girl, but who took Jessie under her wing in many other ways. Sally, who was twenty, missed her own family greatly and understood the newcomer's feelings. She treated her like a younger cousin, telling her all about Robbie and Callie and the others from her own family of ten children. Sally still sent most of her wages home to help out and seemed very proud of being able to do this, though it left her without much money to spend on frivolities like new ribbons for her bonnet.

Jessie, with her mother's strict training behind her, proved an apt pupil in this wider world of housework and within a year had been promoted from cleaning the servants' sparsely furnished quarters and helping with the second floor, to cleaning His Lordship's guest bedrooms in Sally's company.

When Jessie was fourteen, Sally took her aside after supper one night. 'You're the first to know, love, apart from Mrs Coxleigh, but I'm leaving here come the end of the quarter.'

Jessie's eyes filled with tears. 'Sally, no!'

'Aye. My whole family is going to America and I'm going with them. I told you about our Peter emigrating, didn't I? Well, he keeps writing to say we can all do better for ourselves there and offering to help with the fares. Dad isn't too happy working for the new farmer who's taken Eastby Farm – he's a mean old sod, Dad says – so we're all to go to America.' She gave Jessie a hug. 'Eh, I'll miss you, love. I wish you could come, too.'

'I'll m-miss you, too.' Tears were dripping down Jessie's nose.

'Cry baby, cry!' jeered Thomas as he passed by.

'Just ignore that fool! Footmen are all stupid,' Sally said with lofty scorn.

When the time came for her friend to leave, Jessie presented her with a handkerchief she had embroidered herself and the two promised to write – but no letters ever came from America and gradually memories of Sally faded.

Another maid was taken on to work with Jessie, who would be senior to the newcomer. But Young Jane, as everyone soon called her, was not like Sally, not someone to make a friend of. She was a lumpy creature, strong physically and not afraid of hard work, but with no thought in her head beyond getting through her daily tasks without incurring the wrath of the housemaid in charge of that wing and begging extra food from Cook whenever she could, for she was perpetually hungry.

At the end of Jessie's third year at the Hall, Mrs Coxleigh informed the head housemaid that she had marked Burton down for future advancement and Vera passed on this gratifying piece of news as she promoted Jessie to helping with the bedrooms of His Lordship's children. At the same time, the girl's wages were raised to five pounds per annum.

But this lure of future advancement was of little consolation to someone who had never lost her love of the outdoors and could not bear to think of spending the rest of her life shut up in a big dark house, in service to gentry who didn't even notice your existence when they walked past you in a corridor, let alone thank you for all you did for them.

It was the tedium of the job she hated most. The work was

hard, but not unduly so, for the Hall was generously staffed, but there was little to hold her interest, beyond an instinctive pride in doing any job well. Make the beds, sweep the floors, empty the most disgusting of slops, fetch up the hot water, empty it out again – on and on in an interminable cycle.

When she first arrived, Jessie had marvelled at the beautiful things around her, but now she was so accustomed to them that she hardly noticed them. She learned to walk quietly, whether on the thick carpets in the family's part of the house, or the worn drugget which kept the noise down in the servants' quarters. If Lord Morrisham's deep fruity voice boomed in the distance or Her Ladyship's shrill whine drifted down the stairs, she did not even turn her head.

While the other maids chatted and teased one another, Jessie could take little part in most of their conversations, for several of them were related and they all came from the nearby villages, not from Hettonby – and what's more, seemed to think that gave them some sort of superiority. Once again she was the outsider, though at least this time, the others weren't hostile.

The children of the family clattered around their own wing of the house as they pleased, occasionally making forays out to invade the kitchen but only entering the main areas of the house at their parents' invitation. The first time Miss Susannah, the eldest, pinched her arm when no one was looking, Jessie yelped involuntarily. That brought her a lecture from Letty, who was in charge of that wing.

'You silly fool! What'd you yell out like that for?'

'She pinched me.'

'She pinches everyone. The more you yell, the more she'll pinch. Pretend you don't care.'

'But that's not fair. Can't Mrs Coxleigh have a word with the mistress about it?'

Letty rolled her eyes. 'Miss Susannah's *family*. What's *fair* got to do with it? They can do anything they want. Now, get on with your work and don't let me hear you yelling like that again.'

The next time the girl pinched her, Jessie said in a low, angry voice, 'That hurt and I can't pinch you back because I'm only a servant. So it isn't fair for you to do it.'

Susannah stared at her and then frowned down at her fingers as if they were not quite part of her.

Jessie pursued her advantage, but still in a low voice with an eye out for Letty. 'Why did you pinch me, Miss? I haven't hurt you.'

Susannah shrugged. 'I don't know why I did it.' She stared at Jessie, her head on one side, then smiled. 'I shan't pinch you again, though. I like you. I don't like Letty.'

This showed, Jessie thought, good taste, because Letty was a sour, spiteful woman – but she was distantly related to Vera, so you couldn't afford to get on the wrong side of her.

The other maids lived near enough to go home twice a month, but Jessie could only manage that once on her full Sundays off, when she walked the five miles to visit her mother and then five miles back again.

On her half Sundays, desperate to get out of the overheated house, she went for long walks round the estate, except on the most stormy days, when she stayed in her chilly attic bedroom. A little rain did you no harm, after all, and wet clothes would soon dry. She would fill her lungs with great deep breaths and stride along rapidly. Soon she got to know Sutton Woods as well as she knew the woods around Hettonby. Soon all the keepers knew the young maidservant by sight and would give her a cheery hello or invite her into their cottages for a sup of tea or milk.

But this only showed Jessie how right her mother had been for their cottages were poor, cramped places and their lives very hard. For all Lord Morrisham's supposed generosity towards his dependants, he did not pay high wages, nor did he pay much attention to his people's material comfort, apart from ensuring that the roofs of his cottages were kept in good repair, the chimneys swept annually and the cess pits emptied at regular intervals, so as not to offend the noses of the family.

Each summer, though, Jessie had one blissful week of holiday, when she was allowed to go home. That was the high spot of her whole year. She would be outdoors every day, sitting in the back garden where Parson couldn't see her, walking through the woods, enjoying the peace and the absence of other people. Her mother sometimes suggested a trip into Leeds, but Jessie wasn't interested.

'Too many people there,' she would say, wrinkling her nose. 'And the air smells smoky.'

'But there are lots of things to see. And you need some material for a new dress.'

'You get it for me next time you go. There's no hurry. I like to be by myself on my holiday and to get out of doors.' Jessie gave her mother a hug. 'You don't mind, do you? It's just that I spend all my life indoors and I miss the fresh air.'

Agnes shrugged. She, too, found Leeds crowded and ugly. She could see so many tall chimneys belching black smoke as she approached the city that she always wondered how the house-wives there kept their homes clean. Mind, the central markets were good, and so were the shops, and two or three times a year she enjoyed the outing. But that was enough. The rest of the time, she got on with her work, which was to keep Parson happy and well-fed.

Since Jessie had started at the Hall, John Marley sometimes came down to the kitchen during the day to share a cup of tea with his housekeeper and ask her advice about this or that parish matter. It was as if he knew how she missed the child. He was such a good man to work for, Agnes thought, so appreciative of all she did for him. What with Jessie set for life at the Hall and herself here, things could not be better.

Jessie's only self-indulgence was reading. There was a shelf of books in the servants' hall, another example of His Lordship's generosity, Vera said, passing his own books on to the staff. As the books were old and nearly falling to pieces, it was that or throw them away, Jessie reckoned, but she knew better than to say so. She read them all during her short periods of leisure, especially during that last hour of the day, when those servants not on duty were allowed to sit in front of the fire in the servants' hall, where they could chat or sew.

'What are you reading now?' One of the footmen snatched her book and held it up in the air. '*Ivanhoe*. Silly title. What's it about, then?'

'Mind your own business. And give me back that book this minute.'

The butler came into the servants' hall at that moment and roared at the footman, 'What are you doing, James?' Horseplay between the male and female servants was not encouraged.

'He was just looking at my book, sir,' said Jessie, stepping forward to take the precious volume back.

Mr Howard held out his hand for it. '*Ivanhoe*. Do you understand this, girl?'

'Oh, yes, sir. I was educated in His Lordship's own school in Hettonby. It was very generous of him to found the school and I'll always be grateful to him for the education I received there.' She let out her breath in relief as she saw that she had struck the right note.

With a nod, Mr Howard returned the book.

Behind his back, Jessie glared at James.

'Thanks for that,' he said when the butler had left, after a stern warning to the footman not to annoy the maidservants when they were improving their minds with reading.

'I did it for me, to keep my book, not for you, you great fool! Just keep your hands off my things in future, or I'll complain to Mrs Coxleigh.'

James went over to sit with his friend and fellow footman, Thomas. 'She's a strange girl, that one, isn't she?' he muttered.

'Stuck-up bitch, if you ask me. Miss Turn-up-your-Nose, I call her.'

They turned their attention to Young Jane, who was not nearly as pretty as Jessie, but who was friendlier and always very grateful for any small attention from them.

Sometimes Jessie would lie awake in bed and wonder if this was all there was to life. Sometimes she would weep into her pillow for no reason. But she didn't know what else she could do with her life. One day, she told herself. One day I'll leave here, find something else to do. But that would be much later. At present, the years of her youth stretched ahead of her like a long, dark tunnel.

In mid-1835, Elinor received a letter from their old lawyer, enclosing another letter which had come for her to their former home. She fingered the crest embossed in the red sealing wax which held the folds closed and wondered who it could be from. Taking a knife, she carefully lifted the seal and spread open the single sheet of paper.

My dear Cousin Elinor,
I have only just heard of how your father left things and am writing at once to see how I may help you?
    Please write and tell me how you are circumstanced. I'm a little busy at present, but when things are quieter, I would like to come and visit you, if I may.
    I am trusting that someone will know where to forward this letter.

          Yours sincerely,
       Clarence, Lord Morrisham

'Thirza, Thirza!' She ran into the small kitchen, where her maid was making pastry. 'Listen to this!' She read the letter aloud. 'What do you think of that, eh?'

'Who is he?'

'Father's cousin. How kind of him!'

'The proof of the pudding is in the eating.' Thirza was disgusted that only two of her mistress's former friends and neighbours had made any attempt to visit her or even write. She knew what she thought of the rest of them, gentry or not. But in spite of the occasional visitors and Simon's letters, she had watched her young lady grow even thinner since they'd moved to Halifax and begin to look like a lady well settled into spinsterhood. You couldn't buy fancy clothes if you were short of money, but you could wear your hair in a prettier style and buy yourself new ribbons for your bonnet, instead of wearing a plain old thing that wouldn't flatter anyone and screwing your hair back into a severe knot.

'I shall reply to him at once,' Elinor decided.

'Ask him if he's got any pretty cottages to let. This place gets damper every year. I keep telling you to find another.'

'And I keep telling you it's not worth the trouble. The sort of places we can afford are all dingy and damp.' Elinor looked at the letter again and frowned. 'I don't wish to beg for anyone's charity, but it wouldn't hurt to see him.' After all, he might have a cottage she could use, one which wouldn't cost too much to rent. She didn't intend to dip into her small reserves of money to find a better place, just manage as best she could on her annuity, meagre as it was.

'If Lord Morrisham is rich, he can afford to let you have a cottage for nothing,' Thirza said, setting her hands on her scrawny hips and looking at her mistress challengingly. 'And you're not to turn down any offer. He's family, isn't he? Family should look after one another, if you ask me.'

When Miss Elinor was out shopping, Thirza took the letter and wrote a note of her own to the address on it, begging His Lordship's pardon for presuming, but telling him quite bluntly how short of money her young mistress was. He never said anything about that, but he came over right away to see them and looked down his nose at the terraced house, with its three narrow stories.

'Why don't you come and live in Great Sutton, my dear Cousin Elinor? I've got a couple of new cottages lying empty just now. Four bedrooms, two parlours. Nice little places.' He was always very careful to whom he let them. These weren't cottages for working folk, but larger places for those who were more comfortably circumstanced and who could afford to pay their rent regularly.

'I don't like to – ' Elinor broke off, her face scarlet, then said bluntly, 'I haven't much money, Cousin Clarence. I doubt I could afford the rent of anything better than this.'

The thought of one of his relatives being reduced to such circumstances or – worse still! – of any of his acquaintances finding out, outweighed even his desire to maximise his income. He elevated his nose and said coldly, 'I couldn't think of charging my own cousin rent. And one of the houses is just lying vacant.' And he would not take no for an answer.

Elinor was not sure she was doing the right thing, but in the end agreed to move to his house, and thanked him as prettily as she could manage. He was not a very warm person, 'downright bossy' Thirza said later, but Elinor was tired of living in a town. She hadn't realised how much she would miss a village where everyone knew one another, or the wide freedom of the moors.

Of course, there weren't any moors near Great Sutton, from the sounds of it, but there was open countryside where she could go for walks.

Miss Stafford arrived in Great Sutton in 1835, a few months before Jessie's fifteenth birthday. All the servants knew by then that His Lordship was providing the cottage rent-free for his impoverished cousin, though how the information got out, no one could have said.

Simon came over to help with the move and insisted on accompanying his sister and her maid. The furniture was sent by one of His Lordship's drays and a carriage called for them, carrying them out to Great Sutton in considerable style.

'Life will be much easier when we have railways everywhere,' Simon said. 'None of this changing horses and jolting along. You'll be able to get down to London in half a day.'

'I can't imagine that.'

'I can.' The railways excited him. They would change the world, and change it for the better, too. He was quite sure of that. And he wanted to be part of it all, as his teacher and master Samuel Dentinby was.

The countryside was pretty enough, but as the horses clopped to a halt in front of a stark oblong cottage of red brick, with a grey slate roof and small, mean windows, Simon pulled a face at Elinor. 'Not the prettiest place on earth. I'd hoped for better for you. Are you sure you're going to be all right here, dear?'

She didn't intend to betray her doubts to him. He had enough troubles of his own, for the jewels had not brought as much as they had hoped, and he was still not earning any money, while completing his engineering apprenticeship. She knew how careful he had to be of every farthing. 'Of course I will. And think how rich I shall feel with no rent to pay! I shall buy myself some new clothes.' It was the right note to strike. Simon cheered up visibly.

The coachman opened the carriage door and they got out, followed by Thirza. 'Well, the garden's nice and big,' she said in a determinedly cheerful voice when neither of the others spoke. 'We'll be able to do something with that, Miss Elinor, won't we, put in some roses, perhaps, and grow our own vegetables?'

Elinor forced a smile and from then on the two women entered into an unspoken conspiracy to seem cheerful and optimistic about every aspect of their new life.

When a curt note was discovered on the mantelpiece of the small sitting-room, stating that His Lordship would expect them to dine with him tonight at six o'clock and would send the carriage, Simon shook his head over its autocratic tone but Elinor insisted it was a delightful way to welcome them.

He also worried about the smallness of the house and its lack of elegant appointments.

Elinor linked her arm through his. 'I've got the things from home to brighten the inside up and intend to remedy any shortcomings with my own needlework.' She gave him a saucy smile as she added, 'Which I'm sure you'll admit to be adequate to the task.'

'You shouldn't have to do that. Even if we are only second cousins, he was the one who offered to help and should have more respect for you. He could at least have had this place painted and freshened up.' Simon scowled round, not at all won over. 'And it's a mean little house. Mean!'

'It's bigger than the one in Halifax. And setting it to rights will give me something to do, my dear. That and the garden. I've missed my garden.'

He swung her round to face him. 'Are you sure you'll be all right?'

'Of course I will, you idiot! This place is a godsend.' She hesitated. 'There's just one thing. From something Cousin Clarence said, I gather he's very much against the railways. I think it'd be better if you didn't mention that you're working on them.'

'But surely he knows I'm an engineer?'

'Yes, but – well, he assumed it was steam engines and such things.'

'Elinor, I don't know anything about steam engines.'

'Well – maybe you could pretend you're working on roads and bridges, then?'

'I don't like to do that.'

She used the one argument she knew would win him round. 'It'd make my life easier.'

'Oh, very well. It won't last forever, after all.' He gave her a sudden hug. 'I'm working hard and learning so much. One day I'll take you away from places like this, and from depending on stuffy old cousins.'

'Oh, pooh! When that day comes, you'll probably be thinking of marriage and the last thing you'll want is a spinster sister hanging on your arm.'

'I'll always want you. And anyway, maybe by then you'll be married yourself?'

She shook her head, her smile fading instantly. 'No. I've told you before – I have no desire for that.'

Her voice was always so flat and determined when she said that, and she always looked so sad, that he ventured to ask, 'Is there something you haven't told me – something about the past?'

She summoned up her best smile. 'Dozens of things. But do you really want to hear all the details of how Thirza and I managed at Blackholm?' Without waiting for an answer, she took his arm. 'Now, come upstairs and help me choose our bedrooms. The letter said there were four. One each for us, and two for visitors. Thirza can have her choice of the attics. Perfect.'

The carriage arrived five minutes before six o'clock and deposited them at the door of the Hall just before the hour.

'Into the lion's den,' Simon murmured, offering Elinor his arm as she finished shaking out the folds of her skirts.

She dug him in the ribs. 'Shh! Someone might hear.'

Inside, a maid bobbed a curtsey and took their cloaks, then they were ushered into a large, elegant drawing-room. Lord Morrisham was standing toasting himself in front of the fire. He looked up as they entered and studied them thoughtfully, but it was a moment before he moved forward to greet them.

In the soft light of the candles, he looked suddenly so like their father, not in features, but in general deportment, that Elinor's blood ran cold for a moment and she had a sudden urge to flee for her life. Then reason took over and she reminded herself that he was *not* her father, just a man of similar build and attitude to the world.

'Cousin Elinor.' He bowed briefly over her hand. 'And you must be Cousin Simon? It's easy to see that you're brother and sister.'

He was already shepherding them towards the woman reclining on a sofa with a shawl over her feet. 'And this is my wife, Adelaide, who is, I'm afraid, of an invalidish disposition.'

Lady Morrisham twittered a greeting, then looked sideways at her husband as if waiting for him to take the lead.

'We didn't invite any of the neighbours to dine tonight. Thought it best to get to know one another first.'

Did he think they might not be presentable? Simon wondered.

'I agree,' said Elinor coolly, refusing to let that old panic well up as Clarence Morrisham towered over her.

'Take a seat. It's a chilly evening for April, don't you think?' He waited until Elinor had settled in an armchair and took one nearby. 'Well, how do you find things? Neat little house, ain't it? I had a few of them built when I inherited the estate. Brings a better class of people into the villages.'

'The house is very nice, a big improvement on where I was living before. We're very grateful to you for your help, Cousin.' He was definitely the sort of man who'd expect gratitude to be voiced.

He smirked. 'Can't let family down.'

'We were not aware that you'd kept in touch with Father?' Simon commented.

'Oh, I'd lent him a bit of money. After your mother died, that was.'

Simon stiffened. 'Then you must tell us how much you are owed and I give you my word that one day I'll pay you back.'

'Y'r father paid it back the following year. Had a bit of luck on the horses, I believe.'

Elinor nodded. 'Yes, he did win sometimes.' Lord Morrisham must have pressed for repayment, though, or he'd have got nothing. Few of the other debts had been repaid.

'The cottage is in a very convenient position, not too close to the village,' Adelaide Morrisham volunteered, not liking the way the conversation was going. Money was men's business, not a subject for a lady's drawing-room. 'I'm sure you'll both be very happy there.'

Elinor turned to her with relief. 'I'm sure we shall. My brother will be leaving next week to continue his training, but

I hope he'll be able to come back and see me often.'

'Training as an engineer, eh?' Clarence Morrisham tugged at his military-style moustache. 'Yes. Might be a good thing, that. My livings have both got priests in 'em, and neither fellow is old, so I couldn't help you if you went into the church. But an engineer . . . Yes, it might answer. I have a few connections here and there. Come to me when you finish your training. Not that I have any steam engines, but I know folk who do use the damned things.'

Elinor shot a warning glance at Simon, but he merely inclined his head in response. She hurried to fill the gap. 'I hope I'll be able to make myself useful to you in some way, Cousin Clarence. At home, I was used to doing the flowers in church, visiting the poor, that sort of thing.' And had missed the sense of worth it brought.

Lord Morrisham nodded. 'Good, good.' He scowled at his wife. 'Best if a member of the family takes an interest and Adelaide here hasn't the constitution for it.'

During the meal they continued to make laboured conversation, with His Lordship not hesitating to correct any view with which he didn't agree, and Elinor once or twice kicking Simon in the ankle.

When the carriage had deposited them at home and driven off into the darkness, Simon sighed and put one arm round his sister as they lingered on the doorstep to admire a fine display of stars in a clear night sky. 'How can I leave you here with that – that despot?'

'Quite easily. If I could live with Father, I can certainly cope with Clarence Morrisham. At least I shan't have to see *him* every day.'

'You don't deserve any of this, though.'

She started walking towards the front door. 'We take what life metes out to us and make the best of it. I don't mean to repine over my fate, love. And I shall be glad to live in the country again.' Even if this were a tame place compared to her own countryside. A sudden pang shot through her, a longing for a tramp across the moors on a sunny, breezy day, but she did not allow herself to dwell on that.

When Simon left three days later, Thirza peeped into the

sitting-room and, seeing how sad her mistress looked, suggested, 'Let's go out and look over that garden, eh? We'll get someone to dig the front over for us, then we'll do the rest ourselves.'

Elinor stood up and gave her maid a sudden hug. 'What would I do without you?' she asked in a voice made husky by emotion.

Thirza returned the hug. 'I don't know and I don't mean to let you find out, Miss Elinor.' But though she didn't say so, she didn't like His Lordship, either, she couldn't understand why. Perhaps it was the way he ordered you around. As if you meant nothing to him. As if it only mattered what he wanted.

5

Great Sutton: 1836–37

*B*y the time Jessie was seventeen, she was the tallest of all the maids at five feet ten inches. She was now earning eight pounds a year and was in complete charge of the children's wing, a great honour for one so young. Her mother was delighted about that, but Jessie was indifferent. She was still quite determined not to spend the rest of her life in service and when she was twenty-one, intended to leave Sutton Hall. At the very least, she would find herself a position elsewhere, perhaps in a town where there would be more to see and do. But she wouldn't tell her mother that until it was done.

And if fate really smiled on her, she would find another way entirely of earning her living.

In preparation for her escape, she hoarded her money in the tin trunk which stood at the foot of her narrow bed, earning herself the nickname of Miss Miser because she wouldn't buy herself new trimmings for her old clothes, let alone buy new until the old ones were threadbare or she'd grown right out of them. Mr Marley still gave her a Christmas half-guinea each year and she saved that, as well. Fortunately, her uniforms were provided.

Her only other expense was a few pennies spent on second-hand books to feed her starved brain, for she had read all the moth-eaten volumes on the servants' shelf. Some of the ones the pedlar brought to the rear door of the Hall she kept and some she traded back to him in part-exchange for new ones.

Several times, Susannah Morrisham, who was only two years younger than she was, lent her a book to read, amused to find a maid who shared her own hunger for knowledge. Since her Cousin Elinor had come to live in the neighbourhood, Susannah had changed, become much nicer to serve and often stayed to chat to the tall young maid who brought up her hot water and cleaned out her room.

Jessie had met Miss Stafford several times and found her polite and pleasant to deal with – unlike His Lordship, who seemed to grow more grumpy and autocratic each year.

Mrs Coxleigh had hinted that in a year or two's time, when Miss Susannah came out of the schoolroom, Jessie would probably become her personal maid. And if she played her cards right and won her young mistress's trust, then she would be set for life. Or so her mother assured her. And indeed, being Miss Susannah's maid might be one way of escaping.

Once a month on her Sunday off, she still walked the five miles to Hettonby to spend the day with her mother. Often a passing farmer would offer her a lift, but if not, her strong young legs made nothing of this distance and she revelled in the walk and the fresh air. The only times she missed going were when the snow lay too deep for her to risk the journey, for it wouldn't do to be late back, whatever the reason.

Simon Stafford was not finding life easy as he learned about canals and railways. At first he found it hard to adjust to Samuel Dentinby's ways, for his master was a hard brute of a man, who got every ounce of work out of his apprentices that he could and delighted in besting anyone and everyone who came his way. He clearly found Simon too finicky and too gentlemanly, and his scorn showed.

His senior apprentice was of a similar nature and made the younger man's life a misery for a while, with practical jokes and tricks like pinching his notes. However, he took this a bit too far and even Dentinby noticed, putting a stop to the tricks which were costing him time and money.

Gradually, master and apprentice grew used to one another

and Dentinby came to realise that Simon might wash his hands and scrub his nails when he got home from the diggings, but was not averse to getting those same gentleman's hands dirty. He also promised to be a damned good engineer.

When Elinor moved to Great Sutton, Simon had hoped to go and see her every month, since he was working reasonably close to her, but Dentinby seemed to think it ungrateful of him even to consider it.

'What d'you want to hang on your sister's apron strings for?' he roared when Simon mentioned that he was thinking of going over to Great Sutton at the weekend. 'A young fellow your age should be out drinking,' he winked, 'and finding himself a bit of skirt. What's wrong with you, lad?'

At twenty-two, Simon did not feel like a lad. Nor did he feel like following his employer's example. He already knew how often Samuel Dentinby cheated on his wife, and how often the new young apprentice, Robert, slipped out after dark to meet the barmaid from the village inn. But Simon was too fastidious to do that, so he just endured their taunts and continued to visit Elinor whenever he could.

A few months before Jessie's nineteenth birthday, the railway came into the district and the world turned upside down for many people, herself included.

Lord Morrisham exploded with rage when he heard about the projected railway, opposing it vehemently at every turn and refusing to sell any of his land to the company. After dinner, he would stand in front of the drawing-room fire, hogging all the warmth and boring his family to tears with his tirades. 'Those damned railways are creeping in everywhere, which just shows how modern manners are declining. But, by heaven, I'll not have one on *my* land!'

'I don't think they're really so bad,' Elinor remarked once. 'After all, they're very good for commerce.'

'I am not concerned with commerce, Cousin, but with the preservation of a way of life that has stood the gentry of England in good stead for centuries. But I don't expect a woman to understand that.'

She should have known better than to expect him to discuss it with her, she realised, and said nothing further.

When his attempts to stop the railway coming anywhere near Great Sutton failed and the digging began, he took a perverse interest in riding in that direction and watching everything that was done. He still hindered progress whenever he could, for example by insisting as a magistrate that no work be undertaken on the Sabbath, but there was not really much he could do to prevent the work being done. The company, once properly formed, with its own Act of Parliament passed for the line, contracted out various stretches. The contractors then split the work into smaller projects and sub-contracted it to various specialists, a cutting here, a bridge there. And His Lordship, rant and rave as he might, could not really control anything or even keep an eye on all the nearby projects, which added to his frustration.

One evening in March, he seemed even more furious than usual. 'Damned ingrates!' he snorted into his soup.

'Don't know when they're well off,' he declared over a plate of freshly caught trout.

'They'll live to regret it, see if they don't!' he trumpeted as he carved the joint of beef.

'Who will live to regret what?' Elinor asked, ignoring the way Adelaide was making shushing gestures behind her table napkin.

'Those fools of labourers will. Three of them have run away, that's what they've done, just upped and left their jobs, with the busiest time of year yet to come.'

'Where have they gone?'

'To work on the railways, that's what. Call themselves navigators now. I'll give them navigators if I see them!'

'Perhaps they can earn more money on the railways?' Elinor knew they could, for wages on the estate were very low.

'Twenty shillings a week, the bailiff tells me. What is the world coming to when common men can earn so much money? Why, Jack will think himself as good as his master if we go on like this. And they'll only spend it on drink. We'll see a rise in drunkenness in this county, mark my words, we will.'

Elinor sighed, put a forkful of beef into her mouth to prevent herself from disagreeing, and wished she could earn twenty shillings a week. It would make a big difference to her two hundred pounds a year, which did not allow her to do so many things she had once taken for granted. Keep a riding horse, maintain a carriage, travel a little, to name but a few.

By that time, Simon had left Dentinby and was working on his own, which brought in more money. He moved from one job to the next, wherever work was to be found. When he was offered work on the new line which passed quite close to Great Sutton, he hesitated about accepting it. But there was no other work in the offing just then and he could not afford to sit idle. He needed all he could earn if he was one day to take on his own sub-contract.

He had heard one of Clarence Morrisham's tirades against the railways on his last visit and was beginning to worry about what their benefactor would do if he found out that one of the cousins he had befriended was working on them.

After he had accepted, he wrote to tell his sister what he had done. 'I shall keep very quiet while I'm working there and not even come over to visit you, in case anyone connects us. I think we may rub through without *all being revealed*.'

Elinor showed the letter to Thirza, who shook her head. 'There's too many of the folk round here met him when he's been visiting. They'll recognise him easy, him being so tall and thin. I can't see how he'll keep it quiet who he is. Let alone he looks like you.'

'Well, if the worst comes to the worst, we must just put up with Cousin Clarence's wrath. But if Simon is so close, I couldn't bear not to go and see him.'

'You'd be better not.'

'I'll be careful, Thirza, I promise.'

The servants at the Hall were as fascinated by the railways as everyone else in the district. Even the Morrisham children were taking a keen interest – though not when their father was around, of course. Miss Susannah told Jessie one day that her Cousin Elinor thought the railways wonderful and that Cousin Simon was working on them at the cutting just down the road. They had been over to meet him secretly and he had shown them the diggings from a safe distance. Susannah's eyes were alight with mischief as she spoke, for she, too, suffered from her father's autocratic temperament and had enjoyed deceiving him. 'But don't tell any of the other servants that, please, Jessie. I trust you, but they might speak out of turn. Elinor and I haven't said anything to Father about what Simon's doing, of course. You know what he's like.'

'Of course I'll keep it to myself, miss.'

Susannah went to stare out of the window. 'I wish I could get on a train and go far away and never come back. Nothing exciting ever happens here.'

Jessie made a noise which could have been taken for agreement and continued to pick up pieces of discarded clothing.

'And look how fast the trains go. Just think of it – more than twice as fast as horses, Cousin Simon says. Oh, I'm longing to ride on one.'

'Won't that make people dizzy, miss?'

'No. Simon says it's exhilarating.' Susannah beamed at her maid. 'I do like my cousins. I'm *so* glad they came to live here.'

Next time she heard His Lordship grumbling to the butler again about runaway labourers, and the butler parroting the same phrases to the housekeeper an hour later, Jessie smiled. She thought it a wonderful thing for ordinary men to have this chance of earning better money and only wished something similar were available for ordinary women.

Most of the men who fell into the temptation of leaving to work for the railways were young single men, but one or two who followed them later were married with families. 'His Lordship's in a right taking today,' Thomas said during the evening meal one night, after a quick glance round to make sure Mr Howard wasn't nearby. 'He's had to turn Mrs Perrins and the children out of their cottage in Great Sutton to make way for the new ploughman.'

Jessie was betrayed into muttering, 'Poor woman!' which earned her a scolding afterwards from Vera.

Two days later, the butler appeared during the servants'

evening meal, which he usually took in state in Mrs Coxleigh's room. Flanked by the housekeeper, he stood at the head of the table, cleared his throat and waited as everyone fell silent. 'His Lordship wishes me to inform you that you are forbidden to speak to or associate with any person employed on the railways. Any servant who does so will be dismissed instantly. Without a reference!'

A whisper ran round the table.

'Is that clear?' Mr Howard demanded.

There was a chorus of 'Yes, sir!' and 'Oh, certainly, sir.'

Lord Morrisham did not, however, turn away the opportunity to make a nice profit by selling meat and vegetables from the home farm to the diggings at inflated prices.

'Trust him!' said Thomas cynically, when he passed on this titbit of information to the other servants. 'He says it's one's Christian duty not to let one's fellow creatures starve.'

'Mrs Perrins won't be eating well inside the poor house,' Jessie commented.

'They say she's pining away,' Thomas admitted, for once in sympathy with her. His family lived in the village and his mother had told him if it hadn't been for their fear of His Lordship, they might have got poor little Amy Perrins out of the poor house and found her some temporary lodgings and a bit of work until she heard from her husband again. But apparently His Lordship wanted an example made of her and her family as a warning to others, and the bailiff said their own jobs and tenancies might be at risk if they did anything. 'They're upsetting everyone, those navvies are,' Thomas ended gloomily.

'Well, they won't be in the area for long, will they?'

'A few months yet, apparently. It's going to take a bit longer to finish this stretch than they thought it would. His Lordship and Parson Bulmer won't let them work the diggings on Sundays, you see.'

What difference would that make to Lord Morrisham? Jessie wondered. It was just sour grapes, that was all, and in her opinion, a lord ought to be above such things.

When someone banged furiously on the door of their small house one afternoon and kept on banging, Elinor turned to Thirza in amazement. 'Who can that be?'

Thirza peered out of the window. 'It's His Lordship. And he looks furious.'

'I'd better answer the door, then.'

'No. You go and sit in the parlour. I'll answer it.' Thirza did so and gasped in shock as he brushed right past her without a word and stormed into the parlour. Shutting the front door, she crept along the hallway to listen, worried for her mistress.

'Is it true?' he demanded, arms akimbo, not even taking off his hat.

Elinor stared at him in amazement. 'Please take a seat, Cousin Clarence.'

His voice rose several tones and doubled in volume. *'Is - it - true?'*

She sat down again and took her time about arranging her skirts. She could guess what this was about. 'Is what true?'

'That your brother is working on those damned railways?'

There was silence as she looked up at his blotchy red face. 'Please don't raise your voice to me, Cousin Clarence. I don't appreciate being bullied.'

He gobbled incoherently for a few seconds, then got out the words: 'Answer me, dammit, woman!'

'Yes, it's true.'

'You deceived me, then?'

'Not intentionally. You assumed that Simon was working on steam engines. By the time we realised how strongly you felt about the railways, I had already moved here and was dependent upon you for my home, so it seemed best to let matters lie.'

He swept off his hat and plonked himself down on a chair. 'Have you any idea how I felt when Harold Blackworth twitted me about my views on the railways and then threw my own cousin's employment at me? Simon's even working nearby, apparently, rubbing it in people's faces.'

Her heart sank at the expression on his face. His vanity had been damaged. 'I'm sorry you're so upset, Clarence, but I can assure you that Simon is not rubbing anything in people's faces. He's tried not to mention his connection with you.'

'Well, he's failed then, hasn't he?'

'He'll be gone in a few months and then people will stop talking.' It was the nearest she could manage to an apology and even that stuck in her throat.

He thumped one fist on the occasional table that stood between them, setting it skittering across the room and scattering her embroidery silks over the floor. 'I won't have it!'

She waited, very still, her heart thumping suddenly inside her breast, as it used to thump when her father got into one of his passions.

Clarence Morrisham took several breaths, then said in a slightly calmer voice, but one with a vicious undertone, 'I have an ultimatum for you, madam. Either your brother finds himself other employment or he will no longer be welcome on my estate.'

Outside the door, Thirza put one hand to her mouth but kept listening. If he got violent, she'd run in and help her mistress, she would indeed.

Elinor stood up, very pale and dignified in contrast to her visitor. 'I can't believe you mean that.'

'I most certainly do. As long as he's on the railways, Simon is not setting foot on my land again. And if *you* defy me about this, you can choose between your brother and your home.'

Elinor did not hesitate. 'Then I had better find myself somewhere else to live, had I not?'

Silence hung heavy between them and when he did break it, His Lordship spoke more temperately. 'You can't mean that! After all I've done for you.'

'Simon is my brother, my only close relative. There is no way I would cut myself off from him.'

'I'll give you until tomorrow morning to think it over. I fancy you'll change your mind when you consider what it will mean to leave this place.' He looked around him with a return of his usual complacency.

Her temper snapped. 'This cottage, Cousin, is damp and ill-designed. When I moved here, there was nothing but grass growing in the garden. I think you'll find that I have repaid your *kindness* by improving its amenities greatly, as well as undertaking many charitable duties on your estate in Adelaide's place.

I shall miss the company of your wife and daughters, miss them greatly,' especially Susannah, who was her favourite, 'but I have no intention of being bullied by anyone. Or of being forbidden to see my only brother.'

He was making angry, gobbling noises again, shocked rigid that any woman should dare to speak to him like that.

Elinor moved towards the door. 'I'd be grateful if you'd kindly leave now. I'll find somewhere else to live as soon as I can.'

He strode out after her. 'See that you do, then. You're as ungrateful as those labourer scum.'

When the front door had slammed behind him, she leaned against the wall, trembling. 'So like Father,' she whispered, and turned to hold Thirza's arm until the sick, shaky feeling had passed.

The next day Jessie found Susannah sobbing her heart out in her bedroom. Without thinking about it, she went to pat the heaving shoulders, and when Susannah turned and threw herself into her arms, she let the girl weep herself out.

When Vera peered into the room, her eyes met Jessie's and her lips pursed. It wasn't right for a maid to cuddle Miss Susannah like that.

As if she had sensed the eyes on her, Susannah turned round and drew a deep, shuddering breath. 'Oh, Vera. Will you please excuse Jessie if she's late with things? I was - upset. And she - she's been very kind.'

'Certainly, miss.' Vera's eyes said that she would not be excusing Jessie for forgetting her place, but she withdrew for the moment.

Susannah, who was nobody's fool, looked at Jessie. 'I've got you into trouble too, now, haven't I? Thank you for - for being here.'

'Everyone gets upset sometimes. Is it anything I can help with?'

Susannah shook her head. 'No. It's my father. He's forbidden me to see my Cousin Elinor again. He's found out that Simon is working on the railways and says she got the cottage from him under false pretences.' More tears rolled down the girl's cheeks. 'And I don't know what I'll do without her. There's no one else I can talk to.'

'Will she have to leave?' Surely even His Lordship would not be so unkind as to turn her out?

Susannah nodded. 'He said *she* could stay, but her brother was not to visit, so she chose to leave. Only she hasn't got much money and – and she has nowhere to go. I'm so worried about her!'

Jessie did not comment. It wasn't her place. But she felt angry. What did His Lordship think he was? Ruler of the world?

6

⟡

May 1837

*F*or the next week, Miss Susannah moped around the house like someone who'd lost a lover and her eyes were constantly red, as if she'd been weeping. As a result, Lady Morrisham said it was time the chit had a maid of her own and started preparations for her eldest daughter's coming out. Susannah could join her mother on visits to other families in the neighbourhood and start learning to go about in polite society.

'So you, Burton, are to maid Miss Susannah whenever she needs you,' Vera said. 'We'll start training up Young Jane to help you with the bedrooms and the other children. And if you prove satisfactory, you can become Miss Susannah's maid full-time when the family goes up to London. Her Ladyship's maid will give you lessons on how to do hair and such.'

Jessie nodded.

'You don't look all that pleased,' Vera said sourly. She had hoped Jessie would not be acceptable for the post, because her Cousin Letty would love that job, absolutely love it, but that Jessie Burton had taken advantage of Miss Stafford's leaving to worm her way in with Miss Susannah.

'Oh, I am. Very pleased,' Jessie said hastily.

'Well, just see that you give satisfaction, then. It's a great honour. And you're not even nineteen yet.' Vera intended to keep a careful eye on her in future, and if she saw a chance to help Letty, she would.

Nineteen! Sometimes she felt more like ninety, Jessie thought. As if she'd been a prisoner here for a thousand dreary years.

The servants' hall continued to buzz with talk about the railway, new rumours being added daily. 'Of course,' Vera declared one evening, 'there's no fear of any of *us* leaving!' Everyone looked at Thomas and James as she said this. The two matched footmen, both the same height and of roughly the same colouring, were the only ones young and strong enough to be considered candidates for a navigator's job.

'I wouldn't soil my hands with such menial work,' James declared, 'whatever they pay you there. I know which side my bread's buttered on, thank you very much!'

'Me, neither,' said Thomas hastily, when he saw everyone's eyes on him.

From her place at the head of the table, Vera nodded approvingly. 'And, of course, none of *my* girls would associate with such rough fellows as navigators,' she added. The 'girls', some of them pushing forty and growing grey in His Lordship's service, tittered at the mere idea.

But the gossip did not die down and as the days passed, great interest continued to be taken in the progress of the diggings. Only James had actually seen the work when he went to visit his uncle on his day off, and he held centre stage describing it after he got back. 'Filthy place. Piles of muck and dozens of them navvies all covered in mud. Ugly brutes, they are. Wouldn't catch me working in a place like that. Not likely!'

'Who do you think will be the next to go?' James wondered aloud. 'They've all gone as could go from the village.'

'What do you think, Jessie?' Vera asked suddenly. 'What are things like in Hettonby? Is anyone there likely to run off?'

'I don't know. And I don't really care about the railways. They're nothing to me.'

Jessie was glad when it was her Sunday off and she could leave the Hall and its gossiping inmates behind to walk over to her mother's. It was a fine early spring day, the sun was shining and the daffodils were out in the woods. The five-mile walk would be a real treat, filling her soul with peace as it always did. And although she had long ceased to believe in fairies, the woods still held a magic for Jessie that nothing could erase.

She didn't leave the Hall until nine in the morning. In spite of its being her day off, she still had to help carry up the heavy copper cans of hot water to the children's rooms and lend a hand with the beds before she left. But by ten o'clock she was well on her way, dawdling in the woods, deep in daydreams. It came as a shock to realise she was not alone. A tall young man was barring her path.

'Good morning, miss.' His accent betrayed him immediately as a stranger. No one she knew spoke like this.

He was huge, one of the tallest men she'd ever met, well over six feet for sure. He made Thomas and James look puny. He had broad shoulders, strongly muscled, and looked like a man who worked with his body, taking pride in his strength. He was clean, too, his skin ruddy and glowing with health.

She had only intended to say good morning and be on her way, but couldn't help staring and thinking how handsome he was, in spite of the newly healed scar across one cheek! Dark curly hair, vivid blue eyes and a smile that would melt an icicle. Before she realised what she was doing, she found herself returning his smile and listening as he spoke again.

'Could you please tell me, miss, if there's a farm near here as would sell me a breakfast?'

He was too flamboyantly dressed to be a villager, wearing good corduroy trousers, a blue and white striped shirt and a leather waistcoat. He had a bright red scarf knotted around his neck and a jacket slung over his shoulder. She should have followed Lord Morrisham's orders, ignored him and gone on her way. Instead, she found herself asking, 'Are you a navigator, then?'

'A navvy, aye. I'm workin' on the cutting.'

'You should get off Lord Morrisham's land before you ask for food at any of the farms. He doesn't approve of the railway and has told his tenants to have nothing to do with anyone working on it. You'd be best going to an inn. They'd not refuse to serve you there.'

She nodded to him and would have moved on but he turned and began to walk beside her, matching his great strides to her smaller steps. It felt strange to be with a man so much taller.

Suddenly she remembered Lord Morrisham's orders and realised that she was putting her own job in jeopardy. She wondered how to tell the stranger to leave her alone. It would have been easy enough to get rid of Thomas or James. She had their measure and despised them. But this man was different. He was – she searched for the word she wanted – yes, that was it, he was *free*! Look at the way he was striding along beside her, head up, breathing deeply, as if the very air tasted good to him. She felt like that sometimes when she got out of the Hall.

He looked down at her and smiled again, a smile that lit up his whole face and made Jessie feel all strange and fluttery inside. 'And where would His Lordship's land end, so that I can get a meal?'

'About a mile down the road.'

'Your road?'

'I – I beg your pardon?'

'Are you goin' that way?'

'Oh. Well – yes, I am.'

He noticed her hesitation and his smile broadened. 'Shall I walk ten steps behind you, then? I wouldn't want t'get you into trouble with His Almighty Lordship.'

She couldn't help chuckling at that. 'No. Of course not! It's not far. I'll tell you when we get to a road that leads off the estate. But if we meet anyone, I'll have to walk away from you or I'll be in trouble.' After all, he wasn't doing any harm, so why should she be rude to him?

'Me name's Jared Wilde.' He paused expectantly.

'Oh. Well, I'm Jessie Burton.'

He gave a mocking bow. 'Pleased t'meet you, Miss Jessie Burton.'

They walked on for a while, but it seemed he couldn't keep silent. 'Do you work for His Lordship, then? Everyone else round here seems to.'

'Yes. I'm an upstairs maid at the Hall.'

'Upstairs maid?' he repeated, thoughtfully. 'An' what does one of those do, might I ask?'

'Don't you know?' She was amazed at his ignorance.

He flushed. 'No, I don't! Or I wouldn't have asked, would I? But it doesn't matter, if you don't want to tell me. P'rhaps you're ashamed of what you do!'

Now it was her turn to redden. 'I'm sorry if I sounded rude.'

He nodded acceptance of her apology. 'Go on, then. Tell me what an upstairs maid does? I like to learn about things.' And he'd like to learn a lot more about this pretty lass, by heck he would!

'I look after the bedrooms at the Hall. I make the beds, clean the rooms, lay the fires, bring up the hot water – that sort of thing, you know.'

'An' d'you like doing it?'

'No, I hate it!' The words were out before she could stop them.

Now it was his turn to look surprised. 'Then why d'you do it? A strong lass like you could easy get another job.'

She pulled a face. 'I do it because my mother thinks it's a good way to earn your living. It's very *respectable*!' She flung the last word at him defiantly.

Jared shrugged and changed the subject. 'Where are you goin' now?'

'To see my mother. It's my day off.'

'Is she very respectable, too?'

Jessie gasped indignantly. 'What a thing to say! You make it sound as if – as if it's something to be ashamed of!'

He grinned. 'Nay, I didn't mean it like that. But is she?'

'Yes. She's housekeeper to Parson Marley at Hettonby.' She stared him right in the eye. Let him mock that, if he dared!

'Aye, that sounds about as respectable as you can get.'

She decided not to answer. If he made fun of her again, she'd tell him to go away and leave her to walk alone. But he didn't say anything else, just walked along beside her with that easy stride. She somehow found herself speaking to him again. 'If you're working on the railway, what are you doing round here? The cutting's over the other side of Little Sutton, isn't it?'

'I'm just out for a walk. I work in all the muck for six days, then on Sundays I get out of it – an' out of the camp too.'

'What do you do when you get away from the camp?'

'I just walk until I'm tired, then sit down somewhere peaceful an' have meself a bit of a think. A person needs time to think, don't you reckon?'

'Oh, yes.' Jessie found herself warming to him. She liked what he said, even if he did make fun of her. And she liked his easy confidence, unlike Thomas's slyness and his servility to those above him. She'd bet that this man was never servile.

'And when do *you* get time to think?' he asked.

'I don't much. Just on my Sundays off, once a month, like today. There are always too many people around at the Hall. The family keep twenty indoor servants, you know.'

'Fancy that!' he said gravely, but his eyes were dancing with laughter again.

'What's so funny?'

'I'm not laughin' at you, lass. It's just - fancy needin' twenty people to look after one family! Are they helpless, these rich folk? Do they need someone to wipe their bums - ' he saw her stiffen and hastily changed it to ' - I mean, wipe their noses for them?'

'No, silly! They need us to look after the house. The Hall has over fifty rooms. That takes a lot of cleaning.'

'It would. And do they use all them fifty rooms?'

'No.' But they still wanted everything cleaning every week and there was trouble if even a speck of dust was seen during Mrs Coxleigh's inspections.

Jessie didn't know whether to be glad or sorry when they came to her turn-off. She stopped and pointed ahead. 'If you go down there, you'll find the village and you should be able to get a good breakfast at the inn. But don't tell them you work on the railway. They'll guess, but if you don't say it, they won't ask. I have to turn off here.'

She bade him a crisp goodbye and turned on her heel. She didn't look back, or she'd have seen that he stood and watched her until she was out of sight. Then he sighed and made his way down the hill to the little hamlet to buy himself a late breakfast. Eh, she was a bonny lass, that one was. He didn't know when he'd met a bonnier. Some day, he'd find himself a lass like that to marry. When he was better set up. Yes, he really liked the looks of her - tall and womanly, not a snirpy little thing like his friend Alfred Small's wife.

* * *

The rest of the day seemed to Jessie to go very slowly. She had to pass on to her mother all the latest gossip from the Hall, for Agnes could never hear enough about the life there. And, of course, her mother shared His Lordship's views on navvies.

'Jim Todd's run away to join them.'

'We hadn't heard about Jim.'

'It only happened last week, and anyway his family don't live on the estate. Granny Todd's that upset. Everyone feels for her. She says she'll never see the boy again, and him her favourite grandson, and that he'll learn rough ways.'

Jessie tried to look on the bright side. 'He might make a lot of money, though.'

'Money's not everything.'

'No, but it comes in useful and they say those navvies earn a pound a week.'

Agnes Burton sniffed. 'Well, that's as may be, but I don't want to spend all day talking about *them*. Tell me how Miss Susannah is, and how you're enjoying maiding her. Have you got used to doing her hair now?'

'It's only part of the time that I look after her, though it is more interesting . . .'

Later, there was church to be attended. After the service, everyone waited for the folk from the front pews to leave, for a young couple called Nellor had recently rented the old Manor House to the north of the village, a place which had stood empty for years, and they chose to worship in Hettonby. Only when they'd left did the rest of the congregation file out and stand chatting in the churchyard.

It was always nice to see Mr Snelling, the schoolmaster, but Jessie also had to face her former classmates and they were no more friendly towards her now than they had been at school. Most of the girls were married or betrothed, and liked to flaunt their husbands or young men in front of poor Jessie Burton, who might have done better than them at school, but who was only a servant and never likely to get married. Not to anyone respectable, anyway.

After church came the midday meal, which Jessie always

enjoyed. Her mother was a good cook, and it was pleasant to eat quietly together, instead of sitting down at a table of twenty chattering servants. Today, however, the food seemed tasteless and the afternoon dragged on interminably. Even the fluffy scones offered with her parting cup of tea stuck in Jessie's throat and she could hardly choke one down. In the end she left early, making the excuse that she had some mending to do.

The air seemed sweeter outside and Jessie breathed deeply as she swung along at a cracking pace. She could normally think herself out of a bad mood and on to the sensible path again, but today all her reasoning was in vain. She kept seeing a handsome face and a pair of blue eyes twinkling down at her. She kept seeing Jared Wilde's head thrown back in laughter, such hearty ringing laughter. She kept hearing a voice saying, 'Then why d'you do it?'

'Well, I won't be doing it forever!' Jessie didn't realise that she had spoken these last words aloud until a familiar voice broke into her reverie.

'They say it's the first sign of madness, y'know.'

She looked up and there he was, smiling down at her. Drat the man! What she needed was to talk herself into the right frame of mind, but looking at him, at the way he stood leaning against a tree, lazily smiling, she felt the restlessness she'd been suppressing all day surge up again and overflow. Life wasn't *fair*! She stood staring up at him, not knowing what to say or do.

And Jared was the same. He'd had any number of things worked out to say to the pretty lass he'd met that morning, but they all flew out of his head after he made his opening remark, and he stood there as tongue-tied as she was. And that was funny, because Big Jared had a way with women and they usually came to him as tame as doves. But this one was no dove! Her fiery spirit showed in her bright, sparkling blue eyes. She was looking furious about something and he was part of it, he could tell that.

Without a word, Jessie swung round and began to walk on, her lips pressed tightly together. Without a word, he fell in beside her.

'I waited for you,' he said abruptly, breaking the silence and surprising himself even more than her by his honesty.

'I can't think why,' she replied with a toss of her head.

'I can't either. No – I can really. I just – I wanted t'see you again.'

'Oh, yes?' Her tone gave him no encouragement. She had her eyes on the path and was choosing her way with unusual care, as if her very life depended on it.

'Was your mam all right?'

'Oh, yes. She never ails.'

'Good. Good.'

'And did you have your think?' She regretted the question as soon as it was voiced. It was getting too personal to ask him something like that. And it showed that she remembered their earlier conversation.

'Sort of.'

'Oh?'

When she looked questioningly up at him through those thick lashes, he had to fight off the urge to reach out, pull her towards him and kiss her soundly. But he didn't dare touch her. There was something special about this woman that made him want to avoid upsetting her. Abandoning the stilted conversation, he spoke abruptly from the heart.

'Aye. But what I thought about was you, my bonny lass. All day. On and on. That's why I waited for you to come back.'

'Oh.'

'Is that all you can say? Just, "*Oh*"!' His tone was harsh.

She flushed. 'Well, what do you expect me to say? You're a stranger. A navvy. I could lose my place just for talking to you!' But she'd been thinking about him all day, too, much to her annoyance, though she wasn't going to admit that, of course.

'Why *are* you talking to me, then?'

'I don't know. You disturb me – make me feel restless.' She hesitated over her choice of words. 'I've felt downright dissatisfied all day, if you must know. I thought the afternoon was never going to pass. I think – I think it's because I envy you.'

'Envy *me*?' That was the last thing he'd expected her to say. Folk didn't usually envy railway navvies; they mostly despised them.

'Yes, envy you!' Her voice was fierce and tight. 'It's all right for you men. You can go off and dig railways or – or go to sea – or anything!' The words were pouring out, like a dam suddenly bursting. 'A woman like me can either get married or go into service. There's nothing else that's respectable.'

His voice was mild. 'Most women seem happy enough to get married.'

'Well, I shan't be! The only men who'd have me for a wife, because I'm just a servant's brat, are thick-headed lumps of labourers, or stupid footmen with brains like sparrows! I'd rather stay in service for the rest of my life than marry one of them. It's safe and it's respectable.' Her voice was bitter.

'That's your favourite word *respectable*.'

'Well, what's wrong with that? It's better than what my mother went through with my father before he died! Once they get on the booze . . .'

She stopped short, the words dying on her lips in a half-sob. She'd never told anyone before about her mother's early life. Why was she telling this stranger?

'Drank, did he?'

'Yes. And beat her. And gambled away his money, so she went hungry. I shan't make the same mistake she did.'

'My mam died when I were eight,' Jared said abruptly. 'She had consumption. We called it the coughin' sickness in our street, but a doctor came to see her once an' he called it consumption. I've never forgotten the bloody word. He said she were to rest an' eat plenty of light nourishing food. Only she couldn't rest, could she, not with six children an' a man to look after? And we thought ourselves lucky to get any food, let alone "light nourishing" stuff, whatever that is.' He drew in a deep, painful breath. 'So she looked after us as best she could till she couldn't stand up any more, an' then she died as quickly as she could. She kept sayin' she were sorry to be such a nuisance. *Nuisance!* She were a good mother, the best.' He let out a long shuddering sigh, then added bitterly, 'An' then, when she'd gone, me dad married again, only a month later. He couldn't wait, couldn't do without it.'

His voice became as fierce as Jessie's had been. 'It were a woman from t'mill where he worked. He'd been goin' with her since afore me mam died. Kitty were pregnant already, six months gone. I hated 'er, the old sow! She used to hit me with a strap. When I were ten, I were big enough to hit her back, so I did, an' then I left.' He looked down at his bunched fists. 'I were allus big for me age.'

Jessie's heart was touched. She could imagine him, a lump of a lad, grieving for his mother. 'I'm sorry.'

He just shrugged.

'How did you live?'

'As best I could till I were twelve. Then I went to work on a canal. I weren't strong enough to dig, but I made mesen useful to one of the gangs an' they let me stay around. It were a fellow called Clogger Joe as gave me that job.' He smiled. 'He's workin' at the same camp as me now. He's a tough old b— er, fellow.'

He stopped and she said, 'Go on!' finding his tale fascinating.

'When I were eating proper, I started to grow again an' soon I were big enough to dig. When the gang moved to the railways, I did too. It's hard work, but the pay's good – if you don't drink it. An' I don't. An' what's more, I *like* workin' on the railways.' The last was tossed at her just as defiantly as she had tossed her respectability at him.

They stared at one another and the world seemed to slow down around them.

'Jessie . . .'

'Yes.'

'Jessie Burton, I really like you.'

She turned scarlet and took refuge in flippancy. 'Thank you very much, I'm sure!'

He reached out and took her by the shoulders, shaking her roughly so that she dropped her package.

'Don't talk like that! Don't *ever* talk like that when I'm sayin' something that matters!' He shook her again, gently, to emphasise his words. 'I've never said that to a woman before. Never.'

She swayed as if dizzy. 'Let me go!' She was breathless, gasping.

But he didn't let her go. He drew her slowly towards him, eyes fixed on hers so that she couldn't look away. And she could only go to him, her heart fluttering madly inside her. Like a dreamer she raised her lips for his kiss and tenderly he drew her close. She hadn't realised that a kiss could feel like this, could bind two people together, could rouse such a surge of passion in her. And when it was over, when he drew his lips away from hers and just cradled her head against his shoulder, she could only stay there, clinging to him. As he was clinging to her.

How long they stood there Jessie couldn't have told. She only knew that for the first time in her life she had met a man she respected, a man who would be worth loving. When at last she pulled away, she was trembling slightly and stood looking up at him like one mesmerised.

He was just as shaken by the kiss as she was. For all his experience, no woman had ever touched his heart like this. Imagine him, Big Jared, telling a woman that he liked her, feeling a woman respond to him as this one had and making no attempt to take her. He must be mad!

'Jessie Burton, you're a witch!' he said huskily.

She looked straight up into his eyes. 'Jared Wilde, I like you,' she said, deliberately echoing his earlier words.

At that his restraint slipped. He gave a shout of joy and swung her round and round like a child, till she begged him, laughing breathlessly, to put her down again. Then she picked up her package, the biscuits her mother had baked for her, though she didn't really need extra food, and they walked on slowly through the woods, holding hands, smiling from time to time, but saying very little. What did they need to say? They'd found each other and they knew it. For the moment it was enough to savour that knowledge.

Not till they were nearly at the walls of Lord Morrisham's private park did they come tumbling back down to earth. Jessie wanted to stay with Jared, but she had to ask him not to go any further with her, in case someone saw them together. They kissed again, lingeringly, and then arranged to meet in a fortnight's time, when she would have her half day off.

She dreamed of him every night during those two weeks, every single night. And she didn't know whether to be glad or sad about that, whether to be glad or sorry that she'd met him, even. She didn't feel as if she knew anything any more. Only that she would meet him as arranged. And after that – who could tell?

7

Sutton Hall

*E*linor wrote to Simon to tell him that she was leaving her cottage and why, then set about finding somewhere to live. But without the Morrisham carriage, it took a long time to get anywhere and she was reluctant to spend some of her precious savings on hiring a carriage, so the house hunting went very slowly.

She hadn't liked living in Halifax and Leeds was close by, so she started looking there. Thirza went with her on the local stage coach and they stayed overnight, but what they saw depressed them both. Smoky air and rows of houses with no gardens. It was just as bad as Halifax.

'What are we going to do?' Elinor worried that night in the frowsy bedroom they were sharing in a small, inexpensive inn.

'We'll find something, miss, don't you worry. And after all, he's a gentleman. He won't put his own cousin out in the street.'

While Elinor was in Leeds, Lord Morrisham went to dine with an old acquaintance, who had known him long enough to dare to tease him over rather too many glasses of port about his relative, the railway engineer. Clarence controlled his temper, but inside felt swollen with rage by the time his carriage was summoned.

His wife did not dare open her mouth the whole way home, just huddled in the corner and let him rant on.

'How dare Elinor do this to me?' he spat out. 'After all my

kindness to her, too. Taking her in, when she was little more than a pauper.'

'Mmm.'

'And she's taking her own sweet time about finding somewhere else to live.' The memory of his friend's gleeful expression nearly made him choke. 'I'll have to hurry her up a bit. I'll show her I'm not to be trifled with. I'll show everyone I mean what I say. They'll not laugh at me again.'

On and on he went, and after they got home, he stormed into his wife's bedchamber, for lack of anyone else to torment, and made violent love to her, in spite of her pleas and whimpered protests.

When Elinor and Thirza got home the next day, after looking round some villages to the south of Leeds, they were exhausted after tramping the streets then jolting along in a tired old stage coach that smelled of sweat and straw. They were unlucky enough to meet her cousin in the village as they were walking back from the inn, carrying their portmanteau between them.

When Lord Morrisham strode over to them, he looked so enraged that Elinor thought for one minute he was going to strike her.

Instead of dropping back to let her betters talk in private, Thirza had to stay by her mistress's side, holding one handle of the bag. She, too, was terrified that he meant to do them an injury, for he was nearly purple with rage.

He planted himself in front of Elinor, ignoring the maid. 'Well, have you found another place to live, madam?'

'No, I'm afraid not. I – '

'You've had over two weeks to look now, by God! You're just not trying. You think I'll change my mind, don't you? Well, by hell I won't! I meant exactly what I said. No one connected with the railways is going to stay on my land.'

'I'm doing my best to find somewhere, Cousin Clarence, I do ass—'

'Don't "Cousin" me! I repudiate the relationship, repudiate it utterly.'

She stared at him, not understanding what he wanted, amazed and horrified by this public confrontation.

He smiled then, a cruel smile, like a small boy taking pleasure from tormenting a lame dog, and for a moment his voice grew softer. 'You must let me help you to do better, then, madam. I shall send two of my farm carts over to the cottage tomorrow. Have your things packed and they'll be at your service to help you move.'

'But I have nowhere to go!'

His voice increased in volume again till everyone nearby could hear him. 'You can go to hell for all I care, madam. You and your brother, both!' He pushed Thirza out of the way so violently that she dropped the bag and fell over, then strode off, shouting over his shoulder, 'They'll be there at daybreak. Make sure you're ready to leave.'

Tears were trickling down Elinor's face, but she held her head up proudly as she helped her maid to rise and together they took hold of the bag again.

'What are we to do now, miss?' Thirza whispered as they started walking.

'Send a message to my brother. He'll help us.'

'But where shall we go?' For once, even Thirza had lost heart.

'I don't know. But I'll make sure we find somewhere. I'm not staying in that house any longer than I have to.'

The days passed so slowly during the two weeks after her encounter with Jared that Jessie thought she would go mad with frustration. If she had found work at the Hall uncongenial before, how much more so now? Untidy beds, filthy stinking chamber pots, dirty grates, floors to scrub and sweep, endless, endless cans of hot water to carry up morning and evening . . . then the whole process to repeat the next day.

Only the years of enforced self-control made Jessie still able to maintain the pattern of her days and carry on as if nothing had happened: coping with Miss Susannah's fusses, ignoring the teasing of the footmen, pretending to listen to the chatter of the other maids – in fact, behaving absolutely normally – as if the earth hadn't stood still for a precious few moments on her Sunday off, as if she didn't see Jared again every night in her dreams.

Worst of all during those long days were her thoughts. Round and round they buzzed in her head like flies on a scrap of food. One day and two meetings with Jared Wilde had stirred up feelings in her which made her blush to think of them, though as a country girl, she knew perfectly well what happened between males and females, whatever the species. But somehow, she had never thought *she* would be affected like that.

Sometimes she grew angry with herself for reacting so strongly to a handsome face and a pair of bright blue eyes. She was just as bad as any other silly girl, just as bad as those she'd always despised! How could she feel like that after all her mother's careful training?

A voice grated in her ear: 'Jessie Burton, what on earth's got into you today?'

She dropped her duster. 'Oh! I'm sorry, Mrs Coxleigh. I was just thinking about something.'

'You aren't paid to think, but to clean the bedrooms!'

'I've almost finished, Mrs Coxleigh.'

'Indeed you have not! Look at that grate! You'll re-do it before you stir another step, and I'll be back to check it afterwards myself.' She bent down to tug at the carefully set pile of kindling and wood, leaving it in a mess all over the hearth.

Jessie heard the housekeeper muttering something about 'don't know what's got into that girl' as she walked away down the corridor and felt ashamed that she had done her work less than well. But when she looked at the grate, she grew angry. There had been nothing wrong with it, but Mrs Coxleigh had decided to punish her by making her re-set the fire, so it had all to be done again.

As the golden glow of that Sunday receded into the past and the two long weeks dragged slowly by, Jessie grew more and more worried. What, after all, did she really know about Jared Wilde? Why, she didn't even know how old he was! Her temper grew short and her fellow workers looked at her in bewilderment, trying to keep out of her way. What on earth had got into Jessie Burton?

Then, at long last, it was Sunday. Perversely Jessie didn't put on her new dress, but dragged from her tin trunk her old green checked one, a simple dress with long sleeves, puffed at the top, and white lawn cuffs and collar. She had spent hours scalloping the edges of the muslin, and been pleased with the delicate effect, but now the dress seemed limp and ordinary to her. She scowled at herself in the speckled mirror in the attic and crammed her bonnet down anyhow on her head, muttering to herself as she tied the ribbons under her chin. What did it matter how she looked? She was a fool to be meeting him and it could not, *must not*, continue. And so she would tell him.

By the time she left the park gates, anger at herself for getting into this situation was burning high in her and she had almost convinced herself that he would not be there and that she would be glad of it.

She felt shocked to find him waiting for her as arranged, leaning against a tree and chewing a piece of grass, a blue neckerchief at his throat this time, matching the vivid hue of his eyes. Again her eyes lingered on the scar, healed now but still marring one cheek. His skin looked tanned and healthy against the cream of his coarse cotton shirt – a shirt which was crudely sewn and which would have been the better for a good ironing, but which was, at least, clean.

And when his face lit up at the sight of her, her heart began to thud in her breast and she couldn't move a step.

He tossed the grass stalk away and came striding towards her, ready to sweep her into his arms. 'Jessie!'

But perversely she took a step backwards.

Some of the eagerness went out of his face. 'What's the matter?'

'I – I . . .' She couldn't think what to say and made a little movement with her hand, as if to ward him off.

When she looked beseechingly up at him, he was reminded of a bird he had once seen fluttering in a trap, one he had released then had to put out of its misery, because its wing was broken. His expression softened and he asked again, very gently this time, 'What's the matter, Jessie, love?'

'You. Me. Us.' She was looking down at her hands, which were clasped together so tightly that her knuckles had turned white. She did not see him start to reach towards her and then check the gesture.

He spoke softly. 'I won't ever hurt you, Jessie. Don't you know that?'

'I – I don't know anything – about you.' Her words came hesitantly, in little rushes. 'And I – I've never – never even walked out with anyone before.'

'Are the lads round here so blind, then? How did you manage to frighten them off?' He spoke lightly, casually, as if this weren't the most important conversation of his whole life.

She flicked a quick glance up at him through her long lashes and flushed a little. 'I wasn't fishing for compliments, Jared Wilde. I was – I was . . .'

'You were makin' a mountain out of a molehill, Jessie Burton. Look, we met two weeks ago. We liked each other. We arranged t'meet again. That's all! No one's rushin' you into anythin' you don't want. An' I promise faithfully that you'll not lose your precious respectability with me.' He paused to let that sink in, then said quietly, 'How about showin' me these woods of yours, then?'

They wandered along, hiding twice to let people go by, stifling their laughter as they did so, which relieved the tension nicely. They shared the piece of cake that Cook had given Jessie, then drank from a stream and splashed their hands in the water to clean them, laughing at how cold it was, still not properly warmed by the spring sunshine.

She felt just like the water, Jessie thought, staring down at it, cold inside, not warmed by anything.

Once or twice, their hands brushed by accident and both jerked away as if they had been stung. And all the time they were walking, they talked. She had forgotten just how easy he was to talk to, how comfortable she felt with him. She told him about her job and about life at the Hall and in return he told her about the canals and railways on which he'd been working for fourteen years now. He was twenty-eight, but looked younger. He'd got the scar in an accident on the diggings the previous month. 'Carelessness did it. I gave him careless! He'll be more careful from now on.' In an abrupt change of subject, he added, 'I'm a ganger, you know.'

'What's that?'

Pride showed in his face. 'I'm in charge of a team of men. We stay together an' I contract for us to work on different jobs. If I

94

do things right, we make money. If I make too many mistakes, they leave me an' join some other gang, then I'm back to being just a navvy myself.'

'Are you not a navvy, then?'

'Sort of. I still work, but I'm in charge of my lot, d'you see?'

She moistened her lips. 'How – how much money do you make, if you don't mind me asking?'

'It varies. About thirty shillin' a week, usually.'

Jessie gaped at him. '*You earn thirty shillings a week!* Why, all I get is eight pounds a year and all found.'

'Mean buggers, those nobs of yours.'

'What's it like, working on the railways? What's your life really like?'

'Rough. We live in camps an' move on every few months or so. Me an' my gang come here because the engineer, Mr Stafford, asked us. He reckons we're a good gang.'

'He must be the brother of our Miss Stafford. What's he like?'

'He's all right. Knows his job. We call him Bony Stafford among oursen, he's that thin!'

'His sister's nice, too.' Jessie listened, fascinated, as Jared told her about the nicknames they all used. He was Big Jared, for obvious reasons, then there was Red Mike, Squinting Tom and Bull Jones – who had once been chased by a bull that a hostile farmer had let out of his field on purpose.

It was not until they'd started to make their way back to the Hall that Jessie's earlier constraint returned. 'Jared, I – I think we'd better – we'd better not . . .' she faltered.

'Better not what?'

'Better not see each other again.' Unhappiness lanced through her as she spoke the words and she was avoiding his eyes.

'You're ashamed of meetin' me, afraid of them findin' out that you've been speakin' to one of them dirty navvies, is that it?'

She winced at the harshness of his words. 'You know it's not that. I'm just – just trying to be sensible. I don't want to lose my job.'

'You said you hated your bloody job!' He stopped short, seeing the tears rolling down her cheeks. 'Aw, Jessie, I'm sorry! Don't cry, my little love. Aw, don't cry!' As he spoke, he pulled her down beside him in a hollow, cradling her in his arms as no one had ever cradled her in her whole life before. He whispered soothing, meaningless endearments, as one would to a child in distress, patting her and rocking her gently. He made no attempt to do more than hold her, though the proximity of her body made his belly throb with desire.

While she was calming down and wiping her eyes, he did some hard and rapid thinking. He knew why she'd said that. Oh, yes, knew very well. If he did not mean things seriously, it *would* be unfair to expect her to keep on meeting him and risk losing her job. And what did he want with her anyway? He drew in a deep, painful breath. Was he prepared to go as far as marriage? For all his teasing, he knew she was respectable – frighteningly, terrifyingly respectable to a man like him.

So he had to decide quickly what he wanted. He had not intended to marry for years, not till he had made something of himself – but then, he had not expected to meet a girl like Jessie. You had to take risks in life to get what you wanted. And this was something he wanted very much indeed.

He sat up and held her at arm's length. 'Jessie, love, there's no time to do things properly.'

She did not pretend to misunderstand him. 'No.'

'So I'll ask you straight out – will you marry me?' He watched her face as he spoke and his heart was thumping so loudly that he thought she must be able to hear it.

A whole range of emotions played across her face, the main ones being surprise and disbelief. 'You – you must be joking!' she whispered after a moment.

'Nay, that I'm not! I meant what I said. I want t'marry you.'

'But you – I – we hardly know one another. A person can't just marry someone like that!'

'I can. I have to. I shan't be in this area for long. Once we've finished diggin' this cutting, I'll be movin' on. I'm allus movin' on, love. That's my job and will be for a good few years yet, so I can't even offer you a proper home.' He watched her face, trying to gauge her reactions. She looked troubled more than anything, but at least she hadn't said no.

His hand tightened on her shoulder. 'I had me life all planned

out, Jessie. Not to marry for another few years. Not to have any
childer till I could look after 'em properly. But then I met you, an'
I knew I wanted you in my life for ever. It's special, this – this
thing between us, isn't it? You've felt it too, haven't you?'

'Yes.' She put up one hand and touched his cheek. 'Yes, I have,
Jared.' Then she grew frightened and snatched her hand away.

'It wouldn't be easy, Jessie. It's a hard life on the diggings,
make no mistake about it. But I earn good money – an' it's gettin'
better all the time.'

'I don't have an easy life now, Jared. And – and I'm not afraid
of hard work.' If she were with him, she realised in sudden
wonderment, she wouldn't be afraid of anything.

He raised one hand to trace a line down the softness of her
cheek, then held the hand out to her. 'It's like me, this hand is,
love. Rough an' a bit battered, but strong underneath it all.'

She gave in to temptation, pulled his arm round her shoulders
and learned against him. 'I don't know what to say, Jared. It's all
happened so quickly.'

'You do like me, though?'

Her voice was burred with emotion as she answered, 'Yes. You
know I do. More than like you.'

His arm tightened around her at that admission. 'An' you don't
like that job of yours? You told me you hated it at that Hall.'

'I do hate it. I loathe it! But . . .'

'What is it, then?'

'There's a lot to be thought about, whoever you marry. You've
got to be *sure* of things.'

'You can never be sure of anything in this world.' His voice
was dull, sad, full of memories. He started twisting her hair with
one finger, twirling it round and round, then letting the curl he
had formed slip away, before starting all over again. The lightest
touch of his fingertips made her catch her breath.

'My mother doesn't want me to get married – not ever. And I
owe her a lot.'

'You're bound to marry one day. You're a beautiful woman,
Jessie Burton.'

She looked at him in amazement and saw that he meant this.
She had never thought herself anything special, just – all right.

She tried desperately to find the words to explain how she felt. 'What worries me is – you have to be able to make a decent life together. I don't mind working, and working hard, too. I'm young and strong and I'm not stupid – but I don't want to spend my life struggling in a cottage with a pack of brats and never enough to live on. That would sour us both. Can you understand that?'

'Oh, aye, I can understand that all right. I think the same way. I've been savin' me money for a year or two. I've got near a hundred pounds saved, Jessie. One day I'll have enough to take on a small sub-contract. I'll keep me eyes open for a likely chance, an' then I'll make a bid for it an' . . .' He broke off and stared at her in bewilderment. 'What the hell are you laughin' at?'

She was quite convulsed with laughter. And with relief. For she had suddenly realised that he was no different from her or her mother. She spluttered to a stop and looked at him, at the baffled angry expression on his face, sure of her feelings now, not because he had money saved, but because he wanted more out of life than just to exist and had done something about it. 'Jared!' Her whole face softened and she whispered again, 'Oh, Jared, are you sure?'

'I'm sure.' His voice was choked and his eyes were burning into hers.

'I can't believe it's true.'

'Is that yes?'

'Yes, it is. I will marry you, Jared Wilde.'

He gave one of his shouts of joy, pulled her to her feet, and swung her round and round in a wild dance of triumph that brought them both to a halt against the trunk of a tree. There he kissed her as he had been longing to do all day; kissed her until she could hardly breathe. And she returned his kisses with ardour. Automatically his hands began to caress her body and at first she let him. Then suddenly she became aware of what was happening and pushed his hands away.

'*No!* No, Jared! Not here, not yet!'

His face darkened and he made as if to grab her again. She twisted out of his reach and stood there, panting.

Indignantly he let his hands fall and said, 'But we're goin' to be wed! What does it matter?'

'It matters to me. I'm not getting married with a big belly and everyone winking at one another.'

'Your bloody respectability again!'

'Yes!' Her voice was fierce. 'So if it sticks in your gullet, Jared Wilde, you'd better say so now. I'm respectable and I'm staying respectable, and so are you if we get married!'

As quickly as it had risen, the anger died in his eyes, leaving a reluctant admiration. 'All right, all right! We'll do it your way. But I'm not goin' t'wait long. When can we get wed? Next week? There's a preacher comes round the diggings. He marries folk for half a crown. I can ask him to . . .'

Next week! Jared Wilde, we can't possibly get married next week! I have to give in my notice properly – and that's three months. And I'm not going to be married by some travelling preacher in a ditch! I'm getting married in a church, the proper way, at Hettonby, with Parson Marley holding the ceremony.' She had grown fond of the gentle parson over the years. 'And what about a place for us to live? Have you thought about that?'

'Well, no. I hadn't even thought of marriage until today.'

She began to look worried. 'Jared, how do married people live on the diggings? I've never even seen a railway, let alone a cutting. How do the wives manage if you have to keep moving on every few months? What's it like?'

'We live in shanties. Build 'em ourselves out of anything we can find: old timber, stones, any old thing. There are twenty men living in some of 'em. Ten in mine. Just our gang. We're a bit picky, the lads an' me are.'

She was very still, trying to digest this. 'How do they cook and wash, then?'

'Ma Hawkins looks after our lot, cooks an' washes an' all that. She's been with us a while now, at other camps too. She has a big black pot to boil the meat in. We each have our own piece of meat an' we tie a wooden marker to it with a piece of string. Then she boils them all up together, usually with a few taties.' He shrugged. 'As for washing . . . well, most of the lads don't wash much.' He pulled her against him and sighed. 'Eh, how can I ask you to live like that, Jessie? A girl like you. Except – if we don't get married – well, I don't think I can bear it.'

'Oh, Jared, I can't bear it either.' Not now she had met him and tasted the thought of freedom. Jessie hesitated then asked, 'Have you ever thought of – well, of leaving the railways and trying to get yourself another sort of job? In a town, maybe, or on a farm?' The idea died in her mind even before he replied, and died for ever at the fierceness of his reply.

'Never! I'd go mad on a farm, let alone I know precious little about farmin'. It'd be worse for me than workin' at that Hall is for you. It'd be stupid, too. There's no future in it.' His arms tightened round her. 'It's hard bein' a navvy, Jessie. Near breaks your back sometimes, 'specially in the winter, when it's cold an' wet an' the ground's like iron. But they pay you good money, don't you see? They pay you enough to live on. So you eat well. An' if you've got any sense, which most of 'em haven't, you can put a bit by.'

She leaned her head against his chest. 'What are we going to do, then, Jared?'

'Get wed as soon as possible,' he said promptly. 'I'll talk to the chaps I work with. There's one or two of 'em married. Or as near married as makes no difference. I'll ask what they think. Can't you get out to see me next Sunday, just for an hour or two?'

'Not a chance. They keep us busy, even on Sundays. We have to do the work of those who've got a day off. I don't know how I'll wait until the Sunday after to see you, though.'

'Same with me. I'll be frightened you've changed your mind.'

She squeezed his hand. 'I won't do that. Once I've decided something, I'm as stubborn as a mule.'

'Er – ' He cleared his throat. 'Seein' as we're doin' this proper, had you better take me over to meet your mam next time?'

She hugged him. 'Oh, Jared, yes! Only . . .' She hesitated, then the words came out in a rush. 'Jared, she won't make you at all welcome.'

'She won't be the first! A lot of folk don't like navvies.'

'She wouldn't like anyone who wanted to marry me. You won't let her get you angry?'

He planted a kiss on her forehead. 'I'll try not to.' He stood up and pulled her to her feet. 'Come on, then, love. I suppose I'd better get you back to your precious bloody Hall now. But first,' he pulled her into a close embrace, 'give me another kiss. A good one. It'll have to last me two whole weeks.'

She was gasping by the time he let her go.

'Don't forget, Jessie Burton! You're mine now.'

'Don't you forget either, Jared Wilde,' she tossed back at him, hands on hips, eyes challenging his.

He threw back his head, roaring with laughter. 'Oh, I won't forget, I promise you that!' How could he? There was no one in the world like his Jessie.

Neither of them noticed the man walking along a path that crossed theirs stop and stare at them, then grin and carry on. Only a pair of young lovers. The woods were full of them in the summer. He'd never seen Jessie Burton walking out with anyone before, though. Well, she was a pretty lass and nice with it. She deserved to be happy.

When Jessie got back to the Hall, she didn't realise that her face was flushed and her eyes were starry, or that her whole body simply radiated happiness.

Mrs Coxleigh, who was standing by the window, saw her coming up the drive and frowned. 'If that young woman is not in love, then I've never seen one who is,' she muttered. Maids who fell in love and lost the little sense they were born with were the bane of her life, and she hated to lose a good one to such a foolish emotion.

Vera, who was enjoying the privilege of a cup of tea in the housekeeper's room, came across to join her. 'Jessie Burton in love? Why, she won't even flirt with the footmen like the other girls. Surely you're mistaken?'

'I'm never mistaken about such things. Keep your eyes open from now on, Vera. I want to know what's going on and put a stop to it.'

8

June 1837

During the day or two following her return, Jessie had to put up with a lot of teasing from the other young servants, who had also noticed how happy she looked, and that soon brought her down to earth, brought the tight, watchful look to her face again. Thomas was particularly spiteful.

'Been meeting a lover, have you?' he jeered. ' 'Bout time you found out what it's all about, Miss Toffee-Nose!' And he went away, laughing heartily at his own wit. It wasn't often he got a chance to feel superior to that one. And he hadn't forgotten the scratches she'd given him one day when he'd tried to kiss her, or Mr Howard's scornful expression when he'd claimed he got them teasing the stable cat.

So when he happened to be loitering in the yard and overheard one of the gamekeepers joking with a groom about Jessie meeting her young man in the woods, he pricked up his ears and moved forward to join the two men. 'What did you say about Jessie Burton, Ralph?'

'I said, it was about time that nice young lass found herself a fellow.'

'*Jessie? Our* Jessie?'

The gamekeeper frowned. 'And why not?' Although she was as tall as he was now, he remembered when she'd been a little lass, lost and unhappy in the big house. Why, his wife had given her a cup of tea many a time, because they felt so sorry for her.

'She don't like men, that one don't,' Thomas stated flatly.

'Well, she likes one at least. She were a-hugging this one.'

'Who was he?'

'No one from round here. A big, strapping fellow.' His wife reckoned it must be one of them navvies, but given His Lordship's views, Ralph wasn't going to say that. He wished he'd not said anything at all now, for Thomas was looking at him like a cat who'd got the cream. 'You leave that nice lass be!' he said severely.

Thomas had no intention of leaving Jessie be. When the servants were assembled for dinner the following night, he seized his opportunity for revenge. 'I hear you're courting, Jessie?'

She jerked in surprise, then stilled herself.

'Oh, stop teasing her, do!' Vera snapped. 'You've had your fun now.'

'Oh, have I?' He leaned forward, well aware that everyone had stopped talking to look at him. 'Well, so has she had her fun. She's been meeting one of them railway navvies in our own woods.'

A gasp ran round the table.

Jessie stared at Thomas, trying to remain calm. If she said the wrong thing now, there would be trouble. 'You do go on, Thomas Wadkin. You'll have me taking tea with the Queen next!' She poured herself another cup and somehow managed to keep her hand steady.

'You've been seen,' he said, furious that she wasn't reacting.

'Oh, yes?'

Vera's voice cut in. 'I said, that's enough, Thomas. If you don't leave her alone, I'll ask Mr Howard to have a word with you. You should pay more attention to your job and less to teasing the lasses.'

He scowled, but shut his mouth.

Aware of their eyes still on her, Jessie drank her tea slowly and steadily. She had lost her appetite but took a big bite of cake and swallowed it, trying desperately to think of something casual to say. But she could think of nothing, and could still feel Vera's eyes on her.

After the meal, Vera made her way up to Mrs Coxleigh's room, where the housekeeper dined in rather more state than they did in the servants' hall. One day, Vera was determined to inherit that room.

The other senior servants were just leaving, so she knocked on the door. 'Excuse me, Mrs Coxleigh, but you said to keep my eyes open. About Jessie Burton.'

'Ah. Come in.'

Mr Howard returned at that moment, bearing a decanter freshly filled with His Lordship's best port wine.

'I can come back another time,' Vera whispered.

'No. Mr Howard will also be interested in what you have to say.'

So Vera related what had happened at the dinner table. 'There may be nothing in it, of course, that Thomas is so spiteful, but *she* didn't say a word afterwards, And she looked – well, tight-lipped.'

Mrs Coxleigh nodded her head. 'I knew there was something going on when I saw her yesterday coming back from her afternoon off. You can't mistake that look.' She explained the situation to Mr Howard.

He steepled his fingers and said thoughtfully, 'I'll find out where Thomas heard about Burton's young man – if he did hear anything – and pursue matters myself. Leave this to me, my dear lady.'

'Yes, that would be best. Thank you, Vera. And keep this to yourself for now, will you?'

'Oh, certainly, Mrs Coxleigh.' She hurried back to her duties.

'Is there any news about Miss Stafford?' Mrs Coxleigh asked as soon as the door was closed. 'Is she still to leave?'

'Oh, yes. He's ordered the carts got ready tomorrow morning early.'

They exchanged speaking glances, but did not comment further on the doings of His Lordship. Both had noticed how irritable he was getting lately, worse than ever before. But he was the master. There was nothing they could do about his whims and fusses, not even when he behaved irrationally.

During the two endless weeks before Jessie's next day off, Jared made time to talk to some of the married men around the camp.

He found their answers depressing. *Don't do it! Stay clear! By heaven, you'll regret it, Jared lad!* were the most common answers to his questions about married life.

Alfred Small had been married for several years, with two young children and a third on the way, so Jared bought him a mug of ale from Ma's barrel in the hut after they had finished work one night. 'I'm thinking of getting wed,' he said abruptly.

'Eh, never! Who is it?'

'No one you know. I met her when I were out walkin'.'

'Shall you be stayin' on t'railways, then?'

'Aye. What else do I know?'

Alfred's expression grew wistful. 'Well, I hope things work out for you better nor they 'ave for me.'

'That's why I wanted to talk to you. To ask you what it's like – bein' wed, I mean?'

'Oh.'

'I think a lot of my girl. I want to do the best I can for her.'

Alfred smiled, but there was sadness in his eyes. 'Aye. We all feel like that at first. An' things were all reet for me an' Bessie till t'childer started comin'. That's what spoils it, Jared. It's a hard life for a woman on t'diggings. It's gettin' my Bessie down, it is that. She hasn't been well all the time she's been carryin' this one.'

Jared made a sympathetic noise in his throat and refrained from commenting. Bessie Small was a weak reed at the best of times, always imagining herself ill. Alfred had been a fool to marry a woman like her.

'In fact,' his friend glanced round to make sure nobody could overhear them, 'if someone were to offer me a job again as a farm labourer, I'd snap their 'and off. Aye, I would an' all. She's pinin' for a home of her own, one with a little garden.'

Jared tried to hide his surprise. He studied Alfred, who was a strongly muscled man – they all were on the diggings – but was only of medium height. His hair was growing thin already, though he couldn't be much more than Jared's age, and he always had worry lines on his face these days. He sat cradling one of Ma's pots in his hands at the end of the rough board table, looking weary and dispirited. The tallow candles flickered in the draught and gave Alfred's face a pallid sheen, shadows making his receding chin seem even weaker.

Men were sprawled on their bunks behind them: some asleep already, some chatting over a drink, some just smoking their clay pipes. Three men were gathered at the end of the table, discussing the wrestling matches that were to take place the following Saturday night and laying bets on their favoured contenders. Ma was sitting in her rocking chair, her most precious possession which she'd carried from camp to camp for years. Between her rotting teeth was a clay pipe like the men smoked and her beady eyes were watchful for empty pots that might need refilling. She made a bit extra each week selling ale to the lads in her hut. Best gang she'd ever looked after, Jared's lot were. Not boozers, just nice steady drinkers. The other hut keepers envied her.

But Ma must have been listening to what they were saying, for she suddenly came over to join in the discussion. 'Th'art a fool, Alfred Small! I've told thee afore there's no need to get childer if tha doesn't want 'em. Thy wife's no sooner dropped one than thou sets her off again.'

Alfred squirmed uncomfortably. 'Aw, Ma,' he protested, 'a man can't be thinkin' of things like that when he's on his moment!'

'*Thou* cannot! But it'd be better for thy Bessie if tha tried. She's got enough on her plate just now without another babby to mind.'

Jared looked at them both. 'What're you on about, Ma?' he asked. 'How can a man stop the babies comin' if he rogers his wife?'

A pair of beady black eyes focused on his face and Ma cocked her head to one side and cackled. 'Keen t'get wed, but not keen t'get babbies? Aye, that's a man all over. But maybe thy lass'll thank me for speakin' a word. Sithee, Big Jared, if tha doesn't leave thy seed inside thy wife, she cannot start a babby. Leastways, most on 'em don't. Nothin's certain in this world 'cept the grave.'

'I tried it,' said Alfred glumly. 'It don't work, because you can't do it! A man's on'y human, isn't he?'

'But if he could,' said Jared thoughtfully, 'if a man could do that ... How well does it work, Ma?'

'It's not perfick,' she admitted. 'There's some women has only to look at a chap to fall for a babby. But,' she wagged her bony finger at him to emphasise her point, 'it gen'rally works all reet, if tha can but control thysen.'

Jared filed that piece of information in his mind for future reference. If he and Jessie could avoid having any babies for a year or two, they'd have a much better chance to set themselves up proper and carry out all the plans he'd made. And he would do owt to stop her ending up like Bessie Small. Owt he had to.

At last Jessie woke in the early dawn to the knowledge that it was her Sunday off. She would be free of the Hall for the whole day. She rose with the others when the bell rang and helped get things ready, carrying the big copper ewers of hot and cold water up to Miss Susannah's bedroom and stopping for a quick chat. Then she went to dress herself for her day out, unaware that she was smiling.

When Thomas tossed a parting shot at her: 'Have a nice day! Be kind to him!' she rolled her eyes at Letty and ignored him. One day, she thought, one day soon I'll be leaving here for good, and then I'll never need to see *you* again, Thomas Wadkin. As she walked down the drive, she savoured the thought of giving in her notice in a few days' time on Quarter Day, working out how she would phrase it. What a shock that would be for Mrs Coxleigh and the rest of them! Though she'd tell Miss Susannah about it all first, of course.

Jared was waiting for her in the woods and this time Jessie ran to fling herself into his arms. He kissed her hungrily, then held her at arm's length. 'You look lovely,' he said in a rough voice, all his love showing in his eyes. 'I were feared you wouldn't come.'

'Of course I came. I said I would, didn't I?'

He offered her his arm and they walked along in silence for a while. Then they began to talk and suddenly the words were pouring out – hopes, plans, tales of their childhoods. So engrossed were they that neither noticed the man who was hiding at the crossroads, the man who watched them most carefully and followed them for a while. Even the increasing dullness of the day and the light shower that fell could not mar their happiness.

When the man stopped following and went back to report on what he had seen, neither of them noticed that, either.

'I'll have to give notice,' Jessie was saying, 'so in just over three months, we can – '

'*Three months*! This contract will be nearly finished by then. And anyway,' Jared pulled her to him for another quick kiss, 'I don't want to wait so long.'

He grew quieter as they approached Hettonby. He wasn't looking forward to meeting Jessie's mam, the one who set such store on respectability. He didn't need anyone to tell him that it would be an unpleasant encounter. Mrs Burton wouldn't want her precious daughter to marry a navvy and live on the diggings, and who could blame her for feeling like that? He and Jessie weren't going to say anything about marriage this visit, just that they were walking out together, but the old lady would be bound to guess things were serious between them.

'She'll be furious,' Jessie prophesied gloomily. 'Absolutely furious. You won't get a civil word out of her.'

'Well, she'll just have t'get used to the idea,' he replied, more confidently than he felt. 'We'll have t'win her round, like.' He changed the subject and began to tell Jessie what he'd found out about married life on the diggings. He didn't try to spare her the sordid details and they were both quiet and thoughtful as they walked along. Today, they were oblivious to the beauties of nature, though the drops of rain from the last shower were glinting like diamonds on the young green leaves, cow parsley was standing tall and lacy white in the verges and other, smaller flowers were peeping out in all the hedgerows.

Because they didn't try to hide the fact that they were together, they drew curious and sometimes hostile stares from the folk they passed. One woman even went so far as to call out, 'What'll your mam say to you walking out with a fellow, Jessie Burton?'

Jared swung round angrily, but she pulled him on. 'It's best to ignore them.'

'Nosy bitch!' he muttered. 'I hope they don't tell tales on you to your precious lord.'

She laughed. 'Lord Morrisham doesn't associate with people like her. And I don't care now. I'll soon be serving my notice.' She opened the parsonage gate. 'Well, are you ready?'

'Aye. Let's get it over with.'

* * *

Simon was away meeting the directors of the railway when his sister's message arrived at the inn where he was lodging, so it lay unopened in his chamber until late the next day.

When the lad she'd sent with the message returned to say Mr Stafford was away, Elinor nearly gave way to despair. 'What are we going to do, Thirza? Whatever are we going to do?'

The two women, who had been packing while they waited for Simon, went by mutual accord into the kitchen and Thirza swung the kettle over the fire. 'We're going to make ourselves a nice cup of tea, miss, that's what we're going to do. Then we'll have a think.'

'I wonder where Simon is?' Elinor walked up and down while her maid fussed over their cups. She had to think. Somehow she had to think. But her mind seemed full of dull greyness, so she sat down to wait for her tea. 'We can find lodgings for ourselves,' she said slowly as she sipped, finding the warmth comforting. 'It's the furniture we need to worry about. Whatever can we do with that?'

'We could put it in a barn somewhere – only all the farms hereabouts belong to His Lordship, so I doubt they'll be willing to help us.'

'There must be other farms which don't belong to the estate?'

'But will they want to cross a neighbour like him, Miss Elinor?' Thirza remembered quite clearly how afraid the people in Blackholm had been of upsetting old Mr Stafford.

'We can only ask.' Suddenly she looked thoughtful. 'In fact, while we're asking, we'll explain exactly why we're in such dire straits. We'll make sure everyone knows what my cousin is doing and why.'

'That won't help us find somewhere to put the stuff,' said Thirza, ever practical.

'If we ask at enough places, we'll surely find somewhere. And it'll put him in bad repute in the neighbourhood. Deservedly.'

So the next morning, the goggling grooms who drove the carts over from the Hall found two exhausted women, who'd been up all night, and a house full of bits and pieces tied up in old sheets, or packed in bookcases, or just gathered together in heaps. It made them feel uncomfortable.

'Where do you want to go, miss?' the head groom asked politely. He thought this was a shameful thing to do to a kind lady like Miss Stafford, but of course he couldn't admit that to anyone, not if he wanted to keep his job.

'Can you take me and my things off His Lordship's land and then start calling at the farms we pass? I'm hoping someone will have a barn they can lend us to store our things?'

'But – don't you have anywhere to go, miss?'

'No. We were only told to leave yesterday.'

He goggled at her as all the implications of this sank into his mind, but his orders were strict. He was to take the two women and their furniture wherever they wanted and not to bring them back to Great Sutton.

By lunchtime everything was loaded on the carts and the little convoy set off, with Elinor perched up beside the driver on the first vehicle and Thirza sitting on the other.

By mid-afternoon, they had called at several farms and received a refusal at each. Elinor was finding it hard not to fall asleep and Thirza had dozed off several times.

Word spread throughout the district about what was happening and reached Parson Marley by late afternoon.

'Dear heavens, has the man run mad?' he exclaimed when old Judd Pintby caught him on the way back from church to tell him the great scandal. 'Where did you say the ladies were, Judd?'

'Heading down Gabbitts Lane, going towards Wetherby.'

John Marley stood stock still. He owed his patron loyalty, but could not bear to think of Miss Stafford homeless like that, and shamed in front of the world. It took him only a minute to decide to intervene. 'Go and tell them to harness up the gig at The Crown, Judd. I can't leave the ladies in such distress.'

He watched the older man hurry across the green, then rushed into the house. 'Agnes, Agnes, where are you? Oh, there you are. Will you prepare the spare bedroom? I think we shall have visitors tonight.'

He was off again before she could ask who, leaving her standing gaping as he, too, ran across to the green to The Crown. 'Hurry up!' he fretted as the lad harnessed the horse. And as soon as the gig was ready, gave the order to drive 'as fast as you can' – which was so unlike him that the lad only goggled.

They caught up with the two carts just as they were pulling out of yet another farm whose owner had refused this unusual request. The carts stopped at the parson's signal.

'My dear Miss Stafford, may I beg the favour of a word with you?'

Elinor nodded and climbed down again, stifling a yawn. What had seemed like a reasonable idea last night, now seemed as mad as her cousin's behaviour. No one was willing to accommodate her furniture and she seemed to have been driving from farm to farm for a bleak eternity. She was wondering whether she ought to go to the inn where her brother was staying and wait there – but it was a small place. She and Susannah had taken tea with him there, and Elinor couldn't see how they would have room for her furniture.

John Marley offered her his arm and walked up the road a little, away from prying ears. 'I heard what had happened. You must allow me to offer you the shelter of my roof, Miss Stafford.'

She stopped and tears came into her eyes. 'Oh, if only I could accept, but my cousin will throw *you* out, if you do that.'

'He has not the power. The living may be his, but the parsonage building belongs to the church authorities. He can only turn me out for misconduct, which this is not.'

'It's very kind of you, but it doesn't solve the problem of my furniture. You won't have room for that.' She looked up at the sky and tears came into her eyes. 'And it's going to rain. Everything will get wet and my books will be ruined!' Everything she owned was on those carts, everything she had left.

He patted her hand. 'I think I know a farmer who will take in your things. He has no love for His Lordship. But you're going in the wrong direction for his place. If you'll climb up into the gig with me, I'll tell the drivers where to go and we'll hurry on ahead. But I'm sure James Bittle will help us.'

'There's Thirza, too – my maid.'

'I have room for her in the gig as well. Here, let me help you up.'

As she watched him speak to the drivers, she couldn't help a few tears from running down her face, but forced herself to stop weeping. By the time John climbed back into the gig, she had herself under control again and was thinking things through carefully. 'I can't stay with you, Mr Marley. It really wouldn't be suitable. But if you can find somewhere for my furniture, Thirza and I will lodge at the nearest inn.'

'I can assure you – '

'No. I won't put you in such an invidious position.'

By the time they had seen the men start unloading the furniture under the eyes of a gleeful James Bittle, who detested Clarence Morrisham and had promised to make sure nothing was stolen, dusk was falling.

'It's too late to travel across to your brother. If you agree, I'll take you to the inn down the road,' John decided.

At the inn, well off His Lordship's estate, a smiling landlady assured the parson that she had plenty of room for the poor lady. 'Shocking, it is. Shocking. To treat a kind lady like Miss Stafford so.' Clearly the gossip had spread this far.

'I'll return tomorrow morning, then, if you'll permit, Miss Stafford? I think I may be able to help you find somewhere to live. Shall I send a message to your brother?'

'No. I'll do that myself in the morning.'

The next day John Marley arrived at the inn soon after breakfast and was shown into the landlady's own parlour to wait for Miss Stafford. When she came in, he hastened to shake her hand and ask how she had slept.

'Like the dead. Both Thirza and I were quite exhausted. I'm so grateful for your help yesterday. I don't know what we'd have done without you.'

'Do you have any – er – prospects of accommodation?'

'No. We went to look at houses in Leeds, and I suppose we can find one to rent. But,' Elinor pulled a face, 'I'm not taken with city life.'

'Please excuse my asking.' He coloured a little. 'But do you have enough money?'

'Yes. I have a small annuity, enough to manage on, if I'm careful.' And money left still from selling the small things she had taken with her from home, a sum she had promised herself not to touch. And she had added to this during her years in Great Sutton. She had been hoping one day to save enough to buy herself a house with a garden, but now she would have greater living expenses, so maybe she wouldn't be able to save any more.

No one except Thirza knew about her savings, not even Simon. If he had known, he might have wanted to use the money to finance a small sub-contract, for she knew that was his ambition. But Elinor didn't think he was ready for that yet. Much as she loved him, she didn't have a great deal of faith in his business acumen, though when he talked of his work, it was a different thing. His love for and understanding of it shone out.

John Marley's voice interrupted her cogitations. 'If I might offer a suggestion, then, Miss Stafford?'

'Of course.'

'I am acquainted with a gentleman near Rotherham. Charles Butterfield, who is the squire of a small village there, has extensive property in the district. I could write to him and ask whether he has any cottages vacant suitable for a lady like you, or whether he knows anyone else who has. He's well known in the county. If anyone can help you, it'll be him. But perhaps you don't want me to interfere?'

'I'm afraid I need all the help I can get.' Elinor managed a smile, though it was an effort.

John Marley's heart went out to her. 'I'll ask Mr Butterfield to write back quickly. Can you stay on here for a while longer? If not, there is always the parsonage.'

'I'll stay here.'

Simon arrived late that afternoon, having only just received his sister's two messages. He was furious and intending to go and confront Clarence Morrisham. 'Of all the ungentlemanly behaviour!' he fumed. 'He deserves horse-whipping, peer or not!'

Elinor managed to talk him out of that, but it took a while. After all, what good would it serve for him to quarrel with their cousin? The deed was done and as far as she was concerned, she hoped neither of them had to speak to Clarence Morrisham again.

Within a couple of days Mr Marley had heard from Squire Butterfield and came over at once to tell Elinor the news. The

Squire of Mellersley had an aunt who would welcome some company and she was happy to trust to John Marley's judgement about Miss Stafford's suitability. No menial work would be involved, just the provision of a little companionship for an old lady who was well loved by all who knew her, but too independent in her ways to live with her relatives. And afterwards, when the inevitable happened – for Charles feared his aunt was very frail and had not much longer to live – if they all suited one another as neighbours, Miss Stafford could stay on at the house for a modest rent. He would welcome a good tenant for it. He would send a carriage and a dray for her furniture if that arrangement suited everyone. They had only to let him know.

Elinor read the letter and breathed a long, shuddering sigh of relief. She had been lying awake worrying at night and now suddenly, all her problems were solved. For the time being, anyway. And this was a far better solution than she had expected, for she would not even have to expend any of her reserves on moving expenses. Or pay rent.

'It sounds wonderful,' she said, blowing her nose firmly and forcing a smile to her face. 'Please let him know I accept.' Only after it had all been settled did she send a note to Simon to inform him of what she was about to do. She did not intend to be a burden to him.

As she was packing, she wondered how things were at the Hall. She would not miss Clarence and Adelaide in the slightest, but she would miss dear Susannah greatly.

'I wonder,' she said when Mr Marley kindly came to see her off, 'if I could ask your help in another small matter? Could you get a note to Susannah for me – just once, to say goodbye and tell her that I'm all right? I hated to leave her so abruptly. We were good friends.'

'Yes, of course.' John found he didn't mind deceiving a man who could behave in such a way. His Lordship must have heard of his parson's intervention in Miss Stafford's troubles, but had made no mention of it, nor asked after her. What a stubborn, cruel man he was!

As she and Thirza rode towards a place called Yettley in the comfortable carriage of their new benefactor, Elinor stared out at the rain-sodden landscape and promised herself, not for the first time, that she would find herself a real home again one day, a place where she could not be thrown out at someone else's whim, a place where she could make a few friends and be of some use to her fellow human beings.

A vision of her old home rose before her, as it often did. She didn't miss the house so much as the moors and the gardens that surrounded it. She made a soft noise of regret in her throat, saw Thirza look at her anxiously, and resolutely banished the painful memories. 'I'm all right,' she said softly. 'Just thinking about home. It seems such a long time since I walked on the moors.'

Thirza nodded. She, too, had loved walking on the moors.

Elinor's thoughts turned next to Simon, who had remained bitter about losing his inheritance. He had vowed never to return to Blackholm, or anywhere near it, if he could possibly help it, not even to visit.

'At least the place is too small and too remote to need a railway,' he had scoffed once. 'So nothing will make it necessary for me to return there.'

Well, even if she didn't go back to Blackholm, there must be other places near the moors that she could love. When the time came for her to leave Yettley, she would look around carefully for one. Exhaustion made her lean back and close her eyes as she waited for the journey to be over. She only hoped this squire was as amiable as he sounded, and that the old lady was not too bad-tempered. But whatever they were like, she would cope, for she would not be a burden to her brother.

9

❦

Hettonby

*W*hen Jessie turned up at the back door of the parsonage, escorted by a young giant with a scarred face, Agnes Burton reeled back in shock. Her first impulse was to drag her daughter inside and slam the door in the man's face. She managed to refrain from doing this, but if looks could have killed, he'd have been blasted into tiny pieces on the spot.

'This is Jared Wilde, Mother. A friend of mine. I've brought him home to meet you.'

Jared stuck out his hand.

Agnes ignored it and stamped into the house. Jessie looked at him apologetically and beckoned him to follow.

He did so, frowning at the neat, spare woman, so like Jessie but without her warmth. Agnes's hair, streaked only slightly with grey, was scraped back into an unflattering bun, her eyes were a cooler grey-blue and her lips thinner than her daughter's full, soft ones. There was a marked resemblance between the two women, but the older one had been soured by life. By God, Jared vowed, I'll not let that happen to my Jessie!

Grudgingly Agnes pointed to a chair for him to sit on. As Jessie went to kiss her mother, Agnes gripped her shoulders and looked searchingly into her eyes. An impulse to ask what her daughter meant by bringing this great lout home with her was still-born. Lips tightly compressed, every inch of her body radiating hostility, she stood with arms folded, waiting for them to offer some explanation.

'Mother, I'd like you to meet Jared – '

'You told me his name already.' Bitterness welling up inside her, Agnes turned away to stir something on the kitchen range. Behind her back, Jessie pulled another wry face at Jared and mouthed the words, 'I love you.'

Torn between her overwhelming new feelings for him and her love for her mother, she spoke as gently as she could, trying to bridge the great gulf yawning between them. 'Mother, I brought Jared home to meet you because ... well, we're walking out together.' The back turned to them went suddenly rigid and the hand holding the spoon froze, but Agnes said nothing.

'Did you hear me, Mother?' Jessie asked, pain at this treatment clearly evident in her voice.

Agnes couldn't speak, couldn't even move for a moment, she felt so sick with anger. How dared her daughter do this to her?

Jared stood up. 'Mrs Burton, I asked Jessie to bring me here today because I wanted to meet you. I wanted to do everythin' proper.'

There wasn't a quiver in response.

'I'm tryin' to do what's best for her.'

Agnes spun round then, her face white as chalk but with a hectic spot of colour flaring in each cheek. 'Oh, yes! Well, if you want to do what's best for my Jessie, you'll leave her alone. She's not for such as you!'

His anger began to bubble over. 'What's wrong with me, Mrs Burton?' he demanded. 'An' what's wrong with Jessie wanting to walk out with someone?'

'Everything's wrong with it!' She could feel the bile rising in her throat. '*Everything!*'

She rounded on her daughter, because she couldn't bear even to look at *him*. 'How dare you take up with a – a lump like him, you ungrateful creature? After all I've done for you! And you getting on so well at the Hall! You're set for life there. You could do really well for yourself. Be Miss Susannah's maid – see the world – have a comfortable life.' Her voice rose shrilly. 'And what do you do? You fall for the first handsome face that cozens you! If it *is* the first!'

Now Jessie was getting angry, too, but she shook her head at Jared to stop him speaking and for her sake, he bit off the angry words hovering on his lips.

'Just what do you mean by that, Mother?' She glared across the kitchen and thumped the table for good measure. 'He's the first fellow I've ever walked out with. You know he is. And I thought you'd prefer to meet him than have me go with him secretly.'

'Well, I wouldn't.'

Jessie took a deep breath and tried to keep her voice steady, but it shook as she said, 'I knew you wouldn't like it, me walking out. I knew that. But I thought you'd get used to it if we did everything right. And you're not even giving him a chance!'

'I don't need to. I can see what he is. It's written all over him. Look at his hands. Look at that scar. He's a labourer. And he's just after you for what he can get. They're all alike, men are. And it doesn't last, I know that. Whatever they promise, *it never lasts!*'

With the two of them shouting at each other across the kitchen table and Jared trying to make himself heard, the noise penetrated as far as the parson's study upstairs. John, who was going over his sermon for the morning service, laid aside his notes and came hurrying down to the kitchen, afraid that Agnes was being annoyed by gipsies or tinkers.

His appearance in the doorway made them all fall suddenly silent. Jessie stood biting her lip, wondering what to say. Jared was not sure who the stout gentleman was, but naturally supposed it to be the parson, so he stood there silently watchful, waiting for the other man to make the first move. *If in doubt, do nowt*, was a good motto in a strange situation, and he'd never been in one stranger than this.

Caught for the first time ever by her employer in an embarrassing situation, and distraught about her daughter taking up with a common labourer, Agnes collapsed into one of the chairs, buried her head in her arms and burst into loud, angry sobs.

It took John Marley and Jessie several minutes to get her to calm down enough to discuss matters quietly and sensibly. Neither had ever seen her weep before, let alone succumb to hysterics.

John didn't realise that he was holding her hand, patting it, trying to offer some comfort. The only thing he was certain of was that his housekeeper didn't deserve this, whatever it was.

All the time, Jared stood silently in a corner of the kitchen, arms folded. *Bloody old hag*, he said to himself. *I'll keep away from you in future, missus, don't you fret, but your daughter goes with me.* He felt comforted by the glances Jessie threw at him from time to time, her face full of love and anguish. This fuss wasn't changing her mind, any road.

After a few minutes of watching the scene, the humour of it began to strike him. *Bloody old hag*, he thought again, but felt sorry for Agnes all the same, because he could see that the poor bitch was really upset. And the old fellow, who seemed very fond of her, was flapping around like a fish on dry land, trying to comfort her.

Eventually, feeling that he could conduct matters better on his own ground, John insisted they adjourn to his study to sort it all out. He led the way upstairs, where he installed his housekeeper in one of the big leather armchairs and seated himself behind the desk, leaving the young couple standing before him like criminals in front of a magistrate.

'Now,' he said, once all was arranged to his liking, 'what's all this about, Agnes?' He usually called her Mrs Burton in public, but neither of them noticed that slip.

'It's my Jessie. She's taken up with this – this fellow. After all I've done for her!' More tears of outrage rose to her eyes. 'All the advantages she's had! Three years of proper schooling, thanks to you, sir. A good post with Lord Morrisham. Just to throw them away. It's more than I can *bear*!'

'Yes, yes! Quite natural that you should be upset.' John spoke soothingly, shooting a sideways frown at the girl. 'But we can't expect old heads on young shoulders, can we? I'm sure that Jessie will not do anything to upset her mother. Isn't that right, Jessie, my dear? You won't do anything hasty, will you?'

'I won't do anything I'll regret, sir,' she said, her eyes flickering another warning towards Jared.

'And,' continued the parson, 'you can at least be thankful that she's brought him home to meet you, my dear Agnes.'

'I'd rather meet the devil himself!' The way she spat the words made John blink. Could this be his quiet housekeeper speaking? Then he remembered what a good mother she was. He only wished his own had cared half as much for him, but she had sent him off to school at the age of eight, then university had followed, and she had died before he was ordained. Shaking his head sadly at the realisation of how little he had known of a mother's care, he turned back to the matter at hand.

'Jessie, my dear, you can see how much you've upset your mother. It really won't do, you know.' He shook his head at her and frowned over the spectacles which he always donned when he felt the need of an appearance of authority.

But Jessie was not to be cowed. 'Sir,' she said clearly, her chin up and eyes meeting his unflinchingly, 'I've done nothing wrong. Nothing.'

Jared judged it time to speak. 'Sir,' he followed Jessie's example in addressing the fat old codger, 'I asked Jessie to bring me here t'meet her mother. She said her mother would throw a fit, but what else could we do?' He decided there was no use hedging around. 'I want to marry Jessie and she wants to marry me. It's as simple as that.'

Agnes wailed loudly and buried her face in her hands.

Jared had had enough of this. 'What's wrong with that, missus?' His voice rang out loudly in the stuffy room and she looked up to glare at him. Jessie gave his hand an encouraging squeeze and he smiled down at her in a way that made her mother sob quietly and hopelessly into her handkerchief.

'Well, young man,' the parson's fussy, precise voice broke the awkward pause, 'I must commend you on your veracity, indeed I must! The Bible enjoins us all to honour our fathers and mothers, and I think that you have been quite correct in coming to make the acquaintance of your – er – of Jessie's mother.'

Not by a flicker of an eyelid did Jared betray that he didn't understand half the breakjaw words the old fellow had used. It was obvious the parson could handle the old biddy better than they could, so let him get on with it.

John frowned. 'Er – I know most of the young fellows round here, by sight at least, but I can't immediately place your face.

Are you new to the district? For whom are you working?'

Jared and Jessie both tensed. Here it was, the question they'd hoped to avoid this first time.

He looked down at her and shrugged his shoulders slightly, then turned to face the old fellow. 'I'm workin' on the railway, sir.'

If he had suddenly thrown a live snake at them, he couldn't have surprised and shocked the parson and his housekeeper more! Agnes's sobbing rose again to an incoherent shriek and then she began to make broken sounds into her handkerchief, amongst which could be distinguished, 'ungrateful' and 'gutter scum'.

John Marley didn't know what to say next. The last thing he needed was something else to anger his patron. He stared at Jared in fascination, amazed by his powerful muscles and broad shoulders, wondering uneasily what would happen if the fellow lost his temper. But he had to admit, to himself at least, that the young man had been very patient so far, in the face of Agnes's open hostility.

Had Jessie not been involved, Jared would have cursed them all and left. But for her sake, he stood his ground.

It was Jessie who broke the silence. 'What's wrong with him being a navvy? He works hard and earns good money. What's wrong with working on the railways, for heaven's sake?'

'You'll find out what's wrong if you take up with such as him!' Agnes found her voice again. 'Navvies, labourers . . . they're all alike! Earn good money one week, out on their ears the next. Drink most of what they earn, beat their wives, leave their children to starve– you'll find out, my girl!'

'You won't even give him a chance, will you?'

'I don't need to. I know his type. But you're under age, Jessie Burton. You can't get married without my say so and I won't *let* you ruin yourself.'

Jessie let go of Jared's hand and spoke before he could. 'If you don't let us get married, then we'll run off and live together without. And that'll be your fault, Mother! I'm going to leave the Hall and be with my Jared one way or another. You'll not stop us!' Tears were trembling in her eyes and her voice shook as she made her threat, the worst she could think of.

'All right! That's bloody well enough!' Jared's roar startled even Agnes into silence. 'I've tried to do things your way, missus, the *respectable* way, an' it's gettin' us nowhere. Jessie an' me love one another. We want t'get wed. Is that wrong? Well, is it?' His great fist thumped down on the desk, making John jump as much as the pens and papers on it. 'Go on! You're the parson! You tell us! Is it wrong to want to get wed?'

'Well – er – no.'

'And you, Mrs Precious Burton, what about you? Would you rather Jessie just came an' lived with me? A lot of women do that on the diggings, you know. But I don't think that's good enough for a girl like her. I've not even touched her – '

John Marley, who had never touched a woman in his whole life, winced visibly and went bright pink.

' – an' I won't till we're wed. Not unless *you* force us to, that is! It isn't just me bein' a navvy, is it? It's me bein' a man. Any man. Well, you'll not be able to keep the men away from your Jessie! Have you looked at her lately? She's pretty – much too pretty to waste her life emptying chamber pots for rich folk. An' what's more, you should be ashamed of how you've spoken to her today, bloody well ashamed! She's a *good* girl, your daughter is, an' she's done nowt to be ashamed of! An' nor have I.'

Agnes had the grace to flush, but was still not in the least won over. 'Even if all you say is true,' she hissed at him, her face bone white, 'what sort of a life would she lead, married to you, following the railways, with no proper home? I've heard about those diggings. You can't get away from that.'

'I'm not tryin' to. I don't think it'll be easy. I've already told Jessie about it. But I'm not stayin' a navvy forever. I'm already a ganger – the youngest ganger on the line.' He saw her brows wrinkle in puzzlement and leaned forward to emphasise what he was saying. 'That means I'm in charge of a team of men. I earn thirty shillin' a week, sometimes more, an' I don't waste it on booze. So I don't think your Jessie will go hungry, do you?'

'Thirty shillings a week!' murmured the Parson. 'Bless me!'

Agnes said nothing. She was in no way reconciled to the idea of her daughter marrying this man, however much he earned – or claimed to earn.

Jared turned to the old fellow, since Jessie's ma was obviously not going to speak to him. 'I've got near a hundred pound saved,' he said negligently, as if it were nothing, but he didn't miss the expressions of astonishment on their faces. 'I told you, I earn good money. I don't waste it – I save it. Mr Stafford, the engineer on the line, he'll say a word for me. It'd only be fair for someone to check, for Jessie's sake.' He almost laughed aloud at the fury on Agnes Burton's face. *Get out of that, if you can, you silly old hag!* he thought gleefully.

'Well, yes, I suppose we could do that.' John was relieved to clutch at any straw which might persuade his housekeeper to accept the inevitable. You only had to see the way the two young people looked at one another, to realise that. 'Um, would that be Miss Stafford's brother? Miss Stafford who lives – used to live – in Great Sutton?'

'So Jessie tells me.'

'Then I think we should consult him. It's an excellent idea.' John carefully wrote down the engineer's name, though he didn't like the sound of The Bird in the Bush, Cramsley, as an address.

Jared took charge again. 'Now it comes down to this: I can't spend a long time courtin' Jessie. I have t'keep movin' about the country. I can't change that. So it's just a question of settin' the date.'

Mr Marley blinked at him again. Such bluntness! Such determination! And yet the young man had spoken out honestly, had even offered to get someone, a gentleman too, to speak for him. 'Mmm.' He chose his next words carefully. 'Of course, it's for Mrs Burton to give permission, not me, but if you are both so sure and determined . . .' They nodded. 'Well, it would be very wrong to drive you into immorality. So I shall write to your Mr Stafford at once. If Ag— Mrs Burton wishes me to . . .' His voice trailed away as he looked at her.

She stood up and dropped him her usual respectful curtsey. 'Thank you, sir.' Her voice was toneless, despair echoing in every syllable. 'I'd be grateful if you would write. And – it's very kind of you to have helped me today. It was the shock, you see, the shock of it happening so suddenly that upset me.'

John's face brightened. 'Yes, of course. Quite understandable.

The young never consider what they're doing.' He nodded at them all vaguely and encouragingly.

Agnes led the way down to the kitchen and once the door to upstairs was firmly closed, turned to the young couple. 'You haven't won me over. I think you're a fool, our Jessie.' She glared at Jared. 'And don't think your hundred pounds makes me like you any better, young man – *if* you do have that much money. Let's see what you do with it. Let's see where you are in five years. I've heard fancy promises before and they don't butter any bread!'

'Mother . . .' Jessie stepped forward.

'No, let me finish! You've had your say. It's my turn now. You've made your point. You're determined to get married to him.' She jerked her head at Jared, who scowled back at her. 'We'll write to this Mr Stafford and see what he has to say about you. And *if* he says you're a good worker and a decent-living man, then we'll think of you getting married in a year or two's time. You owe me that much, Jessie! It won't kill you to wait a while. You did say there was no need to rush into things, didn't you?'

Jessie gave a quick shake of her head when Jared would have argued with this. Best to let things drop, for the moment.

'I don't think I'll go to church today,' Agnes said. 'Nor do I want you two going and giving folk something to goggle at.'

'Suits me,' said Jared, who had scarcely been inside a church in his life and wasn't keen to change that. The sounds coming out of them were so doleful he often chuckled as he passed one by on a bright summer's day.

After an awkward few moments of halting conversation with her daughter, Agnes insisted on making them a meal, which they ate in an uncomfortable silence.

Jared felt ill-at-ease in the bright, cheerful kitchen, but the food was good. Better than good and he said so, but his hostess just scowled at him, so he kept his thoughts to himself from then on.

The dresser, with its shining rows of plates and glasses, seemed to mock him and his aspirations. Ma kept her plates in a pile on the end of the table and if you broke one, you had to buy yourself another from the camp shop. No two of Ma's plates were alike. Here, every piece of crockery matched and the kitchen range, black with brass trimmings against the wall opposite the dresser, only emphasised the fact that Ma had to do all her cooking on an open fire that vented up a makeshift chimney. A wide window, its many little panes twinkling and its ledge lined with pots of herbs, flooded the kitchen with bright sunlight. In the hut you either left the door open or you lit a tallow dip.

They started back towards the Hall earlier than Jessie usually did. 'Phew!' said Jared as soon as they had left behind the curious stares of the villagers, who had never seen Jessie Burton even look twice at a man, let alone walk out with one.

'I told you Mother would be bad, but I didn't think she'd be that bad.' Jessie sounded near to tears.

'I don't see any need t'wait even one year,' said Jared, after a while. 'I don't know where I'll be in six months time, let alone two years.'

'I don't intend to wait that long, either, but I thought we'd had enough arguing for one day. If you're moving on in another three months, I think we should plan to get married just before you leave. That'll give me time to work out my notice and give Mother time to get more used to everything. If I don't tell her I'm giving my notice, she won't be able to do anything about it until it's too late.'

'Three months it is, then.'

When he had left her near the Hall, he set off back to the diggings, calling at the first inn he passed to drain a single pot of ale.

Phew! he thought to himself. What a day! Then he pictured Jessie's face and smiled. Well, it would all be worth it. They'd get married and he'd prove the old woman wrong. He raised his pot in a silent toast. *Jessie!*

As he set off again, a fellow turned on to the main road from a side track, nodded a greeting and fell in beside him.

'Going far?'

'No, just to the other side of Little Sutton.'

'Live there, do you?'

'No. I'm working on the railway.'

'Ah.' There was a silence. Then, 'Nice night, isn't it?'

Jared looked up at the sun-gilded evening sky and thought of Jessie. 'Yes, a beautiful night.'

'Well, I turn off here. Goodbye.'

Jared went on his way and didn't give the man another thought, but his former companion stood and let out a soft whistle as he watched the young giant vanish into the distance.

'A bloody railway navvy,' he said aloud. 'Eh, that poor lass is in for some trouble.' But he dared do no other than make his report. He had his own family to think of and they all depended on His Lordship for a roof over their heads and bread in their mouths.

10

⸙

Sutton Hall

*T*he next morning Young Jane poked a head round the bedroom door where Jessie was working. 'Mrs Coxleigh wants to see you when you've finished up here. She don't half look mad! What've you been doing?' She realised that Miss Susannah was still there and gasped. 'Ooh, sorry, miss! Didn't see you.' Bobbing a curtsey, she scurried away to her own work.

Susannah frowned. 'Are you in trouble, Jessie?'

'Not that I know of, miss.'

'Well, I hope she doesn't take you away from me for long. You're the only one here who talks sense.' She giggled. 'Can you imagine me having a chat to Jane, like I do to you? Or lending *her* books? I'm looking forward to having you as my maid all the time.'

Her stomach tight with apprehension, Jessie cast a last glance round the bedroom to check that nothing else needed doing. 'I'll be back later to help you change for your callers, miss.'

Susannah nodded happily. Her best friend and her mother were coming over to have luncheon at the Hall, as part of their practice for coming out.

As she walked down to the housekeeper's room, Jessie tried to work out what this summons could mean. It wasn't usual to be sent for in the middle of a morning's work and it felt particularly ominous coming just after her meeting with Jared. Now she came to think of it, Thomas had smirked at her across the breakfast

129

table this morning as if he knew something she didn't, as if he had somehow triumphed over her, but she had ignored him, as she usually did.

Mrs Coxleigh's expression confirmed the fact that this summons did not mean good news even before Jessie approached the large desk. The housekeeper did not speak immediately, just studied the maid, a tactic designed to induce fear.

Jessie stared back, keeping her face expressionless. She knew Mrs Coxleigh's tricks of old and they no longer worried her. It was what was behind this summons that made her wary.

After a minute or two more had elapsed, the housekeeper cleared her throat. 'It has come to my notice that you have been walking out with a young man, Burton.'

Jessie's heart began to thump loudly. Who had seen her? 'Yes, Mrs Coxleigh.' Her voice came out calm, thank goodness. Perhaps she could brazen this out. They didn't like you walking out, but they couldn't do much to stop it on your day off.

'Who is he?'

'His name is Jared Wilde.' She raised her head to look the housekeeper right in the face, using the words the gentry used. 'We're engaged to be married.'

Mrs Coxleigh's lips tightened. 'You know what I mean, Jessie. What does this young man do? For whom does he work?'

A quiver of apprehension was followed by a surge of anger. What business was it of Mrs Coxleigh's who Jared worked for? Did they think they owned their maids body and soul? 'Since he's not employed by His Lordship, I don't see that that concerns anyone but myself. I shall be moving away when we marry.' She tried to keep her voice steady, but it wasn't an easy thing to defy a woman with such absolute powers as the housekeeper.

Mrs Coxleigh gasped in outrage. 'Don't be impertinent, girl! Answer my question at once!'

Was it Jared's influence? Jessie felt positively mutinous. 'I'm sorry, but what he does concerns no one but myself, Mrs Coxleigh.'

'It concerns *me* if you are intending to give notice, after all the training we've given you here!'

'I had intended to give notice on Quarter Day, which would allow you adequate time to find someone to replace me.'

'Oh, had you! Leaving poor Miss Susannah in the lurch after all her kindnesses, I suppose? And you refuse to tell me anything more about this – this person?'

Jessie just stared at her.

'We shall see about that! Stay where you are.' Mrs Coxleigh leaned forward and rang the little silver bell on her desk, sending Letty to ask Mr Howard if he could spare a few moments of his time. She then busied herself with her accounts, totally ignoring the maid.

If this was designed to play on Jessie's nerves, it was having exactly the opposite effect. She was growing more angry by the minute. How dared they treat her as if she had no mind or feelings of her own? How dared they demand her very soul for a mere eight pounds a year?

Mr Howard came in and was fussed into a comfortable chair behind the desk, next to Mrs Coxleigh. Then the two figures of authority turned to confront Jessie, who was still standing near the table, arms folded across her chest now.

'She refuses to tell me anything about this young man,' said Mrs Coxleigh in a hushed and ominous voice.

Mr Howard looked sternly at Jessie. 'Is this so, young woman?' he demanded.

'I can't see how it concerns anyone but myself.'

He turned to the housekeeper, shaking his head. 'Then it must be true.'

'Yes, I fear it is.'

They do know, Jessie decided. Someone's told them about Jared, someone who's guessed that he works on the railways. They're just playing with me. Anger at that stiffened her spine.

Mr Howard leaned forward and glared across the desk. 'Young woman, you have been housed and fed by His Lordship since you were twelve years old. And what have you done in return?'

I've slaved all the hours God sends, Jessie thought to herself, and I've earned all I've received twice over. She was very tempted to tell him that, but said nothing. Best not to make matters worse. If they were going to dismiss her, let them get on with it. To her surprise, she didn't care. She had some money saved. She could manage till they got married.

Burton's quiet self-control was making Mr Howard even angrier. 'Well, answer me, girl!' he snapped when she continued to hold her tongue. '*What have you done in return?*'

'I've done my job as well as I could. To your satisfaction, I think, Mrs Coxleigh? Or so you've led me to believe. Certainly to Miss Susannah's. As to the rest, how can I answer you when I don't know what you're accusing me of now?'

'You have been seen talking to a – a person from the railways, *in direct disobedience to His Lordship's orders*. What have you to say to that?'

'Nothing.'

'*Nothing!*' He was so outraged and red of face that he seemed to have puffed up to twice his normal size.

He looks like a silly old frog, Jessie thought, and felt a sudden desire to giggle, but that soon faded.

More head-shaking. 'I begin to think, Mrs Coxleigh, that we are being over-generous with this young woman. If it were not that we have so far had no complaints about her work, and that His Lordship has expressly requested us to try to help her see the error of her ways . . .' He left the sentence unfinished.

Mrs Coxleigh took over. 'His Lordship has decided to send you up to the London house immediately and to say no more about this deplorable incident – so long as you promise to have nothing more to do with this fellow. Now, what do you say to that, Jessie? It is an extremely generous offer, is it not?'

She looked at them in astonishment. Did they really expect her to renounce the man she loved and intended to marry, at Lord Morrisham's whim?

'Well?' said Mrs Coxleigh impatiently. 'Have you nothing to say for yourself?'

'You can tell His Lordship thank you, but no. I'd rather marry Jared.'

'You can't be serious, girl! What about your future here? You can't just throw everything away for a – a railway navigator!'

'He isn't just a railway navigator, Mrs Coxleigh. He's a ganger. He has a team of men working under him and earns thirty shillings a week. He has a very promising future.'

'Thirty shillings a week!' Mr Howard's face became even redder. 'He's telling you lies, girl!'

'No, sir. He isn't.' Jessie guessed from the sour expression on the butler's face that Mr Howard didn't earn much more than that himself. 'And you have no right to accuse him of lying, since you've never met him,' she added, for good measure.

There was a moment's stunned silence. 'Does your mother know about this?' The housekeeper played her final trump card.

'Yes, Mrs Coxleigh. Of course she does! I took Jared over to meet her yesterday.'

'And are you telling me that she *approves* of your marrying him?'

'No. She wouldn't approve of my marrying anyone. And she has the same prejudices about people who work on the railways as everyone else. But I managed to convince her that I shan't change my mind – as I hope I have convinced you today.'

'I can't believe that this is you speaking, Jessie Burton!' Mrs Coxleigh said bitterly. She had been so sure the girl would be amenable to reason. Such a fine, strong girl, too.

Mr Howard clicked his tongue in disappointment. 'We felt that you had a permanent place here with the family, Burton. We had planned to offer you the permanent position of Miss Susannah's maid. She has grown quite fond of you.'

'Is your young man worth it? Is any young man worth giving up your security for?' Mrs Coxleigh hated having to plead like this, but His Lordship had made it clear that he considered it a point of honour to save the girl from making such a dreadful mistake.

Jessie smiled, an expression of pure happiness. 'Oh, yes! He's worth it, Mrs Coxleigh.' She compounded the insult by taking the initiative. 'So when would you like me to leave?'

There was silence for a moment, then Mrs Coxleigh rang her bell.

Jessie looked at her in puzzlement.

Thomas and James answered so promptly that they must have been waiting nearby.

'Take her up to the small west attic and lock her in,' Mr Howard ordered.

Jessie froze in shock, then shoved Thomas away as he reached out for her, grinning. It took both him and James all their strength to hold her and the noise she made must have penetrated quite a distance, but no one came to investigate.

'Hurry up!' Mr Howard snapped.

As they pushed and pulled her out of the room, Jessie began to scream, deliberately making as much noise as possible. She screamed every inch of the way up the stairs, but none of the other servants appeared to investigate.

At the top of the first flight of stairs, His Lordship appeared. 'Be quiet, girl!' he roared.

Jessie screamed again and shouted for help. Behind Lord Morrisham she could see Susannah, gaping in astonishment. 'You have no right to lock me up!' she yelled. 'I've done nothing wrong. Nothing!'

'I'm giving you a chance to come to your senses.' He jerked his head to the footmen who continued to drag Jessie up the two more flights of steps to the attics.

Her voice was hoarse now, but she didn't stop screaming and protesting all the way up. When they flung her into one of the smaller unused rooms on the far side of the attics, she turned and attacked them with feet and nails.

Mr Howard appeared in the doorway. 'Have you run mad, girl?'

She stopped, panting. 'It's you who've run mad. You have no *right* to do this.'

'We have every right.' He took a step forward. 'And if you don't come to your senses, if this – this madness persists, then His Lordship has mentioned the fact that you might need locking away in the lunatic house, for your own good.'

Horror filled her and she could not speak. Lord Morrisham was a magistrate. He could carry out that threat. They chained lunatics up and just left them in their own filth.

'Yes, I see that's made you think.' He took a step backwards. 'We'll leave you to consider His Lordship's offer.'

Behind him she could see Thomas grinning.

After the door had slammed shut, Jessie remained where she was for several minutes. It was like a nightmare. How could a man like Lord Morrisham treat her like this? It was he who had run mad. Did he think he was above the law? *Was* he above the law?

Eventually, she moved across to the bed and sank down on it. 'I've got to keep control of myself,' she whispered. 'I'll get nowhere if I panic.' But her hands were still shaking and her heart was thudding in her chest.

After a while, she roused herself from her worries to inspect her surroundings. A narrow attic room, two paces wide, three paces long. High iron bed with a prickly straw mattress on it. One small wooden chair with a loose leg. Tiny mirror on the wall above a battered chest of drawers. Slop bucket with lid in the corner behind the chest of drawers. And high in the wall a small dormer window.

She had to push the bed across the room and stand on it to see out of the window, and then all that rewarded her efforts was an expanse of slate roof, with another expanse rising behind that. Sunlight from outside mocked her and made the room too warm. The window would not open. She thumped it a few times, then got off the bed and began to pace up and down, unable to sit still. She was angry, but she was afraid, too. Lord Morrisham was very powerful. Could he really have her locked away and declared insane if she didn't do as he ordered?

The day dragged on and they left her there until dusk before they came again. No food, nothing to drink, in a room that grew hotter and hotter.

When she heard footsteps, she stood up and faced the door. The housekeeper appeared. Behind her lounged Thomas and James, not daring to smile, but managing to look triumphant nonetheless.

'Well, have you thought better of your rashness, girl?' Mrs Coxleigh demanded.

Jessie tried to speak, but only a croak came out. 'I'm thirsty. And hungry, too. Do you intend starving me into submission?'

'I gave orders that a jug of water was to be left here.' She turned to stare accusingly at Thomas.

'Oh, sorry, Mrs Coxleigh. It must have slipped my mind, with all the fuss she made. Shocking way to behave. Shocking.'

'Go and fetch some water immediately!' She turned back to

Jessie, her face flushed with embarrassment. 'I'm sorry about that. His Lordship would not want you treated unkindly, I'm sure.'

Not want her treated unkindly? What sort of treatment was this, then?

'Answer my question, girl! Have you come to your senses?'

'I have every right to marry the man I love, every right to give notice. What *you* are doing is wrong, Mrs Coxleigh. And if you help them to lock me away in the lunatic house, I don't know how you'll ever dare say your prayers at night again.'

The colour drained from the housekeeper's face and without a word she turned and left the room. James waited until Thomas had set down a jug of water, then locked the door again.

Jessie poured herself a glass, looked at it and put it down again. Thomas had poured it from today's drawing, which was always left standing till the bits settled to the bottom, then filtered off before being boiled. She wasn't drinking that stuff. It could give you the gripes. She had never felt so thirsty in her life. Tears of disappointment came into her eyes and she blinked them away again. She wasn't going to cry. And she wasn't going to give in, either. They had no right to do this.

A phrase she'd read at school came back to her and made her shiver. *Might is right.*

When darkness fell, she was visited again by Mrs Coxleigh, flanked this time by Mr Howard.

Jessie took the initiative, her voice husky. 'The water Thomas brought isn't drinkable. You've kept me here all day with no food or water.'

'I assume from your truculent tone, Burton, that you haven't come to your senses,' Mr Howard said.

'I haven't done anything wrong. You have no right to keep me here.'

He looked behind him, a surprisingly furtive gesture for such a dignified man, then said in a low voice, 'His Lordship is very fixed upon this. He's talking about locking you away for good. Says you must be out of your mind to associate with a railway navvy. A girl like you wouldn't do so, otherwise.'

Mrs Coxleigh stepped forward. 'Jessie, *please* think again! You don't think we enjoy doing this to you?'

'And if I do agree, what will happen?'

'His Lordship will send you to the Scottish shooting lodge. He'll make sure that – that people up there keep an eye on you. Until the danger is past. Until you've realised this is all for the best.'

'I see.'

'And – and if you try to escape from there, he'll say you've stolen something.'

Silence.

'Jessie – '

'My answer is still no. I hope *you* sleep well tonight. I hope you're not thirsty and hungry.'

They went out. A short time later, Mrs Coxleigh returned with a jug of fresh water and a piece of dry bread. Thomas stood guarding the door. He had lost his smirk and seemed faintly anxious.

Sickened, Jessie turned her back on them. When Mrs Coxleigh left, taking the oil lamp with her, Jessie drank a glass of water in the darkness and ate the piece of dry bread, for she was ravenous. She used the bucket reluctantly to empty her bladder, then lay down on the bed, but sat up again after a few minutes. 'What am I going to do?' she whispered. 'What if he does lock me away for good? Or accuse me of theft?' If *he* said something was so, no one would dare dispute it.

She wondered, with a stab of pure terror, whether Jared would think she'd changed her mind about marrying him? And what would her mother say? Would Mrs Coxleigh just tell her that Jessie had been sent to the Scottish house? And would Agnes believe them? As Jessie's thoughts whirled round inside her head, her spirits sank lower and lower.

The moon alternately shone into the narrow room, then disappeared behind the clouds, leaving her feeling as if she were choking in the stuffy blackness. Time crawled past, but although she felt tired, she had no desire to sleep.

Suddenly there was a faint sound outside her door. She was off the bed and across to it instantly. The other visitors had just walked in. Whoever was there now was trying not to be heard.

A key was inserted in the lock and turned slowly, so slowly that Jessie felt like shouting, 'Hurry up!'

The click as the lock gave sounded so loud that for a few seconds she held her breath, almost expecting people to come rushing to investigate. But nothing happened, except that the door swung open and someone whispered, 'Shh!'

Jessie blinked. She could see nothing, for the person was not carrying a lamp. Was this someone trying to help her or another of Lord Morrisham's tricks?

11

❧

Hettonby: July 1837

'*W*ho's there?' Jessie whispered. Just then the moon came out again. 'Miss Susannah!'

A small hand was clamped firmly over her mouth. 'Shh! Do you want to wake everyone?'

Susannah moved closer until her lips were right next to Jessie's ear. 'When I saw what they were doing to you, I started eavesdropping.' Her voice was full of suppressed anger. 'I couldn't *believe* what my father was planning.'

'Nor could I when it happened. Miss Susannah, I've done nothing wrong. Nothing. And I'm not mad.'

'Of course you're not! My mother said you'd met a railway navvy and wanted to marry him. No wonder Father's furious.' She gave a low chuckle. 'Serve him right! So I've decided to rescue you. Though I shall miss you. None of the other maids will suit me half as well.'

'*What!*' Relief made the room spin around Jessie for a moment.

Susannah went outside and brought in a portmanteau. 'I can't get your own clothes because it'd wake the other maids, so I've put some of mine in a bag and you can take that. They'll be a bit short for you, but you can sew frills on them or something.'

'*No!*' Seeing the hurt on her rescuer's face, Jessie tried to explain her sharp refusal. 'Your father will accuse me of stealing them.'

'Oh. I never thought of that.' Silence. Then: 'He's a wicked man. You don't know how unkind he is to my mother, how he bullies us all.'

Jessie did. Servants couldn't help knowing things like that. But she didn't say so. 'I'd better go. If I'm not quick, someone might hear us.'

Susannah pressed something into her hand. A small purse. The coins chinked faintly.

Again Jessie shook her head. 'Let me take a small coin or two, but not the purse.'

'You're very clever. That's why I've always liked you better than the other servants.' Susannah reached up and gave her a quick hug. 'Good luck.'

'Go back to your room now, miss. I'll find my own way out.'

'I left the side window open in the library. I don't think they'll have noticed it.'

Jessie could not help hugging her back. 'One day I'll thank you properly for this, miss.'

'One day we'll both be free of him. When I'm in London, I'm going to marry the first man who asks me and insist on an early wedding.'

Jessie suspected, from remarks she'd overheard, that Lord Morrisham had already got one or two men under consideration as husbands for his eldest daughter, whose feelings would not be taken into account when weighed against a prosperous match. But she didn't say that either.

'Wait! I've got an idea.' Jessie went back in and arranged the bedclothes and pillow to look as though someone were sleeping. 'If we lock the door again, they'll not notice I'm missing straight away.'

Susannah giggled. 'Oh, yes. What a good idea! I wish I could see their faces when they open that door.' She locked it, waved farewell and tiptoed away.

Left on her own, Jessie took a deep breath and wished she didn't feel so wobbly and afraid. What if someone heard her? She'd not get another chance to escape.

Making her way through the quiet house seemed to take an eternity. If she hadn't known every inch of it, she'd have had trouble, because the moon chose that moment to hide behind the clouds and the darkness seemed impenetrable. She crept down the attic stairs, sucking in an anxious breath as she carelessly allowed the third one to creak. She waited at the bottom until she heard Susannah's bedroom door click shut. The noise sounded so loud in the darkness that she waited again.

When no one came out to see what was going on, she let out a long breath of relief and set off.

It was easier to tread quietly on the next flight of stairs, because they were covered in thick carpet. From the direction of His Lordship's room came the snorting, grunting sound he made most nights. He sounds like a pig! she thought, then shivered. More like a nasty-tempered, rutting old boar. He was a dangerous, wicked man. If he caught her trying to escape, who knew what he'd do?

She paused again on the first-floor landing, outside Her Ladyship's small parlour, peering down into the big silent space of the entrance hall, itself larger than the parsonage where she'd grown up. When nothing moved, she tiptoed down the stairs which servants were not normally allowed to use. At the foot, there was a sleepy 'Woof!' and she froze again, her pulse hammering in her throat.

Something pattered towards her and with a thankful sigh she recognised His Lordship's dog, which usually slept out in the stables. Jessie leaned down to pat its head. She had let it in and out of the house many times at His Lordship's bidding and it knew her well.

When she pushed it away and whispered, 'Lie down!' it trotted back to its blanket, settling with its head on its paws, watching her.

Relief was almost as debilitating as the terror Jessie had felt when the dog came towards her and it was a while before she could persuade her legs to move. Slowly she crept round the edges of the hall to the library, praying that Mr Howard had not seen the open window when he locked up. Inside the room, coals were still burning in the grate. She thought she saw something move and could not hold back a hiss of indrawn breath. But then she saw it was only a curtain blowing slightly and let out her breath again slowly. That could be because of the open window.

Oh, please, let it open quietly! she prayed. *Let them not catch me!* She crept across and sagged in relief as she found the gap at the bottom of the window.

But she couldn't stand here like a fool. She must escape, get as far away from the Hall as possible. It was the work of a moment to slide the window gently open and swing her legs across the sill. She dropped into the flowerbed, landing next to a clump of big yellow daisies she had often admired for their cheerful colour. About to rush across the lawn, she hesitated, then turned back and dragged the window down again. They'd wonder how she had got out of the attic and would have to look closely to see that this window was not locked.

She followed the darkest shadows to the far side of the lawn, her eyes accustomed now to the dimness but her nerves twitching at every sound that whispered through the still night air. Walking carefully along the grass by the side of the drive to avoid making any noise on the gravel, she headed towards the gates.

She was halfway down the drive before she realised this would not work. The gatekeeper's dog was trained to bark at the slightest noise and even Lord Morrisham himself wasn't immune to its attentions. After a slight hesitation, she turned on to a side path which led to another part of the wall, pushing her way past overhanging bushes, all of which seemed to be rustling loudly, to be moving, to be ... *Stop it!* she told herself. *It's just your imagination.*

There was a small gate somewhere round here. She didn't think it was kept locked. She'd never found it locked on her wanderings through the grounds, anyway. And if it was, she'd just have to find some way to climb over the wall.

Her heart had stopped fluttering in panic now and her mind was functioning better. Where was she going once she got outside? Her first instinct had been to flee to Jared, but he would stand no chance against Lord Morrisham. She didn't want to put him in danger as well. Where could she go, then? It took her a minute or two to realise that there was only one place. *Home.*

But would the parson take her side? He didn't usually go against His Lordship's wishes, but she had noticed several times that he had stood up for things he thought right or necessary - such as when he'd obtained a place for her in the school. And she didn't think he'd countenance their locking her up simply for falling in love with a railway navvy.

When she found the small gate in the estate wall – unlocked, thank goodness! – she went through it quickly, feeling better just to be out of the grounds. She followed the wall round to the road and turned towards Hettonby. It was her only chance. That or running away and never coming back, and she wouldn't be driven to that. She did not intend to lose Jared. But if the parson did not support her . . . she cut off that thought. Surely, surely he would? Or at the very worst, allow her to continue her flight.

She reached Hettonby while it was still dark and could not stop a few tears of relief from trickling down her face as she limped across the green. She was wearing only her felt house shoes and they had worn right through in places, as well as rubbing her right heel to a blister. And although it was a warm summer's night, she felt chilled, somehow, chilled to her soul. She had not thought the gentry could be so wicked.

The village looked strange without people bustling about and she hoped no one heard her pass through in the hush of the false dawn. There was a light on behind the forge, where the blacksmith's lad would be working to get the damped down fire blazing again. Thank goodness she had got here in time to slip inside the parsonage unnoticed!

There was no light showing there, of course. Even her mother did not get up this early. Jessie leaned against the wall by the back door, resisting a strong desire to burst into tears of sheer relief, then reached up to fumble for the key on the top of the door lintel. She missed the lock the first time, because her hands were trembling, but the second time she got the key in and gave a low moan as it turned easily.

The kitchen felt warm and she could see an ember winking in the range. She paused for a moment to turn up the damper, then swing the big kettle across to the middle, where it would soon be warm. She felt like a criminal as she tiptoed up the stairs to the room she had shared with her mother for so long.

As she opened the door, a voice asked sleepily, 'Who's that?' Then her mother sat bolt upright in the bed and stared through the dimness. '*Jessie!* What on earth are you doing here in the middle of the night?'

She ran across to the bed and threw herself on it, sobbing in her mother's arms, gulping and hiccupping as she tried to explain what had happened. But she couldn't stop crying for long enough to get the words out. All the tears and anger and despair she'd held back the previous day, all the terror she'd felt as she'd fled through the night, came bursting out of her, overwhelming her.

Agnes could only pat her daughter's head and wait for an explanation. If that fellow had hurt her Jessie, she'd have the law on him.

'What's wrong?'

The parson's voice made both women jerk round.

'*Jessie?* What are you doing here? Agnes – ?'

She kept her arm round her daughter's shaking shoulders. 'I don't know what's happened, sir. She came in and woke me up, then she just burst into tears.'

Jessie at last found her voice. 'I – I need to tell you what's happened, too, sir. C-could we go downstairs? I've turned up the fire and put the kettle over it. I'm so c-cold!'

'A nice cup of tea,' decided Agnes. 'Yes, that will do us all good.' She looked down and blushed, pulling the sheet hurriedly up to hide her nightdress. And her hair, as thick and unruly as her daughter's when released from its bun, was streaming over her shoulders like a hoyden's.

John Marley became belatedly aware that he was standing there in only his nightshirt, and blushed too. 'I'll go and put on my dressing gown and – and come down to the kitchen. It'll be warmer there than in my study.' He secretly enjoyed sitting in the cosy kitchen.

When they were all settled at the table, Jessie stared down into her cup, cradling it in her hands, not quite knowing how to begin. Then she took a deep breath and started to tell her tale.

Her two companions did not interrupt, because each of them was shocked rigid by what she had to say. John Marley wanted to deny that his patron could have done such a thing, but he knew Lord Morrisham's intense and unreasonable hatred of the railways and what he had done to his own cousin because of it. So John believed the girl. Besides, you could not doubt her sincerity, not when you saw how upset she was.

When the tale was told, Agnes reached out to grasp her daughter's hand and they both turned to the parson.

Jessie spoke, because it had to be asked. 'Will you give me shelter until I can s-sort something out, and h-help me if His Lordship – if he – accuses me of – of – ' Her voice faltered on a sob. 'I didn't dare go to Jared tonight in case Lord Morrisham accused *him* of s-something. I thought – I thought no one could accuse you.'

John Marley looked down at his hands and could not for a moment speak, so filled with rage was he. He disliked confrontations, but he was also a man of God and knew he could not refuse to assist this young woman. Even if she had been a stranger, he must have helped her. Sometimes you had to follow your conscience – wherever it led.

'You did right to come here, Jessie, and you must stay as long as you need.' He turned to his housekeeper. 'Can you – have you some clothes for your daughter, Agnes?'

'Yes, sir.'

'Then I think she should go to bed and rest while I consider how best to approach this.'

At that Agnes did something she had never done before. She reached out and grasped the parson's hand, squeezing it as she said fervently, 'I can't thank you enough, sir.'

He stared at her. At that moment the resemblance between her and her daughter was very strong. He blinked in surprise. Why had he never realised how *pretty* Agnes was? Then he dismissed such thoughts and cleared his throat. 'If I could have another cup of your tea, and perhaps one of those little cakes from yesterday, I'll just sit here in the warmth and think what to do while you see to Jessie. After that, perhaps you would come back down and we'll discuss it further. Better put her in the spare bedroom at the back.'

While an exhausted Jessie was sleeping away the day, John Marley dressed in his severest clerical black and was driven over to Sutton Hall by the lad from The Crown.

He arrived a little before ten and found it a place of silence and whispers. The footman who opened the door looked sullen. The maid crossing the hall looked defiant and nervous at the same time. Even the butler looked wan and strained.

'I wish to see His Lordship, Howard.'

'I'm afraid you've had a wasted journey, sir. His Lordship is very busy today and can see no one.'

John Marley looked the butler in the eye. 'I know exactly what's been happening here and it's imperative that I see Lord Morrisham. Today. Before this foolishness goes from bad to worse.'

Mr Howard realised that the girl must have fled to the parsonage. He stole a quick glance round, then whispered, 'Is she all right, sir?'

'No thanks to you.'

'I was only following His Lordship's orders.'

'And if he orders you to kill someone tomorrow, will you do that as well?'

A dull flush stained Mr Howard's cheeks and he shook his head helplessly. 'Will you wait in the morning room while I apprise Lord Morrisham of your presence?'

'No. Just show me in.' Better to take him by surprise, John decided.

Mr Howard threw open the library doors, to reveal Lord Morrisham interrogating Vera, who was sobbing into her apron. 'Parson Marley to see you, m'lord.'

'Damn you, fellow, I said no callers. Tell him I'm busy!'

John Marley drew in a deep breath and stepped forward. 'I'm here already and I think you'd better send that woman away and listen to what I have to say, Your Lordship.'

Clarence Morrisham stared at him, eyes narrowed, then jerked his head in the direction of the door. Vera fled. He leaned back in his chair and scowled. 'Well, what's so important that you have to force your way in here when I'm busy?'

The parson took a seat without being asked and clasped his hands in front of him, looking down at them for a moment to gather his thoughts and his courage. Then he looked at the man he had once believed to be a friend and anger rose in him.

'What the devil do you mean by persecuting that girl?'

'Persecuting! *Persecuting!* Do you know what *that girl* has been doing? Against my express orders!'

'She's been doing what all pretty girls do – walking out with a young man. Whom, incidentally, she is to marry.'

'He's a damned navvy!'

'That is not, so far as I know, a crime.'

'And I gave orders that none of my staff was to have anything to do with those fellers. On pain of instant dismissal. She disobeyed those orders.'

'Then why didn't you just dismiss her when you found out?'

For the first time Clarence Morrisham's confidence faltered. 'I needed to make an example of her.'

'As you did with your own cousin?'

'Do you know how many men I've lost to that damned cutting they're ruining the countryside with?'

'No. And I don't care. What I do care about is that you are behaving in a shameful manner, imperilling your eternal soul and blackening your family honour.' John Marley might not have the other man's wealth, but he could trace his ancestry back several generations to an earl of some distinction, and all his breeding showed in his face as he spoke. Indolent he might be, and overfond of his food, but he despised men who took advantage of their position and wealth to persecute those under them, despised them utterly – and it showed.

Clarence Morrisham let out his breath noisily. 'How did she get out?'

'I have no idea. She was in no state for me to be questioning her about such irrelevancies. She had fled through the night to Hettonby and was chilled through, with blistered feet. She had been terrified, starved and kept thirsty.'

'Kept hungry and thirsty! That was no part of my orders.'

'What was, then? Threatening to lock her up in the lunatic asylum? Trying to force her to give up the man she loves?' John's romantic soul had been rather impressed by the way the two young lovers had stood up for themselves the previous Sunday. 'Threatening to send her to Scotland and accuse her of theft if she tried to escape from your lodge there?'

Silence pooled around them, broken only by the clock ticking and the sound of Lord Morrisham's finger tracing a pattern to and fro on the ruby velvet of his great armchair.

'Jessie is now at my house, where she is living in fear that you'll accuse her of theft. However, if you do, I shall be able to bear witness that she had nothing with her when she stumbled into my house, that her feet were bleeding and blistered, that – '

'Enough! I take your point, damn it all. Though I'm not impressed by your lack of loyalty to me. Not impressed at all. First my cous— that Stafford woman, now this maid.'

'I have a greater loyalty, sir. I answer first to my Maker. And as His representative, I tell you that your feelings about the railways are getting out of hand, My Lord.'

'They're the devil's toy, those railways! Let alone they ruin the countryside, what do you think will happen to the stability of our country when any Jack or Harry can go gallivanting round? It'll give them ideas above their station. We'll be facing worse than the French Revolution if this goes on, far worse.'

'You know that we disagree about that.'

'Aye.' Clarence Morrisham let out a long sigh, then glared at the parson. 'But she's not coming back to work here.'

'I doubt she'd want to.'

'And I'll still turn off anyone else who associates with those damned railway scum.'

'That is your prerogative. May I take back her belongings?'

His host shrugged.

'And I believe you owe her some wages.'

'I'll be damned if I do!'

'You'd stoop to stealing from a girl of nineteen?'

'I don't pay servants who've been dismissed.'

'Then I shall find out what's owing and pay her in your place. And I shall not be coming to dine here again. To steal from those in your employment is – is dastardly.' John Marley stood up and moved towards the door. He expected – hoped – that the man he had known for so long would call him back, but no sound broke the silence as he closed the door behind him.

The butler was hovering in the hallway.

'Ah, Howard, will you please have Miss Burton's things packed?

I'll take them back with me now. And if you could let me know how much is owing to her, I'll see she gets paid.'

'His Lordship . . . ?' The butler did not quite know how to phrase his question tactfully.

'Your master has given permission for me to take Miss Burton's things with me, but he is still angry.' John raised his voice as he added, 'He has refused to pay her the wages he owes, so I shall do it for him.'

Behind the door to the servants' quarters, Vera clasped her hand to her mouth. They all knew what had happened, and it wasn't fair. Any of it. Whatever her faults, Jessie Burton hadn't deserved to be treated like that. And which of them would sleep easily from now on, knowing how far His Lordship was prepared to go to get his own way? For the first time, she began to consider looking for another position.

In her room upstairs at the back of the house, Mrs Coxleigh wept into her lace handkerchief, for shame sat heavily within her. She had done wrong and she was afraid *he* would ask her to do so again. But she was even more afraid of trying to look for a position elsewhere. She was just too old to change her ways.

Downstairs in the servants' hall Thomas and James found themselves cast in the role of villains by the other servants for their part in the affair. For several days, no one would speak to them or pass them food at mealtimes, let alone lend a hand with lifting something.

And upstairs, Susannah Morrisham watched everything and said nothing, wishing desperately that Elinor Stafford were still here to confide in. She didn't even know where Elinor was, or how to find out – then she frowned as she wondered if Parson Marley knew, or could find out for her. She sighed, wishing desperately that she could leave her father's house. But she would be very careful whom she married. No use leaping from the frying pan into the fire.

Her mother said her father had several men in mind already, and that she and her sisters would get little choice, but Susannah didn't intend to spend the rest of her life with a man she was as terrified of as her mother was of her father. Not even, she realised, frowning, if it meant defying her father. After all, he could not say the words of a marriage ceremony for her. And he might beat her, but he would not murder her – so it was just a question of holding out. Though that would be hard enough.

Later that day, one of the gardeners begged her pardon and said, 'You dropped this piece of paper, miss.'

Susannah looked at him for a moment, then nodded and took it. 'Thank you. It's just a list, but I'm glad not to lose it.'

She didn't read it until she was alone in her bedroom, then wept with relief to know that Elinor was safe. *And if*, the letter ended, *when you are grown up and married, you wish to get in touch with me, I shall always be happy to hear from you. I'll ask Mr Marley to get this note to you and I'll keep him informed of my whereabouts.*

As he drove back along the country lanes to Hettonby, John Marley's thoughts were in turmoil. Disgust was very strong in him. 'A gentleman,' he said aloud at one stage, startling the lad from the inn, 'a *real* gentleman, does not persecute those weaker than he.' He was not sorry that he'd stopped to pass on Elinor's note. The gardener was the son of one of his parishioners and had not even blinked at the request. Everyone in the district was well aware of what had been going on.

The lad driving the trap decided that no answer was needed, but wondered what Parson was so upset about.

'I shall have to find another living,' he said a bit later, by which time the lad had grown used to his mumblings and stopped listening. 'I shall take Agnes with me, of course. She has been a loyal servant. And a good mother.'

And finally, as he neared home, 'And I shall marry that girl to her young man in my church – damned if I don't!'

When John Marley was young himself, he had been very much in favour of universal education and progress. He still enjoyed toying with daring new thoughts and ideas from the comfort of his armchair. Now, suddenly, he realised that the world was not as cosy as it had seemed for the past twenty years. This was 1837, not the Dark Ages, yet Lord Morrisham had acted like a feudal ravager. His Lordship did not own the souls of those he employed. Or his parson's soul, either.

* * *

The following Thursday, John came down to the kitchen waving a sheet of paper. 'Well, your young man was telling the truth about himself, my dear Jessie. He is indeed a ganger, as he claimed, and Mr Stafford says that he is of sober habits and well thought of by his employers.'

She smiled. 'I never doubted Jared was telling the truth, sir, but I'm glad Mr Stafford wrote to you because it may make my mother feel a bit better about everything.' Her smile faded and she looked at him anxiously. 'Will you call the banns on Sunday, sir? And can I ask Jared to come here for that?'

'Yes. We'll send the lad from the inn across to the diggings with a message. If you'll write a note, I'll enclose it with mine.'

She stepped forward impulsively and gave him a hug. 'Thank you, sir! For everything.'

He patted her shoulder in avuncular fashion. 'It was my privilege to help you, my dear. After all, I'm indebted to your mother for a good many comfortable years.' Dear Agnes, he thought, smiling. The very best of housekeepers – almost a friend, lately. They had had several chats, for she was still not reconciled to the idea of her daughter marrying young Wilde, and John thought he had been of some comfort to her.

Jessie stepped back, smiling. 'Thank you, sir. I wanted very much to be married here in Hettonby. The parsonage is the only home I've ever known.'

That touched John deeply and he had to blink rather rapidly for a moment. Then he remembered his duty and looked at Jessie sternly over the tops of his spectacles. 'And please see that you tell your young man in your note he's to come here to church *every* Sunday to hear the banns read. We shall do this thing properly or not at all. And will you ask your mother to come to my study when convenient? I'm sure she'll feel better when she reads this letter.'

'Yes, sir.' Then Jessie was off, flying out into the garden to tell her mother everything.

'Ah!' he sighed. 'What it is to be young!' And went to peep into the mirror in his study, wondering how he had grown old so quickly. 'And yet,' he murmured, 'I'm only five and forty. Surely there's still time to do something more – more worthwhile with my life?'

His sermon on Sunday was so full of fire, and talk of duty and responsibility, that his congregation abandoned their usual slumbers to sit up and gape. What had got into Parson? Perhaps what the lad from The Crown said was true? Perhaps he had had a falling out with His Lordship?

Folk sat waiting impatiently for the service to be over so that they could get outside, compare notes and try to work out what was making Parson thunder at them like this. It had been a strange week, it had that. Poor Miss Stafford turned from her home and Jessie Burton suddenly appearing in the village one day, though no one had even seen her arrive. Something *must* have happened at the Hall to make her lose her place so suddenly. And those villagers with relatives over Great Sutton way had heard that His Lordship was in a foul mood, finding fault with everything and everyone around him.

Agnes, still very stiff in Jared's presence, went with them to church for Evensong, sitting there stony-faced as the banns were read out. The congregation gasped in shock and turned as one to stare at Jessie and Jared. Afterwards, while everyone else lingered in the churchyard or on the village green to discuss this new development, Agnes led Jessie and her young man straight home.

Jared had not been told what had happened, just that His Lordship had dismissed Jessie the minute he heard of her connection with the railways. He didn't mind too much, because it meant they could get wed earlier than they had planned, but he thought it a nasty trick to play on a girl who'd worked for you for years. If that was how the nobs treated folk, he was glad his lass was leaving them.

During the following week, whenever she went shopping in the village, Agnes refused point blank to discuss her future son-in-law with anyone, and snubbed Mrs Plumworthy very sharply indeed when that lady asked her straight out why her Jessie was having to get married and why she had left her position at the Hall so suddenly.

'My Jessie does not *have* to marry anyone, if that's what you're hinting at – unlike *your* daughter.'

Mrs Plumworthy turned bright red. Her Rosie was certainly growing very stout for one so newly married, but no one had dared say this to her doting mother's face before. 'Well, I've heard that your Jessie, your precious little ewe lamb, *has* to get married and that that's why she was dismissed,' she retorted. 'His Lordship wouldn't turn her off for nothing. Not after all these years.'

'She was dismissed because Lord Morrisham doesn't approve of the railways, that's all,' said Mrs Burton loftily. 'Everyone knows how he feels about them. And if you don't believe me, you can ask Parson. What's more, Mr Wilde is not just a navigator, he's a ganger, with ten men working under him. Mr Marley made enquiries for me and found out all about it. You don't think I'd let my Jessie marry just anyone, do you? Mr Wilde has excellent prospects, or so Mr Stafford, who is one of the engineers on the railway, told Parson. And *he* is the brother of Miss Stafford who used to live in Great Sutton – before she, too, was asked to leave because of her connection with the railways. Ah, thank you, Mr Benbow. And I'd also like a pound of raisins, if you please.'

Mrs Plumworthy shoved the rest of her packages into her basket anyhow and stormed out of the shop, routed.

Agnes asked for a piece of cheese she didn't need to give herself time to recover while Mr Benbow was cutting it, for if she moved now, she was sure her legs would let her down.

Jessie was equally uncommunicative with the villagers, except for Mr Snelling, who had been so kind to her and whose gentle enquiries about her young man were not made out of malice, but out of genuine concern for her future. To keep herself occupied, she bought some material and kept herself busy sewing sheets and pillow cases. Agnes, unable to sit and watch, took up a piece of material one evening and began to stitch at it.

'Thank you, Mother,' Jessie said softly. 'I'm sorry to disappoint you.'

Agnes just shook her head and kept on sewing. A little later she asked. 'What are you going to wear?' It was as near as she could get to making peace, and she was still very sharp sometimes, but as Jessie told Jared on the second Sunday, 'She's coming round.'

He rolled his eyes. 'If that's coming round, I never want her to be my enemy.' Then he hugged his wife-to-be. 'Not long now,' he whispered in her ear. 'I'm that glad we won't have to wait three months.' And he said the same words to himself every night as he fell into bed, exhausted from his own wedding preparations, for he had to build them somewhere to live.

During the three weeks which had to pass before she could be married, Jessie still woke in the night, thinking she was locked in, and several times had to get up and fling the window wide open before she could breathe easily. She stayed close to the parsonage, not going out after dusk, for she was constantly afraid that Lord Morrisham would find some way to hurt her or Jared.

She felt she had grown up very suddenly in the past few weeks. It hadn't affected her love for Jared or her desire to marry him, but it had affected her view of the world. Everything seemed less stable, less honest, less fair than she had thought, and she wasn't sure she liked that new understanding.

Even the parson had changed. He had told her mother he was thinking about finding a new parish, and hoped she would stay with him when he moved. And he came into the kitchen more often, as if seeking company. He hadn't been over to the Hall once since he'd brought Jessie's things and her money home, though formerly he had dined there quite often and played chess with His Lordship sometimes.

'When your daughter is married, I shall teach you to play chess,' he told Agnes one day, for he could see how sad she was.

'Oh, sir, I don't think I – '

'You'll like it,' he said, beaming at her.

She smiled back. He was such a boy sometimes, with his little enthusiasms. 'I don't think I'll be very good at something like that.'

'We shall see.' And he walked out, humming. It made you feel good to do the right thing. He had perhaps been too eager to accede to Lord Morrisham's wishes before. But not now. He had no respect left for his patron, none at all. That was why he was making enquiries about another living. And would find one, too, he was sure.

Simon could not help brooding over the wrong done to his sister by their cousin, and although she had persuaded him not to go and confront His Lordship at the Hall, when Simon saw him crossing the street in Little Sutton, he could not hold back any longer. He went and planted himself in front of Lord Morrisham.

'Get out of my way, sir! I have nothing to say to you.'

Simon moved first to one side, then the other, to prevent Lord Morrisham from moving on. 'But I have something to say to you, sir. You are a coward and a disgrace to your rank. Easy to bully those weaker than yourself, isn't it? I heard what you did to that poor servant girl.'

'I will deal as I see fit with any of my people who disobey me.'

'I am ashamed that we are related, and had you not repudiated the relationship between us, I would have done it myself.' Simon flourished a bow and said loudly, 'Pass on, Sir Coward! I hope I never have to speak to you again.'

Someone in the small crowd which had gathered to watch the encounter tittered and Lord Morrisham turned purple with fury, slashing out at the younger man with his walking stick, catching him across the face. Simon dragged it from his hand, leaned it against the wall and stamped on it, breaking it in two. Then he tossed the pieces away and touched his stinging cheek. 'A badge of honour,' he said even more loudly. 'You'd be better sticking to bullying poor little servant girls.'

Lord Morrisham walked round him and into the inn, calling for his carriage. Then, as he was about to mount into it, he stopped and said softly, 'You'll be sorry for that, Simon Stafford. Very sorry.'

12

August 1837

*E*linor felt apprehensive as the squire's comfortable, old-fashioned carriage rumbled through the countryside towards Rotherham, though the coachman was solicitous of their comfort and stopped twice so they might take refreshments. They skirted Rotherham, another place full of smoking chimneys, with ugly heaps of earth mounded just outside the town itself, as if everything was raw and unfinished.

'I hope where we'll be living isn't like this,' she said to Thirza.

'Oh, the gentry allus live away from the muck,' the maid said with a chuckle.

Yettley proved to be a tiny village, stark in its architecture, with a single terrace of small houses being its most prominent feature. The inn was in the centre and it was clearly market day, because half a dozen stallholders were packing up their unsold goods and rotten vegetables were piled in one corner. They drove on through and pulled up at a commodious house built in an old-fashioned style just outside the village.

When the coachman opened the carriage door, he beamed at them and said, 'Miss Butterfield will be waiting for you in her front parlour. She isn't too good on her feet now or she'd have come out to welcome you.' He helped them down, as if they weren't too good on their feet, either, then gestured towards the door, at which a plump maid in a white pinafore was waiting for them.

'Miss Stafford?' she asked.

'Yes. And this is my maid, Thirza.'

The woman nodded. 'I'll take you through to Miss Butterfield – and she'll probably want to meet your maid as well.'

Belinda Butterfield was tiny, with that shrunken look to her whole body which sometimes comes in old age or extreme illness. But her eyes were alive, like two black coals in her yellowing face, and she was not only dressed immaculately, but holding herself very upright. She was sitting on a sofa, and held out one hand to Elinor. 'Come and sit here. Let me have a look at you, girl.'

'Hardly a girl,' she said, smiling and doing as she was told.

'You're a girl to me.' She looked across at Thirza. 'This'll be your maid. Come closer, if you please.' She did not scruple to eye Thirza up and down, and Thirza eyed her back. After a minute, Belinda chuckled. 'Yes, I like your maid, too. Got spirit, which shows you treat her right. Go with Nancy now, Thirza, and she'll show you your rooms. I hope you'll be happy with us.'

Thirza dropped a curtsey and followed the other woman. 'She's very – frank, isn't she?' she whispered as they climbed the stairs.

Nancy smiled. 'Always speaks her mind. But she's a right nice lady.' Her expression turned sad. 'She's not well, though. We all know she hasn't long to live. And we're all going to miss her. You don't often get a mistress like her.'

And then what'll happen to Miss Elinor? Thirza wondered. And me. Will we never find somewhere to settle? But she wasn't going to let her worries show to her mistress, who had enough to trouble her, so she just unpacked everything, then found her way down to the servants' quarters to offer her services.

'I can't abide to be idle,' she explained to the cook-housekeeper.

'Well, an extra pair of hands is allus welcome.'

Thirza nodded to herself as she set to and cleaned some silver. Friendly staff. Well-respected mistress. At least they'd have a while here to recover from the nastiness with His Lordship, but she couldn't see Miss Elinor being able to afford the rent for this place afterwards, if anything happened – or the expense of running it, either.

* * *

At the diggings, Alfred Small helped Jared to enlarge Ma's shanty, partitioning off a corner to give some privacy to the newly-weds. His wife, Bessie, was brought in to give Jared some practical advice on the things Jessie would need to start housekeeping in the diggings and to help him select them at the shop.

'Will you come to the wedding?' he asked them afterwards as they stood for a moment in the doorway of the hut, looking at the setting sun.

'Eh, how can we? The childer aren't old enough to leave. An' if we took 'em with us, they'd only be a nuisance,' Bessie sighed. 'Nor I can't walk that far these days.'

'I'm hiring a cart, so there'll be no need for anyone to walk. An' how about I pay Ma t'look after them children of yours?'

She gaped at him so strangely for a moment that he wondered if she had heard him properly, then she beamed and gave him a hug. 'Oh, Jared, we'd love to come.'

He turned to his friend. 'And you, Alfred, will you stand up for me in t'church?'

'Eh, I'd like to, lad, but I haven't got no fancy clothes. I'd just show you up.'

'Nor have I. But them nobs say cleanliness is next to godliness, so we'll just shine ourselves up a bit, eh, an' make that do?'

'Well.' Alfred shuffled his feet and exchanged glances with his wife, both pleased and embarrassed. 'If you're sure about that, I'd be glad to, Jared lad.'

The prospect of an outing cheered Bessie up enormously, and she washed and pressed Alfred's best shirt and her faded print dress for the occasion. Ma took one look at her when she was ready and produced her own Sunday shawl. 'If tha's going to spend thy time getting childer, tha'll have to get thysen a wider dress, lass.' She saw tears rise to Bessie's eyes and added hastily, 'Not but what it hasn't washed up well. It's a pretty colour, that.'

Jared was resplendent in corduroy trousers and brown woollen jacket, with a new shirt under his old leather waistcoat, and a bright red neckerchief round his throat. His clothes, except for the shirt, had been purchased second-hand and were too tight at some of the seams, though in reasonable condition. The shirt had been made for him by Jessie as a wedding present and that, at least, fitted him well.

Ma had nodded approval when he'd brought the shirt back the week before the wedding and showed it to her proudly, and she nodded again as she saw him dressed in it. 'Fine enough for a gentleman, that shirt is. Thy lass is good wi' her needle.' She reached up to pat his cheek in a motherly gesture.

'We'll have to be calling him Lord Jared from now on,' one of the other men said, nudging his friend.

Jared spun round. 'You can if you want a fight on your hands.' After the way a certain lord had treated his Jessie, just dismissing her out of hand, he wanted nothing to do with such titles. 'An' when we get back, you'd better all remember what I said last night. I don't want my Jessie embarrassing with silly remarks or rude language.' One huge clenched fist waved threateningly at them and the scar burned livid across his cheek. 'Mind on, or you'll be sorry.'

After which the rest of them left him in peace.

Jessie was touched when Jared arrived with a posy of wild flowers he had picked for her on the way over. 'They're lovely.' She smiled at him, a smile that excluded the rest of the world for one warm, tender moment.

'Not as lovely as you, lass,' he said gruffly. 'You're a real beauty, I reckon. An' I'm t'luckiest chap around.'

She knew she was looking her best, wearing a new straw bonnet, trimmed with blue and white ribbons, and a dress of blue lawn with two lace-edged flounces round the hem. And although it wasn't the most practical style, she had made her sleeves fuller than usual, in imitation of Miss Susannah's. Under the dress she wore three starched petticoats to give herself a bit of fashionable fullness at the hem.

Her mother sniffed and made a scornful noise in her throat at Jared's comments, but everyone ignored that.

When the bridal pair didn't move, Agnes said pointedly, 'We don't want to be late.'

Jared turned to beckon his two friends forward and brief introductions were made. Agnes Burton's lips pinched together at the sight of the Smalls in their shabby clothes, but she shook hands civilly enough and asked how their journey had been. Bessie, who had already been warned about Jessie's ogre of a mother, was looking terrified and answered the question in gasping monosyllables that made Agnes speak more softly to her thereafter.

Then they all walked along the side path to the parish church, took one of the rear pews and sat through the service, only too aware that people were turning to take quick looks at them. Agnes did not fail to notice that neither Alfred nor his wife was able to read and just stared blankly at the open hymnbooks she handed them. She did fail to notice that Jared held his hymnbook upside down because Jessie righted it for him quickly.

After what seemed an interminable wait, the service ended and people shuffled out. Then Jessica Mary Burton was summoned to the front of the church to be married to Jared Wilde. She would rather have been married more privately, but Jared could only come over on a Sunday, so they had no choice but to hold the ceremony straight after the normal service.

Quite a few villagers lingered to watch. Nosy things! thought Jessie as she walked to the front of the church, so she held her head up proudly as she took her place before the parson. Inside she felt strange, very unlike her normal practical self. She was not usually fanciful, but this was a marriage born in trouble and she could not help wondering whether the trouble would cease once she became Jared's wife.

Then he nudged her and she realised that Mr Marley was waiting for her to respond, so she said, 'I do!' loudly and clearly, and banished such foolish fancies.

Agnes Burton, who was wearing her usual navy Sunday silk and a small bonnet with a new lace trimming, was not observed to shed a single tear by those watching the wedding. This was felt to be typical of her! Anyone could see, however, that she was not best pleased by the match – and it served her right, said Mrs Plumworthy spitefully, for setting herself and her precious daughter so high!

The bride and groom signed the parish register afterwards and no one watching them would have guessed that Jessie had had to teach Jared to sign his name properly. Her discovery that he could neither read nor write had caused a major row between them the previous week when he insisted he could get along perfectly well without such skills. But although he'd returned to the camp in a bad mood, ashamed to be found lacking, he'd brought back the piece of paper on which she'd written his name and had been practising the signature in secret all week.

After the ceremony the guests gathered for a meal in the parsonage kitchen. John Marley produced a bottle of wine and proposed a toast to the newly-weds' health, but he could see that his presence made everyone feel uncomfortable, so left before the food was served.

He felt lonely as he sat in state in his own study listening to the buzz of conversation from below. Ever since the trouble with Lord Morrisham he'd felt out of place, as if the earth had moved and set him down out of his accustomed sphere. He'd already written to a friend higher up in the church hierarchy, asking if Matthew knew of any decent livings going. He had not given his real reasons for wanting the move, just said he had perhaps been in Hettonby too long and needed a change.

No one thought it at all strange that Mrs Burton took up her employer's meal before serving the guests. While she was doing this, everyone admired the wedding presents: the lacquered tea-caddy full of best Lapsang Souchong that the parson had given them, the saucepans and blankets from Mrs Burton, and a small watercolour painting of the Lake District from the schoolmaster.

These presents had impressed Jared more than he would admit. They were a symbol, somehow, of the step upwards in the world that he was taking by marrying Jessie. Who'd ever heard of a navvy on the diggings getting wedding presents, let alone a picture to hang on the wall of his hut, or a wife so fiercely respectable? Well, his lass wouldn't regret it, he vowed yet again. He'd make sure of that.

She'd been very quiet these past three weeks. He was sure something besides being dismissed had happened to upset her at that Hall, but she refused to discuss it. He intended to find out, though, when they had more time together.

The guests ate heartily of the good food provided. The women and Mr Snelling drank the best China tea that Mrs Burton had procured specially for the occasion. Jared and Alfred drank ale. But Jessie and her mother barely touched the good ham and home-made cakes. Agnes Burton hid her sadness under an extra display of sharpness and her daughter didn't try to hide it at all.

When it came time for them to leave, Jared tactfully took the Smalls outside to the trap first.

'Oh, Mother!' Jessie's eyes were brimming with tears. 'Mother, you don't . . . you're not still . . .' She was unable to finish.

Tears were trickling down Agnes's cheeks too, tears she'd held back all day. She tried to speak, but could only sob and hold out her arms to her daughter. They clung together wordlessly, then broke apart as Jared called out from outside that he was ready to go.

'I'll be back to see you, Mother. As often as I can. And – and when we move on, I'll write. I'll write wherever we go.'

'See that you do! And don't forget – if you need me, need any-thing – you just let me know. I've got a bit of money put by and – '

'Now, Mother! Jared'll look after me all right. He's not like my father with money. Stop worrying about that, at least!' Jessie kissed her mother again and, unable to bear another minute of this parting, ran out through the garden to the village green where a group of women had gathered to gossip and goggle at them.

There was none of the usual good-natured teasing, just the silent stares of Granny Todd and her cronies to face. So Jessie straightened her shoulders and called farewell to them.

Granny turned to her friend. 'Didn't I tell you? Didn't I?' she demanded triumphantly.

The friend nodded.

'I knew those eyes would never sit quietly in a cottage. Eh, she's in for a few troubles, I don't doubt, for he's not the meek sort, either.'

Unaware of this gloomy prediction, Jessie kept up a cheerful flow of conversation all the way to the diggings, making the others laugh and leading them in singing, for she had a tuneful contralto voice. But they all fell silent when they came to Eastby, and on the other side of it, the navvies' camp. Jessie had a hard time hiding her dismay at her first sight of a half-completed railway cutting and its attendant shanty town.

'She's coming along nicely,' said Jared, pulling up to admire the fruits of so much labour. He cast a professional eye over the scene. 'Another couple of months to complete this stretch, I'd say. What do you reckon, Alfred lad?'

'Aye. 'Bout that. Give or take a few days. Depends on t'weather.'

Jessie, sitting rigid with horror by her husband's side, managed not to show her feelings. She had never seen anything like this great raw scar, running across a landscape denuded of grass and trees, and dotted about with heaps of muck and piles of planks and equipment. As it was Sunday, no one was working, which gave the bare slopes a forlorn look. The scene made a grim contrast to the beauty of the lanes through which they had just driven.

Jared waved his arm, pointing out the salient features and explaining that he and his gang had the end patch over there. She nodded to show she'd understood, but could not at first frame a single word, frightened that she might show him how she really felt.

Narrow wooden runways led down the steep slopes for the barrows to run along. The pulleys and ropes at the top were to help draw the barrows up when they were full of muck. Once there, they were tipped into carts and the fill was taken further down the line to where the contractors needed to build an embankment, for you couldn't have a steep incline on a railway line, it seemed.

'A good contractor,' Jared wound up, 'plans it all out in advance, so that none of the muck is wasted. Take from a high bit, fill up a low bit.'

Jessie eyed the narrowness of the wooden runways and the steepness of the slopes. 'Isn't – isn't it dangerous?'.

'Only if you play the fool, love. An' I don't. Nor do any of the lads as work with me.' He saw her looking at his scar and touched it. 'This were caused by a drunken sot as isn't working on the diggings any more. An' I've made improvements since the accident, too. See them ropes? My gang uses a harness on the man as well as on the barrow.'

'It speeds things up as well as makin' it all safer,' put in Alfred. 'He's a rare one for bein' careful, is Big Jared.'

Jared saw that she was still looking worried and gave her a crushing hug. 'I know every job there is on a cuttin', love, and I can do 'em all as well as the next man. That's why I'm the ganger.' His eyes lingered on the huge depression in the ground as he mentally estimated the next few days' work and the bonuses they could earn if they made good time.

Bessie reached out to squeeze Jessie's hand. She knew why the girl had fallen silent. She remembered only too well her own first view of a diggings and how ugly it had all seemed after the Leicestershire village where she and Alfred had grown up. You got used to it. You had to. And eventually you forgot how ugly it all was – until newcomers came and you saw it again through their eyes.

Jared had warned Jessie about the shanty in which they were to live, but even so, she wasn't prepared for the sight that met her when he stopped the cart and helped her down. The huts around her were mere hovels, built of a motley collection of materials, some roofed in sods, others with pieces of tin weighted down by stones to keep the rain off. No one she knew would even have housed their cows in them, let alone fifteen or twenty human beings. Some were just holes in the ground, covered with a roof made of whatever was handy, with drainage channels to carry away the water.

He opened his mouth to speak, then shut it again. What could he say? The contrast between the pretty little village of Hettonby and this wasteland of dried mud was only too fresh in his own mind. He looked at her pleadingly and she managed a brief smile.

The two men unloaded the trunk and the other packages, and carried them inside. Reluctantly, Jessie followed them. A couple of men were lying about in the shadowy room, men who stared at her but said nothing. There was no sign of the woman known as Ma. Jessie walked across the hut as quickly as she could and was thankful to get out of sight of those staring eyes; thankful for the dimness inside their room, too, as Jared fumbled for a candle and went outside to light it at the fire.

When he returned, shielding the flame, she had herself under control and was able to inspect the room he had built for them at the side of the hut. It was tiny and would be dim, even in the daytime, though it had the rare luxury of a minute window the size of one pane of glass. There was scarcely space to move, with the trunk and all the bundles lying on the hard earth floor, and even after they were cleared up, there'd be only a narrow space to walk between the trunk and the bed.

'I've got to take the trap back,' Jared said gruffly. 'Will you – will you be all right on your own for a few minutes, love?'

'Yes.'

When he had gone, Jessie pressed her hands to her face for a moment and then forced herself to look round again. He'd tried to tell her – he really had – but words couldn't describe the shanty camp. You had to see it for yourself. However was she going to keep cheerful in a place like this?

When she heard Jared coming back, she turned to greet him and forced another smile to her face. She wasn't going to let him see how horrified she felt.

He wasn't alone. With him was an old crone with a blackened clay pipe clamped between her lips.

'This is Ma.'

She smiled at Jessie, showing gums nearly deprived of teeth. A sour, unwashed smell emanated from her person and from her dun-coloured clothes.

'How do you do?' Jessie took the grimy hand that was held out to her and shook it gingerly.

After looking the young woman up and down, Ma cackled. 'Ha! Tha's getten thysen a fancy piece there, Jared lad. Pretty, ain't she? Too pretty, me lad! Tha'll 'ave trouble keepin' th'other bees from this honey-pot.'

'I'll manage. Where is everyone?'

'Watchin' t'fight.'

'Oh? Anyone I know?'

'Clogger Joe. Can't stay out o' trouble, that one. If your Mester Stafford hears about it, he'll be mad as fire, and he ent been in the sweetest mood lately, anyway. He's warned Joe about fightin' afore. That daft bugger don't know when t'stop.'

'Silly old bastard!' said Jared. But he wasn't really interested in what she was saying. He had eyes only for Jessie.

Still cackling and mumbling to herself, Ma left them and

disappeared behind a ragged curtain that half covered a corner of the main room. This was, Jessie presumed, her private domain.

A couple of men wandered into the hut, nudged each other and came to stare into the little room at Big Jared's new wife. They were filthy and unkempt, with long, straggling beards, and their trouser bottoms were caked with old, dried mud.

If it was like this in summer, what was it like in winter? wondered Jessie.

'How'd it go?' asked Jared.

'Clogger won. Allus does. But this time, they kep' him off th'other man once the poor sod went down. We don't want no trouble wi' old Bony Stafford. Clogger were a bit wild, but some-one give him a drink o' gin, an' he soon cheered up.'

Their stares reminded Jared of a duty. 'Er – this is my wife, Jessie. Love, this is Bull Jones and Three Finger Billy.' He frowned at the men. 'Remember what I told you, you two!'

Jessie nodded to the two men. 'Pleased to meet you.' She shook the grimy hands they proffered, but if she'd met them on the road, she'd have turned aside and hidden, so villainous did they look.

'Ah, no one'd touch your woman, Big Jared,' said the one called Billy, 'let alone your *wife*!' He bowed to Jessie. 'Welcome to your new 'ome, missus. You've got a good man there.' He pronounced the word 'thee-ah'. Indeed, each man she met seemed to speak with a different accent, which added to the strangeness of the day.

Another man came in and threw his jacket down on one of the bunks that lined the walls of the hut. He then went and sat astride a bench next to the rough plank table and shouted for Ma to bring him a pot of ale. She came scurrying out of her corner. Three more men came in. Jessie allowed Jared to introduce her to them all, then retreated into their tiny room on the excuse of unpacking and making up the bed. He followed her, to the accompaniment of a few good-natured guffaws and a falsetto voice asking if he needed any help.

'They don't mean anythin' by it,' Jared assured her. 'They're a good bunch of lads, my lot. They can move more muck in a day than any other team, come rain or shine.' He was a bit embarrassed and dreading what she would say to him for bringing her to such a place. 'Are you all right, love?'

'Yes, Jared,' she said softly, and leaned her head against him. 'I'll get used to it, don't you worry. We'll manage fine.' What it cost her to say that, to remain cheerful in the face of the dreadful squalor around them, no one would ever know. But she couldn't bear to see that anxious, shamed look in her husband's eyes.

He put his arms round her and began to kiss her. Nothing held Jessie back now. She was as ardent as he was. With the tin trunk behind the door, so that no one could get in, they were soon oblivious to the world outside. And apart from one or two joking remarks about love-birds, the men in the hut were more interested in their ale, pipes and cards than they were in what was happening behind that closed door.

As Jared held Jessie in his arms and caressed her eager body, he blessed whatever fate had given him such a girl for a wife. He was almost afraid to make love to her, afraid of hurting or disgusting her, and it was she who now encouraged him, with hands, with lips, with whispered words of love. Even the first time it was good for both of them, but from that first time Jared also remembered Ma's advice and exercised self-control. He wanted no babies yet to spoil things for them.

When it was over and they were lying in each other's arms in the bed he had made himself, he said earnestly, 'It won't always be like this. I'll get on, you'll see. One day you'll have a proper house, a big one, with a maid to wait on you.'

'We'll get on together,' she replied confidently. 'I'll help, too. I'll find work. You'll see as well, Jared Wilde.'

'You're a Wilde yourself now, love. Jessie Wilde.' He repeated the name several times, savouring the sound of it, then gathered her to him again. But he was just as careful this second time. It would hurt him to see her with a big, swollen belly. Look how pulled down Bessie Small always seemed nowadays, though she had been a bright, cheerful girl once. No, he wanted a wife, not a family. And he would make sure that was all he got. Bloody sure.

13

⟨ornament⟩

Eastby Cutting: August 1837

$\mathcal{T}$he next morning Jared was awake as soon as it was light. Jessie kept up a cheerful front until he left for work, joking as she packed him a midday meal of bread, ham and wedding cake in his battered tin box. She filled his 'bottle' with cold tea. It wasn't really a bottle, but a tin can with a lid that was also a cup and a wire handle to carry the whole contraption. She pulled a face at the battered condition of it and scrubbed it out thoroughly before she put anything into it, which made Ma cackle with laughter.

'It'll taste twice as good today,' Jared joked.

Jessie watched him eat breakfast, a massive chunk of bread and a piece of cheese, smiling back at him when he beamed across the rough table at her. She still felt shy with the other men in the hut, but they took little notice of her this morning, being more concerned to drive away the mists of sleep and get off to their 'patch', as they called it.

'Right, lads, let's be havin' you,' called Jared.

When the hut was suddenly empty, Jessie went into her room and sat down on the edge of the bed, clasping her hands together in her lap and looking round the dim little space which she must now call home. This was a dreadful place to live, as bad as anywhere she'd ever seen. An image of Meg Dunnerby's cottage in Hettonby flashed briefly into her mind. It was a palace compared to this. Her mother would go mad if she saw it. For all her brave words of the night before, tears formed in Jessie's eyes.

Oh, Jared! she thought. How can I bear to live here? More important, how long could she hide her feelings from him?

Before she had time to give way to any more self-pity, there was a knock on the door and a cackle of laughter that announced the presence of Ma. Jessie reached over listlessly to turn the handle and the old woman walked in, holding a steaming tin mug.

She looked knowingly at Jessie, but didn't comment on the over-bright eyes. 'Tea!' she announced. 'Nothin' like a cup t'set a body up in t'mornin'. I allus sit an' have a drink when t'lads have gone off.' She held out the mug, which was covered with greasy fingerprints and contained a strong-smelling black liquid.

Jessie recoiled a little. 'I can't . . . I mean, I don't . . .' Her protests died before they could be uttered.

'Thou drink it down, lass! Tha'll 'ave t'get used to black tea. Can't allus get milk on the diggin's an' George Snader only sells two sorts o' tea – the strong sort, which my lads like, an' t'sweepings.'

Wordlessly Jessie took the proffered mug and sipped its contents. It tasted awful, stronger than any tea she'd ever tasted, but she didn't want to offend Ma or to reject an overture of friendliness.

'Won't you – er – sit down for a moment? There's only the bed, but you can . . .'

'Beds is nice an' soft on old bones.' Ma sat down and gave a sigh. 'Bit of a rush in t'mornin', gettin' them lads off. Eh, that Billy takes some wakin' up, he does an' all!'

Jessie nodded and took another sip. At least the warmth was comforting. She tried not to think of the greasy fingerprints beneath her lips.

Ma reached across to pat her arm. 'I promised Jared I'd keep an eye on thee. He's worried about how tha'll settle in.'

The young back next to her stiffened. 'Oh? Is he?'

'Now, now! Don't take a huff! It's on'y natural he'd worry, ain't it? He's told us about thy mother and that parsonage. Right little palace that sounds. Can't get much more respectable than a parsonage, can you?'

'Being respectable doesn't mean being helpless,' protested Jessie, affronted. 'I can assure you that . . .'

'Oh, lord, don't get on thy high horse, girl!' Ma wiped away a tear with the corner of her stained apron and stood up. 'Me, I gotta think about food for my lads, buy some bread an' taties, an' check me ale. They're terrors if they ain't fed proper, them lads are. They don't mind a bit o' dirt, but they get terrible hungry by th'end o' t'day.'

She hauled herself to her feet. 'Before I start, though, I'll show thee where to empty thy slops – show thee where t'clean watter is, too. We got good watter i' these diggin's. Real nice stream, it is. That young fellow, th'engineer, he's got a bee in his bonnet about watter. Says dirty watter breeds disease. As though a bit o' dirt ever hurt anyone! Still, this watter do taste better, I'll give him that. Makes a real nice cup o' tea.'

Jessie spent the morning rearranging their possessions. Sanitary arrangements were primitive, to say the least, and she'd been embarrassed at first to use the bucket in their room while Jared was there. She was relieved to get rid of its malodorous contents. She would have to get a new slop bucket, one with a tighter fitting lid. This one wouldn't do at all. A good thing she had another bucket for water and a jug for drinking water. She was going to boil everything they drank, just like Cook had at the Hall.

A little cheered by Ma's visit, she set to work to clean their room. It might only have an earth floor, but the rest of it could be immaculate, couldn't it? By midday everything had been scrubbed, including the rough planking walls. Even the cracked glass in the window was shining and she'd found a scrap of material to make a curtain. She'd get Jared to put up a piece of wire to slide it along. The window was too high for people to look in easily, but she wouldn't put it past some of the men who'd grinned at her knowingly to stand on a box and try to peer inside.

Her frequent visits to the stream seemed to amuse a pair of slovenly-looking girls little older than herself, but with raddled, painted faces and tawdry finery, who were hanging about the door of another hut. She ignored their ribald comments and suggestions, and went on with her toils. Ma found her efforts amusing too, but she didn't make a comment, just smiled to herself. Jessie was beginning to find Ma's perpetual amusement a trifle irritating.

After a midday snack of bread and jam, she refused Ma's offer to take her down to the camp shop, having already accepted a similar offer from Bessie. When she'd finished the room, she tidied herself up and took off her coarse working apron. She went to the door of the hut several times during the next half hour to see if Bessie were in sight, but there was no sign of her. Eventually Jessie decided that she'd have to find her way to the shop herself if she were to have time to cook a meal for Jared.

She woke up Ma, now dozing by the fire upon which a big black pot was bubbling. How old was she? She looked far older than Granny Todd in Hettonby, and she was sixty. 'Bessie hasn't come and I need to go to the shop. Would you tell me how to get there?' Jessie wasn't looking forward to going out on her own, but the men would be working, so maybe it wouldn't be too bad. And she'd have to get used to it.

Ma cackled. 'Can't miss the shop, lass. Just turn left outside the door and go downhill. Snader's, it's called.'

The shop was the most solid-looking building in the camp. It was made of wood, good, heavy planks, and had two small windows, with bars across them. SNADER'S STORE was painted in large uneven letters on the wall. The door stood open and through it passed a trickle of slatternly or worn-looking women, sharp-faced children, flies, the odd dog, and anything else that cared to enter the premises.

Jessie hesitated, not liking the look of it, but she had no choice. It was the only place she could buy food unless she walked into Eastby, and she didn't want to go anywhere near His Lordship's territory. She went inside and hesitated again. It was dark and dirty, with a pungent odour of rotting food, tobacco and sharp cheese. A woman shuffled forward to serve her. She was as dirty as the shop, her greasy hair straggling over her face and her dress almost as filthy as her sacking apron. She looked exhausted.

There was a man at the back of the shop. He was cleaner and appeared well-fed, with a comfortable paunch curving out over his trousers. He had a shrewd face, with a bushy pepper-and-salt-coloured moustache to match the sparser hairs brushed carefully across his balding head. After studying Jessie for a moment or two, in the manner of one who knows everyone and suddenly sees a new face, he stepped forward, gave the woman assistant a shove to one side and told Jessie it would be his pleasure to serve her himself.

'New to the camp, dear? Looking for a good pitch?' His eyes seemed to see right through her clothing to the body beneath. 'Girl as pretty as you is sure to get plenty of customers.'

She flushed and answered sharply, 'New to the camp, yes, but I'm not looking for a pitch!' She waved her wedding ring at him.

He was in no way put out by this reply. 'Ah, then you must be Big Jared's wife. I heard he was getting wed yesterday. My apologies for the mistake, Mrs Wilde.'

He proffered a hand and kept hers in his as she responded, patting it a few times with his other hand. Not an advance, just a way of keeping her close while he scrutinised her, she realised.

'Pleased to meet you, my dear. Very pleased. George Snader is the name, proprietor of this shop.' He paused expectantly.

'Mrs Wilde.' Why should she tell him her first name?

He chuckled to himself, his paunch wobbling a little. 'Oh, my! Jared certainly picked himself a sharp one! Pretty, too. Now, what can I get you?'

'I want meat, flour and some shortening. Also some potatoes and onions.'

He picked up a lump of meat. 'How about this?'

She leaned forward and examined it, shaking her head. 'I'm not buying rotten meat.'

He waved one hand. 'Why don't you select a piece yourself, then? Newer stuff is on the left – but it costs more. Still, Big Jared can afford it, I'm sure.'

She ignored him and began to poke among the bloody chunks on the wooden table until she found a marginally fresher piece. She treated the other goods in the same way, pushing aside rancid shortening and weevily flour in no uncertain terms.

The other women in the shop watched open-mouthed. Had anyone told Jessie that George Snader was greatly feared by most of the women in the camp, she would have been surprised. She was later to discover that he acted as pimp to several of the camp whores, finding them a shack, taking a large proportion of their earnings and ruling them with a rod of iron. He also lent the men money, at extortionate rates of interest, for their wages were often paid late, or he accepted goods in pawn from those of the navvies' women who found themselves short of ready money while waiting for the next pay.

Later she came to understand that his shop was the least profitable of his many enterprises, but it provided a respectable excuse for his presence here, so that he could operate on the diggings without upsetting the railway company's representatives or the local magistrates.

At this first meeting, he seemed to Jessie no more than a cheating shopkeeper – and Agnes Burton's daughter had no hesitation in pointing out to him an error in his addition of her bill.

'Tut, tut! Silly me!' He grinned at her and handed over another penny ha'penny.

She put the change away carefully and was about to gather up her goods when an arm caught hold of her waist and swung her round. A ruddy face with bushy grey whiskers, topped by a balding head, leered down at her as a meaty hand came up to paw at her bosom.

'New stock, George? Put me down for tonight.' The voice was hoarse and she could smell the fumes of gin even above the rank smell of the man's body.

Outraged, she swung her free arm at her captor's face, only to have it caught in mid-air by a large hairy hand. Having made both her arms fast, the owner of the hand then resumed his exploration of her body.

'Tell 'er to behave, George! Tell 'er who I am!'

But the man was too confident and was holding her carelessly. Before Mr Snader could say anything, she'd brought her knee up into her captor's groin and had scraped her boot down the front of his shin for good measure. His grip loosened involuntarily and he roared with pain. Jessie whirled out of his grasp, seized a heavy frying-pan from a nearby shelf and brandished it in his face.

'I'll smash this over your head if you lay one finger on me again!' she panted.

An ugly look appeared on his face, but he made no immediate

move towards her. 'Who is she, George? Introduce me to Lady Muck, won't yer?'

Snader stepped forward with an ingratiating smile on his face. 'Tch! Tch! All a big mistake, I do assure you, Joe. This is Mrs Wilde, Big Jared's new wife, not one of my girls. But I do have one or two new ones coming in soon, and I'll make sure you get first choice.' He kept a wary eye on the huge brute as he spoke, afraid that Joe would go berserk and wreck everything, as he had done once before in another camp.

Joe breathed deeply and took a step backward. 'Aye, George, I'll take you up on that offer.' He swung round again towards Jessie, making her jump in fright and clutch the frying-pan more tightly. 'But I won't forget you, *Mrs* Wilde,' he said thickly. 'No indeed! Better stick close to your man on dark nights, you had! When I fancy something, I usually get it – one way or another.' On this menacing note he seized a loaf, muttered, 'Put it on my slate, George!' and walked out of the shop.

George Snader let out an involuntary sigh of relief and fumbled for something under the counter. Jessie lowered the frying-pan with an arm that had begun to tremble. She could feel her knees shaking, too. She shut her eyes and took a few deep breaths. When she opened them, she became aware that the proprietor was holding out a glass to her.

'Drink that. Best gin. It'll help pull you together.' She shook her head, but he pushed it towards her. 'Go on. No charge. You look shook up. Don't like my customers to be upset. Especially new ones. Bad for business.'

Jessie took a reluctant sip. She had tried gin before, but didn't really enjoy the taste of it. However, like Ma's tea, it was a goodwill gesture and you couldn't toss that back in someone's face. The warmth as it slid down her throat was as comforting as the warmth of Ma's tea had been, in spite of the taste.

'Who was that man?' she asked. 'He acts like he owns the place and everyone in it.'

'His name's Clogger Joe. He don't own the place, I do. But it's dangerous to cross him.' Snader gestured around. 'I'd likely get my shop smashed up. My face too. He's famous for that. He's killed his man before now. Uses his clogs when he fights. Iron-tipped. Very damaging to soft skin.' He sucked in breath thoughtfully. 'That's a bad enemy you've made there, lass. First time I ever saw a woman stand up to him. He won't like that to get around.' He looked at a couple of women customers muttering to one another in a corner. 'And it's bound to.'

Jessie frowned. 'Surely he can't expect a married woman to . . . to . . .' She paused, not knowing how to put it into words. She frowned. Clogger Joe? Where had she heard that name before?

'Depends what you mean by *married*. There ain't many here that can boast a preacher at their wedding, let alone a proper church service. We heard about yours from Bessie Small last night. Fair set up about her day out, she was, couldn't stop talking about it. An' she told us about that fine house where your mother works.'

He seemed to be enjoying talking to her so she let him ramble on, wanting to learn as much as she could about the life and people on the diggings.

'Most women here just live with a man as long as he'll have them.' He grinned. 'Or as long as nothing better turns up. They don't object to a man like Joe. He's a bit heavy-handed, but he's a good provider. Earns a top wage when he wants, does Joe. He can dig twice as much muck in a day as most men. Used to work on the canals before they started building railways.'

'Well,' said Jessie, 'he'll just have to accept the fact that I'm Jared's wife.' She set the half-empty glass down. 'So I'll thank you for your help and get back to cook my husband's tea.'

Just outside the door, she remembered where she had heard the name. Clogger Joe was the man who had given Jared a chance when he was a runaway lad. Surely he wouldn't pester a friend's wife? But in spite of her confident words, she shivered as she walked away, remembering the expression on Joe's face, and the threat he had made. More trouble! Why could people not let her get on with her life in peace?

When Jared arrived home that night, there was a shining new cooking pot filled with stew simmering gently on the extra hook he had fixed over the fire next to Ma's huge black pot. There was also a bowl of water in their room ready for him to wash in.

'You're a treat to come home to!' he exclaimed, kissing Jessie on the lips but making no attempt to touch her with his dirty hands. 'I reckon I'm goin' to enjoy married life.'

She bullied him into changing into some old things that she'd found and mended, and hung his muddy things up to dry on a line she'd strung across their room. She'd brush the mud off them later, before they went to bed.

When Jared went into the main room and called for a pot of ale from Ma, he laughed at Jessie's disapproving expression. 'It's all right, love. I'm no boozer. But you get thirsty when you're diggin' an' you sweat a lot. There's nothin' sets you up as right as a pot of ale after a day's work.'

Once he'd drunk his pot, he was ready to take a closer look at their room, praise her housekeeping, hammer in two nails and fix up a bit of wire for the curtain, then wolf down three helpings of stew with loud expressions of appreciation. The other men, most of whom hadn't even bothered to wash the mud from their hands, kept looking at his piled plate enviously, for each of them had only a chunk of boiled meat, a puddle of greyish gravy and a piece of bread before them. But they saved their comments till Ma was out of hearing.

Jessie felt a little shy, being the only woman in a crowd of men, most of whom, though dirty and unkempt, were youngish and well built. Although Jared had introduced her to them the previous day, she still had trouble remembering their names. Three Finger Billy was easy enough, because she only had to look at his hand, but London Harry looked little different to Bull Jones or Banto Jim to her – until he opened his mouth and she heard his accent, which she could barely understand.

'Cockney,' explained Jared, seeing her bewilderment. 'Comes from London.'

'Born wivvin the sahnd o' Bow Bells,' added Harry.

They took her mistakes in good part and roared with laughter when she misnamed someone. After they'd all eaten, some of them settled down with pots of ale and Billy approached Jared. 'Can you lend us a bit, lad?'

'Have you spent up already?'

Billy shrugged. 'I put my bets on the other fellow in the fight.

Clogger's drinking too much. He's headin' for a fall. But this young fellow as challenged him weren't as tough as he looked. *You* should fight Clogger, Jared lad. I reckon you're the only one as could take him.'

Jessie scowled.

Jared just laughed easily. 'Well, you know me. More interested in money than fightin'.'

'But you'd *make* money . . .'

Jared saw his wife's expression and cut in. 'Let it drop, Billy.' He fumbled in his pocket. 'How much?'

'Five shillin'?'

'No. You already owe me ten. You'll have spent your next pay before you get it. Three shillin'.' He took out some coins. 'An' I'm givin' it to Ma for food and ale, else you'll be bettin' it on somethin' else.'

'Aw, Jared – '

He slapped the coins down on the table. 'Take it or leave it, an' don't go borrowin' more from George. I've told you afore: I'm not havin' my gang payin' that sharp sod through the nose.'

Billy sighed and Ma, who'd been listening in, like everyone else, stepped forward and scooped up the money.

Jared put his arm round Jessie. 'Now, what were we sayin'?'

'Do you often lend them money?' she whispered.

'Now an' then.' He leaned a bit closer and said quietly, 'We'll talk about it later, love.'

He drank a second pot of ale, then pronounced himself well set up. As he watched Jessie scour the cooking pot and put their things away, he exchanged a few bantering remarks with Ma, who was kept busy refilling the men's pots from her barrel. She made a chalk mark on each man's tally as she did so. She might not be able to read or write, but she was a careful businesswoman, and no man would get a drink the next night if he hadn't paid up and wiped his tally clean. When Jared had handed her the money for Three Finger Billy, she'd put an appropriate number of dots on his tally.

'Some of the women let their lads buy the ale on tick,' Ma told Jessie, who could not help staring. 'I don't, 'cos then you 'ave to chase 'em for the money when they get paid. I run an honest hut an' I 'ave no trouble fillin' me beds, so them as don't like me ways can allus go somewhere else. Nor I don't allow no rough-yids in my hut. I'm not havin' me bits an' pieces smashed up.'

Jared saw that Jessie didn't understand the last remark. 'Rough-yids means rough heads,' he explained, grinning. 'Lads as fight too much.'

'Oh.'

Once Jessie had cleared up their things, she turned to Jared. 'I thought we might take a stroll, look in on the Smalls, perhaps? Bessie didn't turn up today, as we'd arranged.' She found the heat and the smell of unwashed bodies in the hut unpleasant, but did not say so.

'Good idea.' He stood up and stretched, then led the way outside. It was still light and quite warm, and the camp was thronged with folk coming and going, talk and laughter alternating with angry shouts from the huts.

'Whatever is it like in winter?' Jessie wondered.

'Quieter. They stay inside mostly. It gets bloody cold.' Jared put his arm round her shoulders and they strolled across the camp.

The Smalls lived in the fenced-off corner of a bigger hut and their room, which was little bigger than Jessie and Jared's, had to house them and their two children. Jared knocked on the warped door, behind which a child was crying weakly and voices were muttering. The voices and crying stopped abruptly and the door opened a few inches. Alfred peered out from behind it, then opened it wider when he saw who was there.

'Er – come in,' he said, looking embarrassed. 'We – er – there's not much room, but, well – come in.'

They edged into the tiny space, to find Bessie lying on the bed, her face pale and sweat glistening on her brow. In the corner, on a bed that was little more than a pile of rags, a sickly-looking child began to fret softly to itself again. Next to it, a baby was sleeping soundly.

'Eh, I'm that sorry I couldn't get round to see you today,' said Bessie, making an attempt to sit up. 'I've been poorly. I expect it were all th'excitement. Eh, I did enjoy mysen yesterday! It were lovely to get out o' the camp for a bit.'

'You should have let me know, Bessie. I'd have come over to help you.'

'Nay, you've enough on your plate settlin' in. Are you managin' all right? How's your room?'

'I'm managing fine, thanks,' said Jessie. 'And the room's – fine.'

Only Jared noticed her slight hesitation. 'She's been through that room from top to bottom. I never was so comfy in all me life! An' cook! She's a real good cook, is my Jessie.' His voice rang with pride.

An awkward silence fell, which Jared broke by clearing his throat and saying that they must be going now.

They strolled on when they left the Smalls, past an occasional shanty which was more brightly lit. 'Ale-houses,' said Jared. 'An' worse.' He scowled. 'They're feckless, most of the lads are! Think of nothin' but drinkin'. And the women are as bad. They egg their men on to spend all their money, then they get advances on the wages an' spend them, too, afore they've even earned 'em. *We* aren't goin' down that road. Nor we aren't goin' like Alfred an' Bessie. A kid every year an' her none so strong!'

'Why are they so – well, so poor?'

'Because they're savin' their money to get out of the camp. Bessie won't cope for much longer with this sort of life. Alfred keeps her belly too full of bairns to live in huts.' He gave Jessie a sudden hug. 'I won't do that to you, love.'

'As long as Ma's way works.'

'We'll *make* it work.' He changed the subject abruptly. 'I saw Mr Stafford today. Told him we were wed an' thanked him for speakin' up for me t'your parson. He sent you his regards.'

'That's nice.'

'He was tellin' me about the next job he's goin' after.'

'Where's that?'

'Willingdon. In Hertfordshire. I might go there next. It sounds all right.'

'It's – a long way away.'

'Aye. You never know where you'll end up next.' He shrugged. 'But I like seein' new places.'

'How long would we be there?'

'Nothin's settled yet, mind, but it'd be a good few months.

Longer than here, mebbe. There are two cuttings to be dug close together, so they're going t'set up a camp between 'em, to save movin' it all. I prefer to work on cuttings. They're better'n tunnels. I don't like to feel shut in. Stafford's goin' to let me know more about it later, but don't say owt to the lads yet.'

She squeezed his hand. 'Tomorrow I'm going to start looking for work for myself.'

'I told you – there's no need. I'm earnin' enough for us both.'

'I want to play my part, just like you do. And anyway, Jared, I couldn't just sit around all day doing nothing. I'd go mad!'

Rather hesitantly she told him of the incident in the shop with Clogger Joe.

He frowned. 'I'll have a word with him. He can be a nasty bugger sometimes. If he tries anythin' else on, he'll have me t'reckon with. But I don't suppose he will, not now he knows you're my wife. I've allus got on all right with Joe, and I'll allus be grateful to him for giving me a chance when I were a lad. I've never clemmed since that day. An' he knows I can stick up for mysen because he taught me a few tricks when I were a young 'un.'

Jessie shivered suddenly.

'What's the matter? Are you cold, love?'

'No. Only, I don't want you fighting, Jared.'

'There are times when a man has t'fight. If I ever have to, you'll stand clear an' let me get on with it. I don't pick fights, but I know how to take care of mysen, never you fret. Now mind what I've said, for I mean it!'

'Yes, Jared.' When he spoke like that she could see why he could handle a gang of men. He had an air of authority about him and in some ways seemed older than his twenty-eight years, yet he was ignorant about so many things which she took for granted. She had learned already to hide her surprise when he asked for explanations of things she mentioned and had noticed that he never forgot anything, once told. His next words made her jump in shock.

'It's about time you told me what really happened when you gave in your notice at that Hall, isn't it?'

'It doesn't matter now. Least said, soonest mended.' She tried to walk on.

He pulled her to a halt. 'It matters to me.'

She couldn't think what to say.

His voice was stern. 'I want the truth, Jessie. No hiding things from one another.'

So she told him, listening to his rumbles of anger, worried that he'd try to get back at Lord Morrisham. As if he could. They had all the power, the gentry did.

'I'll not forget that,' he said at last. 'And if I can ever see a way to harm that bastard, I will.'

'Jared, it's not worth it. *Please* don't harp on it.'

'I shan't harp on it – but I shan't forget it, neither.' With a sudden change of mood, he swung her round till her feet left the ground and then set her down to kiss her passionately. 'Eh, you're the wife for me!' he said thickly. 'We'll do all right for ourselves, you'll see. It won't be easy at first, but one day you'll be dressin' in silk an' ridin' in your own carriage, like that bloody lord of yours.' He held her at arm's length as he made this vow, then whirled her round again and laughed aloud. 'But in the meantime, Mrs Wilde, your husband needs his sleep. Come on! Back to our castle!'

At the Hall, Adelaide Morrisham jerked into an attentive position as her husband walked into the room. She could not help feeling a flutter of anxiety. Clarence had been so bad-tempered lately. There was no one at the Hall, servant or family, who had not been the butt of his anger.

She knew why, of course. Well, the tale of his confrontation with Simon Stafford had spread everywhere and even her friends had not hesitated to tease her about it. Whatever had got into Clarence to throw poor dear Elinor out of her home like that? Susannah was still moping about, had been ever since her cousin left.

'I've had an invitation to stay with Bowers and his family in Cheshire,' Clarence said. 'You, me and Susannah.'

'Oh?'

'We'll see what Peter Bowers thinks of her and we'll look him over while we're at it. His father's got a tidy little fortune and he's the only son. It'd be a good match, and if he's going to offer, there'll be no need of a season in town for her.'

Adelaide's face fell. 'But Susannah is looking forward to seeing London – and – and isn't she a bit too young yet to marry?'

He thrust his big red face next to hers and growled, 'She's sixteen and well grown. Now, go and make sure she has plenty of pretty dresses.'

14

⟨ornament⟩

Eastby: Snader's Store

*A*bout nine o'clock the next morning a shadow fell across the doorway of Ma's hut, making the two women, who were sharing a cup of tea, look up.

George Snader paused a minute by the door to take in the pleasing picture of Jessie, with her hair tied back and her face freshly washed. He paid little direct attention to her when he first spoke, however. 'Got a spare cuppa tea for an old friend, Ma?'

'Thou's nobody's friend but thine own, George Snader, but watter's just on t'boil. Got that new cask of ale wi' thee? We're gettin' a bit low.'

'Aye. Same price as last time. I'll just go and roll it in.'

When he'd fixed up the new barrel on its rickety wooden stand, he came and joined them by the fire, nodding pleasantly to Jessie as he took the mug Ma offered.

'Things goin' all right here, Ma?'

'Aye. I've got a few nice, steady drinkers – the right sort, though, quiet but get through a good few pots of ale of an evening.' She chuckled. 'Jared's lads wouldn't dare randy about. So tha's no need t'worry about selling th'ale.'

He smiled at them both. 'I don't worry, Ma. You run a good hut. You helped me when I was startin' up, an' I don't forget things like that, which is why I take you along with me. An' my ale always sells because I pick my suppliers carefully. Brings in a nice regular profit, ale does.' He winked at Jessie. 'Not as high as some other things, but not to be sneezed at.'

She tried to think how she could excuse herself, but he turned and included her in the conversation. 'And how are you settling in, Mrs Wilde? You'll be finding life on the diggings a bit different, I daresay. Now, what did you say you were doing before you met Jared?'

'I didn't.' She didn't see why she should tell everyone the story of her life and had no desire whatsoever for folk to link her to Lord Morrisham. 'And in answer to your question, yes, it is different here, but I'm coping all right, thank you.'

'Coping!' echoed Ma. 'This one does more nor cope, George lad. Cleaned out their room beautiful, she has – an' ready to start in on me next, if I don't watch out!' She chortled and rocked to and fro on her chair. 'I reckon I'll not be safe till she finds hersen some work, no, I won't, not till she's got summat to keep hersen busy with all day. She'll learn, though.' She wiped a tear from one eye. 'Bit o' dirt never hurt no one!'

George Snader cocked his head to one side, ignoring Ma completely. 'Lookin' for a job, are ye then, Mrs Wilde?'

'Yes. I thought I might find some day-work at one of the local farms.' It then occurred to her that he might have contacts in the neighbourhood and she looked at him speculatively. 'Perhaps you might hear of something?'

She stared in bewilderment as both he and Ma burst out laughing. 'What did I say?'

'Oh! Oh, my!' Ma was holding her stomach and tears of laughter were rolling down her cheeks. 'Oh, dearie me! Local farms!' And she went off into a fresh paroxysm of mirth.

Jessie looked at George Snader for enlightenment and he managed to subdue his merriment and answer her question.

'The local farms have as little as possible to do with us railway folk, except to sell food to us at double the normal price. And they have *nothing at all* to do with the navvies' women, if they can help it, let alone employing one of them on their farms. They'd be more likely to set the dogs on you, Mrs Wilde!'

Jessie flushed in mortification.

'No, my dear,' he went on more gently, 'when you married Big

Jared, you crossed an invisible line. The only place you'll be able to find work will be in the camp itself.' He paused expectantly. 'Now, it might just be possible I could find you something.'

'Oh, no!' Jessie shook her head vigorously. 'I'm not interested in that sort of work.'

'Tch! Tch! Naughty girl! You haven't even heard my offer.'

'And I don't want to! I'm not becoming one of your girls. I love my husband.'

'So impetuous!' He sighed. 'Hasn't even listened to my offer, Ma. Thinks I've only one idea in my head and only one string to my bow.'

'Well, that was the offer you made when I came into your shop,' Jessie snapped.

'You can read and write, I take it?' he asked her, with a sudden switch from mockery to seriousness.

'Of course I can!'

'And you're quick with figures. I noticed that yesterday.' He paused again.

He seemed, Jessie decided, to be fond of keeping people waiting, of letting them hang upon his words, as Ma was doing now. Mrs Coxleigh had been the same.

'Might be able to find you a place in my shop,' he offered after the silence had gone on for long enough, then sat back to observe Jessie's reactions.

'In your shop?'

'It's respectable enough, shop work is!'

'Yes, I suppose so, but . . .' She shrugged.

'But what?'

She spoke off-handedly. He wasn't going to have her falling over herself to do as he wished. 'But I couldn't work in such a dirty place.' She could still remember the smell – and the rotting food.

'My, ain't she the fussy one!' exclaimed Ma. 'Tha should just be thankful, lass, that tha's got such an offer from George 'ere.'

Jessie shook her head, secretly relishing the freedom to pick and choose that marrying Jared had given her. It was that same freedom she had noticed in him the first time she met him. The same freedom she had felt when she'd stood up to Mrs Coxleigh.

'Can't sell food without some of it spoilin' a bit,' said George aggrievedly. 'That's just a fact of life.'

Jessie threw caution to the winds. 'Well, I don't see why so much has to spoil! That's downright bad management, if you ask me! It *loses* you money. They had storerooms full of food at the Hall where I worked, yes, and fancy stuff too, but it didn't go bad, because they stored it properly. And so did my mother. If you keep food clean and cool and don't buy too much at once, it doesn't go rotten.'

'Let me tell you, young lady, that I buy some of that spoiled stuff on purpose, because it's cheaper. The women round here don't have fancy tastes, like you, and they don't object to a few maggots, or a strong smell, if it saves their purses.'

'The prices you charge them, you could afford to get better stuff in the first place. Don't tell me you don't have a lot of wastage when you buy spoiled goods, because I won't believe you!' Jessie was revelling in this exchange.

'So what about the job?' he asked.

'You mean, you still want me to work for you, after all I've said about your shop?'

'Could have a try, see how we go on?' George sighed as she still made no answer. 'Look, these camp women can't add up. I'm losing pounds every week, pounds! And there might be something in what you say. You could tidy up the shop a bit, if you liked. I wouldn't mind. How about it?'

'Well – maybe. What pay are you offering?'

'Five shillings a week?'

'Not enough.'

'Six, then.'

'Ten.'

'*What?*' The word was a yelp of pain.

'You heard me. Ten shillings a week. I'll be worth it.'

'Seven for the first week, then we'll see if you *are* worth ten. And that's my final word!'

Jessie gave him a taste of his own medicine and kept him waiting for a moment or two. 'Well . . .' Then she could not keep it up a minute longer. 'All right. When do I start and what are the hours?'

'Seven in the morning till nine at night. Closed on Sundays, order of the bleedin' magistrates.'

Her face fell. 'Oh, I couldn't! That's too late! I have to be home to get Jared's tea.'

'She'll be the ruin of me,' George Snader told the ceiling. 'I must be goin' soft in my old age! All right. Seven till seven – but mind you're not late!'

Jessie's face lit up. 'You won't regret it. When do I start?'

'Now. One of them dratted women has gone off on the tramp and I'm short-handed.'

'Right. I'll get my pinafore. Ma, will you tell Jared where I am if he gets home first?'

'Aye.'

Jessie came back a moment later, wearing a coarse twill pinafore she'd used for rough work at the Hall, with a shawl round her head. She felt jubilant. Now she, too, would be contributing to their savings. And she'd be earning more money than she ever had before in her life.

That day was a revelation to Jessie. She hadn't realised how much a centre of camp life the shop was, or how everyone relied on it for their food. A constant stream of slovenly looking women passed through its open door. At first they regarded Jessie with suspicion and hostility, but after a few days they got used to her and became a bit friendlier.

In a slack period during the first morning she sorted through the meat – a repulsive task, but she couldn't stand the smell of it any longer. She washed the most offensive pieces, rinsed them in vinegar and put them to one side. These she persuaded George Snader to sell at a reduced price. She then set to and scrubbed the wooden counter on which the meat was kept, rinsed out a piece of cheesecloth and covered the meat with that to keep the flies off. This innovation was regarded with suspicion by the customers, who were used to poking unhindered among the meat. But Jessie wouldn't let them touch a piece until they'd bought it. All the cheap pieces were sold within the hour, however.

At one o'clock Snader came and asked her to look him out a few bits and pieces for his dinner. 'Fry me up a couple of eggs, eh, and get me some of that cheese? Oh, and you can make a pot of tea for us all. I haven't had a decent cup of tea for days. See if you can make me one that doesn't taste stewed. The other woman always managed to spoil it.' He would have turned away, but Jessie stopped him.

'What about *our* dinner, then? Me an' Mary have been working hard, too, you know. We're hungry as well.' She ignored a gasp from her companion and a tug on her sleeve.

'You don't mean you expect me to provide you with dinner as well! I never said anything about meals being found. I'm not made of money, you know.'

'You never said anything about me cooking your dinners, either,' retorted Jessie. 'But I wouldn't mind doing that, if you treat me right. I'm a good cook. Only I'm not going hungry myself while I cook for you.' She looked at him and added coaxingly, 'I was thinking of doing you a French omelette, with cheese in it. There are some hard bits that won't sell well. They'd taste lovely chopped up in an omelette, though.' She didn't know what had got into her today. She would have been out on her ear if she'd spoken to anyone at the Hall like that.

'A French omelette, eh? I don't think I've ever tried one of those.' George licked his lips. 'Take long, will it? What do you need?'

Jessie realised that she had him hooked. 'Be ready in ten minutes, Mr Snader. It'll only take three eggs and a bit of cheese. But you'll like it, I know you will.'

'Right then. Get going!' he ordered, in an unconvincing attempt to regain the upper hand.

True to her word, Jessie had everything ready within ten minutes, with a cup and plate that she'd washed carefully. She called him in from the front of the shop, then returned to serving, saying casually in passing, 'I did you a few fried potatoes to go with it.' She peeped through the doorway a couple of times to see if he was enjoying his food and chuckled to see how quickly it was disappearing!

George mopped the plate clean with a piece of bread and spread another piece thickly with some honey which Jessie had thoughtfully placed on the table. He drank a final cup of tea, then sat back and loosened his belt. Now that was a good meal! He'd done well to hire Big Jared's wife, he reckoned.

When Jessie next peeped in and saw the empty plate, she asked, 'How was it?'

'Not bad.'

'When you come back into the shop, I'll make one for me and Mary.'

He looked at her, opened his mouth, then shut it again. 'Don't take long.'

By six in the evening Jessie was ravenously hungry again, and tired, too. Working in the shop was no sinecure, continually weighing two ounces of this, half a pound of that and four ounces of something else. The only foodstuffs people bought in any quantity were meat and bread for the navvies. The bread came in twice a day from a local baker and George said the navvies were not satisfied with anything less than a pound of meat each per day.

'Most folk where I come from don't get that much in a week!'

'Aye, but they don't need to dig bloody great holes in the ground. It's hard work, digging is. You need muscles for that.'

'Well, there are certainly plenty of muscles round here.'

As the hands on George's rickety clock approached seven, she went up to him. 'I have to go. Jared'll be back and he'll want his tea. So I'll need some steak and onions, also some stewing beef and some carrots for tomorrow's meal. Do I weigh it out myself, or do you want to do it? And if so, you'd better wash your hands before you touch my meat.'

George Snader was nothing if not an opportunist. 'Steak, is it?' He licked his lips. 'With onions, eh? Your Jared's a lucky man. I'm partial to steak and onions myself.'

'Oh, yes?' Jessie could see what was coming, but was not going to offer.

'Er – I'm a bit busy, with you leaving so early. Suppose I was to let you have the meat at cost, could you cook my tea as well? I'll be tied up here serving. It'd be a great help.'

'How much is cost?'

'Twenty per cent off.'

Mean devil, she thought and frowned, as if about to refuse.

'Well, I do believe - yes, I think I could let you have - how about forty per cent off? How would that do you?'

'All right. Send Mary over with a plate in about an hour. You do like onions with your steak?'

His eyes gleamed. 'Yes, that would be nice.'

Just outside the shop, Jessie bumped into a large figure, which smelled of sweat, gin and mud, and a hoarse voice said, 'Well, if it ain't *Mrs* Wilde again!' She gasped and drew back in alarm, then sighed with relief as Jared's voice came out of the shadows behind Joe.

'That's right, Clogger, lad - my wife.'

As Clogger grunted and lurched on into the shop, Jared put his arm round Jessie's waist and she leaned against him with a sigh. 'What's this? No wife at home to greet me! No cup of tea ready!' He was trying hard to sound indignant, but failing. 'Eh, you didn't waste much time in getting a job, did you, lass!'

'You don't mind, do you? It'll make me a bit late in the evenings, but I want to earn some money, too. We'll be able to pay for our food out of my wages and save all of yours - I'm to get ten shillings a week soon - *and* I'll get all our food cheaper *and* something to eat provided free in the middle of the day.'

She stopped for breath and he said exultantly, 'How did I ever get so lucky, finding a wife like you? No, of course I don't mind! As long as it's not too much for you?'

'Too much! You should try lugging cans of hot water up and down two flights of steps. Anyway, I'm as strong as a horse.' And she wanted to prove to her mother that marrying Jared had not been a mistake. Needed to prove it. Not only to her mother, but to everyone in Hettonby.

Simon walked into the building where the railway company had its main office. What the hell had they summoned him here for today? He wasn't due to make his progress report for another two weeks. Supervising several small sites for them on this, his biggest project so far, kept him on the move all the time.

On a hard bench in the outer office, he sat and fumed as he was kept waiting for nearly quarter of an hour, then gave an audible sigh of relief as he followed the clerk into the large inner room.

Three of the Committee were sitting there behind a table, and they didn't look to be in a good mood. He paused to stare at them in surprise. The Committee weren't due to meet for another three weeks.

Pearson, the Chairman, spoke. 'Sit down, Stafford.' He barely waited until Simon had settled in his chair before continuing. 'Now tell us what the hell you've been doing to upset Morrisham?'

Simon could only gape for a moment. This was the last thing he'd expected to hear. Then he began to frown. What mischief was Clarence Morrisham stirring up now? Wasn't it enough for him to bully women and throw them out of their homes?

'Well? Answer me, Stafford! What have you done to upset that old sod? As if we hadn't enough trouble and delays on this line without having to answer his complaints.'

15

Eastby: August–October 1837

*T*he next two months flew past. Jessie went on working for George Snader and got the ten shillings she'd asked for, even the first week. George was not a generous man, but he could recognise a bargain when he saw one – and his profits had gone up appreciably. He soon came to trust her with a lot of the routine business, which left him more time to attend to his other, more lucrative interests.

There was never any question of Mary's resenting Jessie. 'Eh, it's good to have you here,' she said at the end of the first week.

'I'm enjoying myself.'

Mary gaped at her. 'Don't you get tired?'

Jessie shrugged. 'A bit. But I think of the money I'm earning and that makes me forget my aching feet.'

'I wish I could forget mine! When I've finished here, I've the children to see to, an' I never seem to stop running round till I get to bed.'

'Children?'

Mary's tired expression was suddenly transformed by a glowing smile. 'Two. Little devils, they are. An' you might as well know now that I've no man to look after us.' She shrugged. 'Not that I've ever been wed, like you. I weren't even sure who were the father of the first 'un. I were working for George at night then an' the sponge didn't work.' She eyed Jessie sideways, waiting to see if that gave offence.

'Oh.' Somehow, Jessie would have expected someone who'd done *that* for a living to look – different. But Mary was just a woman, one who had worked hard by her side all week.

'Mind you, I'd have stayed with the fellow who fathered my Susan, but he moved on to some new diggings and never sent for us.' She sighed, then stared into space. 'So I told mysen that's it! I've done with men. Done! I've got two children and that's enough, thank you very much! Well, my Tim is enough, if truth be told. He's a right little sod sometimes, that one is.'

As she got to know Mary better and coaxed the other woman into cleaning herself up a bit, Jessie wondered once or twice how long this resolution to have no more children would last, for as Mary cleaned herself up, men started to eye her with interest again. But she gave them no encouragement and one day, during a slack period, confided in Jessie that she didn't see why men made all that fuss about lying with a woman. 'The fellows go mad for it, but I don't reckon much to it, mysen. And who gets landed wi' babies, eh? Not them, never them! No, I'll sleep on me own from now on, thank you very much!'

Thinking of her own rapture with Jared, Jessie made some non-committal remark. She was thankful not to have fallen for a baby, though. It was only two months, but some women got started straight away. Either Ma's advice worked and Jared's self-control was paying off, or she wasn't the sort to have a lot of children. She only wanted two or three. Having too many not only ruined your figure, it kept you poor. And she and Jared didn't intend to be poor.

The camp, just like the Hall, was a world of its own, in which outside events, unless they were connected with railways, made little impact. It was thought worthy of comment that the Liverpool and Manchester railway line was being relaid with wooden, not stone sleepers, that the London–Birmingham line had nearly reached Tring and that Birmingham was being linked to the Liverpool and Manchester Railway. Otherwise news of outside events barely impinged. The women in the camp took a distant interest in their new Queen and an even more distant interest in fashion, those who had been out of the camp laughing at the ridiculous wide sleeves ladies were wearing now. 'Won't be able to lift their skirts for a pee,' one old woman chuckled to another outside the shop, her voice carrying like a foghorn, for she was getting deaf.

When some less fashionably dressed ladies came to the camp to hand out Bible tracts, they were told in very forthright language what they could do with their bits of paper and even Jessie was hard put to be polite to them when they came into the shop.

Times were bad and men kept turning up at the camp, desperate for work, but few of them were taken on, for they were mostly too weak to handle a shovel all day. There was often a handout of food or a few pennies to help them along the road, though. When they had money, most of the navvies were generous to a fault and knew well that common people were suffering and hungering everywhere. And even the most illiterate navvy knew how badly paupers were treated in many places, which was why so many folk preferred to go off on the tramp rather than seek help.

'The only way they'd get me into one of them poor houses,' Billy said one day, 'would be feet first.' He turned to Jared. 'Have you decided yet where we're goin' next, lad?'

'I'm thinkin' about it. There's one or two possibilities. Leave it to me.' At least on the railways there was always employment for experienced navvies, and Simon Stafford had said that he wanted them to follow him. He'd been a bit short last time he came round and had confided in Jared that Lord Morrisham had been stirring up trouble again.

'Luckily, I was able to explain why he was so hostile towards me.'

'Aye, Jessie told me how he'd turned your sister out of her house, Mr Stafford. Is she all right now?'

Simon's scowl changed into a smile as he turned to leave. 'Oh, yes. She's very happy indeed.'

The news Jessie most liked to hear was about the girl who was Queen, for Victoria was near her own age. George passed newspapers on to her sometimes and she read all she could about her new monarch, telling Jared what was happening and making him take an interest in the world outside the camp, too.

'You're a wonder,' he often said to her. 'An' you read it all so easy.'

'So would you, if you'd let me teach you.'

'One day, when we've got a bit of time to spare. I'm a bit pressed at the moment.' He avoided her eyes as he said that. The question of his learning to read was a sore point between them.

They went over to see Jessie's mother twice in those two months. Jared wanted to hire a cart to take them over, but Jessie laughed at the idea of wasting their money, so they walked the six miles to Hettonby. Time enough to hire carts when they were too old to walk! she teased. And he was showing no signs of old age.

'You're a minx sometimes!' Jared's eyes were hot and admiring on her.

'And you're a devil of a lad.'

Since she was even more careful with money than he was, their savings were mounting rapidly, for they really could live on her wages, if they were careful.

'I don't know how you do it, love,' he said one day, when they were counting their hoard.

She laughed. 'It's easy when you've been brought up by my mother.'

There were over a hundred and twenty pounds now locked in the black money box buried under the bed, what with her life savings and his. They were trying to build up enough to take on a small sub-contract, which would mean having enough to pay the men's wages until a piece of work should be finished, for the bigger contractors were rarely quick at paying out to their sub-contractors, blaming it all on the railway companies, who were also slow to lay out their money.

'Looks like Stafford will be taking on his first contract,' Jared told Jessie as they walked. 'That's why he wants us with him.'

'Is it worth going all that way? I mean, wouldn't there be work nearer to home?'

'I don't have a home,' he said flatly. 'And it might be useful to be close to a rising engineer.'

The first time Jared and Jessie walked over to Hettonby, she sent a message to her mother a few days before by a carter whom George Snader knew. The man passed the note to Sam Lubb, who passed it to her mother. It was brief, saying only that they were well and asking if they could come over for a visit on the following Sunday.

The answer was even briefer. Agnes Burton would expect them at ten-thirty for church, followed by luncheon at the parsonage.

'Oh, hell!' said Jared when Jessie read the letter out to him. 'I'm no churchgoer. I can count on me fingers the number of times I've been inside one of them places, apart from gettin' wed. It's all standing up and kneeling down and moaning those miserable bloody hymns. No, you go to t'church with your mam, love. I'll go for a walk in the woods an' meet you at the parsonage afterwards.'

'Oh, no, you won't, Jared Wilde! I'm not facing the Hettonby gossips on my own! If you don't come with me to church, I'm not going to my mother's at all, and that's that!' She set her hands on her hips and glared at him.

'Aw, Jessie!'

'It's up to you entirely. I wouldn't want to force you.'

Silence.

'Well?' She was scowling and tapping one foot. 'Do we go or not?'

'Oh, all right!' He scowled back at her. 'But you'll have to tell me what t'do, mind! An' – an' – what about the hymns?' He flushed a dull red and avoided her eyes. 'I won't know t'words.'

This was treading on thin ice. People who couldn't read usually knew the hymns by heart. But in his wandering life, Jared had not had the chance to learn them.

'I've offered to teach you to read, but there's always some reason why you can't make a start. You're tired, or you're busy – always something! And it's just excuses, we both know that.'

Jared stared down at the ground. He, who was frightened of no man, was terrified of making a fool of himself by trying to learn to read. And he was even more terrified of shaming himself before her. He also broke out in cold sweats at the thought of the other men in the hut finding out and laughing at him. 'No need. I manage all right without.'

He risked a glance at her and sighed. He could tell what she was thinking. When she opened her mouth, he shouted, 'Leave it be, woman!' and stormed off out of the hut.

Ma peered through the doorway of their room. 'What's got into him?'

'Nothing. Just – just a bit of a disagreement.'

'Aye, well, you're bound to have those.'

Jessie nodded, but when Ma went back to serving her ale, she swallowed and sat down on the bed. They had never disagreed about anything before. And he'd never walked out on her. Tears filled her eyes.

A shadow fell across her. She looked up. 'Jared.' She tried to sniff away the tears.

'You're crying, love!'

'I wasn't. I just had something in my eye.'

He sat down beside her and took her hand. 'I'm terrified of reading.'

She leaned her head against him. 'Oh, Jared, you've no need to be. It's not that hard.'

'Let me think about it.'

'What's to think about? I could – '

'*Will* you leave it be?'

They got ready for bed in silence and when they lay down, she turned her back on him. Both of them lay there in a stiff, fraught silence, till suddenly he pulled her round roughly and said, 'All right, then! *All right!* But no one's to know about it! No one at all.'

They started the next evening, with Jessie drawing the ABC on a scrap of paper and Jared laboriously copying out the letters on other scraps. She began taking home every piece of waste paper she could find in the shop, however small or crumpled, for Jared to practise on. After some hesitation she confided the reason for this to George Snader. She had a feeling that he would be on her side and she was right.

'I've wondered if he could read. He's so quick with figures, I thought he must be able to.'

'No.'

'Well, you can't go far in this world if you can't read or write. No one can! And your Jared's a likely chap, all right. He's lucky he's got you!' He was not the only one to think that, he knew, for the lovely Mrs Wilde drew all eyes in the camp. But who would risk angering Big Jared by pestering her? Only one man that George knew.

'You won't say anything about it to anyone else, will you? I mean, Jared doesn't want people to know in case they – well, in case they laugh at him.'

' 'Course I won't. Think I've nothing better to do than gossip about your husband? And any road, if a chap wants to improve himself, that's his own business.' He had improved himself, George thought smugly. His own parents wouldn't recognise him now, or believe how much money he'd got tucked away in a bank. And in a few other places, too, because he didn't trust anyone. He smiled at her benevolently. Very useful to him, Jessie Wilde, and would be even more useful in the future, he hoped, for he had a new plan in mind, which depended on her and which would increase his profits at the next camp.

The reading lessons continued and as Jessie had expected, Jared proved to be a good learner. Once his fears of failure were shown to be groundless, he made rapid progress.

'Eh, lass, if only the rest of life were as easy as this!' he said one night. 'Everything's goin' so well for us that I wake up in a sweat sometimes, worrying.'

'Don't be silly! We're *making* things go well, not standing back and waiting for good luck to favour us. That's different.'

'If anything happened to you, love, I'd go mad,' he said, still in a sombre mood.

'Why should anything happen to me?'

He shrugged. 'Life can be a bugger.'

He tried to cheer up, but from then on she became more aware of that undercurrent of being prepared for the worst that ran beneath his outwardly cheerful approach to life. And when she listened to the women in the shop, heard their stories, saw what they had to put up with, she realised how lucky she had been so far. The incident with Lord Morrisham had been nothing compared to what some of them had lived through. Nothing.

For the first visit to Hettonby, they both wore their wedding clothes, to give them confidence. They set off before eight in the morning, to a chorus of catcalls and jeers from the men in the hut who were awake.

'Not gettin' married again, are yer, Jared lad?'

'Ain't he just *pretty*?'

'Hey, lads, I know what's goin' on! They're goin' t'church! Ya, ya, ya! Big Jared's goin' t'church!'

'That's women for you. Soon as you marry 'em, they ruin your Sundays.'

As this was too close to Jared's own feelings for comfort, he scowled and marched over to the last speaker. 'You shut your trap about my woman, Billy, or I'll shut it for you!' he threatened, fists clenched.

Billy backed off. 'No offence, lad, no offence! Just havin' a bit of a joke!'

'Well, I didn't think it were all that funny.'

It took Jared two full miles to simmer down again. Jessie let him walk off his anger and didn't comment when he muttered things to himself. She was revelling in the beauty of the countryside, after the camp.

Then they got a ride with a farmer driving a cart for a couple of miles and Jared forgot his troubles as they all chatted about the weather and the harvest.

'Folk often used to pick me up when I went home from the Hall,' Jessie said cheerfully as they waved the farmer goodbye. 'But I enjoy a walk on a nice day like this.'

They stopped just before they got to Hettonby to brush the dirt from their boots and tidy themselves up, then they went on, arm in arm, to face their ordeal.

They went in at the kitchen door of the parsonage and found Agnes waiting for them inside, with the door open, sitting bolt upright on a hard wooden chair, dressed in her Sunday navy silk. The fire in the range was banked up and a copper kettle was simmering gently on the hob. The table was laid for three.

'Hello, Mother.' Jessie kissed her cheek. 'Here we are, then.'

'Hello, Mrs Burton.'

There was a moment's silence, then Agnes said, stiffly and grudgingly, 'You look well, at any rate, our Jessie.'

'Why shouldn't I? I've not been so happy for years.' She smiled at Jared.

Watching their loving looks, Agnes thought, Well, their happiness has lasted longer than mine did, at any rate. A pang of sadness pierced her. Since Jessie had left home to go into service, she had found the evenings so empty. It was even worse now with her lass so far away. She couldn't help worrying. If it hadn't been for the parson coming down to share a cup of tea in the kitchen occasionally and chatting to her about parish affairs, there'd be many a day when she didn't speak to another soul. Still, if that was all she had to complain about, she should be thankful for what she'd got. 'There's just time for a cup of tea before church. The kettle's on the boil.'

Jared watched her studying Jessie, as if trying to make sure that her daughter really was all right, but she hardly even glanced at him. She still hadn't asked them to sit down, so he leaned against the doorpost. What a way to spend a precious Sunday!

Jessie broke the silence. 'Aren't you going to ask us to sit down, then, Mother?'

'Oh – yes, of course. Er – won't you take a chair, Mr Wilde?'

'Jared!' Jessie said firmly. 'I'm your daughter and he's your son-in-law now. So it's Jared.'

Mrs Burton went bright red and the kettle shook in her hand, spilling some boiling water on to the hob, where it spat and hissed like an angry cat.

At the sight of her trembling hand, Jared suddenly felt sorry for her. 'Here, let me take that heavy kettle, Mrs Burton.' Gently he removed it from her hand. It had just hit him once again, standing in the gleaming, well-appointed kitchen, how very much Jessie had given up to marry him. He patted Agnes's shoulder awkwardly. 'Your lass *is* all right, you know. Where we're living's not what she's used to, you don't need to tell me that, but it won't be for ever. We're making good money and I'll look after her.'

Agnes's lips suddenly trembled and tears spilled down her cheeks. She whisked out a handkerchief and blew her nose, annoyed at herself for betraying her weakness to him, but a little appeased by what he had said.

Jared turned away and busied himself brewing the tea, which

he did with his usual deftness. 'How long d'you like it to brew?'

'Three minutes. Thank you – Jared. I'll see to it now.'

Behind her back, Jared and Jessie raised their eyebrows at one other. Phew, he was thinking, it's like walking on bloody eggshells! Four hours is going to seem a long time.

Drinking and eating helped fill a few minutes. Jared washed down a couple of scones with three of the tiny cups of tea. It tasted funny with milk in it, and he'd rather have had a glass of ale any day after such a long walk, but he said nothing except to compliment his mother-in-law on her scones. He followed that by praising her daughter's cooking, which obviously pleased the old lady. This nearly led to disaster, though.

'What do you have to cook on, Jessie?' Agnes tried to stick to safe, domestic topics of conversation.

Jared choked on his tea and Jessie tried not to look guilty. 'I – er – there's only an open fire. I told you that we'd have to share our – er – lodgings.'

Her mother looked at her suspiciously. She hadn't missed Jared's reaction and could always tell when her daughter was prevaricating. 'It's about time you told me exactly how you are living,' she said grimly. 'I can see you're not proud of it, or I wouldn't have to drag it out of you.'

'I *am* proud of it! Jared's done the best anyone could, in the circumstances, and all with his own hands!'

He laid one of those same hands over hers, saying with great dignity, 'We have a room built on to the side of a lodging hut, Mrs Burton.' He described it, ending, 'I don't know how Jessie manages, but she does, an' I've never eaten so well in me life. It's a start for us, d'you see? We're savin' money every week, too, a pound or more.'

Agnes goggled. '*Saving* a pound a week?'

'Aye. More now that Jessie's contributing.'

'I've got a job too, Mother. I work in the camp shop. And when Mr Snader's out, I'm in charge.'

'Well, that doesn't sound too bad, I suppose.' Agnes caught sight of the clock and gasped. 'Look at the time! We'll be late for church if we don't hurry! You can tell me all about your shop afterwards.'

Jessie caught Jared's hand as they hurried along behind her mother. He rolled his eyes at her. It was a relief to slide into a pew and follow his wife's example by bowing his head and pretending to pray.

After two hymns had been sung, John Marley climbed up to the pulpit. 'My sermon today is on St Matthew, Chapter 25, Verse 35: *I was a stranger and ye took me in.*' He watched his congregation shuffle uneasily and saw a few glance towards Jared. Yes, I have been remiss, he thought, not offering them as much guidance as I should have, not being firm enough about moral issues. But I shall change all that in my next parish.

His gaze lingered for a moment on Agnes's face, so like her daughter's but without the glow of happiness. Surely Lord, he thought, she too deserves a little joy in her life? Just occasionally, when they were talking, he managed to make her laugh and then her whole face lit up and she looked pretty again. She'd said very little about her husband, just that he was dead, but John guessed that she had been very unhappy in her marriage.

Well, at least she had Jessie, who was a lovely young woman. He had no one. No relatives left that he knew of, apart from the elder brother whom he detested, and no child to carry on his name. That made him feel sad sometimes, very sad.

Susannah was feeling sad at that moment, too, sitting in church in Cheshire next to Peter Bowers, a stolid young man whom she had detested on sight, for no reason that she could understand. Maybe it was because he had never really looked at her, after the first thoughtful scrutiny. And he never really listened to her, either. He asked her questions and his eyes glazed over as she answered, as if he felt duty obliged him to make conversation but she had nothing to say worth listening to.

When they got home, she turned with relief to her preparations for London but her mother was very evasive about when they were going.

One day, her father summoned her down to the library, which was very much his own private territory. As Susannah knocked on the door, she felt her heart speed up and wondered yet again what he wanted. Her mother was unavailable, 'lying down asleep', the maid said when she'd knocked on the bedroom door. 'Come!' said a voice and she took a deep breath before obeying the order.

As she walked across the room, she felt her father's gaze upon her and he, too, was studying her, as Peter Bowers had studied her, as if she were a complete stranger.

'Sit down. Now, I've just received a letter from Cheshire. Young Bowers has offered for you.'

She gaped at him, then shock turned to horror as she saw how complacent he was looking.

'He's coming over next week to make the formal offer, then we'll hold an engagement party next month. This means we won't have all the fuss and nonsense of a London season.' He paused and stared at her again. 'You've done well for yourself.'

She felt terror roil around her belly as she said it, but didn't let that stop her. 'But I don't like him. I don't want to marry him.'

'*What!* Why, you impudent young madam! You'll do as you're told.'

'I'm sorry, Father, but I cannot like Mr Bowers.' Then the world turned into black nothingness as he knocked her from her chair and she hit her head on the leg of a small table.

16

Hettonby

At long last the service was over. Jared started to get to his feet, but Jessie pulled his sleeve and whispered, 'The gentry leave first.'

His stomach rumbled and Jessie let out a soft chuckle, though her mother shot him a look of tight-lipped disapproval. He resigned himself to another wait. The folk in the front pews were certainly taking their time about gathering their things together and leaving. Why the hell should the rest have to wait for them? He studied their fine clothes and glanced sideways at his wife. One day he'd buy shiny material like that for Jessie. She'd look better in green silk than that fat young madam did – she'd look good in anything, would his lass.

Abruptly, he became aware that someone had stopped at the end of the pew and was speaking to him. With an effort he gathered his wandering wits and focused on the speaker.

'I'd never have expected to see *you* here, Jared Wilde!'

He reached across his mother-in-law to shake the hand that was held out to him. 'Hello, Mr Stafford. This is my wife, Jessie.'

Conditioned by her years in service, Jessie almost curtsied, then realised that Mr Stafford was holding his hand out to her as well. She leaned across her husband to shake it gravely, staring up into his thin, elegant face, the sort of face only rich families seemed to produce. He was tall, but not as tall as her Jared, and he had a kind smile. When he was dressed up like this, she could see a clear resemblance to Miss Stafford, but that bony sort of body looked better on a man, somehow. 'I'm pleased to meet you properly, Mr Stafford. I've heard a lot about you from my husband and we're both grateful for your help.'

'It was my pleasure. Your husband's a hard worker, with a good gang behind him. He's got a feel for the railways and the sense to take precautions when he works. I wish there were more like him, then we wouldn't have so many accidents.' The Committee might not let Lord Morrisham bully them into sacking their engineer, but they took a dim view of accidents, which reduced their profits.

Simon realised that he was holding people up and earning disapproving looks from his young hostess, Mrs Nellor, whose husband he had known at school, so he nodded and passed on.

He was surprised that Wilde had managed to woo and win a girl like that. She was quite a beauty and was surely not a village girl, because her voice had no local burr in it and anyway, no village girl would have had her self-possession. Did a girl like her live on the diggings? If so, it was a good thing she had Big Jared to protect her! Navvies were a rough lot and no respecters of women.

On the way back to the house, he tried to listen to his hostess's bright prattle and put Jessie Wilde out of his mind, but he didn't succeed. It wasn't easy to forget a woman with such glorious russet hair and expressive eyes. A fine tall woman, too, not a plump little doll like Diana Nellor with her simpering, pouting ways. How had Ralph come to marry her? But he knew the answer to that, of course he did. Diana had had money, and that made up for her silliness. He ought to marry money himself but didn't think he could do it, not if it meant facing a shrill voice every morning for the rest of his life.

Pleased by the encounter with a member of the gentry, Agnes led the way out of church with her head held high when their turn at last came. She didn't usually linger in the churchyard to exchange gossip, for she had Mr Marley's meal to get ready. But today even she found it hard to get away. Mr Snelling wanted to have a world with Jessie, and you couldn't snub a nice man like him. So they lingered for a few minutes while Jessie told her old teacher about her new life and job.

Once back at the parsonage, the two women set about preparing the meal while Jared sat in the corner, feeling awkward and useless. 'Can I do anythin' to 'elp? Fetch water or summat?'

'No, thank you,' said Agnes curtly, her eye on the clock.

'I think I'll take a turn in the garden, then,' he said.

'You can't. Mr Marley's home.' She didn't even look at him as she said this and he began to grow annoyed.

Jessie hastily intervened. 'We don't use the garden when Mr Marley's around, but you could walk across and have a look round the churchyard. It's very old. There are some funny inscriptions on the headstones.' Her eyes carried a silent plea for him to keep his temper.

He sighed loudly. 'All right, love. At least the folk in the church-yard won't be starin' at me. How long will the meal be?'

'About half an hour. Isn't that right, Mother?'

'Yes. There's a clock on the church tower. Don't be late.'

Jared raised his eyes to the ceiling, planted a defiantly loud kiss on his wife's cheek and went out of the kitchen, whistling.

Agnes muttered something over the pan of gravy she was stirring. Jessie sighed and went to put her arm round her mother's shoulders. 'Be a bit kinder to my Jared! He's walked all this way on his day off to bring me to see you. He was even going to hire a cart.'

They were interrupted by Mr Marley ringing his bell. Agnes hurriedly wiped her hands, took off the plain apron she was wearing to protect her lace-trimmed Sunday one and went up to see what her employer wanted. She was back almost immediately.

'He'd like to see *you*.'

'Me?'

'Yes, you! Go on! Don't keep him waiting!'

Jessie removed the apron she'd borrowed, smoothed her hair and went upstairs to the study. She knocked on the door, still feeling puzzled about the summons. Mr Marley usually liked to rest after a service.

'Ah, Jessie.' He stood up and indicated one of the big leather armchairs. 'Won't you sit down for a moment? I've been wondering how you were getting on.'

'Very well, thank you, sir.'

'I was speaking to Lord Morrisham the other day.' Their quarrel had been more or less patched up, but the parson's relationship with his patron had lost its old ease and warmth. John was hoping he'd be accepted for the new living for which he had applied. 'He – er – His Lordship asked me to tell you that his bailiff could probably find work for Mr Wilde somewhere on the estate. And a cottage too, of course.'

Jessie didn't try to hide her anger. 'I can't imagine why he would bother about me any more. And I thought he hated railway navvies?'

John Marley decided that she was too intelligent to be fooled. 'He doesn't like to be bested. He thought perhaps your husband would be tempted by a chance to lead a more – a more normal sort of life.' John had promised to reason with her, but his heart wasn't in it.

Jessie felt anger rising in her like yeast working through a batch of dough. What was wrong with Lord Morrisham that he couldn't bear to lose even one insignificant maidservant? But she couldn't blame Parson Marley, who was plainly unhappy about relaying the offer. 'We're very well content with our life, I promise you, sir. And I have a job at the camp too, now.'

'Really?'

'Yes, sir. I'm working in a shop. I earn ten shillings a week.'

'My goodness! Ten shillings! As much as some men!'

Jessie breathed deeply. Women worked just as hard as men – harder if the men were footmen – so why should they be paid so much less? 'And my Jared has another job waiting for him when this contract ends. With Mr Stafford.'

John Marley blinked at her like a gentle owl, then smiled. 'I'm glad for you, really glad.' He knew Clarence Morrisham would be disappointed by her response. And angry. But John didn't care about that any longer.

'Thank you for your interest, sir.' Jessie's voice was cool and self-assured. 'Shall I bring up your luncheon now?'

'Yes, please.' He sat musing as he waited for it. What a contrast she was to poor Susannah Morrisham, who had looked extremely unhappy the last time he saw her, face pinched and white, starting when her father bellowed something at her across the hall. It was a good thing she was to marry soon. She'd be better away from that bully.

When Jessie went back down to the kitchen, the meal was ready, so she went out to find Jared and left her mother to serve Mr Marley first. She went into the churchyard, walking slowly and enjoying the sunny quietness of the day. She couldn't see her husband at first, then she caught sight of him by the side of the church, talking to someone. As she drew closer, she saw that it was the railway engineer.

'Hello, love,' Jared called when he saw her. 'Is that food ready yet? I'm as empty as an old beer barrel.' He put his arm round his wife.

'Do you like old churches, Mrs Wilde?' Simon wanted to delay their departure, to chat a little to this beautiful young woman with the warm contralto voice. 'This one is a fine example of fifteenth-century Perpendicular architecture, if only on a small scale.'

'I've never thought about them,' she confessed, taken aback. The things the gentry went on about!

'And you think I'm mad for bothering about such things?' he teased.

'Oh, no, I wouldn't – I mean . . .' Her voice trailed away. 'You're making fun of me, Mr Stafford!' she accused, but couldn't help smiling back at him.

'We'll have to remember to go round lookin' at old churches when we're rich an' have the time, like you, sir.' Jared grinned. 'It'll impress folk no end.'

'How is Miss Stafford?' Jessie asked. 'I saw her a few times at the Hall and was sorry to hear how she'd been treated.'

'My sister's living near Rotherham. She seems very happy there.' And had settled down firmly to being an old maid. Which was not what he'd wanted for her. He had to make more money, and as quickly as possible, so that he could give Elinor a chance to live a fuller life.

Jared looked towards the parsonage and sighed. 'I reckon we'd better get back for our dinner now or me ma-in-law'll chalk up another black mark against me.'

'I'll see you tomorrow, then, Jared. Goodbye, Mrs Wilde.'

'Now, that's what I call a gentleman,' Jared commented as they strolled back. 'He's a good engineer an' he's beginnin' t'make a name for 'imself, but he doesn't talk down to you. I reckon he'd be just the same if he met that young Queen of yours.' His grip tightened on Jessie's waist. 'You can keep your Queens for me, though. I've got the woman I want.'

Agnes greeted them with, 'The food's getting cold.'

'Sorry we're late, Mrs Burton,' said Jared. 'I were talkin' to Mr Stafford an' I forgot the time.'

'Well, sit yourselves down now.' She began to pile food on his plate. No need to tell her that he was a hearty eater. With such a huge frame to maintain, he must cost the earth to feed.

When he had eaten his fill of the roast beef, with potatoes and cabbage and a dumpling gravy, followed by apple pie with thick cream on the top, Jared sat back and beamed at his mother-in-law. 'That were the best meal I've ever had in me whole life!'

Agnes Burton was startled. 'I'm glad you enjoyed it, but there's no need to exaggerate.'

He leaned forward, annoyed that she couldn't even accept a compliment from him. 'I'm *not* exaggeratin'! I left home when I were ten. Till I married Jessie, I just ate what were put before me an' glad of it. Nor I'm not used to places like this, all shining and bright – as you well know.' He gestured to the kitchen.

She was a little mollified. 'Well, I'm glad you enjoyed your dinner. I do pride myself on my pastry, I must admit.'

They stayed for about an hour after the meal, then, with the excuse of the long tramp back, they took their leave. Agnes had made them a big fruit cake and also insisted on tying up in a cloth some buttered scones, in case they got hungry on the way back.

'Phew!' said Jared, once they'd left the village behind. 'I'm glad that's over. Did I do all right, love?'

'You were splendid, Jared. Thank you for bearing with her. She's beginning to come round a bit.'

He stopped walking to gape at Jessie. 'You call that comin' round?'

'She never shows her feelings.'

'Aye, well, I'll have to take your word for it, then.'

But Agnes did show her feelings after they'd left. When John Marley received no answer to his ringing of the bell, he went down to check that everything was all right and found her slumped over the table, head on her arms, sobbing her heart out. He hesitated, but couldn't leave her like that. He went across and put his arm round her thin shoulders. 'My dear Agnes!'

And without thinking, she flung herself into his arms, needing for once some human contact and sobbing even more loudly.

When he had got her calmed down, he insisted on making her a cup of tea and was so inept that he made her laugh. In the end, she made it, and they sat down to enjoy it together.

'I love this kitchen,' he said suddenly, 'the way the brasses sparkle, the herbs on the window sill and the flowers on your table.'

'Oh. Well, thank you.'

'I think I shall join you down here more often. It can get very lonely up in my study.'

'But – that wouldn't be proper!'

'What's proper or not is changing greatly in this world of ours, don't you think? That husband of Jessie's is a fine example of the modern working man, isn't he?'

She nodded. 'Jessie says he earns thirty shillings a week and they're saving money all the time. I can hardly believe that.'

'I'm sure she wouldn't lie to you.' He sat back, enjoying their companionship as much as she was. 'When there is just me, I would like very much to take my meals down here from now on, Agnes – if you don't object, that is?'

'No. Of course I don't object.' John had surprised her again, though, as he had done a few times lately, ever since the night Jessie fled from the Hall and he had stood up to His Lordship. If he got this new living, he had assured her he would take her with him. But she'd been here in Hettonby for nearly twenty years. She was not sure she wanted everything to change, not sure she could cope with the upheavals.

The Wildes' second visit to Hettonby, a month later, followed a similar pattern to the first, except that Agnes showed just a trifle less hostility towards her son-in-law. Well, Jessie said she did anyway. Jared wasn't so sure. But he enjoyed another superb meal and said so, and this time his compliment was accepted with a tight smile.

On their way back to the camp they were overtaken by a gig, which drew up to wait for them. Simon offered them a lift back, but they refused as politely as possible. If they got back too soon, they would only have to sit around in the malodorous hut.

'But it's three miles still to the camp!' he protested.

'A nice stroll, Mr Stafford. Y'should try it sometime.' Jared laughed up at him.

Jessie stood smiling next to him, her hand in his. 'We like walking, Mr Stafford. And it's good to get out of the camp sometimes.'

'Every man to his own!' As he drove off, Simon turned his head and looked back. Jared's huge frame was bent protectively over Jessie. She was looking up at him, listening carefully to something he was saying. Simon suddenly felt lonely. It must be wonderful to have a wife to work alongside you and share your life like that! Diana Nellor had been in a foul mood today, and Ralph had looked hang-dog. I shan't go over there to visit again, he decided. Then he pulled a face, knowing himself. Give him the prospect of another long, boring Sunday in his room at the inn and he'd accept an invitation anywhere. It was just a pity Elinor was too far away to visit and get back in a day.

One day he'd be married and have a home of his own and never be lonely again. But not someone like Diana Nellor. Someone more like Jessie Wilde. He envied Jared, he really did.

That same day, Elinor tapped on the door of the front parlour and frowned when she received no answer. She hesitated. Miss Butterfield didn't like to be interrupted when she was working on her correspondence. But it had been over two hours since they'd heard any sound from the parlour, so the maid had asked her to peep in.

Belinda Butterfield was slumped over her desk and was so very still that Elinor guessed what had happened even before she touched the frail, age-spotted hand and found it cold and lifeless. Tears came into her eyes. She had known that it wouldn't be long now, but Belinda was such a wonderful person, so lively to talk to, that you had trouble most of the time remembering that she was ill.

The doctor had said the growth on her breast was very large now, and that it must be giving her a great deal of pain, but Belinda was not the sort to give in to pain, or even to betray it to others. She had remained upright and alert right until now. Indeed, she had made her companion chuckle over breakfast that very morning with a tale of her girlhood.

'I shall miss you,' Elinor said softly as she closed the staring eyes. 'Oh, I shall miss you quite dreadfully.' She stretched out to tug on the bell pull and when Thirza, who had slipped easily into the role of parlourmaid here, came to answer it, found she could not say the words, only gesture to her dear friend and mentor and let the tears rolling down her cheeks pay their own homage.

For the rest of the day, the elegant little house was full of people coming and going. Squire Butterfield was sent for, of course, and brought his sensible wife with him to help them all through this, for he was a tender-hearted man underneath all that bluster.

The funeral was held two days later and the church was crammed with people paying their last respects to Miss Butterfield. The Priory was just as full afterwards, but the guests were more cheerful now, making a great deal of noise and getting through huge amounts of food.

When the time came for the reading of the will, Elinor would have left to go home and begin thinking about her future, but the squire came over to her and asked her to attend the reading.

'Are you sure?'

'Of course I'm sure.'

'But I'm not a member of the family.'

He patted her shoulder. 'You're a beneficiary, though.'

She gaped at him and he chuckled, then looked round guiltily in case anyone had noticed this lapse from solemnity. 'Don't look so worried. My aunt confided her wishes to me and I thoroughly approved of them. Come along, now, my dear.'

As the lawyer droned on, it became clear that Miss Butterfield had managed her money with considerable astuteness. The bequests were large and all the members of her family were soon smiling and nodding at one another.

'And for Miss Stafford,' the lawyer read, 'who has kindly kept me company in my declining months – and good company she is, too – I leave the house in Heptonstall. There are tenants in it now, but it is my sincere hope that she will go to live there herself as soon as it can be arranged.'

The squire turned to beam at her.

Elinor gulped and swallowed hard, but could not keep back the tears. She had not meant to reveal how much she was missing the moors, but somehow had not been able to help telling Belinda Butterfield things. She was that sort of woman. No one's fool, but kindly, in an astringent way.

'. . . and to maintain the house, an annuity of two hundred pounds per annum,' the lawyer finished.

Now Elinor was weeping in earnest and the squire's wife came over and led her from the room.

'I didn't mean to take her money,' Elinor gulped, terrified that these kind new friends would think she'd been scheming to obtain something.

'Of course you didn't. If you had, Aunt Belinda would have seen straight through you and sent you packing. She'd travelled the world in her time and only came here when she grew old, so she was not easily fooled.'

'But the money should have gone to her family.'

'Nonsense! There's plenty to go round. None of us is lacking.'

They sent Elinor home in the carriage, although it was only a two-mile walk across the fields, and she sat in it feeling numb, like a boat without a rudder.

It was not until the next day that she really began to recover and to appreciate her good fortune. 'We can go back to live near the moors, Thirza,' she said as the two of them sat talking quietly about what they would do next. 'Squire Butterfield says we can stay here, if we want, but once the lease is up, I shall ask the tenants in Hetonstall to leave and we shall move in.' She exhaled in pure happiness.

'You've been missing them dratted moors ever since you left

home.' Thirza gave her rich chuckle. 'I do believe you even like the wind up there.'

'I do. It makes you feel so alive. I didn't know how much I missed it all until I had to leave.'

'Heptonstall is very close to Blackholm.'

'Yes.'

'Do you think folk round there would welcome you back, Miss Elinor?'

She shrugged. 'I don't know. I think some of them will, for Hannah and Jean still write to me, but even if they don't, I'd still be glad to get back there. And, oh, Thirza, we'll have a real home again! I can't wait to tell Simon.'

In response to Elinor's letter telling the good news of her inheritance, Simon came across from Eastby the following Sunday.

She ran to the door as soon as she heard a pony trap coming up the lane, beaming as she flung it open. But he was scowling, and his voice as he made arrangements with the lad driving him to be picked up again in the afternoon, was curt and angry-sounding. Nor did he give her his usual rib-cracking hug.

'Is something wrong, Simon?'

'Can we go inside before we talk?'

She led the way, passing Thirza, mouth open to greet Mr Simon had he even noticed her. But he didn't. He just stalked into the parlour after Elinor and slammed the door shut behind them.

Now, what's got into him? wondered Thirza. She hesitated, then went to press her ear to the door. Sometimes it was better if you didn't have to ask what was happening.

Elinor went to sit on the sofa, but he stood in front of the fire, warming his hands behind him, scowling down at her.

'What's wrong, dear? I thought you'd be happy for me.'

'I'm pleased about the money, of course I am,' he didn't sound it, 'but I'm not pleased about your plans to return to Blackholm. You can't do it, Elinor.'

'I don't understand?'

'We can't ever go back home. Not after the shame of having to be sold up, of knowing how deep in debt to everyone Father was.'

'But I'm not going to live in Blackholm – my house is in Heptonstall.'

'A few miles away! What's the difference? I tell you, you'll be an object of scorn in the district. And it'll bring back memories of *him*. I don't know exactly why, for you'll never discuss it, but I do know he made you very unhappy.'

She'd thought she had laid to rest the ghosts that had haunted her at first after her father's death, but now everything came rushing back at her and she had to stop and breathe deeply as she fought for control.

Simon didn't notice, for he was scowling down at the floor. 'No,' his fingers were tapping restlessly on the small table next to him, 'you aren't thinking clearly. We *can't* go back there. Never.'

'I'm not so sure about that – '

They argued about it for nearly an hour, and in the end he thumped the table and said loudly, 'Well, go your own way then, but I'll tell you one thing – I won't be coming to visit you there. I vowed not to return and I meant it. So you'll have to choose between me and that house. And damn the old lady for doing this to us!'

Before she could stop him, he'd flung out of the house and gone striding down the lane, not waiting for the trap to come and pick him up again.

She rushed to the front gate and called after him, but he didn't even turn his head. Elinor stood for a moment, then walked slowly back into the house. 'You heard?' she asked Thirza, who was waiting for her in the hall.

'Yes. I listened at the door.'

A sob escaped Elinor, then another, and she flung herself into Thirza's arms. 'Simon and I have never quarrelled before. Never.'

Thirza said nothing, just patted her back. To her mind, Mr Simon was being unfair. He'd been hurt by losing his home, perhaps more than they'd realised, but he'd no right to stop Miss Elinor from going back now, no right at all. And so she would tell him next time he came. She would that.

17

❦

Willingdon: October 1837

*A*t the beginning of October, the camp at Eastby started to show the first signs of breaking up. Some of the gangs would be moving fifteen miles down the track to another cutting, but Jared called his group together and asked them to go south with him and Simon Stafford, who had his first job as engineer-in-charge of a whole section of line.

'We could get taken on just down the road,' Banto Jim objected.

'Aye. But that's only a small job. Stafford's job will last a bit longer. An' besides, he's a good engineer. There are less foul-ups with him in charge.'

'I like it in the south,' Bull commented. 'It's not as cold. I'm never going up to Scotland in the winter again. Freezes your balls off, it does, there.'

When Harry gave him a dig in the ribs and Jared glared at him, Bull suddenly remembered that Jessie was within earshot. 'Oh, sorry, missus.'

'What's the pay like?' asked London Harry, who was nobody's fool.

'Regular. Stafford says the contractor's promised fortnightly.'

'All right, big lad. I'll go with you. This lot's bad payers an' they won't be no better down the line. An' anyway, they say there's shale around the next cutting. It's a bug— ' he remembered Jessie's presence, 'er, a bloomin' nuisance to work, shale is.' He grinned across at Jared, who gave a snort of laughter. They might

219

speak a bit rough, his lads, but they were a good lot and meant no harm.

In fact, most of the men in the gang treated Jessie with careful respect, and there was only one man on the diggings who worried her. Clogger Joe still had a tendency to pop up in odd places, and leer at her or make suggestive comments. She hadn't mentioned this to Jared, because she didn't want him to get into a fight with Joe, but it was beginning to wear her down.

When George Snader told her one day that Clogger was going to work down the line, she felt a sense of relief. She didn't know why that man upset her so much, but he did. There was something frightening about him – to her, anyway – like a wild animal who'd been more or less tamed, but whom you could never quite trust. But she couldn't talk about it to Jared, who had a fondness for all old navvies, and Joe in particular. He liked to listen to their stories and think about the old days, for he'd worked on one or two canal extensions himself when he first started and still enjoyed the sight of a barge moving along a man-made waterway.

George was also making plans to move on. Stafford had invited him to run the camp shop on the next contract and he'd been away for a few days to check the lie of the land in Hertfordshire. It looked as if it'd take several months to complete the work there, which suited him just fine. It was more trouble than it was worth to take on the job of setting up a shop and finding suppliers for short pitches. He'd done it when he was first starting, because that was all that was going, but he had a few other fish to fry nowadays and could afford to be more choosy about what he got into. And he intended to settle in the south sometime soon, so this would give him a chance to look around.

He cocked a knowing eye at Jessie one day.

'Still intending to work?' He looked at her stomach suggestively.

'Yes.' She didn't like his tone. 'Why shouldn't I?'

'Oh, you know. Young woman. Not long married. Might be starting a family.'

'We're not planning to have a family yet,' she said coldly, looking, had she but known it, just like her mother.

'Very sensible, my dear, very sensible indeed,' George approved. 'Mmmm.' He looked up at the ceiling, playing his usual trick of keeping his listener waiting. Jessie turned away and began to tidy the counter.

'Do you still want to work for me at Willingdon?' he said at last.

'Same sort of job?'

'More or less.'

'How much more and how much less?'

'Well, I was thinking that you could do most of the running of the next shop for me. I've got a few other things I'm interested in.'

'Oh, yes?' She didn't sound very enthusiastic.

'Don't you *want* the job?'

He sounded hurt, but she knew he was just putting on that pained look to gain an advantage. After working with him for more than two months, she'd learned never to underestimate him. Under that affable exterior was a needle-sharp brain, motivated by pure self-interest. She'd be willing to bet that he had a very tidy sum of money stacked away somewhere. She had a fair idea by now of the comfortable profits he made in that shop of his, and then he had the girls as well. They were even more profitable, apparently.

'I do want a job,' she admitted. 'And I don't mind working for you again, but I've been wondering if I wouldn't make more money running a hut.' She set her hands on her hips and stared at him challengingly and he suppressed a sigh. Like Jared, he'd come to recognise that look.

'Shouldn't think you'd like that. Very tying, running a hut. Don't get Sundays off, like you do with me.'

'But if I made more money, it might be worth it,' she persisted. 'Me and Jared, we're very keen to make money.'

'I'll tell you what,' he countered, with the air of a man making a big sacrifice, 'I might just be able to pay you twelve shillings a week at the next place.'

'For being in charge?' She feigned amusement. 'That's not much! Besides, I couldn't work the longer hours. You know that. I have Jared's meals to cook.'

'Mmm.' He rubbed his nose thoughtfully. 'Might be a way around that.'

221

'Oh, yes?' Her tone was casual, almost disinterested, and her hands were still busy tidying.

'Put those bloody currants down and listen to me, woman.' He waited, breathing deeply while she did as he asked and clasped her hands over her pinafore. 'Now, suppose I were to put a lean-to on the back of the shop for you and Jared to live in? You could cook the meals then for all of us and still keep an eye on things in the shop.'

Yes, and you'll get yourself a free night watchman! she thought. 'I don't know. It's still a lot of responsibility. My Jared's a busy man.'

His patience was suddenly exhausted. 'Damn it all, woman!' he shouted, thumping the counter, then thumping it again for good measure. 'You know you want the job! Stop playing around with me!'

Jessie dimpled a smile at him. 'All right, then. Fifteen shillings a week and free lodgings.'

'*What!* Do you think I'm made of money?'

'You're not short of a bit.'

'Fifteen shillings a week *and* free lodgings!' George repeated, as if shocked to the core. 'It's too much! You'll be the ruin of me!' His face took on the plaintive expression she had learned to recognise as the one which meant he was nearing his final offer. 'Fourteen shillings a week *and* you cook my evening meal for me when I'm in the camp. And that's my last word!'

'You'll supply the food for your meal?'

'*You can take it – out of – the sodding shop!*'

'All right, then!' She tried not to look too triumphant. She had never expected him to go as high as fifteen shillings and had only asked for it out of sheer devilment. Fourteen shillings a week *and* free lodgings! Wait till she told Jared! She was beaming as she walked home. Life was wonderful, just wonderful.

Then she nearly bumped into Clogger Joe, who was leaning against the wall of their hut, and her heart sank. What did *he* want?

'Evenin', Mrs Wilde,' he said, eyes running up and down her body in a way that always made her shudder. 'I've just come over for a bit crack wi' your Jared.' He turned as someone came to the door of the hut behind him. 'Ah, there you are, lad. I've decided to take you up on your offer.'

'Good.' Jared held out his hand and the two of them shook solemnly.

Joe nodded to Jessie and ambled off.

'What offer?' she demanded.

'He's coming to the next place with us. Not in my gang – none of my lads are leaving me – but in Ruddy John's lot. He's a bloody good worker when he sets his mind to it, Joe is. An' he's promised to cut down on the drinkin'.'

She couldn't speak, couldn't say a word, just stared at him in horror. And by the time she'd pulled herself together, he'd gone inside the hut and was talking to Banto Jim. She stood outside in the chill darkness, feeling sick, arms clasped across her chest. She knew Joe spelled trouble, she just knew it.

George Snader moved from Eastby to Willingdon a couple of weeks before Jared and Jessie. He ran most of the shop's stock down and then left her to sell the remainder off for him.

'I'll be back as agreed to pick up the shack and whatever's left.' He studied his dirty fingernails with great concentration. 'If your Jared will help me to dismantle the building and load it on the carts, I'll transport you and your bits and pieces down to Willingdon free of charge.'

'And Mary's things?'

'Mary? What do you mean, Mary?'

'Surely you're taking her with you?'

'If she can get there, I'll employ her.'

'I want to make sure she gets there. Why should we have to train someone else? Mary knows our ways.'

'I don't think . . .'

'Oh, come on, George! It won't cost you anything.'

He puffed up his cheeks, let the air pop out and shrugged. 'Well, all right, then. But she's to help with everything. And to keep her kids out of the way.'

Mary, eavesdropping from the shop, wiped away a tear. Jessie was wonderful. Mary had been dreading trying to get herself, her children and her bits and pieces to another camp-site. It was at times like that you missed having a fellow around. I won't let her down, she vowed. No, I won't.

Jared laughed when told of the offer. 'That's no problem. I've helped him pull that hut down afore. He got a carpenter to make it for him a few year ago specially so it could be pulled to pieces and used again. It's been all over the place, that hut has. I heard tell he's having a new one made now, for himself an' his best girls. He looks after his own comfort, does old George.'

So they made the move to Willingdon, travelling as fast as they could with the wagons, setting off at first light and finding inns only when the daylight faded. When they got there, they slept under the canvas cover of the wagon for two nights while the shop was re-erected and the new lean-to built on for Jessie and Jared. It looked a mess, but was waterproof, which was the main thing.

Within the week they were both working flat out. Jared took his responsibilities as ganger seriously and there was always a lot to do at the start of a new contract. In spite of the fact that they had only recently been paid, some of the gang had already spent their earnings, and he had to make advances to last them until next payday. He charged a halfpenny in the shilling interest per week on this, a low rate for the camp. He only made loans to his own gang, though, as George Snader acted as moneylender to the rest of the camp, and you didn't try to poach on George's preserves.

To Jessie's dismay, in spite of all she had said to Jared – and she had not minced her words – Clogger Joe had also moved to Willingdon. Why could Jared not see how the man upset her?

'I ain't forgotten you, Jessie Wilde,' a hoarse voice whispered to her one day unexpectedly when she was alone in the shop, making her jump like a startled rabbit.

She swung round and glared at Joe. 'And I haven't forgotten you, either. I think my husband's mad to bring you here. Mad.'

Joe chuckled. 'Oh, I've promised to be good, don't worry.' But his eyes said he still wanted her, they always did.

'Clogger Joe's been in the shop leering at me again,' she raged to Jared that night. 'Why did you invite him to come here and work with you?'

'We've been through all that, but I'll say it one last time, then I don't want to hear you complaining again. I asked him to come because he's bloody good. No one can move as much earth as him. An' I want my share of that bonus Stafford promised for an early finish.'

'No one can move as much gin as Joe, either! I never feel comfortable when he's around.'

Jared just chuckled. 'You've got nothing to worry about, love. He wouldn't dare touch my woman. Him an' me have known one another for a long time.'

But she couldn't accept that. It was one of the few things they disagreed about.

Their new living quarters were a distinct improvement over the corner of Ma's hut, because George Snader's shop was solidly built to discourage thieves and withstand drunken mobs on the randy. They had sole use of the small lean-to as sleeping quarters and it was curtained off from the main area by one of Jessie's sheets. There was just room for their rackety chest of drawers in it as well as her tin trunk.

They also had the use of the back room after the shop was shut. George often worked there during the day when he was not dealing with suppliers, spending a lot of time poring over accounts and lists in his small crabbed writing. The back room had a table and four chairs in it and they all ate tea there in the evening, for Jessie was still catering for George. There was also a roll-top desk in one corner, which George kept locked, and often piles of goods overflowing from the storeroom. Jessie did her cooking on a pot-bellied iron stove, which George had acquired from somewhere, and it proved very efficient, though she'd have loved a real oven.

And at night, when George had gone 'home' to keep an eye on his girls, and the shop had at last closed, they were on their own. This privacy, in a big camp, was a treasure beyond price to Jessie, and Jared had never known such a thing, except for the peace he could find on his walks through the countryside. For him, this lifestyle was positively luxurious and he revelled in their hour or so together each night after the shop had closed.

He was beginning to read more easily now and could write

very neatly. Jessie was amazed at the progress he had made in such a short time. He was even beginning to change the way he spoke, modelling his speech on hers and practising at nights, but speaking broadly still on the job, for fear of being laughed at.

Not that they had a lot of time for lessons. The magistrates in this area were not as fussy as those at Eastby, because there was no Lord Morrisham to remind them of their moral duty, and although they had threatened to insist on Sunday closing, they didn't carry out the threat. The railway company was in a hurry to get this stretch finished, so there was no break in the working week and there were the usual bonuses to be earned if they finished the contract ahead of time.

Unfortunately these bonuses remained on paper for a long time before being paid, because the main contractor was not keen on parting with his money and did not keep his promises.

One wage day, Jessie had her first experience of the men going on a randy. After waiting six weeks for their pay, the navvies spent most of it getting roaring drunk and indulging in a lot of senseless horseplay that left a trail of damage and cost many of them a day or two's pay as they recovered from their excesses. Saint Monday, they called their day of recovery, laughing as they added, 'Saint Tuesday, too!' A man had a right to a bit of fun after such hard work.

On hearing about the payout, George Snader hired several guards for his shop. When the drinking started, and one group decided they wanted the shop opened, Jared managed to joke them into moving on to find other butts for their mischief with the gift of a small barrel of ale. Money well spent, even George agreed.

Jessie didn't dare set foot outside the shop for two days and even Mary complained that it was a bad do and thankfully accepted Jared's offer to escort her home at nights to Ma's new hut, where she had a corner behind a curtain. She kept herself and her children in there overnight and didn't set foot outside again till Jared or George came to fetch her in the morning.

In spite of the gruelling hard work, Jessie was happier than she'd ever been in her life before. There were only two clouds on her horizon. One was missing her mother and the other, much more serious, was Clogger Joe. She always seemed to be bumping into him and knew that this was not mere chance. He was mockingly polite on these occasions and made no attempt to touch her, but she could feel his eyes on her, boring through the layers of clothing, boldly appraising her body. She tried again to talk to Jared about her fears, but he just said curtly, 'I've told you before – none of 'em'd *dare* touch my wife!'

'You're very sure of that, Jared.' She wished she were so sure.

'Of course I am!'

'Well, how did we do last week?' They closed the shop earlier on Sundays and it was their treat in the evening to sit counting their savings and dreaming of the future.

'We did well enough, love. An' I'm makin' an extra shillin' or so a week on the advances to the men, as well as what you're earning.' He sat looking thoughtful. 'It's gettin' a start that's going t'be the hard thing, d'you see, gettin' the first sub-contract – one small enough for us to afford. I'm hopin' Mr Stafford'll help me with that. I were speakin' to him the other day about it an' he says he'll keep his eyes open for me when we've finished here.'

Then they hit shale and work slowed down to a crawl. Shale was a devil to move. Rock you could at least blast; clay was heavy; but with shale you had to chip and worry away while the ground shifted beneath your feet and the streams of rock chippings had a habit of slithering back on you. And since no one knew how long it'd last, tempers grew frayed as the gangs struggled to keep up their pace.

One day Jared came home with a black eye, a cut on his cheek and bruised knuckles. He cut short Jessie's exclamations and slumped into a chair.

'Bloody rat!' he said.

She got him a pot of ale in silence and waited for him to explain.

'It's Banto Jim,' he said, after a minute or two. 'He's quit on us, just when we need every man to do his best. An' he tried to get the others to quit too – *my* gang! Said it were better to cut their losses now an' move on to a new pitch wi' him. So I cut his losses for him.' He laughed mirthlessly. 'It'll make the others think twice afore they try quittin' on me in the middle of a job. Not that I think they would.'

'You did right to thump him, then!' Jessie said hotly. 'I'd like to smack his face myself!'

His expression lightened a little. 'You would an' all!' he said admiringly. 'I've seen you in that shop, puttin' the chaps in their place if they try t'get cheeky.'

'Them!' She sniffed scornfully. 'They don't try it on twice.'

There was a knock on the door.

'I'll go,' Jessie said. It was not unusual for some desperate woman to knock on the door after the shop had closed, if she had spoiled her man's meal (an unpardonable offence) or if she had a sick child and wanted some poppy syrup to quieten it so that her man could get some sleep. Jessie didn't encourage this or the more feckless of the women would have been knocking on the door at all hours of the day or night, and she charged an extra penny on whatever they bought for her trouble, but she was known to be sympathetic to a genuine emergency.

'What do you . . .' she began crisply, but the words died on her lips as she saw the burly figure of Clogger Joe, unmistakable even in the feeble light from the back room. She made as if to slam the door in his face, but a meaty hand shot out and held it open.

'Matter o' business,' said the hated, hoarse voice. 'Come t'see your 'usband, missus.'

'Jared. It's for you,' Jessie was thankful that her voice didn't betray her by quavering. She felt intensely uncomfortable, even standing next to Joe, because although his request had been politely phrased and reasonable enough, his eyes were fixed on her breasts.

'Well, ask whoever it is to step inside. It's bloody cold with that door open!' called Jared, still not in the sweetest of humours.

'It's Clogger Joe.'

A sigh echoed from inside the room, then footsteps clumped across bare boards and Jared came over to join her at the door. He put an arm protectively around Jessie's shoulders and she put her arm round his waist, relieved.

Jared could feel how tense she was. It was funny how she felt about Joe; unreasonable, really. The man wasn't going to attack Big Jared's woman. There were other men who lusted after her just as openly. He'd seen them himself. Why did she get so upset about this one?

He was tired after a hard day's work and a fight to top it off, so spoke curtly, anxious to get this over and go back to sit by the stove. 'What can I do for you, Joe?'

'Matter o' business,' repeated Joe. 'Mind if I come in for a minute? Bleedin' cold out tonight.' He had stopped eyeing Jessie up and down the minute Jared appeared.

Jessie nipped Jared's arm. She didn't want that man in her home. She looked at the two of them and shivered. Two giants. They were of much the same height and build, though Joe was probably about fifteen to twenty years older than Jared and was thicker round the waist. Like Jared's, his face bore the marks of a hard life – a puckered scar by his mouth, a dent on his forehead – and she knew his arms were the same. I hope we earn ourselves some money before my Jared gets any more injuries, she thought suddenly. Few navvies escaped accidents. But his complexion was still fresh and he looked healthy, while Joe's face told of years of hard drinking and fighting in his bloodshot eyes, jowly chin and heavy expression.

'Aye,' Jared was saying, 'come in, then, Joe. But make it quick, eh? I'm tired. We've hit a bastard of a patch of shale on the heights at our end.' He shut the door and, arm still round his wife, gestured the visitor towards a chair.

Joe clumped across the room, his iron-shod clogs echoing loudly on the wooden floor. He sprawled next to the table and looked at Jared's half-empty pot of ale meaningfully.

'Will you get Joe a drink, love?' asked Jared, giving Jessie's shoulder an encouraging squeeze.

She nodded, not trusting her voice, but knowing better than to argue with him in front of Joe. She went through into the shop to draw another jug at the barrel on tap there, straining to hear what the men were saying in the back room.

'I 'ear you got rid of Banto Jim today,' said Joe.

'It didn't take long for that bit o' news to spread.'

'Never does.' There was a moment's silence, then, 'You'll be lookin' for someone else t'join your gang, I suppose?'

Jessie dug her nails into her hands to prevent herself from

crying out in protest, for it was suddenly obvious what was coming next.

'Aye, I suppose we will. Can't afford to be a man short just now.'

'Well, I'm not best suited with Ruddy John. I might be glad of a change.'

Jessie went back into the room and banged the jug and another pot on the table in front of Jared, ignoring Joe.

'Your missus don't fancy me joinin' you,' Joe commented, making it sound as if Jared were hen-pecked. 'She's still remembering that little mix-up we 'ad at the last camp.' He gave a wheezing laugh. 'It's all right, missus. I've got meself a nice little bed-warmer just now, let alone you're Big Jared's woman.'

Jessie flushed, looked pleadingly at her husband and muttered something about tidying up the shop counter. She lit another candle and went back into the cold, dark shop, praying fervently that Jared wouldn't set Joe on. She walked loudly over to the counter and then tiptoed back to eavesdrop on what they were saying.

'How about it, then, Jared lad?'

'Why?'

'I told you, I'm not best suited where I am. There's one or two chaps as is careless. I don't want a bloody great barrowload o' muck crashin' down on me head! I haven't lasted this long on the diggings by bein' careless.'

'Aye, there are some stupid buggers about,' agreed Jared. 'Deserve all they get, some of 'em. Pour yourself another drop of ale.'

'Thanks. Good stuff, this. She keeps it well, your missus does.'

'You know about the shale,' Jared warned him. 'Might not be worth your while joinin' us this end.'

'I been an' looked it over. I don't reckon that shale will go on for much longer. Seen patches like it afore.'

Jared nodded, but still shook his head doubtfully. 'They say you've been goin' it a bit on the gin lately. You told me you'd cut down. I'm not havin' no men in my gang who lose time from drunkenness.'

'Ah, I were just havin' a bit of fun. I'm not on the booze so heavy,' said Joe. 'Can't take it like I used to, an' that's the truth. Besides,' he winked, 'this woman's more fun than boozin' all night. She knows a few good bed tricks, Bet does.'

Jared hesitated. If Joe meant what he said, if he really would cut down on the booze, then he'd be a welcome addition to their gang. 'I'll think about it. The others have to agree before we take on anyone new. I don't suppose they'll object, though. You're a strong bastard.'

Jessie, in the cold shop, clasped her hand over her mouth and swayed backwards and forwards in anguish. No! He couldn't take on Joe! He couldn't! Not in his own gang. She knew nothing good would come of it. And she knew also that where his work was concerned, Jared would never listen to her, would grow angry if she even tried to interfere.

'Shouldn't be any trouble there,' Joe was saying. 'I know most o' your chaps.'

'And I wouldn't put up with no Saint Mondays, nor fightin' or arguin' on the job neither!' warned Jared. 'We're a team. Fightin' among ourselves is a waste o' good money.'

'Never thought of it that way. But I don't fight on t'job. Never 'ave.' Joe laughed. 'I save me pleasures for me spare time. Win a bit o' money at the fairs between jobs with me fightin'.' He flexed his muscles and banged one clog against the other.

'I'll put it to the others, then, but you'll have to square it with Ruddy John yourself.'

'Ah, he won't dare say owt,' boasted Joe. 'Knows I could beat 'im with one hand tied behind me back. Soft, he is! An' stupid, too, for all his big talk. I can't thole carelessness.'

The chairs scraped back and the clogs echoed across the planks of the shop floor. Jessie kept her back turned, fiddling with things on a shelf. The door opened, a blast of icy air blew in and a voice called out, 'Goodbye, missus!' then the door banged shut again.

Jessie followed Jared into the back room. 'How could you?' she demanded, her voice choking with rage.

He scowled at her.

'How could you set on a man like that Joe? You *know* how I hate him!' Unshed tears glistened in her eyes and her cheeks were flushed.

'Now, just a minute, Jessie.' Jared strove to keep control of his temper. He wasn't having anyone telling him how to run his gang, not even her. And though he didn't realise it, Joe's mocking words, 'Your missus don't fancy me joinin' you,' had cut him to the quick. His authority over his men would soon be lost if they thought his wife had a say in who joined the gang. 'I know you don't like Joe, love, but he's a good worker, none better, as long as he keeps off the gin.'

'He's scum!' snapped Jessie. 'And I wouldn't trust him as far as I could throw him!'

A pulse began to beat in Jared's aching temple. Those words held a nasty echo of her mother's.

'Joe's a navigator!' he threw back at her, thumping his fist on the table and spilling some of his ale. 'Like me! Like Alfred Small! Like the rest of us! An' he's been a navigator since the old days, long afore they started on the railways. I don't need no woman to help me tell a good navvy from a bad 'un! It's me as is the ganger, not you. An' don't you bloody forget that!' He emphasised his words by giving her a good shake and she gasped as his fingers bruised her shoulders. When he let her go, she almost fell over and had to grab the back of a chair to stop herself from falling.

'Oh, Jared, don't,' she begged. 'Don't let's quarrel!' If any other man had touched her so roughly, she'd have bitten him or kicked him or hit him over the head with the first thing that came to hand, but this was Jared, her big, gentle Jared, and she was shattered by his anger.

The catch in her voice and the tears on her cheeks checked his rage. He'd never seen Jessie look so defenceless. He stepped forward and swept her into his arms. 'Nay, love, I'm sorry! I should never have – ' He rained kisses on her face and tenderly bared her shoulder to kiss the bruise that was already forming. And she, shaken by their first serious quarrel, pressed against him.

Desire flared suddenly in them both and they were pulling at each other's clothes within seconds, murmuring, kissing, caressing. They made love there on the bare boards in front of the fire, so urgent was the need, and neither of them noticed the roughness of the planks or the chair they overturned.

Nor did they notice the face at the window. Joe, watching their passion through a gap in the curtains, swore fluently, but couldn't tear himself away from the sight of Jessie's naked body, pale in the shadows, gilded here and there by the light of the oil lamp. Never had he wanted a woman so desperately. 'An' I'll have her, too,' he muttered as he walked away. 'One day I'll have her.'

He made up for it all when he got back to his hut by thumping the woman he'd lately allowed to move in with him and then slaking his lust as best he could upon Bet's scrawny body, trying to block out from his mind the picture of Jessie's soft white skin and tumbled mass of russet hair in the flickering light of the fire.

In the face of Jared's persuasive arguments that what they needed at the moment was more muscle, and after a promise from Joe not to stir up any trouble and to lay off the heavy boozing, the men in the gang agreed to let him join them.

They were all a bit sceptical of his tale of carelessness at the other end of the cutting until, exactly a week after he'd joined them, there was a serious accident down there. One man was killed outright and another lost his arm. The screams of the latter echoed round the camp, both before and after the amputation of the mangled limb. This was performed in a perfunctory manner by a surgeon who came in reluctantly from a neighbouring town. The screams continued intermittently, growing steadily weaker and hoarser, for several days, until the second man died of the gangrene that had set in. The hospital in the town would not accept him, so he had to stay right there near the diggings that had caused the injury.

This was a side of camp life that Jessie had not seen before, and it shook her. What if it had been Jared injured like that? How could she have borne it? For the first time she became aware of how high a risk they ran to earn the good money they did. Too high? No. She still shared Jared's dream of amassing enough money to buy their own business. But still, a small knot of anxiety formed inside her and she knew it would never disappear until they left the railways. And that might be years, even if things continued to go well for them. But would Jared ever want to leave? He joked sometimes that he had railways in his blood now. And Jessie wondered if it was really a joke, or just the simple truth.

Lord Morrisham looked at his eldest daughter and felt rage hum through him. 'You will do as I say,' he shouted suddenly. 'You're marrying young Bowers an' that's flat. We put him off last time, told him you were ill but that you'd accepted his offer. This time you'll see him and you'll behave yourself.'

Susannah shook her head, trying not to show the trembling that was making her knees feel they wouldn't hold her up another minute.

'Are you defying me, miss?'

In her little parlour, his wife buried her face in her hands. 'Do as he asks, do as he asks, do as he asks,' she moaned.

Again Susannah shook her head.

Clarence Morrisham reached out and grabbed her shoulder, making her cry out as his fingers dug into it. Then he dragged her up the stairs, not worrying whether he banged her against the wall on the way, or about the little whimpering noises she was making. He could see nothing for his rage. The whole world seemed to have turned red and hazy around him. All that remained in focus was this impudent chit who had dared to defy him. Well, they had known how to deal with disobedient daughters in the old days. People were too soft nowadays. The whole country was going to rack and ruin. But he wasn't soft. No. And he'd make her bow to his will.

He threw her into her bedroom, slammed the door behind him and picked her up from the floor, where she lay sobbing. He held her by the back of her expensive gown, hearing the fabric rip and caring nothing for that, and shook her like a rat. 'Last chance.'

'P-please, Father. Please don't ask me to. I c-can't marry him.' The mere touch of Peter Bowers's hand was repulsive to her. Anything more would be torture.

'Right.' In a few swift movements, he ripped the dress from her back, ignoring her moans of terror, and stripped her down to her petticoats. Then he threw her on the bed and began to thump her, hitting her hard enough to make her scream. Every few thumps, he stopped and asked, 'Well?'

At first she said no, then she stopped speaking and just tried not to sob. But she couldn't prevent the tears and the moans, for he had hurt her badly.

After a while, he paused again and looked at her with a calculating expression on his face. 'It seems your clothes are giving you protection from the pain. Take the rest of them off.'

She lay and stared at him in stark terror, unable to believe he meant that. Then, when his great hurtful hand cracked down on her cheek and then his fingers fumbled at her petticoat ties, she tried desperately to escape. He just laughed and threw her back on the bed.

When he ripped off the top layers of petticoats, leaving only one thin piece of lace and lawn between her and the starkest humiliation she had ever known, she thought she would die of the shame. But she didn't. And when he looked at her, it seemed she saw death staring her in the face. He would not stop until he had won, however he had to do it. She remembered the series of broken and dispirited horses the head groom had had to sell, the servants who jumped to obey his every order, her poor weak mother who would have leaped off the roof if her father told her to, and knew then that she was beaten. She held up one shaking hand. 'Don't t-touch me again. I'll marry him.'

'Ah.' He moved back at once. 'Say that again. I want to be sure I heard it aright.'

Susannah swallowed hard. 'I'll marry him.' Nothing could be worse than staying here with *him*.

'Again.'

'I'll marry him.'

'Now apologise for your disobedience, on your knees.'

She did that, too, heaven help her.

Triumph lit Clarence's broad fleshy face. 'Good.' He moved towards the door. 'We'll plan for a Christmas wedding, then. And if any of your bruises show when Peter comes to visit, we'll say you had a fall from your horse. You're a poor rider, anyway.'

And he walked out without a backward glance.

She dragged herself to the door, began sobbing quietly,

slammed it shut and locked it. And not even for her mother would she open it until the next morning, when she appeared at breakfast at her usual time, stony-faced, visibly bruised and wincing when she moved incautiously. She did not try to discuss what had happened and nor did her mother.

18

Willingdon: November–December 1837

Everyone was affected by the accident, the women who came into the shop as well as the men who had to go on shovelling muck near where it had happened. Such gloom filled the camp that work slowed down and the company ordered their engineer to investigate the conditions under which the men were working. If those in charge of each section couldn't manage better than that, the company would be forced to take steps to replace them.

Simon was already in a bad mood because he hadn't heard from Elinor, apart from one short note that said nothing, since he had delivered his ultimatum about the house in Heptonstall. He was feeling guilty about that, but could not help how he felt about his old home. He felt she should respect his feelings, not try to drag him back there.

He turned up at Willingdon unexpectedly, just after midday, furious that the overseer had ignored his safety advice. He watched what was going on through binoculars from the cover of a grove of trees, anger rising rapidly, then moved purposefully into the diggings.

The north-end deputy overseer lost his job on the spot for not making sure that elementary precautions were taken. Simon continued round the camp, looking like a thundercloud, berating the men on the slopes for the careless way they'd set up some of the runways for the wheelbarrows and for the inadequate attention given to the way they dumped their spoil. The gangers came in for a particularly fierce tongue-lashing each time.

The groups of navvies stood in sullen silence and listened to his tirades, then grumbled to one another about the bonuses they'd lose if they did all that the stinking engineers asked them to.

Only Jared's gang was exempt from criticism. Simon Stafford strode up to where they were working with a scowl on his face and lips tightly compressed. His scowl gradually faded as he inspected Jared's patch.

'You run a good gang,' he admitted, after a while.

'Thank you, Mr Stafford,' said Jared quietly, relieved that all was in order. He winked at Billy, who ambled away and passed on the news to the rest of the men that things were all right on their patch.

'That's a good idea, the safety harness your men use to dig the steep bit. I haven't seen one quite like that before.'

'I designed it myself. And it's not just for safety reasons. I can't claim my lads care more about safety than the rest of 'em,' admitted Jared. 'The change in the harness makes workin' easier on the slope. See, they can lean against the ropes an' still swing their shovels, which is all they care about. We're into a bad patch here.'

They spent half an hour examining the shale and, like Joe, Simon Stafford was of the opinion that it wouldn't last. By that time it was dusk and the end of the shorter winter working day.

Stafford yawned. 'Is there anywhere round here where I can get a bite to eat? It's a ten-mile ride to my lodgings and I missed my midday meal.'

'Nay, there's nowhere close,' said Jared. 'The nearest village is two mile away an' that's not much cop. You'll pick up more fleas than food in the ale-house there.'

'Damnation!' Stafford frowned, then brightened up again. 'Surely I remember a shop in the camp? I'll buy some bread and cheese there.' He stretched his neck and shoulders, feeling himself relax now that the worst of his unpleasant task was over. 'It won't be the first time I've eaten as I rode.' He looked up at the sky. 'Let's hope the rain holds off a bit, or I'll get soaked.'

Jared cleared his throat. 'If you don't mind takin' pot luck, then I daresay my wife can fix up something for you to eat. She sets a fair table.'

'Done!' Stafford replied promptly. 'If you're sure she won't mind, that is?'

'Nay, my Jessie's equal to anythin'. Only – well, it'll not be fancy. We live behind the shop and . . .'

'It'll be a palace if there's some food and warmth. Look, you go ahead and warn Mrs Wilde I'm coming and I'll just have another word with that red-headed ganger before I go. One more problem with him and he's out.'

Grateful for the chance to give Jessie a bit of notice, Jared hurried off.

'What? Jared Wilde, you've never!' she wailed. 'Just look at this place! I haven't had time to clear it up properly today, we've been that busy.' She pushed past him and stuck her head into the shop. 'Mary! Can you see to the customers? Jared's invited that Mr Stafford to come and eat supper with us.'

'Eeeeh! He never! Well, you see to the food, love, an' I'll manage here all right.' In Mary's book, a railway engineer ranked only slightly lower than God. She turned back to her customer, tucking a strand of hair behind her ear. Five months of working with Jessie and a rise in wages had made a big difference to her. She was better fed, cleaner, and had begun to take pride in herself and the way she did her job. And Ma was happy to look after her children while she worked. Ma would do anything to earn a bit of extra money.

Jessie turned back to Jared. 'You get a wash and put a clean shirt on. Quick! Don't stand there staring!'

'What?'

'Go *on*!' Jessie gave him an impatient push and followed him into the bed-corner to change her work-soiled apron for a clean one and check her own appearance as well as she could in the little mirror. Then she rushed back to the fire and began to mutter to herself as she stirred her pans.

By the time a goggling Mary showed Mr Stafford in from the shop ten minutes later, the table was set with a snowy white cloth, a little crumpled but immaculately clean. Jessie had sewn it herself after she left the Hall and was waiting to get married, and it had been stored in the tin trunk ever since. She had also got out the few good plates and dishes they owned.

Jared watched all this in amazement and did as he was told.

When Simon arrived, Jessie shook hands. 'Would you like a quick wash before you eat, Mr Stafford?'

'I'd love it.'

'Jared,' a dig in her husband's ribs had him paying attention, 'get a bowl and some water for Mr Stafford. And I've put a clean towel out on our bed.'

She went back to stirring her pots. 'It won't be long.'

When he had chucked away the dirty water, Jared went and sat by the fire with his guest, feeling lazy now. 'It's been a bad few days. That accident upset the lads.'

'Yes. I noticed the atmosphere in the camp.' Simon looked around him, frankly curious. 'I can't think how you've managed to create such a cosy home here, Mrs Wilde. And you run the shop as well.'

'I'm used to working, Mr Stafford. Jared and I have our way to make in the world.'

'You'll do well, I'm sure. Your husband has some good ideas, and with you behind him, well . . .' He turned to Jared. 'Have you ever thought of trying to sell your safety-harness idea to the railway company, Mr Wilde?'

'Sell it? Could I do that?'

'I think so. You've got a better design there than any other I've seen.' Belatedly he remembered his manners. 'I hope you don't mind us talking about work, Mrs Wilde?'

'I prefer it. What does Jared have to do to sell it?'

'Write to the Chairman of the railway company and offer him the harness. You could say that I've seen it and recommended you to write. In fact, I'll take one over with me when next I go to the office, if you have a spare, and give it to him.'

'And he'd pay me money for it?' Jared questioned.

'I'm sure he would. He's like the men in your gang – in favour of anything which increases the rate of work. We're always on the look-out for new ideas.'

'I don't know.' Jared frowned, then looked across at Simon.

'I'm not so good with words. I wouldn't know how to set it down. Besides, you suggested an improvement to it today, so it's partly your idea now. I couldn't take full credit for that. Er . . .' He paused, feeling this to be a crucial moment and searching desperately for the right words. 'I get other ideas from time to time. Only I don't allus – *always*, I mean – know the best way to set about using them. If there's money to be made from ideas, well, we could mebbe do better together? You're more in a position to approach folk than I am – and they'll listen to you when they wouldn't to me. If you're interested, that is?'

'Definitely. We could . . .'

Jessie served the meal and sat back to listen as the two men talked. Jared was at first hesitant about expressing his opinions and offering his ideas, but gradually he lost his diffidence as he saw that the engineer was taking him seriously.

She cleared up quietly, trying not to disturb them more than she had to. This was a side to Jared she'd never really seen before and she marvelled at how much he seemed to know about building railways. And she saw, too, how intently Mr Stafford listened to what he had to say.

There couldn't have been a much greater contrast than between these two men. For all he worked as a railway engineer, Simon Stafford was a gentleman. His thin face and beautifully kept hands, the very way he held himself, all showed his breeding. And her Jared, whatever he did with his life, however much money he made, would never have that air about him. But by the same token, there was a power and a vitality about him that Simon lacked, and a virility that drew women's glances and made men respect him as a leader.

It was Mary who brought them down to earth. She tiptoed in to ask Jessie in a loud whisper if she could leave now. 'That rain's keeping folk indoors. I reckon we're goin' to have a storm tonight.'

Simon stood up. 'Goodness! I hadn't realised how late it was. And there's no moon tonight! Do you think there'd be a spare bunk in one of the huts? I don't much fancy a long ride back in the dark with a storm brewing.'

'*You* sleep in a hut!' Jessie spoke before she thought.

He laughed. 'I know what to expect, Mrs Wilde. I've had to sleep rough before.'

'Not in one of those huts!' She looked at his clothes.

He had a twinkle in his eyes that made her smile back. 'I've done it several times, and I've slept in barns, too, and out in the woods once or twice in summer when we were surveying lines. I'm not such a hothouse plant as you think.'

'There's not much room to spare,' said Jared doubtfully. 'The company was stingy with the material for huts and they're all bursting at the seams.'

'He'll have to stay here, then.' Jessie could read her husband's mind. 'It'll better than the huts. It's clean, at least.'

'But I can't put you to such trouble!' protested their visitor. 'Besides, do you have a spare room?'

'No, but you can sleep on the floor here.' Jessie looked round, mentally measuring the space. 'If we push the table back there'll be room to make you up a bed on the floor – if you don't mind that? I haven't got a spare mattress, but there's a big pile of empty sacks to soften the boards and there are no rats or fleas in my house!'

'I'd be more than grateful. My mount will be all right with the camp horses. He's a placid creature as long as he's well fed.' Simon smiled across at her, looking suddenly like an overgrown lad on a spree. 'I daresay you can even sell me some oats for him? He has more expensive tastes than the other horses do.'

'Your horse won't like our oats, I'm afraid,' she told him, keeping her face straight.

'Why not?'

'They're very poor quality. The gentry's horses are used to much better fare than that, I'm sure.'

He shouted with laughter. 'I can assure you my horse is not fussy. And nor am I.'

Later, as he lay in front of the dying fire, listening to them settling down to sleep behind the curtain, he envied Jared Wilde yet again. Jessie made even this place seem a real home. Women could do that.

His sister was the same. He turned over, trying to get more comfortable, feeling guilty as he thought of her. What was Elinor doing tonight? Had she come to a decision about that damned house? He wished, as he had wished before, that he could do more for her. But he also wished, and quite desperately, that she would not go to live in Heptonstall. He'd meant what he'd said about that.

At the beginning of December, Simon Stafford turned up again with the good news that the company had got another contractor to try out Jared's harness on a steep cutting and he'd been so pleased with it that he'd immediately had more of them made. The company had therefore decided to award Jared the princely sum of ten guineas as a reward.

'It's a bit stingy, I'm afraid.'

Jared brushed aside the apologies. 'That's not important this time, Mr Stafford.' He smiled down at the coins in his hand. 'It's the first brass I've ever earned with this.' He touched his forehead. 'You can sweat and toil all your life, but it's brains what earn the big money, aye, an' keep it, too.' He jingled the coins in his hand, then extracted two and offered them to Simon. 'I think that's about a fair share for your efforts.'

'No, I couldn't take it! I'm already ashamed I wasn't able to persuade them to give you a better price.'

'Nay, I insist.' Jared's voice was soft but firm. 'And any time you feel like it, Mr Stafford, we'll put our heads together on a few of the other ideas I have brewing.' He tapped his head again. 'Put this to work.'

'You're very keen to make money, Mr Wilde.'

'Yes. Me an' my Jessie both are. An' we'll do it, too, one road or another.'

'I'm just as keen. Desperate, in fact.'

Jared could not hide his surprise.

'I'm not rich, Mr Wilde. My father wasted all our family's money. I have only what I can earn.'

Jared looked at him thoughtfully. 'Then mebbe we should see what we can do together?'

Simon immediately held out his hand and they solemnly shook on the promise.

After that, Simon took to dropping in occasionally to see them, accepting a cup of tea or a meal and chatting with Jared about railway matters. Jessie kept in the background at these times, but she liked to listen to them talking, even when she didn't understand the technicalities of what they were discussing. She didn't interrupt, except on the rare occasions when she had something to contribute herself, but she often questioned Jared afterwards about things that had puzzled her.

She had learned a lot about the building of railways by now, but knew little about the way a line was proposed and financed.

She turned to Mr Stafford one day, as they were waiting for Jared to come home. 'How does a railway start? I've often wondered.'

'A group of local businessmen usually get the idea that a railway would be good for their town and would make their businesses more profitable. They form a company and have the line surveyed, after which they sell shares in the company to raise money. The most difficult part is to get a bill through Parliament, which will give them an Act of Incorporation.'

Whatever that meant! thought Jessie, but didn't interrupt his enthusiastic explanation.

'Only then can the actual building begin. As you know, the work on a line is let out to a series of contractors and subcontractors – half a mile here, a cutting there – and bridges usually go to someone else, because they're a separate speciality.'

'And navvies, like my Jared and his gang, do all – er, most of the hard work?'

He chuckled. 'Yes, you could say that.'

The navvies earned none of the fat profits, though, Jessie thought, but didn't say that to him.

'Even among navvies, gangs of hardened, experienced men like your Jared's are at a premium. They're the backbone of our trade and they train the newcomers for us, too. But there are other trades needed. Bricklayers to line the tunnels, carpenters, men who can look after and drive horses.'

This time Jessie didn't keep back her comment. 'And there are the women, too. Don't forget us. There are lots of women following their men around, living in harsh conditions. We're not all whores.'

Simon was a little shocked to hear such a word on her lips, but it was inevitable, he supposed. She was no hothouse flower, sheltered from life. She was – wonderful. Jared was a lucky devil.

They were both silent for a few moments, standing in the shop doorway looking out at the busy scene on the diggings beyond the camp. Then Jared came into view, striding across the riven landscape as if he owned it, tossing a word here and a wave of the hand there. No one failed to notice his passing. And Jessie, standing by the door, completely forgot the man by her side, just beamed at her husband as he came up and shook Simon Stafford's hand. He put an arm carelessly around her shoulders for a minute, giving her an absent-minded hug, then led the engineer back inside.

She stayed out in the weak sunshine for a moment or two longer. Goodness, they'd only been married for five months but she could not imagine life without him now, and when she remembered her days in service, she shuddered. How could she have borne it for so long?

She hadn't heard from her mother for a while and was a bit worried about her. Not that Agnes's letters were very satisfactory when they did arrive. They were stiff little notes, in which Mr Marley sent them his best wishes and blessing, or Mr Snelling asked to be remembered to them.

She had been a good mother, though, as one day Jessie would be to her own children. She was looking forward to that. Of course, Jared was still very careful when they made love, but sometimes she wished he would be careless, for she had a hunger growing in her for her own child – Jared's child. Well, that would come in time. For now, she'd better get back inside and help Mary.

Two other women were fretting on that chill winter's night. Agnes Burton was lying in her bed worrying about the parson. He was anxious, she could tell that. He waited for the mail each day and his shoulders sagged when he didn't receive the letter he was expecting. He had failed to get two other livings for which he had applied. Oh, she did hope he'd get this one!

'It'll not make it come any sooner,' she burst out the next evening.

'What?'

'You worriting. It won't make that letter come any sooner, John Marley.'

He smiled at her. 'I know, but I can't help it. His Lordship is continuing to be very difficult. I think he expects to wear me down and – and bully me back into conforming with his wishes. But I won't.'

Agnes knew what she thought of His Lordship, but she didn't say it aloud. A rumour had gone round that he'd had to beat his daughter into submission before she would agree to marry this man from Cheshire. And they'd all seen how the poor lass had changed, become thin and brittle, looking far older than her years. Eh, you could be rich and still be unhappy, that was sure.

Elinor Stafford lay in her warm bed in Yettley and watched the same moon appearing and disappearing behind the scudding clouds. Thirza was angry with her, very angry, but she couldn't lose the one relative she had to love in the whole world. Thirza said Simon was making empty threats, that he'd never stay away from her if she moved. But she didn't dare risk it. She just didn't dare.

In the morning she got up and wrote the letter before breakfast. It was raining outside now, chill sleeting rain that alternately hissed against the window panes and then whirled round in wind-tossed confusion. She would get wet when she walked to the inn, which acted as the postal receiving office for the village, but she didn't care about that, only about healing the rift with her brother.

Dear Simon,
You will no doubt be glad to know that I've decided to stay here in Yettley, after all. It was a hard decision, because I am missing home – that part of the world will always be home to me, I think. However, I don't want to hurt or alienate you, so I'll respect your wishes. Squire Butterfield is to let me rent a smaller house than this on the outskirts of the village.

I shall now end the letter and start my Christmas preparations. I'm looking forward very much to seeing you then for more than just a few hours.

Your loving sister,
Elinor

19

December 1837

*I*n the middle of December, John Marley rushed down to the kitchen, waving a sheet of paper. 'Agnes, Agnes, listen to this!' He beamed at her as he read aloud:

> *My dear Mr Marley,*
> *Thank you for your recent communication. I am interested in discussing matters further and wonder if you could oblige me by coming down to London within the next week? I consider it urgent to find a new parson for my little parish, but even more important to find the right sort of person.*
>
> *I shall be here in London for the next two weeks. You have only to arrive and I shall see you within the day. Your expenses for this trip will, of course, be reimbursed, whatever the outcome.*
>
> > *Yours sincerely,*
> > *William Roysby*

'There, what do you think of that?'

'I think it sounds very promising, sir.'

'I shall go to London immediately, Agnes, immediately.'

Then he realised that she had been weeping and his face lost its glow. 'Bad news from Jessie?'

'No, sir. I just miss her - worry about her. And I can't

write what I feel. So I seem to be – cut off.'

Within the hour he was clattering down the stairs again. 'Agnes, Agnes, I've got a wonderful idea.' He rushed across to seize her hands, flour-covered as they were. 'Why don't you come to London with me? Then you can go and see your daughter while I meet Mr Roysby.'

She could only goggle at him.

'Do say yes! I can't bear to see you so unhappy.'

'I – yes.'

He waltzed her around the room, then blushed and let her go. 'Oh, I'm sorry. I was so excited. But you will come?'

'Yes, I will.' The thought terrified her, but if it meant she would see Jessie, see for herself that even though her daughter was far away, Jared was still treating her right, well, she would walk barefoot through hell itself. Then she noticed his hands and tutted. 'Look at you, sir. Flour everywhere. Let me get a damp cloth. I'll soon have it off your clothes.'

He watched fondly as she sponged him down. 'You're very good to me, Agnes.'

She flushed slightly. 'Well, you've been a good master to me, sir.'

'I wish you'd call me John.'

'I've told you before: it wouldn't be right.' She took a step back. 'There. You go and write back to Mr Roysby. It'll take us a day or two to sort things out for our journey.'

Ten days before Christmas, the gig from the local inn drew up in front of the camp shop and Agnes Burton got down from it, skirts gathered up to avoid the mud, sharp eyes missing nothing of the squalor around her. She paused for a moment, then tutted softly to herself at the chaos she saw. 'You keep an eye on that basket!' she told the lad who'd driven her over, and then she marched into the shop.

Standing in the doorway, unnoticed by Jessie, she watched as her daughter weighed some potatoes, gave a woman her change and put a leering man smartly in his place. Then Jessie saw her.

'*Mother!*' she shrieked, dropping the piece of cheese she was holding and pushing through the group of gaping customers. 'Mother! However did you get here?' She kissed the cheek that was offered and hugged her mother twice for good measure. 'Goodness, I never thought to see you down here in Hertfordshire!'

Agnes gave Jessie's cheek a quick, dry peck in return. 'If the mountain can't come to Mahomet, then Mahomet must come to the mountain, as Mr Marley would say.'

'He's not here, too?'

'Of course not!'

'Then how did you . . . ?' As far as she knew, her mother had never taken a holiday, never left Hettonby since they first arrived there, except for an occasional day's shopping in Leeds.

'It's a long story. Can you leave things here for a while so that we can talk? I wouldn't normally interrupt your work, but . . .'

'But this is special. I can't tell you how glad I am to see you, Mother. It's a wonderful surprise. Absolutely wonderful.'

'Could you get an hour off?'

'Oh, yes. And we can go and talk in the back.' Jessie became suddenly aware that all commerce had stopped in the shop and that everyone was watching and listening to her and her mother with great interest.

'I'd like to get my things from the gig first.' Agnes went outside, took a well-laden basket off the gig and turned to the lad. 'You're to return for me at four – sharp on the hour, mind.'

'Yes, ma'am.' But his eyes were on the camp, which his mother hadn't let him visit before. Now he'd have a few tales to tell the other lads.

Jessie introduced her mother to George Snader, then led the way into the back room. 'You sit down and I'll make us a nice cup of tea.'

But Agnes wouldn't sit down until she'd examined the living arrangements. Then, she took one of the chairs and watched Jessie putting the kettle on the stove and getting out the best teacups. 'You look well, love.' Her voice was softer than usual.

'I am well.' Jessie had never felt so well in all her life.

'You're not – er – not . . . ?' Mrs Burton patted her stomach suggestively.

'No, I'm not having a baby.' Jessie resigned herself to a

catechism about their life and prospects. 'I told you, Jared's careful. We don't want a family yet.'

'Well, that's something in his favour,' allowed Mrs Burton. 'Rosie Plumworthy had hers seven months to the day after they got wed. Said it came early, but it's a great big boy.' As she drank her tea, she passed on all the news from Hettonby, interspersing it with comments and questions about life in the camp.

'How on earth do you manage to get your washing done?'

'I manage.'

'Isn't it noisy at nights? I don't like the look of those women in the shop. Proper slatterns, they look.'

'They're all right. They don't give me any trouble.' Jessie waited for an explanation for this visit, but it didn't come.

'We'd better unpack that basket. I brought you a few things from Hettonby.'

'A Christmas cake. Oh, Mother! It's exactly what I want. I haven't got a proper oven.'

'It's been soaked in port wine. Better than brandy, I always think. So it'll keep.'

'And jars of your jam!' Jessie picked up the last one and beamed. 'Is this your rum butter? I've been telling Jared about that. Mother, you're too good to us.' She knew that the love Agnes Burton could never put into words was shown in the presents she gave and the things she did for her daughter. When the basket was empty, Jessie asked softly, 'Now, are you going to tell me why you came here?'

Agnes started fiddling with the edge of the tablecloth. 'Well, Parson was coming down to London, so when he suggested I come too, I thought, why shouldn't I? I – I've been worried about you, love.'

'No need. But I'm glad you came. What's Mr Marley doing in London?'

'Seeing about a new living. A Mr Roysby has one vacant, but nothing's certain yet, just a possibility.'

'So how long can you stay here?'

'Two days. I came down on the coach from Leeds with Parson – I'd have been afraid of travelling so far on my own – and I'm to go back with him.' For some reason, she blushed, but her daughter didn't notice. 'I've taken a room at the inn in Willingdon.'

'Then I'll arrange to have tomorrow off and come over to spend the day with you.'

'I don't want you upsetting that nice Mr Snader.'

'I won't upset anyone.' Jessie hid a smile at that description of a man who would do anything for money, a man who was the camp's main pimp and moneylender – and who knew what else besides? – for all his affability.

The next day, while Jessie and her mother were strolling round the pretty little market town, John Marley was being interviewed about the living.

After an hour's chat, William Roysby sat back and frowned. 'I'm going to be frank with you, Marley.'

John looked at him anxiously. Was something wrong? He had thought the interview to be proceeding well.

'You've got sound views and a reasonably modern attitude, but – '

John tensed.

'I always prefer a married man. There are tasks women do better than men – dealing with women parishioners in certain circumstances.'

'Oh.'

'You've never been married?'

'No. I was engaged once, but she died.' Goodness, how long ago that all seemed now!

'Don't mean to pry, but I think this is important. No one else you're interested in at the moment?'

John looked down at his lap, surprised to see a sudden vision of Agnes as she had looked the night her daughter had escaped from the Hall, or the night Jessie got married, when she had wept on his shoulder. She had been his housekeeper for a long time, but it seemed as if he had only got to know her properly in the past few months. 'Well,' he said cautiously, then broke off, struggling for words.

Roysby nodded encouragingly. 'Go on.'

John stared across at him. He liked this man. Really liked him.

And the thought of going back to live under Lord Morrisham's thumb was repugnant to him after his hopes of finding another living had been raised so high. 'There is someone I've grown fond of. I've been thinking of – of saying something, but I haven't spoken to her – and it's all – well, still up in the air.'

Roysby smiled. He could recognise a shy man when he met one, and also one with sound morals. 'Suppose you go back and talk to her, ask her to marry you? If she says yes, the living is yours and a pretty house to go with it.'

'Oh.'

'Unless you're no longer interested?'

'Oh, I am. Very much.'

Mr Roysby stood up. 'You go back and ask her to marry you, then. A good wife is a treasure, John Marley. And a necessity for the incumbent of Shilwick.'

Bemused, John left the house, but didn't go straight back to the hotel. Cold as it was, he strolled round the streets for a long time, lost in his thoughts.

As Agnes and her employer sat in the coach, travelling back to Hettonby, she could see that he had something on his mind.

'You said yesterday you might have got the living. When will you know?' she ventured, as they were stretching their legs in a village street while the horses were being changed.

'I may have got it. There are certain conditions to be fulfilled first.' He looked round in irritation as the coachman sounded his horn to warn them to get back on board. 'I'm beginning to think those railways are a good idea,' he grumbled, as they took their places. 'I'd forgotten how uncomfortable travelling is.'

'But worth it,' she said with a soft smile. 'I needed to see my Jessie, make sure that he was treating her right. I feel a lot better about her now.'

He patted her hand. 'I'm glad about that, Agnes.' Then he looked down at their joined hands, felt the interested gaze of the old woman sitting opposite them and blushed.

When they got back to Hettonby the next day, both of them were tired and hungry. Agnes bustled about getting a meal ready, while he went upstairs to his room, to pace up and down and worry about how to approach her. In the end, when they had eaten their meal in the kitchen and she was about to clear up, he said, 'Please leave that for a moment, Agnes. I really do need to speak to you.'

She saw how agitated he was and her heart sank. What was wrong? Could he not take her with him to the next living? The mere thought of finding herself a new post made her shiver. She'd got out of the habit of dealing with the world - well, she'd never got into it, really. Mellersley, where she'd grown up, had been as small as Hettonby. And she didn't want to leave John. She'd miss him quite dreadfully. But she told herself that if he did tell her he no longer needed her services, she must be brave. He'd give her a good reference, she was sure, and she had some money saved. She sat down by the table and folded her shaking hands in her lap.

'Now - ' He took a deep breath. Heavens, this was so difficult! 'I'll ask you not to say anything until I've finished, Agnes. It's - this is hard to say. I'm not good at this sort of thing.'

He *is* going to give me notice, she thought, and was surprised by how much that hurt. She bent her head over her hands, so that he should not see the fear in her eyes.

'Mr Roysby is only willing to give me the living if I am married. And - and I can quite see his point. So - '

Who is it? she wondered in amazement. Why, he never sees any women in that way. Not that some haven't tried to catch him, but he's not shown the slightest interest.

' - well, I have decided to take his advice. If - if the lady is willing.' He took another deep breath and began to pace up and down the room. 'I did wonder once or twice about getting married when I was younger. I was even engaged once, but she died suddenly, poor girl.' He couldn't even remember Joanna's face clearly now. 'But lately - well, I've been feeling very - lonely. Yes, lonely. And you - you've been very kind to me, letting me eat in the kitchen with you, learning to play chess with me - ' His voice faltered to a halt and so did his steps.

Now she was utterly bewildered.

He stopped in front of her, took a deep breath and said rapidly, 'In short, my dear Agnes, I wonder if you will do me the honour of becoming my wife?'

If the devil himself had risen from the floor, horns and tail and all, Agnes could not have been more surprised. There was total silence in the kitchen, then she heard him gulp, saw how his hands were shaking. Why, he's terrified, she realised, and tried to bridge the great echoing space between them. 'I – don't know what to say. You've taken me by surprise.'

Agitation showed in every line of his body, every twitch of his limbs. 'Yes. Yes, indeed. I've – I've taken myself by surprise, too.' He sucked in more air and said in another rush of words, 'And it's not just because of the new living, my dear Agnes, you must never think that. It's because – because I respect you – and like you. I get lonely sometimes – and I'm getting on and – and ... ' His voice faltered away.

She could not bear his faltering anguish and took charge, as she had been taking charge of people of her own class for years. 'Sit down here, John Marley.'

He sat, looking at her, his eyes pleading as much as his words had. She hadn't said no, at least. 'I know I'm getting on – a bit older than you, I think. But we deal comfortably together, don't we?'

She had a sudden vision of her husband, Frank, the first time they had made love, then she dismissed the vision angrily. Yes, Frank had been handsome, had made her bones turn to jelly – and look where it had led. John Marley would never make her thrill with excitement, but perhaps ... 'I'm not a lady,' she said abruptly. 'You'd be marrying out of your class.'

'I've always been a bit afraid of ladies. You see, my mother died when I was very young and I had only a brother, so I grew up in a house of men. And then I went to school, so I – I never quite learned how to get on with ladies.'

'Folk might think the worse of you for marrying your housekeeper.'

'I shouldn't care about that and I'd never let anyone speak ill of you.' He looked at her sideways and added humbly, 'I'd really like to marry you, Agnes.' Never to sit alone in the evening, wondering how to fill the empty hours. To have someone to talk to at every meal, someone who belonged to him.

'I don't know whether I should – but then who's to say what's right or wrong?'

He jerked out of his chair and came to kneel awkwardly beside her, taking her hand in his. 'Agnes, does that mean you're thinking about accepting my offer?'

She stretched out one hand to pat his cheek and say softly, 'Get up, do, John. It isn't fitting for you to kneel to me like that.'

He seemed surprised to realise where he was, then got up, but still kept hold of her hand.

Eh, she thought, he's a boy still in so many ways. And to think of him feeling lonely all these years, and me sitting on my own down here, feeling the same.

His voice was wistful. 'You haven't said no, at least.'

She smiled. 'Of course I haven't. I'm very flattered. And – and I like you, too. But a change like that – well, it takes some thinking about.'

Hesitantly, he pulled her up and towards him, planting a clumsy kiss on her cheek, then, growing bolder, placing another on her lips, equally boyish and clumsy.

Agnes felt warmth run through her. It had been so long, so very long. Frank would have had his hand up her skirt by now, but this man was so shy, so fumbling, that her heart went out to him. She put her arms round his neck and smiled encouragingly.

His answering smile was full of relief as he hugged her to him. 'Oh, Agnes, I do hope you'll say yes.'

She laid her head on his shoulder with a sigh and they stood there for a few moments, holding one another close, both feeling utterly moved by the sensation of another body, another person caring about them. At last she broke the silence. 'Before we decide anything, John, I think you should write to your new employer and tell him – tell him my background. That I'm your house-keeper.'

'He made no stipulations about the type of wife I should marry.'

'Nonetheless, it'd only be fair, don't you think? For I'm not a lady and never will be, and I'm no good at pretending.'

And then he surprised her again. 'No, I shan't do that. Definitely not. If you're the wife of my choice, that must be good enough for Roysby. Otherwise I'll seek a new living elsewhere. Only I can choose the woman I want to marry. And that's you.'

Tears filled Agnes's eyes. To hear him speak of her like that, to hear the respect in his voice, made her feel suddenly precious – and loved. She blinked at him in astonishment. He was just seeking a marriage of convenience, surely? When she saw how warmly, if still shyly, he was looking at her, something inside her which had been frozen for years began to thaw. She could not speak, could not think clearly. But she knew that she did want to marry him. Oh, she did! Only – would it be fair to him? He was a gentleman and she was just a servant.

She looked down at the floor, then up at John, shaking her head. 'I can't decide all at once. There's a lot to be thought of. It'd be such a big change.'

'But you haven't said no. You are considering my proposal? Seriously?'

She smiled at him, a soft smile, so unlike her usual self that he was delighted and took heart.

'Yes, John, I am considering your proposal. Very seriously.'

He patted her shoulder. 'Then take as long as you wish, my dear. But remember – I shall be hoping you will accept my offer, for believe me, I do want to marry you. Only it took Mr Roysby's saying I needed a wife to make me realise it. I'm a stupid sort of fellow, really. About things like that, anyway. Always have been.'

'I think you're a lovely fellow.'

He blushed bright red.

When he had gone Agnes sat for a long time, staring into the flames of the kitchen fire. Then the clock struck and she jumped to her feet. She was an hour past her usual bedtime and stiff with weariness. But as she walked upstairs and got ready, as she lay down in her soft feather bed, the smile still lingered on her face. And she looked more like her daughter than ever before.

Almost before they knew it in the Willingdon diggings, Christmas was upon them. There was only another month or so's work and then they would all have to move to another camp.

The contractors were to pay out on the twenty-fourth of December and most of the men would no doubt go on a gigantic randy that would last for two or three days, and for which George would supply the ale and gin. Jessie and Jared decided to give a little party on Christmas Day, to which they invited George

Snader, Mary and her two children, and the Smalls with theirs.

They were all worried about Bessie. She'd had her baby, a boy, but it had been sickly and had lived for less than a week. Since then she had fretted and pined, convinced that this tragedy wouldn't have happened if they lived in a proper cottage and led a normal life – though that was, of course, nonsense, for farm cottages were often damp and unhealthy.

Alfred's work had inevitably been affected. Jessie helped them as much as she could, out of pity for their sadness, but it seemed to be a losing battle. The two other children grew steadily more neglected, as did Bessie, and the place they were living in was downright dirty nowadays. Alfred had aged five years in three months, losing the last of his youthfulness in his worry over his wife and family.

Jared hadn't Jessie's tolerance, or maybe he had seen too many other men come and go to spare any sympathy for this one. 'You'll do no good,' he warned her when she tried to help. 'There's some like that. They're born to lose, whatever they do. You'll not change things.'

'I thought he was your friend. Don't you *care* what happens to him?'

'I care as much as I can. But this is no job for weaklings an' you should know that by now, love. If he doesn't look after himself better an' stop that woman of his from frettin', then Alfred'll be no good to anyone, an' that's a fact.'

'Well, I think it's a shame!' she protested. 'And if I can help Bessie, I shall.'

'If you can make Bessie Small pull herself together, it'll be a bloody miracle,' he growled. 'An' you've got enough on your own plate without takin' on anyone else's troubles.' He hated to see how tired she was some evenings.

'Am I not looking after you properly, Jared Wilde?' she flung at him, hands on hips, eyes flashing.

'Aye.'

'And am I not looking after the shop properly?'

'Aye. You know you are.' Just as he knew when he was beaten. He'd not be able to stop her doing this, but she was heading for heartbreak. And she was getting all too attached to Bessie's youngest child. In fact, she seemed fond of children generally and often slipped them a titbit when they came into the shop, or stopped to talk to the little ones as they played nearby. She'd make a wonderful mother one day.

She linked her arm in his. 'You leave Bessie to me. We'll have them over for Christmas dinner *and* we'll do it properly, with oranges for the children, *and* we'll have Mary and her children too!'

After that he gave up trying to reason with her and left her to do as she wanted.

But he was proved right when, in spite of all Jessie's efforts, the Smalls left the railways in the spring to go and work on a farm. And it hurt Jessie to see them go, as if she had failed, somehow.

Twelfth Night was the date set for Susannah's wedding. She endured the preparations stolidly, spoke politely to Peter Bowers when he visited – though she could not hide her shudders of revulsion at his touch. Once he whispered how much he was longing to show her there was no need to be afraid of him, but his eyes weren't kind, only gloating.

Perhaps he was like her father – the two of them seemed to get on very well. Or perhaps he only cared about the dowry she would bring. What did it matter anyway? She had told herself she would never leap from the frying pan into the fire by marrying a man like her father, but here she was, being pushed into the heart of the same fire and utterly helpless to prevent it.

Her mother never mentioned the beating, but then, her mother always tried to ignore unpleasantness. Thinking about it, the newly mature Susannah realised it was probably the only way Adelaide Morrisham managed to endure her life.

Christmas passed in an unhappy blur. When the day of her wedding arrived, Susannah felt so panic-stricken that she lay feigning sleep for a long time after the maid had come in and lit the fire. She felt cold and alone, and underneath it all afraid of what would happen that night.

Eventually Tess, who was maiding her now, but who was too subservient for her taste, tapped on the door and came in. 'Oh, you are awake. You'll need to be getting up now, miss, if we're to get you ready on time. I'll bring your breakfast up, shall I? Cook has everything ready and your father said it was all right.'

'I don't want anything.' But the breakfast arrived anyway, a tray filled with enough food for a whole family. Susannah picked at it, threw some of it in the fire surreptitiously, so that it'd look as if she'd eaten, then rang for Tess again.

Her father was waiting for her when she walked downstairs, clad in her satin and lace, with the full flounced skirts making a swishing noise and the sleeves so fashionably wide that she felt as if she had been stuffed like a capon for the table. He stood squarely in the middle of the hall, studying her and looking so big and red-faced that he seemed like a stranger.

He frowned. 'You look pale, girl. Haven't you got any rouge?'

'No.'

'Has your mother?'

She shrugged.

He took her arm in a tight grasp that hurt, and shook her hard. 'Not going to make any trouble, are you? Because if so, I'd advise you to think again. If you do one thing untoward today, your mother will suffer as well as you.'

He was breathing fast, as if he'd run a race, and his complexion grew even darker as he spoke.

When he let go of her arm, she took a step backwards and tried to smooth the creased satin. 'I shall do nothing to cause trouble. It's too late for that now, anyway.'

'Good. Young Bowers and I had a nice chat last night. I explained that you can be a little flighty, that you need a firm hand.' He grinned at her horrified expression. 'You don't think I'd give one of my daughters to a soft idle fellow, do you? You're the first to go and it's a useful match. From now on, I'll be investing in the Bowers mills and should get a good return for my money there. When Amy is old enough, I'll find someone suitable for her, too.'

Susannah felt sick to the pit of her stomach. What had he been saying? Surely Peter wouldn't take too much notice of her father? If she had thought she'd succeed, she would have run away before now, but where could she go that he would not be able to follow?

And how would she be able to live? She was as much a prisoner in this luxury as the meanest felon in a prison.

The journey to church passed all too quickly. The small building was crowded with people, who all turned round to peer at Susannah as she stood at the end of the aisle. When the organ music changed, her father tugged at her arm and they set off towards the front of the church, where Peter stood waiting, a smug smile on his face.

Halfway down the aisle, her father stopped and grunted, as if in pain.

Susannah looked sideways at him, surprised, but he shook his head and started walking again.

As they came to a halt next to Peter, her father grunted again, clutched at his chest and fell sprawling at her feet.

Behind her Susannah could hear a buzz of voices as she took a step backwards, moving her white kid boot away from his still, outflung hand. Peter bent quickly over her father, stood up again, and gestured to his own father to join him. She could only watch in frozen hope. Was he? Oh, dear Lord, let him be dead!

Mr Bowers knelt beside her father, the parson joining him, and the two of them shook their heads. As they stood up, Mr Bowers turned to her and said gently, 'He's dead, I'm afraid, Susannah. You must be very brave.'

A muffled shriek from her mother brought Susannah out of her shock and she moved across to sit in the front pew beside her, stepping carefully around her father's body with its dreadful staring face.

'What shall we do?' moaned Adelaide. 'Whatever shall we do now?'

Mr Bowers came and leaned over to whisper, 'If I may advise, my dear lady. We can halt the ceremony for a few moments while your husband's body is carried away, then I think we should continue with the wedding service. You will need your son-in-law beside you to help you through the next few days.'

Susannah shook her mother's arm and said, 'No!' in a very loud voice.

Adelaide let out a mew of surprise.

Susannah spoke very loudly and clearly. 'I shan't be marrying your son now, Mr Bowers.'

He began to look angry and menacing. 'What do you mean by that, young woman?'

She looked beyond him to Peter and made sure that her voice carried across the whole church. 'Were you looking forward to having a reluctant bride, Peter? One who had to be beaten into accepting you? Well, God has spared me that, at least.'

There were gasps and exclamations from the congregation behind her and the air was suddenly charged with tension.

Peter's face might have been graven of stone. 'You're not thinking clearly, my dear.' He stepped forward and tried to take her arm.

She slapped his hand away. 'I'm not marrying you, not now and not ever. Mother, come home with me. I'll see to everything and look after you.'

Adelaide hesitated and glanced at Mr Bowers and his son. 'But – '

Susannah shook her mother's arm, terrified she would hand them all into another man's power. 'Mother, this is your one chance to live a peaceful and happy life,' she hissed. 'Don't waste it.'

The church was filled with whispers, rustles of silk and tiny movements, none of them loud enough to prevent people from hearing what was said at the front.

Susannah stood up and pushed Peter away, taking him by surprise. 'Come on, Mother. Let's go home. I'll help you and – '

Mr Bowers grabbed her arm and swung her round. She screamed, deliberately. 'Oh! You're hurting me!'

One of their neighbours stepped forward, her friend Deborah's father. 'Susannah, is this true? Have you been forced to agree to this – this wedding?' His daughter had hinted as much, but he had not believed her, not wanted to believe that Morrisham could have been so cruel.

She turned to him gratefully, beating at Mr Bowers's arm. 'Yes. And I'm afraid now that Mr Bowers will try to make me continue this farce.'

'Why didn't you tell anyone?'

'What could you have done while my father was alive?'

He moved to her mother's side. 'Lady Morrisham, please allow me to help you to your carriage. And if there's anything else I can do to assist in this sad time, you have only to ask.'

Susannah did the asking. 'Would you come home with us now, Mr Grevney, and make sure that Mr Bowers and his son leave without . . .' she allowed a sob to escape and dabbed at her eyes, '. . . without trying to force me into anything?'

Mr Bowers moved closer to Mr Grevney and said in a low voice, 'She's hysterical. You shouldn't believe a word she says.'

'All the more reason,' Mr Grevney said quietly, 'to leave her to recover quietly.'

'Everything's been arranged, all the papers signed!'

'They can be unsigned, then.'

As she followed her mother and Mr Grevney down the aisle, Susannah turned round. 'I'll have your things brought to the front door of the house, Mr Bowers.' Then she walked out of the church.

She had never felt so happy in the whole of her life! Never! And she was going to make sure that her mother did not weaken and do anything to jeopardise that happiness. In fact – she dabbed at her eyes again to hide a smile – she was going to become the most devoted daughter the world had ever known. At thirteen, her brother Donald was too young to take over anything yet. By the time he reached his majority, she would have made a new life for herself. And that would not include a husband like Peter Bowers.

20

20

January 1838

The job at Willingdon lasted until the end of January. There were no more deaths and only a few routine injuries on the diggings, but there was another unpleasant randy that delayed the work. Simon Stafford was furious with the contractors in charge of that section for paying so irregularly.

'They're too blind to see beyond the ends of their noses!' he raged, surveying the havoc caused by the too-long-delayed payday. 'I've told them a dozen times to pay the men weekly, but they won't listen to me!' He looked at Jared. 'I don't blame you for making money out of it with your lending, but if I had my way, that'd not be necessary.'

Jared was not in the least offended. 'It's not my favourite way of earnin' brass, but better me than George Snader, eh? And just at present, me an' Jessie'll turn our hands to owt that's goin'. I'm not havin' her workin' in that shop forever, but now's the time to set ourselves up for life.'

'Where are you going after this?'

'Up the line, wherever there's work.'

'But no definite plans yet?'

'No, Mr Stafford. It's mostly a matter of chance. You hear of a good place an' you go there to look it over. They say the Pensworth cutting should be a good bet for a long job. I were thinkin' of tryin' there. I've got a fair old gang together now an' most of 'em'll probably stick with me. But that'd mean giving up the shop.'

'Don't decide anything just yet. I may know of something better.'

Simon's tone was casual, but Jared could see that this was important to him, for his body fairly radiated tension.

'I'll be coming back next week, Wilde. Can you wait until then to decide?'

'Aye. There'll be a couple of weeks' work here for us yet. I'll tell the lads I'm on to something an'· they'll leave it to me. They always do.'

Simon Stafford returned the next week with an air of suppressed excitement, but he contained himself until the day's work and inspections were over. 'All right if I pop round to see you tonight, Jared? I've got some things to clear up first. Say in half an hour?'

'Fine by me.'

He was round as arranged and left his cup of tea untasted on the table so eager was he to tell Jared and Jessie what it was all about. 'Working on the railways is good, steady work for an engineer, but that's not where the real money lies, is it, Jared?'

'No. It's the contractors an' sub-contractors who make the most money.' Jared drained his mug of tea and held it out to Jessie for a refill. She poured it quickly, anxious not to miss anything.

'You're right there,' Simon was saying. 'So – I've decided to become a sub-contractor myself.' He hadn't even told his sister yet, because he didn't want her to know the risks he was taking until he'd managed one successful contract, however small. He did not intend to let her finance him.

There was still a coolness between them, something that only time would dispel. But Thirza had had no right to write to him like that. Elinor *wasn't* fretting to move back near their old home or she wouldn't have moved into the new house. She was probably just missing Miss Butterfield, which was only to be expected. She'd soon find herself some other interests and he liked the thought of her still being near Squire Butterfield, for he knew that kindly man would keep an eye on her and help her if she were ever in need.

Now he went on with his explanation to Jared. 'It's not a big contract, mind, just a small sub-contract. I haven't enough money to finance a larger one yet. But it should bring in a tidy profit – as much in three months as I'd normally make in three years.' A trace of anxiety crept into his voice. 'It'll take all I have in the world,' and how painfully he had saved it, almost shilling by shilling at first, adding it to what little was left from selling Elinor's jewels, 'but I've surveyed that stretch of line several times and I don't think there are likely to be any snags. It's a cutting on the Rotherham to Sheffield line. It should be a fairly straight-forward job.'

'Sounds reasonable,' said Jared non-committally.

'I think it's a good chance for me,' said Simon seriously. 'The thing is,' he paused and looked at Jared, 'would you like to come and work on it with me?'

'It's a long way to go for me and the lads for a short job. We've just come down from Yorkshire. I was thinking there'd be more work in the south.'

'There might be more opportunity for advancement in the north, though.'

'Advancement, eh? What exactly do you mean by that?'

'I mean, I'd like you to become my overseer and general assistant on this project. I'll be running it myself, but I'll need someone I can trust to keep an eye on the everyday work and to be there if I get called away. I shall be doing some other work for the same company.' Needed to, to cover his own expenses.

Jessie held her breath. Overseer! This would be another step up for Jared. She looked at him sharply. Why wasn't he answering? Why didn't he accept the offer straight away?

Jared's expression registered nothing more than polite interest. 'Well now,' he said slowly, 'that might be worth a try. What were you thinkin' of payin'?'

Simon took a deep breath. 'A pound a week and a percentage of the profits.'

'Why, Jared's earning more than that now!' exclaimed Jessie indignantly.

'Shut up, Jessie!' said Jared quietly and she did so at once. She knew that tone of voice, as did his men.

'What percentage an' what are the profits likely t'be?' he asked, still in that calm tone of voice.

'I stand to make about four hundred pounds, more if we finish the contract early because there's a bonus offered. I was thinking of offering you five per cent . . . ?'

'Ten!' said Jared. 'I'll earn it. We'll get that bonus.'

Simon hesitated. He had not intended to offer that much. 'Seven?' he suggested.

'Ten. I'll not come for less. It's only a short job an' then we'll have to move on again. The lads don't like that.'

Another pause, then: 'All right. Ten.'

Jared allowed the smile that had been hovering to settle briefly on his face. 'Don't worry, Mr Stafford, I'll earn it.'

Jessie let out the breath she'd been holding while the bargaining was going on. She watched the two men shake hands and hid her excitement until she could be alone with her husband.

'What about my gang?' Jared asked then.

'Your gang? But you can hardly run a gang as well as act as overseer! No one can be in two places at once!' Simon protested.

Jessie held her breath. Could this mean the end of their association with Joe? Oh, please, let it be so!

'Oh, there'll be no problem about that. Joe'll run the gang for me. They're a grand team of lads an' I'd not like to lose them now. Besides, I want something to fall back on if this doesn't work out.'

Jessie's heart plummeted and all the brightness went out of the moment. She closed her eyes and bit her lip to prevent herself from crying out in protest.

'Usual terms for the gang?' Jared was asking.

'Yes. Payable weekly.'

'Weekly? That'll make a nice change!'

'You know what I think about holding back the men's pay. I've seen the results of their going on a randy. I can't afford that on my cutting. If we're to get that bonus, we'll need to work every day we can – though it's another place where they fuss about Sundays, unfortunately.'

'An' what about a camp shop?'

Jessie turned her head sharply to watch Simon's face.

'Shop? It's not going to be a big camp. No more than fifty men. I hadn't thought we'd need a shop. There's a village only a mile away.'

'Tired men don't want to walk a mile at the end of the day for a loaf or a jug of ale. And they won't be welcome in the village anyway. Besides, why should other folk make profits when we could do that ourselves?'

'And the women won't be welcome in the village during the day, either,' put in Jessie, quick to see the opportunity and follow Jared's lead. This time he didn't stop her speaking, just gave her a sly wink. 'We won't need something like Snader's store, but I could run a small place for you – buy stuff from the local farmers and sell it in the camp.'

Jared sat back and watched her make short work of convincing Simon Stafford, first that they needed a small camp shop, and second that she was the one to run it.

When their visitor had gone, Jared picked Jessie up and swung her round jubilantly. 'This is it!' he cried. 'This is *our* big chance as well as his, love! Oh, he's a good engineer and he'll do a proper job on that cuttin', but he doesn't see the little opportunities to make a bit more money. If I were in his place as sub-contractor – an' I will be one day! – I'd be runnin' a shop myself. There's a nice, steady profit to be made in a shop. An' I've a few other ideas too. What about an ale hut, where the men can go an' have a drink or two of an evening? We'll get someone in to run it for us, but *we* can supply the ale and take most of the profits.' He laughed aloud. 'This is it! Our chance.'

'Oh, Jared, I'm so proud of you! *Overseer!* Just wait till I write to my mother!' A thoughtful look crossed her face. 'I wonder where exactly this cutting is? My mother came from that part of Yorkshire.'

'Have you still got family there?'

'Oh, no. All her family are dead and I don't know anything at all about my father's side, though they came from the south, I think.' She fell silent, then looked up and beamed at him. 'I'm proud of you, love! So very proud.'

He gathered her close to him, rocking her slightly. 'Eh, Jessie, my love, I'm glad I met you that day. With you by my side I can do anythin'!'

She nestled against him. '*We* can do anything,' she amended.

His laughter rang softly in her ear. 'Aye, we can that!' He held her at arm's length suddenly. 'But one day, Jessie Wilde, you'll live like a lady in a house of your own. You'll not always have to work so hard. Then we'll have our family. Sons I want – but they'll not be navvies! They'll go to proper schools an' they'll grow up to be gentlemen.'

'We'll see about that.' She didn't even want an idle life, but she didn't spoil his moment by saying that.

The next day a letter arrived from Jessie's mother, as terse as all her others, but its contents made Jessie cry out in amazement.

Jared, who'd brought the letter from the village, turned round in the doorway. 'Is owt wrong?'

'Not – not wrong. Jared . . . oh, I can hardly believe it, but my mother's going to marry Parson Marley. And she wants us to – to go back to Hettonby for the wedding.'

'She's going to *wed* him!' He chuckled. 'Eh, I don't think I envy either of 'em. They're both a bit set in their ways. Still, she'll be all right now for the rest of her life.'

'And there's more. Jared, Lord Morrisham's dead. He dropped dead at Susannah's wedding.' Jessie gasped and could not speak for a moment.

'Well?'

'When he died she stopped the wedding, Miss Susannah did, and refused to get married – my mother says she told everyone in the church that she'd been forced into it.'

'I bet that caused a fuss?'

'Poor Miss Susannah. Still, it's an ill wind. I do hope she's happy now. Well, what a letter!' Jessie re-read it, but it was infuriatingly brief and didn't give any more details. 'Jared, is it possible – can we get back for my mother's wedding? I do want to be there.'

'When is it?'

'In two weeks.'

He wanted to say no, but one look at her face and he changed his mind. 'We might be able to fit in a quick visit. We'll talk about it tonight. I've got to get back to the lads now.' Well, he thought as he strode across the diggings, what next?

A few miles away, Simon also was reading the news about

Susannah Morrisham in a letter from his sister. He whistled in amazement as he read it. Who'd have thought that little Susannah had it in her to cause such a fuss? Still, Elinor sounded happy to be in touch with her again, and anything that made Elinor happy pleased him. Except, a little voice whispered, her moving to Heptonstall. But he didn't listen to that voice. In her letter Elinor sounded just like her old self, so she'd obviously forgiven him and settled down at Yettley.

During the next two weeks Jessie watched Jared grow in stature and confidence, like a flower that had been waiting tightly curled in its bud for a sunny day. She began to think that even she had underestimated her husband's potential. He gathered his gang together one night, furnishing them with a few jugs of ale, and put it to them that they should all stay together and go north to work on Mr Stafford's new contract near Rotherham.

As usual, it was Billy who voiced their feelings. 'Aw, Jared, we've just come down from the soddin' north!'

'An' it's winter. It'll be even colder up there,' London Harry complained.

'Freezes your piss before it hits the ground up there,' Bull growled.

Joe just blinked, looked sideways at the others and took a slow pull at his ale.

Jared's voice was calm, but persuasive. 'But we'll be the leading gang at the diggings an' the rest of 'em will have to work our way. If you stick with me, lads, you'll all be running gangs of your own before we're done.'

Billy was still sulky. 'Who's to look after us, if you're turning into a bleedin' overseer? I don't want the job, thank you very much.'

'I thought Joe might do it.'

There was absolute silence for a moment while all heads turned to stare at Joe, who just stared back with a wooden expression on his face. Jared had already spoken to him, and he'd said he'd consider it. But he still wasn't sure.

'He's a bloody hard worker, I'll give him that,' Billy admitted, nodding at Joe. 'But it takes more nor muscles to lead a gang. An' he'll have t'stay off the booze.'

Bull pulled at his whiskers, as he did when thinking hard. 'Joe saw the problem with that soft patch an' he sorted that out all right.'

Heads nodded.

'Oh, hell,' said Red Mike, 'we could give him a chance. I certainly don't want to do it.'

'Nor me.'

'What do you say, Joe lad?' Jared asked quietly.

'I'm still not sure about becomin' a bleedin' ganger.' He grinned at the men around him. 'An' anyway, who wants to take on a scruffy lot like you?'

There was a chorus of ribald calls and suggestions.

Jared watched carefully as Joe took the ribbing in good part. 'Well, think about it now, will you? We need to make a quick decision. You've been workin' on diggings for how long? Ten, twenty year?'

Joe nodded. 'About that. More nor twenty, I reckon.'

'An' you've still got all your fingers and thumbs.' Jared grinned at Billy as he spoke and Billy made a rude sign with one hand, but grinned back.

Joe seemed mildly surprised at this question and peered down at his hairy hands and stubby, dirt-encrusted fingers. He spread them out. Big hands. Scarred but intact. 'Aye, well, I see no need to act stupid.'

Jared waited patiently for that comment to sink in and for the others to nod their agreement. 'So we'll all think about it, eh? About Joe becoming ganger – but still under me?'

'Aw, hell, why not do it, Joe?' Bull demanded, grabbing the nearest jug of ale and sloshing some more into his pot. 'An' if you'll still be around, Big Jared, you'll be able to tuck us up in our beds every night like you do now.'

They roared with laughter and then raised a cheer for Big Jared and swore they'd go with him to hell itself.

When they had all left, Joe lingered behind to speak to Jared. 'Seems like Mr Stafford's not the only one as is goin' to do well for hisself.'

With the older man squinting at him out of his little piggy eyes, Jared took the opportunity to set a few ground rules. 'I've offered you this opportunity, Joe, but you'll be out on your ear if you muck it up. No more randying an' fighting. An' remember – I've trained my lads to work quickly *and* safely. We've got ourselves a name for doin' a good job an' I want it to stay that way. Most of the lads have been with me for two years now an' we've never been short of work. That was why you came in with us, wasn't it? You wanted t'work with a good, safe crew.'

Joe nodded his bullet-shaped head, but his eyes flickered quickly towards Jessie. And because of 'er, he thought. I'll have that bitch one day! For nothing seemed to drive away the obsession that the sight of her white body in the firelight had reinforced in him that night.

'An' you'll stay off the gin? A ganger can't afford to take a Saint Monday because he's been on the grog. A ganger has to be there every day, come rain or shine.'

Joe shrugged. 'Aye. Why not? I been stayin' off it, haven't I? Stickin' with the ale.' He spat into the fire and Jessie, who had been listening in the shop, grimaced with disgust at the sound. 'Must be gettin' old,' he gave his hoarse chuckle, 'settlin' down at last. All right, Jared lad, I'll do it.'

'It's the times as is changin', an' you'll change with 'em, if you've any sense. When you started on them canals, it were brute strength an' nowt but brute strength, an' fightin' for a bit of fun an' extra money on the side. Now – well, there's not the same call for cloggin' matches, an' chaps fight more with their fists.' Jared laughed. 'Perhaps havin' a young girl on the throne is makin' us all a bit softer, eh?'

Joe ignored the last remark. He didn't give a damn who was on the throne of England and, although he'd used Victoria's accession as an excuse to get drunk, he hadn't thought about her since. She was only a woman and to him, women were good for one purpose only. He stood frowning, his brow wrinkled. 'Why are you askin' *me* to lead your gang? That's what I don't understand. You've got some good lads there. They've been with you longer than I 'ave.'

'They're too young yet. You're the most experienced chap

273

around. I've been watchin' you work for a while now.' Jared slapped Joe on the back. 'Well, you're the one as taught me the trade in the first place, aren't you? You don't do stupid, dangerous things. I want my lads led by someone who'll keep 'em safe, someone who's strong enough t'stop the others from gettin' hurt.'

Joe spat again and nodded. That made sense to him.

Jessie, standing quietly in the shop doorway, clenched her hands, but said nothing.

Joe picked up a jug, found it empty, grabbed another and found only a trickle of ale. He stared at his pot and Jared nodded to Jessie, who came across and took the jug to refill it. When she returned, she kept as far away from Joe as she could while she poured another ale for both men.

'Your missus don't look 'appy about it, though,' Joe said suddenly, grinning. He even dared to pat her hand. Soft and warm it was, like her body would be.

'No, I'm not happy!' snapped Jessie, jerking her hand out of his reach. 'But it's Jared's business who he takes on. You just keep away from me, that's all I ask!'

He burst into wheezing chuckles, as if real laughter were something that had rusted inside him. He laughed still harder as the colour rose in her cheeks and she tossed her head at him. One day . . . He banished the thought quickly. *Bide your time, Joe, lad*, he told himself, *bide your bleedin' time*. Aloud he said, 'You've got a right spitfire there, Jared, me boy, a right little spitfire.'

'Nothin' I can't handle,' said Jared, smiling at his wife. But he had no answering smile from her.

Joe showed his stained and broken teeth in a wolfish grin. 'I like 'em a bit meeker, myself,' he said, still not addressing Jessie directly. 'My Bet's a good little bed-warmer. I'm thinkin' of takin' 'er on to t'next place with me. She don't cook so bad, neither.'

'Why don't you get 'er to earn somethin', too?' asked Jared, keen to make it more profitable for Joe to come with them, but not keen to raise his wages any higher.

Pot halfway to his mouth, the other man looked across at him. 'Not a bad bleedin' idea,' he said slowly. 'You're a smart bastard, Big Jared. You've 'ad your woman workin' for you right from t'start.' He poured the rest of the ale down his throat, belched loudly and nodded. 'Aye, you're a right smart bastard, an' no mistake. Worth followin' you for a bit. What've you got in mind for Bet, then? Runnin' one of the 'uts?'

'No, better than that. Runnin' a little ale hut for the men,' said Jared. 'I supply the hut an' the ale, she runs it an' gets 'er wages an' a portion of the profits. With you there to keep order of an evening, we shouldn't get a lot of breakages. Keep it quietish an' you'll make more money. Cash on the nail. No puttin' things on the slate. Do it like Ma Hawkins does. Pity she's staying on with George. She runs a good hut.'

'Ah, she's been with old George for years, Ma has.'

'Mind, you'll have to be firm if you run the ale hut. We don't want the men getting roaring drunk an' missing a day's work. There's a bonus if we finish the job quickly an' you'll get your share.'

Joe smacked one meaty fist into the palm of his other hand then offered it to Jared. 'By hell, you're on! She'll do it!' It didn't occur to him to ask Bet whether she wanted to run the ale hut. She'd do as she was told, or she could get out and he'd find himself another woman. She was getting on a bit, was Bet, and she was no looker, but she was good in bed and her belly had never swelled (or so she told him) which was a bloody good thing as far as he was concerned. The thought of her earning some extra money pleased him enormously. But the thought of following Jessie pleased him still more. His chance would come one day. He'd make sure of that.

During the next week the camp slowly emptied of men, the stocks in the shop were run right down, and Jessie and Jared made plans for moving north, with a quick trip to Hettonby on the way for the wedding. George Snader grumbled when he found that Jessie wouldn't be available to run his shop at the next camp, but she didn't care. She knew that his loyalty to her, like hers to him, was founded purely on profit and that he'd have ditched her just as quickly if something better had come up.

'You should train Mary up in my place,' she told him.

'*Mary?*'

'Yes. Mary. She's coming on well, Mary is.'

He frowned at her. 'Do you think she could handle it?'

'She'd need more help than I do, the first time at least, but she's as honest as they come an' she doesn't make mistakes with the money. So I reckon it'd pay you to train her and keep her with you.'

'I might just do that.'

Which brought Mary round to the hut one night, worrying about whether she should accept George's offer, whether she could cope.

'Of course you can,' Jessie told her. 'It's a big chance for you, Mary. Take it with both hands.'

Mary hugged Jessie and shed a few tears at the thought of their parting. 'It's all thanks to you, love. And I'll never forget it. If I can ever pay you back, I will.'

'I shall miss Mary,' Jessie said to Jared that night.

'It doesn't do to get attached to anyone on the railways.' He snuggled up to her in bed. 'I keep telling you that.'

'I can't help it.' Since she'd escaped from Sutton Hall, she'd found so many people to like, sturdy independent people who were making a life for themselves. And she wasn't going to deny herself these friendships. She'd been lonely all her life until now, it seemed. And she didn't want to be lonely again – never, ever again.

21

Yorkshire: February 1838

'**R**ight,' said Jared. 'We'll leave the lads to ride up to Leeds on the wagons with the heavy stuff and we'll go and spend a day or two in London.'

'*London?*'

'Aye.' He planted a kiss on her cheek. 'London. Capital of England. Where your precious Queen lives in her fancy palace.'

'But – the expense?'

'Won't come to much. And you have to have a holiday sometimes. All work and no play, you know, Mrs Wilde.' And she had worked hard, was looking tired. He wasn't having that.

'I can't believe it,' said Jessie. 'Me, going up to London.'

'And what's more, we'll start our journey by train. You ought to have a ride on one.'

'By train!' She grabbed hold of him and whirled him round the empty hut. 'We're going to London tomorrow!' The impromptu dance ended in a kiss that lasted much longer.

'If it wasn't daylight and the lads nearby,' he muttered in her ear, 'I'd show you a thing or two today, never mind tomorrow.'

She nestled against him and made a warmly approving noise.

Joe, hovering near the door, scowled and made angry fists of his hands, but neither of them saw him. And when the kissing began again, he stumped off to find Bet, muttering to himself.

* * *

Jared, of course, had already seen London and ridden on trains many times, but to Jessie it was all new, and she bubbled with excitement at everything they saw, from the neat little station at Tring, with its carefully tended garden, to the huge hissing monster of a locomotive. She hadn't expected the train to be so big – or to make so much noise. 'Are you *sure* everything's all right?' she whispered to Jared.

'What do you mean, "all right"?'

'Can that engine really pull all those people and carriages at once?' She stared at the front end of the train. 'The front carriages look silly, like three stage coaches joined together.'

He tugged at her arm. 'Never mind staring at them. Let's get ourselves and the luggage on to the train.' He waved away a porter and picked up their bags, helping Jessie into the open-roofed third-class carriages at the end. 'Good. This one has benches. Some of them don't.' He nodded to their fellow passengers, a few of whom looked very nervous.

A whistle sounded and the train began to move slowly away from the station. Jessie, who had never considered herself a timid person, felt a sudden need to hold Jared's hand tightly.

'You all right, love?'

She nodded, eyes darting here and there. She didn't want to miss a thing, even if it scared her. As the train left the station, she relaxed a little. Apart from the rattling and the jerking, it seemed no more dangerous than riding on a cart, though much faster, of course. It continued to gather speed and she began to worry again. 'It's going very fast.'

'And'll go faster when it's at full speed. Don't worry, love. It's quite safe.' He flicked away a smut that had landed on the back of her hand. More smuts rained down.

'I hadn't realised how dirty it would be.' Her tone was disapproving now. 'The people in those posh carriages are lucky having roofs over them.'

'Aye, well, one day we'll ride in them, too. But for the moment, it's better to be a bit careful and save our pennies for London. And this isn't a long trip. One day you'll be able to ride from one end of the country to the other by train.' Jared laughed. 'When we've done a bit more digging, that is.'

She leaned her head against his shoulder. 'It's like riding in a wooden box, isn't it?'

'An uncomfortable box. These benches are hard on the bum.'

'Jared! Shh! Someone'll hear.'

'What, with this racket going on around us?'

'Why have the cheaper carriages got open tops, though?' she whispered indignantly as the journey continued and the freezing wind whistled around them, making noses and cheeks glow. 'They must know about the smuts. We're both wearing our good clothes and they're going to get filthy! And what would we have done if it was raining? We'd have got *soaked*!" She looked up but there were only a few clouds in the sky, although the day was quite cold.

'Oh, it's not so bad. And at least we'll get there fast!'

And they did. Jessie was rendered speechless by her first sight of London as the train rumbled past the backs of houses, workshops and more houses. Even the New Road Station at Euston intimidated her, with its platforms full of bustling people and porters. She clung to Jared's arm and kept her hand on her skirt seam at the opening under which her purse swung from her waist on its cord. She had never seen so many people – and so well dressed, too! The ones who got out of the best carriages looked like Lord Morrisham's visitors, elegant and self-assured.

But even the ordinary women were much smarter than those in Hettonby or Willingdon! Her simple bonnet and best blue dress looked countrified compared to theirs, and she decided within minutes that she must at least buy some braid and ribbon to trim her flounces up a bit, and she would wear all her petticoats the next day to give a fuller appearance to her skirt. And sleeves were more puffed here. Goodness, some of them were so large that you wondered how the wearers managed to do anything! She sighed. What was she doing looking at fashions? She was no fine lady, but a working man's wife. Still, it was nice to look the best you could, and ideas were free, weren't they?

'Something wrong?' Jared whispered in her ear.

'No. Just looking at the clothes. Mine are very plain.'

He smiled down at her. 'Other women's clothes might be

fancier than yours, but you're much prettier than them. I wouldn't swap you for a duchess.'

'And I wouldn't swap you, either.' For a moment they stood smiling at one another, then they moved on.

They found a cab and Jared asked the driver if he could recommend a hotel, somewhere decent for himself and his wife, but not too expensive. The man looked them up and down, studied their luggage, then took them to a hotel a few streets away, which, he said, was the best for their purpose, as it was centrally located. It was reasonably clean and undoubtedly respectable, but the cost of a night's stay there quite horrified Jessie, who was not used to spending money on anything but the barest necessities. She tugged Jared's sleeve and shook her head, but he just grinned and ignored her.

'It's too expensive!' she whispered once they were alone in their room. 'Surely we could have found somewhere cheaper?'

'There are cheaper places – I'd go to one if I was on me own – but they're not usually very clean. They wouldn't do for you, love. Besides, we're on holiday. Let's enjoy ourselves, eh? We won't go mad, but what does it matter if it costs us a few shillings a night? We've more than earned it. If you like, we'll go out this afternoon and see if we can catch sight of that young Queen you're so fond of reading about.'

Jessie didn't answer. She had caught sight of herself in the mirror. 'Why didn't you tell me my face was dirty?' she wailed, pouring some water from the ewer and washing off the smuts with many anxious glances in the small mirror on the wall. When she was satisfied, she tidied her wind-swept hair and sponged down her dress with one corner of the towel.

Jared made similar repairs to his own person, then carried her off for a lightning sightseeing tour. First, they bought a belated midday meal at a threepenny ordinary, then set out to tramp the streets and see as many sights as possible.

By evening, they were both exhausted.

'It's far worse than digging all day.' Jared patted his stomach. 'And I'm starving hungry.'

'You're always hungry.' Jessie stifled a yawn.

'We'll go back to the hotel. I've had enough of traipsing around for today. We'll have a meal there and go straight to bed.'

She was shocked once again by the prices, and by the service, too. 'I could have cooked a better meal myself on Ma's fire,' she grumbled once they were back in their room.

'Well, it was filling enough.'

'And that's all it was. And at one and sixpence each, it was robbery, sheer robbery!'

He caught hold of her. 'Never mind the food. We're alone, with a nice soft bed and no one to interrupt us. I have a mind to pleasure my wife a little . . .'

They woke at their usual early hour and then had to wait around until breakfast was served. 'One more day's sightseeing,' said Jared as they finished eating, 'and then we leave for the north.'

So Jessie tasted her first ice-cream and walked by the famous River Thames, which was disappointingly ordinary and muddy-looking, not to mention foul-smelling. They found out that the Queen wasn't in town, so they looked at the outside of Westminster Abbey, which Jared declined absolutely to enter. He was not going to church when he was on holiday. Later, they went to see the Tower of London, where, Jessie told him, many kings and other important people had been imprisoned or even beheaded.

Jared was disinclined to accept this, but a man standing nearby corroborated what Jessie had said. As he seemed to know what he was talking about and was obviously an educated gentleman, Jared was forced to believe him. 'Which just shows,' he told Jessie afterwards, 'how much progress the world's made since those days.'

Then he looked thoughtful. 'Let's find a bookshop and buy a book about the history of England. If children can learn about it in school, as you did, it's more than time I learned summat, too.'

The young man in the first shop looked so supercilious when they told him what they wanted that Jared walked straight out again.

'You'll not keep customers if you look down your nose at them!' he tossed over his shoulder at the gaping assistant.

They found another bookshop whose owner was more pleasant to deal with. When he found out what they wanted, he waxed enthusiastic about 'the common man' educating himself by means of the printed word. There was a moment when Jessie wondered if Jared was going to walk out again, for he clearly did not like being called a 'common man' in quite that tone, but then the owner produced a short history of the realm, and went on to suggest a book of simple arithmetic and accounts, as well as a plain man's guide to the correct usage of the English language.

Jared warmed so much to the owner that he confided as he paid for his purchases, 'I've never bought a book before, you know.'

'Then I hope, sir, these will be the first of many.'

'So do I.'

'Jared,' said Jessie sleepily in bed that night.

'Mmmm?'

'It's all very interesting – London is, I mean, but – Jared, I don't think I'd like to live here. I'd rather live in the country.'

'Would you?' He was almost asleep.

'Yes, I would. There are too many people here in London and I didn't know any of them. I don't like that. And they stared so. As if they thought me a country bumpkin. Jared . . .'

'Mmmm?'

'One day, when we get a house of our own – let's make sure it's in the country or at least in a very small town. I don't think I could be happy in a big city.'

'All right, love. G'night!' And Jared let himself sink into a delicious sleep. It would be years before they were ready to settle anywhere.

They left London early next morning, taking the mail coach to Leeds, because only a few sections of the London to Birmingham Railway were finished and it would be easier to go straight through by mail. The coach took nearly a whole day of bumping and rattling over a variety of roads, some well repaired, others deeply rutted, before it reached its destination. By that time, Jessie was as convinced as Jared that the railways were an infinitely superior method of travel. She felt as if she were black and blue all over from the jolting and hadn't felt truly warm, in spite of her thick cloak and Jared's arm round her shoulders, since they left London.

* * *

The next day, they took a much slower local coach out to
Hettonby and found the roads so bad that one hour of travelling
over them seemed more like five. Jared, not in the sweetest of
moods before he started, because he could have done without
this detour, grew steadily more irritable as he listened to the
conversation of their fellow passengers.

'One day,' he muttered to Jessie, 'there'll be railways running
between all the big towns, aye, an' between the small ones as
well, and you'll not have all this bother and time-wasting when
you want to get somewhere.' He was addressing only his wife,
but the loud-mouthed gentleman opposite chose to interrupt.

'My good man, you are quite mistaken in your views. These
railways will come to nothing. Steam is an unnatural and
dangerous means of propulsion and will wreak untold harm on
the human constitution, which is not designed to travel at such
perilous velocities. Moreover, the mischief that the sight of these
infernal machines rushing past will do to hapless animals grazing
peacefully in the fields is not to be thought of.'

Jared opened his mouth to reply.

The gentleman did not allow him time to refute these oft-
repeated fallacies, but continued with barely a pause for breath,
'And I have it on the best authority that these locomotives leave
a trail of sparks behind them, which set fire to the very crops in
the fields. Imagine that outrage! It is not to be borne, I say. The
government will have to intervene and stop this senseless activity.
They will be *compelled* to do so in the interests of the farming
community. Indeed, I cannot think why they have not taken
action already.'

Jared did not understand half these long words, but he
understood enough to know that he was being patronised and
that this silly old bugger didn't know what the hell he was talking
about. He leaned forward and said, slowly and distinctly, 'My
wife an' I travelled up to London from Tring only a few days ago
by railway. It were quick an' easy, an' there's no doubt in my
mind that that's the way folk'll travel in the future.'

'My good fellow, just because you have once ridden on one of
these damned contraptions and – '

Jared lost his temper completely. He leaned forward and poked the other man in the chest. 'I'm not your – *good* – *fellow*,' he said, emphasising each word with another jab of his finger. 'I owe nothin' to such as you. I'm a railway man. I've not only ridden on trains, and many of 'em, too, but I've *built* some of the tracks they run on! An' I'm goin' over to Sheffield in a few days to help build another. It annoys me to hear ignorant people, who know *nowt* about the modern world, tellin' such lies, *downright lies*, about one of the – the marvels of the age.' Jessie had read that phrase to him out of the newspaper and it had stuck in his mind. 'Set fire to crops, indeed! If you knew owt worth knowin', you'd not sit there and spout such bloody tarradiddles!'

'How dare you speak to me like that!' spluttered the man. 'I shall complain to the guard. I am a man of the cloth and as such, should command your respect.'

'I dare do a lot more than that,' said Jared very softly. 'We railways chaps get angry when we hear rubbish bein' talked about us. An' I respect fellows for what they've got inside their heads, not what sort of clothes they're wearing!'

There was dead silence inside the coach. Although Jared had lowered rather than raised his voice, so large and menacing did he look that the officious gentleman shrank back into his seat and did not speak for the next ten minutes. Nor did any of the other passengers risk a comment.

It was a relief when the coach stopped at The Crown in Hettonby to let them off, but to Jessie's amazement the pompous gentleman got out, too. He pushed in front of them without a word of apology, demanding a room, and at once.

When the landlady had dealt with him, she turned round and blinked at Jessie. 'Why, it's Agnes Burton's lass, isn't it? I hardly recognised you, love.'

Jessie knew that only curiosity had inspired this greeting, because she had never had much to do with Mrs Roberts, but she just kept hold of Jared's sleeve and said, 'This is my husband, Mrs Roberts. Could we borrow your handcart, do you think, to take our things over to the parsonage? And we'll need it again tomorrow, after the wedding, because we're catching the afternoon coach back into Leeds.' They had brought all their personal possessions with them, because Jared didn't want the lads getting careless with things that mattered.

'Certainly you can, love. Eh, to think of your mother marrying the parson!' Then Mrs Roberts realised that this might sound as if she disapproved and added hastily, 'So romantic.'

Jessie smiled as they walked across the green. 'Romantic, indeed! Can you imagine my mother being romantic, Jared?'

'No.'

'Or Mr Marley?'

He chuckled. 'I think he'd be more bothered about his dinner and his glass of port.'

While Agnes hugged Jessie, exclaiming over how well she looked, the parson came out and pumped Jared's hand.

'It means a lot to Agnes that you could come,' he said quietly.

'It means a lot to my wife, too.'

John looked up at the young giant, who seemed to fill the hallway. 'Come into the parlour. It's the only room that's still decent. We're leaving in another few days, as you know.'

'Before you do that,' Agnes interrupted, 'let me show you to your bedroom. And, Jared, could you and John carry the things upstairs, do you think? Otherwise they'll be cluttering up the hall – as if it isn't cluttered enough already.'

It seemed funny to Jessie to occupy the front bedroom across from the parson's; even funnier to go and sit in the parlour with him. Within a few minutes, however, she and Agnes had gone down to the kitchen to see about a meal, leaving Jared on his own with his host.

'I don't know how we'll get everything done in time ...' Agnes's voice faded into the distance.

Hell, Jared thought, whatever am I going to talk to him about?

Just then there was a knock on the front door.

'Oh, excuse me. I'm expecting the next incumbent,' John realised from Jared's glassy expression that he didn't understand the word, and amended it to, 'the parson who'll be taking over this parish when I leave. He's coming a few days early so that he can marry us. We both have a fancy to be married in Hettonby church.'

He went to open the door and Jared heard him speaking to someone. When the front door closed and two pairs of footsteps came towards him, he stood up and braced himself to talk to another nob.

'This is Roger Tidesby,' John announced in his quiet way, 'the new parson. Roger, my son-in-law.'

The newcomer stopped dead in the doorway.

A smile twitched at the corners of Jared's mouth as he saw fear flicker in the eyes of the pompous gentleman from the coach. 'I think we've already met,' he said in his deep voice, 'though we didn't exchange names.' He held out one large hand. 'Jared Wilde, sir.'

'Oh. Er – pleased to meet you.'

'Jared and Jessie have come up from London early to attend the wedding,' John explained.

'Eh, I don't know how I didn't burst out laughing!' Jared told Jessie gleefully later. 'That Tidesby fellow treated me as if he were afraid I'd smack him in the face at any moment. Marley didn't notice anything – he's not a bad old fellow, is he?' For John had treated them since their arrival with nothing but the most exquisite courtesy, as if they were already related to him.

'I still can't believe my mother's going to marry him.'

'Well, why not? He seems fond of her, in his own way.'

'And she of him – she's already starting to boss him around, which is a sure sign.'

'I think he likes it. And he certainly likes her cooking. Well, who wouldn't? I do, too. But most of all, I like her daughter.'

The day of the wedding was fine, if frosty, and although a few curious villagers crammed into the back of the church to watch the ceremony, the only invited guest was Mr Snelling.

Jessie helped her mother put on a new dress of cornflower blue silk, which John had chosen with her in Leeds. 'Why don't you wear your hair looser today, Mother? You could let some curls hang down at each side. See, I can twist them into fashionable ringlets over my fingers.'

'It's too fussy for me – and too young.'

'No, it's not,' Jessie coaxed. 'Just let me try.'

When she had finished, she stood back and watched her mother study her own reflection.

'It looks quite nice, doesn't it? You're sure it's not too young for me?'

'Of course not! Why, you have hardly any grey in your hair at all.'

When John saw Agnes, he blinked in surprise. 'My dear, you look delightful.'

And for once, she was flustered and pink and lost for words.

They all walked across to the church together. The ceremony was brief, but Jared thought there was something rather touching about the way the old fellow kept Agnes's hand in his, and smiled at her when they were pronounced 'man and wife'.

Tidesby had not been able to refuse the invitation to return to the parsonage and drink the newly-weds' health, but he kept well away from Jared and was noticeably quieter than he had been in the coach.

'You frighten him,' Jessie whispered to her husband, her eyes dancing with laughter.

'Good. He needs frightening, that one does.'

Mr Snelling rose to his feet. 'I'd like to propose a toast.' He waited until the others had stood up and John had poured some wine for his bride, then the schoolmaster raised his own glass and said simply, 'To Mr and Mrs Marley. May they live many years together in happiness and in health. And may you, John, enjoy your work in your new parish.'

In response to a nudge from Agnes, John cleared his throat. 'My wife and I,' he blushed a vivid red as he said those words, 'would like to thank you all for being present. And particular thanks to you, Roger, for coming here early and marrying us. It was most kind.'

Tidesby managed a nod and a sour sort of smile.

'I'm grateful to you too, Tom, for joining us today.'

Mr Snelling inclined his head and blew his nose vigorously to hide his emotion.

'And to you, Jared and Jessie, for coming so far out of your way to be with us.' John raised his glass and drank to them all and

Agnes followed suit, sipping at hers. 'And now, I believe my wife,' he beamed at her again, 'has prepared some refreshments for us. I'm afraid we'll have to eat them in the kitchen, though, because much of our furniture has already been sent ahead, but I'm sure you won't mind that.'

Tidesby cleared his throat. 'I don't – '

'Oh, do come down with me, Mr Tidesby,' Jessie gushed, seizing him by the arm. She found it hard not to laugh aloud at his nervousness as, still with a wary eye on Jared, he escorted her downstairs.

After lunch, Jessie and her mother went upstairs on the excuse of packing the Wildes' things.

'Be happy, Mother,' said Jessie in a voice grown hoarse with the struggle to hold back tears of both joy and sadness. This day marked the end of so much, and was probably the last time she would ever see Hettonby.

'I will.'

'I was a bit surprised when you wrote to say you were marrying him.'

'I was surprised myself when John asked me,' Agnes admitted. 'But Mr Roysby, who holds this new living, only wanted a married man and John thought of me.'

'Oh. I wondered whether you – he might be in love with you?'

'I don't hold with love.' Then Agnes fiddled with the edge of the counterpane, straightening it unnecessarily. 'Not but what I'm not fond of John. I hadn't realised how we'd – well, grown close, grown to know one another's ways. He's a good man.' Which was as near as she could come to admitting her affection.

Downstairs, Snelling and Tidesby had excused themselves and Jared was left with his new relative. He held out one hand. 'I hope you'll be very happy, sir.'

'Oh, I'm sure I will.' John beamed at him as he shook it. 'I never thought to have a family of my own, you know – you won't mind if I think of you as a step-son?'

'Of course not.' Jared hesitated. 'And I'd like to thank you for standing up to Lord Morrisham when he tried to keep Jessie away from me. Eh, I still get angry every time I think of it.'

'Yes. So do I. He was an arrogant man, but there, he's gone to face his Maker now, so we must not speak ill of him. And they tell me that Lady Morrisham is bearing up very well and that dear Susannah has become her mother's right hand.'

He looked sideways at Jared. 'I think, if I may say so, you make Jessie a very good husband. Anyone can see how happy she is. You're two of a kind. I'm sorry if I seemed – well, a bit disapproving before.'

'That's all right, Parson.' Jared clapped him on the back. 'She's a wonderful woman, my Jessie. I just hope you're as happy with her mother.' Though he doubted it. Agnes Burton – no, Agnes Marley now – would never be an easy woman to live with.

'I think I shall be. Perhaps – perhaps you'll come and stay with us in Shilwick, if you can spare the time between contracts? Agnes misses her daughter very much.'

'We'll definitely do that.' Jared turned at the sound of footsteps coming down the stairs. 'Right then, love. Let's get our things across to that inn again.'

With her new husband's arm around her shoulders, Agnes held her hand out to him. 'Look after her, Jared.'

He took the hand, then pulled Jessie's mother closer and hugged her. 'I shall. She means everything to me, you know. And I hope you'll be very happy, Mrs Marley.'

As they stood watching them leave, John said softly, 'I like him.'

Agnes sniffed. 'He's not as bad as I thought, but handsome is as handsome does. Let's see how he shapes when there's trouble.' For she would never be able to believe that life could run smoothly for anyone.

John cleared his throat. 'I think you look very well with your hair like that. Why do you not wear it so all the time?'

'Do you think so? It's not too fussy? Or – or too young?'

'It looks lovely. And so do you today, my dear. You should wear more bright colours.'

'Oh. Well. If you say so.'

They were both very shy as they went back inside, not knowing how to handle their new roles. But by the time Agnes had cleared up, then chivvied him into sorting out the contents of the last of his bookcases, they were beginning to relax again.

When it was time to go to bed, the constraint returned, however. John hummed and hawed, clearing his throat a few times, opening his mouth, then shutting it, till Agnes said sharply, 'Just say it, whatever it is!'

'I wanted to say – if you would prefer not to share a bed – just at first, you know, till we're used to one another – well, I shall quite understand.'

She stood stock still, then shook her head. 'I think we should start our life together properly. If we're married, we're married, and that's that. So, John, I'll go up first and give a thump on the floor when I'm ready.'

It was only when he got into bed and she felt him trembling that she realised how nervous and unsure of himself he was, so she snuggled into his arms and took the initiative by kissing him. She had forgotten how wonderful it felt to have another warm body to cuddle up to, whisper to, wake up with in the morning. Absolutely wonderful.

When he awoke, he beamed at her and said quietly, 'I do love you, you know, Agnes.' And was at first horrified when she burst into tears. But when he had petted her and been assured that she was weeping for sheer happiness, he relaxed again.

'I love you, too, John Marley,' she said as she mopped her eyes. 'I never thought to love a man again, but I do.'

22

❧❧❧❧❧

Atterby: March 1838

*I*n Sheffield Jared and Jessie, both heartily tired of travelling by
now, took a room at the coaching inn and fell into bed as soon as
they had eaten. And if the room was not as clean as Jessie would
have liked, at least the food was plentiful and hot, and they were
no longer jolting about. The next day they found a carter to take
them and their luggage over to Hatley, which Simon had told
them was the nearest village to the projected cutting.

The landlord of the inn greeted them warmly at first, then turned
surly when he found out they were connected with the railway. 'We
haven't got no rooms. An' we don't want your sort in our village.'
He walked away, leaving them standing in the entrance hall of the
inn surrounded by their luggage. The carter had already left.

Jared glared at the door and then turned to Jessie. 'Sorry, love.'

'What for? You haven't done anything.'

'It's because of what I am.'

'I'm a railway person, too. You go and find us somewhere else
to stay, and I'll keep my eye on the luggage. I don't think they'll
throw a woman out of this place forcibly.' Her eyes flashed. 'I'd
like to see them even try.'

But when Jared had gone, the landlady came into the entrance
hall. 'My husband told you we haven't got any rooms. So you can
just leave. At once, if you please.'

Jessie gestured to the luggage. 'How can I? I can't carry this lot
by myself.'

From the look the landlady threw over her shoulder, someone was watching. 'I'll find help for you.'

'Can't you even let me stay here until my husband comes back? It's going to rain any minute.' The landlady hesitated, then shook her head.

Jessie, who was beginning to feel angry, sat down on her tin trunk. They'd have to carry her outside first.

A lad shambled into the entrance hall. 'I'm t'help you carry your stuff outside.'

'It's raining and I'm not moving from this spot until my husband returns.'

He gaped at her, then called over his shoulder, 'She won't go!'

There was silence in the hallway. Jessie crossed her arms.

The lad looked at the smaller pieces of luggage lying on the floor next to her.

'You'll have to fight me for them.' She spoke too quietly for the others to overhear, staring him right in the eyes.

After opening and shutting his mouth a few times, he shambled away again. Silence fell. No one came near the entrance hall, but Jessie felt sure someone was watching her and was relieved when Jared returned.

'It's the local landowner's fault they won't let us stay, love. A Mr Rishworth. He owns most of the village and he's forbidden them to lodge us in the inn, on pain of losing their lease.' He brushed the raindrops from the shoulders of his coat and shook his hat, scattering a shower of droplets.

'What are we going to do, then? They sent a lad to carry our things outside, but I sat on the trunk and dared him to move me. Since then, nobody's been near.'

His expression lightened for a moment. 'I wish I'd been there to see it.'

'But what *are* we going to do?'

'I've found us lodgings with the local cobbler, who owns his own house and land, and isn't indebted to this Rishworth for anything – in fact, he seems to detest the fellow. I think Beevers has been a bit of a rebel in his day. And he says that Atterby, the next village, is just as near to the railway line. He thinks we might get rooms in the inn there.'

Jessie raised her voice. 'Pity about this one, eh? We'll have to buy our ale elsewhere. They'll be losing a lot of money.'

Jared chuckled as he picked up the trunk and carried it outside to the handcart loaned to them by the cobbler's next door neighbour.

Dan Beevers, an elderly man with a bald head and a pronounced limp, was waiting for them in his tiny shop. He shook hands with Jessie, patting her hand several times before releasing it. 'Eeh, what a welcome to Hatley! My wife's got the kettle boiling. We can leave your things in the shop for now. No one'll touch them.' He led the way along a narrow passage to the rear of the house.

Mrs Beevers, plump and twice his size, with a surprisingly girlish face, was equally welcoming. 'Eh, look how wet you are. Dratted rain's set in for the day. Come an' sit by the fire, lass.'

Jessie hesitated, remembering the absolute power Lord Morrisham had wielded in Sutton and Hettonby. 'Are you sure you won't get in trouble for helping us?'

Mrs Beevers shrugged. 'My husband thrives on trouble, allus has. It'll be nothing new for us. Besides, Rishworth doesn't own the whole village, only the northern half. He's a mean old devil, he is.'

'Why do some people hate the railways so?' Jessie wondered.

'Because they're a sign of progress, that's why,' Dan said immediately. 'An' because they'll mean the common man will get to see what's happening elsewhere, then he'll be wanting the vote an' all sorts of things the privileged classes already have. An' he'll get them, too!'

Mrs Beevers sighed and rolled her eyes at Jessie. 'He's that set on gettin' the vote, my Dan is. He never stops going on about that Charter of his.'

'Not *my* Charter,' her husband said stubbornly, 'a Charter of Rights for the common man.'

'What about the common woman?' Jessie asked.

He blinked at her. 'Their men look after them.'

'I earn my own way in life and I reckon I deserve a vote, too.'

'She certainly does.' Jared put his arm round her. 'She'll be running the shop at the diggings on her own, making more money than most men. You're not telling me she wouldn't have enough sense to use a vote properly?'

Dan cackled and said triumphantly, 'Then you're *not* a common woman, Mrs Wilde, not common at all.' And everyone dissolved into laughter.

They were fed royally, then given their hosts' own bed for the night. The following day, Jared walked over to Atterby and came back in the gig from the inn there. 'They're friendly,' he told his wife as he helped her up into it, 'and grew even friendlier when I told them about you buying ale and such from them.'

The Green Man in Atterby was a smaller inn, but looked well kept, with windows twinkling in the weak sunlight. The potman hurried out at once to help Jared carry their things inside.

'This is Mr Malterby,' Jared said, nodding in the direction of the doorway. 'And Mrs Malterby.'

This landlady was plump and looked pleased with herself and life. She shook Jessie's hand warmly. 'I'll show you up to your room. I've given you the big one at the front. I think you'll like it.'

She puffed her way up the first flight of stairs, then flung open a door to reveal an airy room with a big comfortable bed to one side. Near the hearth, two large armchairs invited the weary traveller to sit and toast his feet at a warm fire. 'I was sorry to hear you'd had trouble in Hatley. Rishworth is a right bossy sort of fellow. Nor he isn't proper gentry, neither. Made his money in the India trade, he did, then bought up the old Horsfall estate. Been acting like he's the King of England ever since. Mind you, it's an ill wind. They had to change the route of the railway because of him an' now it's coming closer to Atterby, so I daresay we'll benefit, here at The Green Man – at least we will if they put in a station nearby.'

Her husband was less optimistic. 'We heard as how them navvies caused an unholy lot of trouble over Rotherham way.'

'Well, *these* navvies won't!' said Jared. 'It's only goin' to be a small camp an' Mr Stafford, the engineer, will be payin' their wages weekly, so there'll be no drunken randies on our diggings.'

'I'm glad to hear that.' But he didn't sound glad. 'Er – what exactly is your connection with the railway, Mr Wilde?'

'I'm the overseer of these diggings. I've come on ahead to get things set up. An' Mr Stafford, the engineer, will be coming later. He'll need a room as well.'

Mr Malterby brightened marginally. 'Ah. Well, you've come to the right place, then. Nowhere else in Atterby has rooms as good as ours.'

'And we'll need a supplier of ale for the men. Do you have any casks to spare? And can you get us more? They're thirsty chaps, navvies are.'

'Might be able to help you. What exactly will you need?'

Jared jerked a thumb in Jessie's direction. 'My wife will be arranging all that, so you'll need to deal with her. What I want to do now is look for a camp-site. The men have to live somewhere. We'll need a water supply, too.'

'Dan Frewiston's north meadow.' Mr Malterby sighed as if telling them bad news. 'He could use the money.' He looked sideways at Jessie, still frowning. '*You* buy the ale?'

'I run the camp shop.' She turned to include his wife. 'I buy provisions, too, bread and baked goods generally.'

Mrs Malterby beamed. 'I'm well known for my pies. I could bake extra if you put in a firm order.'

'Then later we'll talk about prices.'

From that moment on, they found their hosts more than eager to do business, though Mr Malterby never looked less than gloomy and punctuated all their conversations with sighs and predictions of trouble ahead.

When their hosts had left them, they stood looking out of their bedroom window across a peaceful scene. Jessie said softly, 'It's a pretty little place, isn't it? Such a pity we'll spoil all that.'

Jared leaned against the window frame. 'We'll only change it for a while.The scars will soon heal over.' But he, too, acknowledged the quiet beauty of the moment and for a while they just stood there, she leaning against him, he enjoying the feel of her hair against his chin, her soft warmth against the whole length of him.

At last, he stirred. 'If we don't move away, I'll be taking you over to that bed instead of going out and looking for a camp-site.'

'The bed'll still be there tonight.'

* * *

After a brisk bargaining session that afternoon, in which he halved Frewiston's asking price, Jared hired the north meadow for the men to camp in and made a further agreement to take water from the nearby stream. He didn't get back to the inn until late afternoon, by which time Jessie had made a start on her own arrangements. As it was market day, she got Mrs Malterby to introduce her to some of the local farmers' wives, who would be likely to have eggs, dairy and garden produce to sell, and whose husbands might have beasts to slaughter for meat.

The next day Jared and Jessie hired the landlord's gig and drove round all the hamlets in the area. He found several wood merchants and purchased a dozen wagon loads of wood, second-hand stuff with big knots or other major faults that had been lying useless in corners for years. The sellers were jubilant at the price they got for such rubbish, though they regretted it a few months later, when seasoned wood grew scarce and prices soared because of the railways.

Jared was equally delighted at the low price he'd paid. 'We'll take the best of it,' he said jubilantly when he got back, 'an' make ourselves a movable hut, like George's shop, one we can use over an' over. Not as fancy, though. Just one big room at first, split into two – the shop at the front an' a place at the back for everything else, with our bed in a lean-to at the side. I've been speaking to the village carpenter about it and he's going to work with me.'

'It'll be nice to have our own place again.'

He wasn't really listening. 'Mmm. We'll keep the rest of the wood for building huts for the lads and an ale hut for Joe an' Bet. Stafford told me to look out for some building materials. He'll never believe how cheap I got this lot after London prices, but I'll add a bit to what I paid an' make something on it from him, all the same. He should have been doing this work himself to get the best profits. I would have, in his place.'

Jared spent two more days on such buying trips, looking for sheets of tin for roofs, and for nails and tools of various kinds. Again, while most of the things were for Simon Stafford, there was often something that he could make a small profit on for himself, or that they could sell later in the shop.

Next he hired some local men and with their help, began to

set up the field as a camp, digging latrines in one corner, well away from the stream, and marking out sites for huts. Then he set to work on the shop, with the help of the local carpenter and his journeyman.

On the Saturday evening, before they went to bed, Jessie said thoughtfully, 'I think we ought to go to church tomorrow.'

'*What?* Oh, no! I'm not starting that lark.'

'Well, you're wrong.'

'What do you mean, wrong?'

'If you want people round here to co-operate with us, you need to show them we're respectable.'

'Back to your bloody *respectable* again. You've been showing them that all week. It'll have to do.'

She glared at him. 'You're the one who wants to make a lot of money. What are you going to do when you get it – carry on living in a hut?'

He just stared at her in bewilderment.

'We need to *show* everyone we're respectable, Jared, we really do, and go on showing it. If that costs us a couple of hours in a church every Sunday, what does it matter?'

'A couple of wasted, boring hours!'

'We're going, Jared.'

'You look just like your bloody mother when you talk like that.'

'I feel like her, too. Very determined.'

He let out a long, aggrieved sigh, but stopped protesting. He was beginning to recognise that look of implacable determination. He smiled at the thought. Give and take, they called it, an' his Jessie could certainly give as well as take!

It was a small church, more modern than the one at Hettonby, and not nearly as pretty. The church warden tried to show them to a pew at the very back, for whatever Mr Malterby said, and however pleased some of the women in the village were about the chance to earn extra money by selling things to the camp shop, the warden had a low opinion of railway folk. Jessie shook her head firmly and held Jared back from the pew. 'Somewhere further forward, I think.' She wasn't going to sit with the farm labourers and casual workers. That wouldn't look at all well.

After a moment or two's hesitation, the man showed them to an empty pew halfway up the aisle, and this Jessie accepted with a gracious inclination of the head.

The service wound on interminably, but when Jared started to fidget, Jessie's foot kicked his ankle hard and he subsided with a suppressed sigh.

Afterwards, they lingered in the churchyard.

'What are we waiting for?' he demanded in a loud whisper. 'I want my dinner.'

'Shh!'

The parson, who had been watching them, hesitated, then came over to speak to them. 'You're new to the area, I believe?'

As if he didn't know exactly who they were, thought Jessie scornfully.

'Aye.' Jared's voice was curt. He was thinking longingly of a thick slice of Mrs Malterby's excellent roast beef.

'Yes, we are.' Jessie gave the parson her sweetest and most innocent smile, the one Jared already recognised as another sign that she intended to get her own way about something.

'Then allow me to welcome you to our congregation. I'm James Pardew.' The parson had been astonished when the church warden had whispered to him that *that fellow* and his wife had come to morning service.

He realised that Mrs Wilde was staring over his shoulder expectantly and understood exactly why. 'Er – you must meet my wife. Dorothy, my dear.' He beckoned to a thin-faced lady, who was talking to two other ladies in the church porch and trying to watch her husband and the newcomers at the same time without betraying it. 'I'd like you to meet Mr and Mrs Wilde, who are to reside in Atterby for a while.'

'I'm *so* delighted to meet you,' cooed Jessie.

Jared shot her a suspicious glance. What on earth was she up to now?

They all shook hands solemnly and expressed a fictitious pleasure at meeting each other.

There was an awkward silence, which Mr Pardew hurried to fill when he saw that his wife did not intend to make the effort.

'So you're with the railway, eh? My goodness! Such changes! Where will it all end? Er – what exactly do you do, Mr Wilde?'

'I'm the overseer,' said Jared yet again, his mind still more on his Sunday dinner than on what this fussy old sod was saying. 'In charge of the diggings.'

'Oh, yes. My, my! A responsible position.' Mr Pardew obviously had no idea what an overseer did, but was trying to maintain some flow of conversation in the face of his wife's stubborn silence, one that was heavy with disapproval.

'I was *so* glad to find that there was a church nearby,' said Jessie as Mrs Pardew began to fidget and look up at the clock on the church tower. 'I like to attend whenever possible. I found your sermon very interesting, Mr Pardew. My step-father has just moved to a parish near York. He, too, has used that text for a sermon, but he developed it differently.'

'Your step-father is a parson?' Mrs Pardew looked at her sharply. 'And yet Mrs Dean from Bottom Dip Farm was telling me that you were – have I got it right? – going to run a shop in the camp for the railway people.' Her tone indicated what she thought of a woman who did that sort of thing.

'But of course!' said Jessie as if this was the most natural thing in the world. 'I always do. My husband's men must eat, after all. The village will benefit greatly from our stay here, for I mean to buy as much as I can locally.'

'This village,' said Mrs Pardew, in a voice that defied anyone to contradict her, 'would be far better off if railways had never been thought of!'

Jessie breathed deeply and bit back a sharp response. 'Oh, I think you'll find most people disagree with that. You can't stop progress.'

'And anyway, that's hardly our concern,' said Jared, bristling visibly at the way his wife was being spoken to. '*We* don't decide where to put the railways, we just build 'em for the companies.'

'Well, I hope you do your job quickly, then, and keep your men under control,' retorted Mrs Pardew, undaunted. 'One hears dreadful tales, quite dreadful.'

'Oh, aye, we'll do that, never fear.' He was bored by this hatchet-faced old hag. Who did she think she was, talking like this to his Jessie? He raised the new hat that Jessie had made him buy in London, which looked more like an upturned flower pot to him, and winced as he thought what the lads were going to say when they saw him all fancied up like this of a Sunday. Nodding to the parson, he offered his arm to Jessie in a way he wouldn't have known how to do a year previously, and led her away.

'What the hell was that all about?' he asked, once out of earshot. 'I want my dinner, not a lecture from a sour-faced old biddy.'

'I *told* you. We're showing off our respectability,' said Jessie. 'Mostly mine. And we'll be doing the same thing every Sunday from now on.'

The first time she heard the noise in the night, Elinor assumed it was simply the wind blowing a piece of wood around. Early next morning, however, Thirza, placid sensible Thirza, screamed when she went down to the kitchen.

Elinor rushed downstairs to find her maid being sick into the sink and saw something bloody on the table covered with a cloth.

'Don't look at it, Miss Elinor. Don't look!' Thirza retched, but took a few deep breaths and managed not to be sick again.

'What is it?'

'The cat. It's dead. Someone's been,' Thirza gulped, 'tormenting the poor thing. And – they came inside and put it on the table. While we were asleep. We could have been murdered in our beds.'

Elinor gazed at her in horror, then went to peep beneath the cloth. What she saw made her gasp and throw the cover over it again, nausea roiling through her stomach. She had to lean against the wall for a minute. Then she felt a draught on her back and turned to see the window thumping gently against its frame. 'Did you leave that open?'

'No. You know how careful I am to lock up.'

'The catch was a bit loose. We must check the rest of the windows and doors.' She turned, dreading what she might find in the parlour, but determined to face the worst at once. Nothing there had been damaged there, just rearranged, although two small figurines were missing.

The two women looked at one another, both feeling horrified to think that someone had been creeping about downstairs while they were sleeping peacefully in their beds.

'Go and fetch the village constable, Thirza.'

'That stupid lump won't be able to do anything.'

'Nonetheless, he must be informed. I'll get dressed while you're doing that.'

'Oh, no! You go and get dressed now, while I search the house and make sure he isn't still around, waiting to cut our throats.'

'We'll both search together.'

They went round the house, Elinor holding a walking stick and Thirza her carving knife. No other room had been touched and there was no one hiding under the beds or in the attics. Elinor got dressed and then, still with a walking stick in her hand for protection, waited for her maid's return with Tom Pikely, who acted as constable from time to time and, much more important to himself and everyone else, was the best ploughman in the village.

'Disgusting!' he said, and carried the cat's body outside for them.

'And that's all the use he'll be,' Thirza muttered. A few minutes later she shot a triumphant glance at Elinor when she was proved right, for all he could do was mutter phrases like, 'Can't hardly believe it,' or 'Don't know what the dangy old world's coming to, that I don't!'

When Tom had seen everything twice, he cleared his throat. 'I'll go an' tell Squire, see what he says. It can't be someone from round here, though. We've never had no trouble like this afore. It'll be some tramp passing through, that's what it'll be.'

'You said that already,' Thirza declared, ushering him towards the door. 'And on your way over to see Squire, you ask old Job Bartley to come and fit us some new bolts on our windows.'

Charles Butterfield drove round to see them as soon as he heard what had happened, but he was as little use as the constable. 'Never seen the like,' he kept saying. 'Shocking! Shameful! You ladies must come and spend a few days with us. You can't stay here until we've caught whoever did it.'

'And what if you don't catch them?' Elinor asked quietly.

He was silent.

'No, Squire, I think we'll stay in our own home. But we've arranged to get new bolts fitted and you can be sure that we'll be very careful to lock up at night.'

Elinor didn't write to tell Simon what had happened, for there was nothing he could do to help and it would only worry him unnecessarily. But the Squire assumed she had and took it upon himself to write to Mr Stafford as well, to assure him that they would keep an eye on his sister.

'Why didn't you tell me?' Simon raged the following Sunday, turning up without warning. 'You said nothing about it when you wrote, absolutely nothing.'

Elinor shrugged. 'It doesn't matter. We've got new bolts fitted, so we'll be all right now.'

'You can't be sure. The fellow is obviously deranged. He might smash in the windows.'

'If he does, we'll certainly hear him.'

But in the end Simon had to get back to the new contract, which looked like taking all his time and energy for the next month or two and which he had now told her about. Neither of them had said anything about the house in Heptonstall. But it had lain between them, nonetheless, causing a stiffness in their relations which had never been there before and which was hurting them both.

That evening, Elinor sat in the parlour and wondered once again if she'd done the right thing staying here in Yettley. Perhaps Thirza was right. Perhaps Simon would not have carried out his threat of not coming to see her. But she didn't dare risk it.

After a while she sighed and decided to go to bed. Who was to know what was right and what was not? Certainly not her. But she wasn't having anyone breaking in again and killing poor animals in her house. Like Thirza, she felt angry about the affair. And if she woke more often in the night, worrying that she had heard a noise, well, Thirza didn't know about it, did she? And there were no more break-ins in the village.

23

***

Atterby: March–April 1838

Jared let out a great shout of delight when the first four members of his old gang drove up with the two wagons he had purchased to transport all the gang's goods and chattels.

'Joe and Bet will be here in a day or two,' Bull said. 'He stopped off for a cloggin' match.' And a last booze-up before he got to the camp, but Bull wasn't going to tell Big Jared about that. Their ex-ganger had a rather narrow view of heavy drinking.

'Well, we can move in properly now, thank goodness,' said Jessie. 'Carry those boxes inside more carefully, Bull. We don't want my crockery broken, do we?'

He pulled a face at his companions, but did as she told him. 'Got any ale yet?' he asked as they carried the last lot in.

Jessie nodded. 'You can have one pot each free. After that, you pay me for what you drink. No credit.'

'She's a sharp bugger,' Bull muttered to Harry.

'Aye, but she keeps good ale.' He held out his hand for a pot and downed its contents in one, before holding it out for a refill. 'I needed that.'

Supplies had begun to arrive on the site now: barrows, timber for shoring, pickaxes, a small supply of dynamite in case they hit any unexpected patches of rock, and a myriad other bits and pieces Jared had purchased on Simon's behalf. On the next contract, there wouldn't be so much to buy, but this time they were starting from scratch with tools and equipment and Simon had given Jared the money for that.

More men began to trickle in. Old acquaintances and a motley collection of strangers, seeking jobs. It hadn't taken long for word to get around that there was work available near Atterby. Jared was very choosy about the men he set on, however, and turned away several whose looks he didn't like. 'Poor muscles,' he muttered to Jessie as one group trudged disconsolately away. 'An' we can't spare the time or money to train 'em. Besides, we'll have no trouble getting the numbers we need. It's not as if it's a big job here.'

He put the men of his own gang in charge of the newcomers and got them to finish setting up the site. They did the necessary jobs like diverting a water supply from a nearby stream and digging rainwater drains around each hut. All was done according to detailed instructions from Simon, who would tolerate neither polluted water supplies nor men relieving themselves anywhere except in the places designated.

'He's another fussy bugger, that engineer is,' Bull grumbled.

'Aye, an' so am I,' Jared snapped, 'so stop standing around an' get on with it.'

Simon arrived in Atterby a day late because of his hurried visit to his sister. He stood in the doorway of Jessie's shop, watching her serve a customer and smiling across at her with what she always thought of as his nice, shy gentleman's smile. 'I can see that you've worked your usual miracle here, Mrs Wilde.'

'No miracle. Just a lot of hard work.' She handed the customer her change and gestured to Simon to follow her into the back.

Although they hadn't been long in the hut, it already had a look of home, with Mr Snelling's delicate watercolour hanging on the rough wooden wall and a well-scrubbed, if roughly made table set for tea with a bunch of wildflowers in a jar in the middle. Half-finished shelves would form a partition between the living and selling areas when filled with goods and the bed alcove was already screened off by a sheet. The bed was another example of Jared's handiwork, a wooden frame with canvas webbing, carrying two mattresses, a straw one overlaid by a feather mattress. To sit on there were two rough stools and a bench, also made by Jared. 'No use gettin' proper furniture yet,' he'd said. 'We'll be movin' from one small contract to another for a while, so we can't hump too much stuff around the country.'

'How on earth have you got everything done so quickly?' Simon asked.

Jessie shrugged and waved one hand at the removable pegging in the corners of the walls and the cotton waste that filled the gaps to keep most of the wind out. 'We've copied Mr Snader. Jared built this hut so we can pull it to pieces and take it with us to the next diggings.'

'Wonderful!' said Simon enthusiastically, then frowned. 'I wonder if I ought to do something similar? I'd thought to lodge in Hatley, but they said at The Traveller's Rest they were full. Perhaps I ought to live on the site?'

'No need,' said Jared's voice behind them. 'The Green Man in Atterby will take you. I've already told them you'd be coming. It's closer to the diggings anyway. The Traveller's Rest wasn't full. Just a local landowner who's against the railways.'

'Not Risherworth again!' Simon groaned. 'Hasn't he caused enough trouble on this line? He's just as bad as Morrisham was.'

Jared shrugged. 'He enjoys meddling, they tell me. But it'll look better when the company's agent comes to inspect the work if you can entertain him at an inn afterwards. They'll be more impressed by a private parlour than by a hut like this. How about a cup of tea, Jessie?'

While the two men sat down at the table, she busied herself at an iron stove similar to the one they'd had in Willingdon, listening as they talked about the work that would soon be under way. The company surveyors were coming in two days' time to check that everything was in order, so as soon as they had drunk their tea, they went off to inspect what had been done so far.

Jessie was left in the hut, happily busy, but her peace of mind lasted only an hour longer, then a familiar hoarse voice said, 'Good day to ye, *Mrs* Wilde!'

She started at the sound and dropped the packet she was holding, which set Clogger off into his usual wheezing chuckle.

'Sorry if I startled you, missus. Bit jumpy, ain't you? You're not frightened of me, are you?' He leered at her across the counter. 'I wouldn't hurt a pretty piece like you.'

'You made me jump, that's all.' She ignored his would-be gallantry. 'I thought all the men were down at the other end of the field. My husband is there, if you want him.'

'Aye, I seen 'im. I'll go over there in a minute.' He made no move to leave the shop.

'Did you want to buy something? We haven't got a lot of stock yet.'

'No, I don't want anythin', but my Bet will. She's stopped in the village to buy summat at that little draper's shop. Women's stuff. I walked on ahead. She'll be here in a few minutes with a cart we brung our things on. Got the cart cheap an' a nag to pull it.' He winked. 'Got Bet cheap, too. Your husband's not the only one with an eye to business. She'll be 'ere in a few minutes. All right if she stays with you in t'shop till I find out about a hut for us?'

Jessie knew she couldn't refuse this reasonable request, but she didn't really want Joe's woman in her shop. It wasn't Bet's lack of respectability that stuck in her throat, for most of the women who were trickling into the camp were the same: not married, not respectable, not overly clean, but indispensable to the men working there. No, it was the fact that Bet was Joe's woman. That tainted her, so far as Jessie was concerned.

He clumped off to look for Jared. Bet and the cart drew up outside soon after, with Three Finger Billy, whom she'd met in Atterby, driving it. He, too, went off to join the other men, and Bet came into the shop, hesitating by the door.

Jessie looked at her and felt a surge of hostility, but this soon faded. She couldn't help feeling sorry for the poor woman, who looked exhausted and was clutching a very damp shawl around her thin shoulders. 'Would you like a cup of tea?'

'Aye. If you've got one goin'. Bad day to travel.'

'Come round here and sit by the stove. You look frozen.'

'There's the 'orse to see to.'

'There's a barrel of water next to the shop for it to drink from. I don't know what arrangements Jared's made for housing the animals yet, so it'll just have to stand there. At least it's stopped raining now.'

Bet nodded and clumped outside to attend to the animal. When she came back, she hesitated by the door and looked doubtfully down at her muddy skirts. 'I'm all mucky.'

'No matter. Everyone trails the dirt in. You can't do much about it. Come and get warm.'

Bet went over to the stove and held out her hands gratefully to its warmth. 'Nice place you've got 'ere.' She sighed with pleasure as the warmth began to seep into her chilled body. She gulped down the mug of tea that Jessie offered her and accepted another, a little colour returning to her face.

'They 'aven't started diggin' out the cutting yet, then?' Bet asked.

'No, they're still setting things up.'

'I see they've got some of the 'uts up, though.'

'Yes.'

'Joe says him an' me are to run an ale hut.'

'So I believe.'

Bet beamed. 'I'll like that. I used to work in an inn, afore I come on the railways. Be like old times.' She looked pleadingly at Jessie. 'I'd welcome any advice, though. I – it's me chance, don't you see? Joe's gettin' older. He might want t'settle down a bit. Really settle down. I'd like t'settle too, stick wi' one man. I'm not so young as I was.'

'*With Joe?*' Jessie couldn't keep the surprise out of her voice. She would have done anything rather than live with such a brute and bully.

Bet shrugged. 'He's a bit rough, but he's a good provider. Generous, too. I've never bin hungry since I took up with 'im. Not once. He allus makes sure I've got summat to eat.'

Jessie was silent for a moment. How lucky she'd been, with a mother like Agnes Burton and a husband like Jared! She felt a sudden sympathy for the tired, filthy woman next to her, who had such modest ambitions.

'If I can help, you'll always know where to find me.'

'Thanks.' Bet sipped the tea again, slowly and appreciatively, making loud slurping noises.

Half an hour later Joe poked his head in at the door. 'There you are, you lazy bitch! Come on out o' there! We've got an 'ut to finish off an' you might as well 'elp me. Sooner it's done, sooner we'll 'ave somewhere proper t'sleep. I'm sick of that bleedin' cart.' For once, he had no time to taunt Jessie.

Within the week, a shanty town had sprung up of huts cobbled together from the rough timber Jared had bought. The company agent came on his regular weekly inspection and told Simon that he had a good man in his overseer, young as he was. The agent was also impressed by Jessie's shop and sound business sense, not to mention the cups of excellent tea she had made for him.

There had been two weekly paydays already for the early-comers, and both Jessie's shop and Bet's ale hut were doing a brisk trade. Jessie's prices were higher than those in the village, just a little, but as she'd expected, the camp women weren't made welcome in Atterby and they preferred to buy from her. Only now did she realise exactly how much profit George Snader had been making from his shop in the big camp. At the end of her first real week of trading, with the camp still only half full, she looked across at Jared and gasped, 'I've made over a pound this week!'

He grinned. 'Never mind. You'll do better when we really get going.'

'*Never mind!* I – oh, you're teasing me!' She looked down at the money gloatingly. 'Over twenty-one shillings, as near as I can work out. I can't believe it!'

'It'll be more from now on. We'll soon have a full team working. But you're looking tired. You'd better get yourself a lad to help out. I don't want you killin' yourself.'

She swallowed hard. 'Me? Hire someone!'

'Well, I 'aven't time to do it, 'ave I? An' it is your shop.'

'Have,' she corrected automatically. 'Don't forget the aitches.'

'No, ma'am.' He planted a kiss on her soft cheek. 'So, you'd better find someone. Try in the village.'

Words failed her. Jared had promised her a house and servants one day, but that would be in the future, when she was older. This was here and now, and she was still only twenty. Could she employ someone? Boss them around? She took a deep breath and smiled at him. If he thought she could, then she could. 'All right.'

'That's my girl.'

The next morning she paid Bet to look after the shop for an hour or two and walked up to the village. She went first to see Mrs Malterby at The Green Man. That lady could not do enough for Jessie, because the extra trade in ale and other produce for the camp was proving very lucrative indeed, and Mrs Malterby had her eye on a new silk dress to wear to church.

'I need someone to help in the shop,' said Jessie. 'I thought maybe a lad from the village might . . .'

'I don't think you'll get anyone from round here, Mrs Wilde. They're all keeping their sons as far away as they can from those diggings. They don't want them to get any silly ideas and run off.'

'Well, perhaps a lass? The work's not all that heavy.'

Mrs Malterby shook her head even more vigorously. 'That'd be worse! Them as can do have sent their daughters away till that cutting's done. And them as can't are keeping their lasses close to home. Eeh, no! You'll not get anyone from here to work in your shop.'

'But I must have someone! What'll I do? The shop's so busy I can't manage on my own.'

'Well – you could try the House – though I'd not fancy taking anyone from there myself.'

'The House? What's that?'

'The poor house. Where the paupers go. Shiftless devils, most of them, if you ask me! Those poor rates are a scandal. Never been so high! But you can buy a lad from there. Only too glad to get rid of them, they are. Don't mind where they send them.' She realised how bad this sounded and flushed. 'No offence intended,' she added hastily.

Jessie hadn't even noticed the implied insult. 'I – don't know. I'd better see Jared first, I think. No, he's too busy. I must do it myself.' She took a deep breath. 'Where is this poor house?'

'Over Betterton way. Only half an hour, if you take the gig. The one House serves the six parishes. Do you want the stable lad to drive you?'

'Er – yes. That'd be best, I think.'

So Jessie found herself being jolted over some rough back lanes in The Green Man's gig, driven in a very dashing manner by the stable lad until she told him sharply to slow down or she'd return at once to the inn and ask for another driver.

A mere half hour later she was knocking on the door of a red-brick building three stories high whose rear grounds were surrounded by unusually high walls. Once her purpose was known, the reception she received was very flattering.

The supervisor, a scrawny man in an old-fashioned brown suit, with grubby linen and an equally grubby neck, showed her into his office and got straight down to business. 'You can buy an apprentice for a mere two guineas. The boy will be indentured to you for seven years, after which he'll be free to make his own way in the world – or else you can keep him on and pay him wages.'

'But I don't want anyone for seven years, Mr Soames!' protested Jessie, thinking it sounded like worse slavery than going into service. 'I only want someone for a few months.'

'In that case,' he looked like a cat with a bowl of cream, 'you can put him back in here again when you've finished with him. But you won't get your two guineas back.'

Jessie sat thinking furiously. What was she to do? She certainly needed help and just as certainly wouldn't get it from anyone in the village. But two guineas was a lot to pay out. She'd been doing a great deal of paying out lately.

'I didn't want to spend as much as two guineas,' she said at last, testing the ground. 'That's a lot of money to pay for a boy I don't even know.' She saw a flicker of interest and cupidity in the man's eyes and went on, as if talking to herself, 'No, I don't think I could go to two guineas. I'm not rich. I have my living to make. Even one guinea is a lot of money to risk, too much. No, I believe I shall have to look elsewhere.'

'We-ell, I don't like to let an honest woman down or deny a boy his chance in life. I wonder, now, if this isn't a case for making some accommodation to both our needs?'

'I wouldn't want you to get yourself into trouble with the authorities.' She took two silver coins out of her purse and began toying with the money.

The man's smile was a mirthless grimace that merely stretched the skin on his face. 'Well, we do have one lad that I'd like to put out to a good place. I could tell the Guardians that he was feeble-minded. There's nothing at all to pay for those.' He saw this did not please Jessie and hastened to add, 'He's not feeble-minded, though. Anything but! Too sharp for his own good, that one is. Mind, I won't deny he's a bit of a handful, but with the right person he could be made to do a good day's work. Take a strap to him. Can't spare the rod with young lads, believe me. I've dealt with a few and it always answers.'

'I'd have to see him first,' said Jessie, reluctant to take a child who came with such a poor recommendation. 'I'd want to talk to him. I couldn't take a half-wit, no matter how cheap.'

'I'll go and fetch him.'

He was gone for nearly ten minutes according to the loudly ticking clock on the mantelpiece, which seemed rather a long time just to fetch someone. When he returned, he was pushing a struggling child before him. The boy was blinking as if the light hurt his eyes.

'What's wrong with his eyes?' Jessie asked at once.

'Nothing. Nothing at all. He's been misbehaving – you know what boys are like – so my wife had him shut up in the cupboard. They don't like the cupboard, children don't. Frightened of the dark, they are.'

The boy wiped his ragged sleeve across his face and glowered at the supervisor. 'Ah wean't answer to John!' he declared in a shrill voice. 'Not if you leave me in that cupboard all night, ah wean't!'

The supervisor cuffed him across the head. 'You shut your face or I'll shut it for you! Now, let the lady look at you!' He pushed the lad forward.

Jessie was not impressed by the scrawny ragged child. 'What's your name?' she asked.

'John,' said the supervisor.

'Me name's Elisha!' The boy looked defiant again.

'A ridiculous name for a pauper brat!' sniffed the man. 'But he won't answer to a nice, straightforward name like John.'

'Ah'm noan *called* John!' yelled the boy, quivering with rage. 'Me mam called me Elisha an' ah'm noan changin' it!' He turned to stare at Jessie just as keenly as she was looking at him.

'I'm looking for someone to help me in my shop, Elisha,' she said quietly.

'A shop!' The supervisor stared at her in astonishment, for she had merely told him that she wanted a lad to run errands and help generally. 'I don't think *he* would suit that type of work! Now, for two guineas . . .'

'I told you, I'm not made of money and I'm not paying two guineas. How did you come to be here, Elisha?'

'His mother was brought in here *in extremis*,' said the supervisor at once. 'A dancer, she called herself. Tinkers, if you ask me! Left behind by her own people when she fell ill. No sense of responsibility . . . The parish had to pay for the doctor *and* all the funeral costs. *He* was ill too, but he recovered.' He scowled at the boy, not sounding at all pleased about that.

Elisha was scrubbing at his eyes again. 'He wouldn't let me see our mam after they took her away. She died an' ah never saw 'er again. It were his fault, so ah wean't work for him, no matter what! An' ah wean't change me name, neither.'

Jessie's heart went out to the child. 'Would you work for me, Elisha?'

'He'll do as he's told!'

'I'm grateful for your assistance, Mr Soames, but I'd prefer the boy to answer my questions himself. Well, Elisha, would you work for me?'

Solemnly the boy stared across at her. 'In a shop?'

'In a sort of shop. It's in a camp, next to the railway diggings. We move to a new place every few months.'

The supervisor nodded, pleased to have the mystery explained. That was why she'd had to come to the House for a boy. No respectable person would send their child to work in a railway camp. And for all her decent appearance and manners, the woman herself was probably no better than she ought to be.

Elisha stared at her for a minute longer, eyes old in an emaciated monkey face, then he nodded gravely, like one adult striking a bargain with another. 'Aye, then. Ah'll come with yo'.'

Jessie turned to Mr Soames and pushed the coins across the table.

The money vanished and the supervisor produced a piece of paper as if by sleight of hand. 'You'll have to sign for him. Pauper child. Feeble-minded. And there'll be no bringing *him* back. He's yours for however long you want to keep him.' He turned to the child as Jessie signed. 'And you, boy, see you obey your new mistress!'

For answer the child stuck out his tongue, then dodged behind Jessie.

'Filthy tinkers! Glad to see the back of that one. Not from our parishes, anyway. Shouldn't have had to keep him.'

Jessie handed him the signed form, then a thought struck her. 'Has he no other clothes?'

'No. They were sold to help with the expense of the burial. However, should you wish to purchase some clothes for him, we do have stocks and the price would be very reasonable.'

Fifteen minutes later Jessie and the boy left the House and got into the waiting gig. As soon as they were out of sight of the place, the boy's truculence vanished and he seemed to shrink into a sad little bundle of rags. He smelled terrible and Jessie was terrified that something would crawl on to her from his lousy body. When they got back to The Green Man, she turned to the stable lad who'd been driving her. 'I'll give you sixpence if you'll help Elisha to wash himself under the pump. *Thoroughly*, mind! And then you can burn those filthy rags he's wearing.'

The stable lad's eyes lit up. 'Yes, Mrs Wilde. Come on, you!'

'Go with him, Elisha,' said Jessie gently, 'and when you're clean, you shall have a pie to eat and a glass of milk to drink.'

'Yo' wean't leave me?' He scowled up at her.

'Of course not! I need you to work for me. I'll be in the kitchen, talking to Mrs Malterby.'

Half an hour later, a pink-skinned, shivering figure with wet hair, dressed in clean clothes too large for it, was led to the kitchen door by a grinning stable lad, who pocketed the sixpence with a wink and walked off whistling.

Jessie, who had just finished a meal similar to the one she had promised the boy, beckoned him inside. 'This is Elisha, Mrs Malterby. He's coming to work for me. Could he warm himself by your fire and have a bowl of your delicious soup, please?'

All traces of the truculent rebel were gone. Elisha, feeling that he must have landed in paradise, drank the soup in loud, appreciative gulps, then began to tackle a meat pie and a big glass of milk. He knew the two women were talking about him, but he couldn't take in what they were saying because all his attention was concentrated on the food and the warmth.

'He looks a poor scrap of a creature,' said Mrs Malterby. 'Don't they feed them in that place?'

'Not very well, obviously.' Jessie's eyes were on the waif at the table. She felt an almost maternal sense of protectiveness towards the poor lad.

'Are you sure he's what you want?' whispered the landlady, pushing a plate of cake towards her visitor. 'Have a piece, do. I'm rather proud of my fruit cake.'

'Thank you. I'd love one. As for what I want, he's all they had. Besides, they were ill treating him. I couldn't leave him there.' Jessie smiled ruefully. 'Jared'll think I've run mad.'

'Well, I hope you don't regret it, that's all.' Mrs Malterby watched the unlovely specimen of humanity stuffing itself with her good meat pie, with a complete disregard for such niceties as knives and forks. 'He hasn't got any table manners, that's for sure!'

Elisha crammed the last bit of pie into his mouth, gulped down the milk and sighed happily as he licked the white moustache from round his lips. He leaned back and within seconds his head was nodding in the warmth of the fire.

Jessie finished her cake and laughed as she had to shake him awake. 'Come on, Elisha! I've been away long enough. Bet'll be wondering what's happened to us.'

'Who's Bet?' he asked sleepily as they walked back from the inn.

'She lives at the camp and she's looking after my shop for me. I've got to get back now and see that everything's all right. And *you* look as if you could do with a sleep!'

'It were dark in that cupboard.' He shot a quick sideways glance at her. 'An' I were frit, so I daresn't sleep. But I weren't goin' to let *him* know that.'

'Certainly not.'

Elisha staggered along beside her, vainly trying to suppress a series of yawns. As they approached the camp, he stopped and stared at it. 'What's everyone doin'?'

'Building a railway. Cutting a hole through the hill because trains can't go uphill.'

'I seen a train once. Puffin' out steam, it were. Me mam promised me we'd ride on one if she got lucky.'

She watched him stare around, sleepiness forgotten in his interest. Not a stupid boy – and not a meek one, either. She hoped Jared wouldn't mind, but whether he did or not, she wasn't giving Elisha back to that terrible man.

24

Atterby: April–May 1838

'*W*ho's the lad?' Jared asked, appearing suddenly from inside the shop.

'This is Elisha. He's going to help me.'

The boy gaped up at the huge figure towering over him.

Jessie's heart sank at the expression on her husband's face.

He took Elisha by one shoulder and turned him round, inspecting him with a grimace. 'Is that the best you could find?'

'No one in the village would come to work on the diggings. I got Elisha from the Union Poor House.'

'Well, you can just take him back there again. He's too small. And underfed. He'll not be able to do the work.'

Jessie heard the boy's gasp of terror and put one arm round his shoulders. 'He'll manage, I'm sure.'

'He won't be able to carry the bigger stuff.'

She breathed in carefully and let the air out slowly. 'Elisha, go and have a look around inside, will you? I want to talk to Mr Wilde.'

He clutched her arm. 'Yo' wean't send me back!'

Her eyes met Jared's defiantly. 'No, I won't.'

Elisha opened his mouth, caught Jared's gaze and shut it again. He scuffed his way up the steps, turning at the top to look back at Jessie in appeal.

Jared shook his head as the boy disappeared inside. 'He won't do, love.'

'He'll have to do. He's all there is.' Jessie hesitated. 'And anyway, I can't send him back. They were ill treating him.'

Jared made a scornful noise in his throat.

She drew herself up and gave him back glare for glare. 'I'm *not* sending him back, Jared!'

'We'll see about that . . .'

She grabbed his arm. 'Jared, *no!*'

'We can't afford to support those who don't work.'

'He'll earn his way.'

'He's a half-wit!'

'No, he's not. He was just frightened of you. Anybody would be when you glare at them like that.'

For a moment, his scowl turned into a near grin. 'You aren't.'

'No, Jared. And I'm not giving in on this.'

A voice yelled, 'Big Jared!'

He turned his head. 'Coming!'

'Give him a week's trial, love,' she begged. 'If he's no good, we'll find him somewhere else to go, but he's not going back inside that place.'

'Hey, Jared!'

'*Coming!*' He looked down at Jessie solemnly. 'A week's trial, then. But I'll be watching him carefully.'

She let out a sigh of relief as he strode away, then turned to see Elisha peeping at her from the doorway. 'You heard?'

He nodded.

She went over to put an arm round his bony shoulders. 'We'll show him, eh? By the end of the week, he'll realise what a good, hard-working lad you are.'

He nodded again, but didn't seem convinced.

'Come on, then. Let me show you around.' There was no question now of Elisha's resting, though he looked exhausted. In a quiet voice, Jessie explained the business of the little shop.

'He's a bit small,' Bet said disapprovingly. 'I thought you wanted a strapping lad?'

'There aren't any.'

Bet rolled her eyes.

'Been busy here?'

'No, not really. Just a steady trickle.'

318

Jessie paid her the agreed amount for watching the shop and the woman slouched off. Somehow, her shoes never seemed to fit properly, just as her hair was always falling down and her shawl slipping off her shoulders. She might have been pretty when she was young. There were traces of it in her face, but mostly now she looked worn, as if life had been hard for her.

'Me mam used t'sell things,' Elisha volunteered suddenly. 'An' I used to help 'er. She used to diddle the customers sometimes, the ones as were daft an' had a bit o' money, like.'

'We don't diddle anyone in our shop.' Jessie saw his disbelief and added firmly, '*Never*. We don't have to. We make enough money without diddling. And anyway, if you diddle folk, my Jared will send you straight back to the House.'

He just shrugged, clearly thinking her foolish but accepting the implied threat. 'All reet, then.'

'How are you at counting money?' She tested him on various amounts and he proved sharp enough with figures, though he could neither read nor write. They spent the next hour going over the stock in the shop and letting Elisha count out change for customers under Jessie's supervision. The women who came in were good-natured about that, joking about her 'new feller'.

'Where's *he* going t'sleep?' Jared asked when he came back for tea. He stared at Jessie. 'I don't want any interruptions.'

'He'll sleep in the shop, under the end of the counter.'

She wasn't over-pleased with this solution, but it was all they had – and the boy himself seemed quite happy with this humble resting place and a pile of sacks to sleep on.

'I'll get you a mattress and proper blankets later,' she promised.

'*If* he stays,' Jared put in sharply.

She said nothing, but felt upset. It was rare that they had a serious disagreement, although she had no intention of backing down. Still, she had persuaded Jared to learn to read and would persuade him to keep the boy, as well. She only wished she could persuade him to send Joe away.

During the day, Elisha made himself useful in dozens of different ways, both around the shop and with anything else that needed doing. He would fetch water and empty slops, deliver messages to men on the diggings for Jared or run errands into the village, where he soon had a most enjoyable feud going with the village lads. He never forgot a task, once he had been shown how to do it, though he was appallingly ignorant at first of the most common everyday chores. Jessie concluded that the supervisor at the House had been correct when he said that the lad and his mother were tinkers, but as Elisha seemed reluctant to talk about the past, she didn't pry.

It didn't take the lad long to run foul of Joe, to whom he took an instant dislike, though whether this was on his own account because the old navvy shoved him roughly out of the way the first time he came into the shop, or whether it was because Elisha sensed Jessie's feelings, was not plain. He refused point-blank either to take messages to Joe or to serve him in the shop, and nothing would shake him from this stance. Whenever the man came into the shop, Elisha would start muttering under his breath, words that sounded like gibberish and which no one understood.

The first time it happened, Joe roared, 'Shut up, you!'

'Leave the boy alone,' Jessie snapped.

'What's he sayin' at me?'

She shrugged. Elisha had refused to explain the words he sometimes used, even to her, insisting they were secret and he'd die horribly if he told her. 'Just some boy's talk.'

'It sounds like tinker gibberish to me. An' I'm not havin' no tinker cursin' me.'

'Why should you think he's cursing you?'

After that, even if Elisha were in the back room, you could still see his lips moving whenever Joe came in. Once Joe cornered the boy near the privvy trenches and clouted him round the ear. If Jared hadn't come along just then, he would undoubtedly have given him a thrashing.

Jared, whose own feelings for Jessie's protégé were equivocal, found himself suddenly cast in the role of defender.

'What d'you want with such a varmint?' Clogger demanded.

'Jessie needs help in the shop.'

'He don't help much as I can see. Whenever I go in, he's just standing around, staring like a loony.'

Jared fought a battle with himself and honesty won. 'He does help.'

'Well, he refuses t'serve me.'

'He's probably frightened of you.'

'That one's frightened of nowt!'

'Look, let's get one thing plain, Clogger. I'm not having you thumping him. He's my responsibility, mine and Jessie's. If he cheeks you or causes trouble, you bring your complaints to me.'

Joe rumbled angrily, 'Right. But you tell him to watch hisself. An' to stop that mutterin' at me.'

'I will.' Jared tried to part on better terms. 'Christ, Joe, you're surely not bothered about a child like him? You don't have to prove how tough you are to us – we know.'

Joe muttered something and lumbered off.

Jared turned to the boy. 'You heard him, lad. Mind what you do from now on!'

'Ah'm noan feared of 'im!' Elisha said shrilly, rubbing his ear.

'Then you should be! Grown men are afraid of that fellow.' Jared sighed and tried another approach. 'Besides, you'll make things difficult for Jessie if you cause trouble with him. When you run a shop, you have to serve everyone who comes in. He's just a customer, like anyone else. So you'll cause no more trouble for Jessie?'

'Ah wean't do nowt to hurt her.' Elisha's accent became very thick whenever he was upset, but the rest of the time he had taken to imitating Jessie's accent, and had proved a good mimic. He stood scowling in the direction Joe had taken and said suddenly, 'You shouldn't let 'im come near 'er, Big Jared! He's bad. An' he stares at her.'

'He won't hurt my wife. Now go on! Back to work!'

At the end of the week, Jessie waited till Elisha was busy serving in the shop before confronting Jared. 'He's staying.'

Jared shrugged. 'It's you who needs the help.'

'And he does help me. He's a quick learner. And besides, I've grown fond of him.' He had begun to seem like a younger brother, or a cousin maybe. She had always known she wanted a proper family, and although it was wise to postpone having children until she and Jared were better set up, she still found herself looking at babies longingly and scolding the camp women when they neglected their brats.

'Oh, do as you please.'

She had expected to have to fight for Elisha. 'You've changed your mind?'

'I've watched him work.' And Jared had begun to be irritated at the way Joe stared at Jessie sometimes. It would, he'd decided, be better for her to have a companion and there was only Elisha available. Not that Joe would dare do anything, but he was obviously attracted. Jared sighed. If he'd realised how attracted, he'd not have invited the man along, but it was too late to do anything about that now. And give the fellow his due, he was working hard and had cut right down on the booze.

Oh, hell, he was probably worrying about nothing. Joe was just looking. A lot of men looked at Jessie.

The first six weeks of work on the cutting went well, with few accidents, none fatal, and the work ahead of schedule. Then they hit a rocky outcropping and the work slowed right down. The navvies became ill-tempered as their easy job turned into a struggle, and their promised bonuses receded into the distance. They grumbled and took it out on their womenfolk, several of whom soon sported bruises or black eyes. The women accepted this philosophically, but it made Jessie angry. For once, Bet didn't suffer Joe's wrath, because the ale-house profits continued to be good.

'Ye're a smart one, Big Jared,' Joe admitted one day. 'Gettin' a woman t'work for you is a good idea.'

'And having you in the ale-house is a good idea, too.' Jared grinned. 'We've never had so few disturbances.'

Joe bunched one hand into a fist and looked at it approvingly. 'They wouldn't dare.'

'Exactly.' And Joe seemed to have stopped looking at Jessie so hungrily. So maybe Jared had just been imagining things, because of what the lad had said.

One bright sunny day, however, one of the men grew careless, lulled by the warm breeze and the feel of the sun on his back. A barrow full of muck and rock crashed down on Joe, causing him to roar with fury. He lay where he had fallen for a minute or two, cursing anyone who came near him and threatening to gut the fellow who had been so careless.

After a bit, he allowed a couple of the men to help him back to his hut. His face was twisted in pain and he took to his bed for a day or two, which showed that he really had hurt himself, for Joe didn't believe in giving in to pain and boasted that he rarely lost a day's work.

The man whose carelessness had caused the accident didn't wait for dismissal, or even try to get his wages, but left precipitately before vengeance could descend on him.

When Joe went back to work, it was not with his usual vigour and it was obvious he was still in pain.

'Must be hurtin',' Bull said, spitting to one side. 'Poor old sod. Looks older, don't he?'

'Ah, he'll be all right in a few days. Let's get at that muck again.'

Profits or no profits, Bet soon had a bruised face. And it was noticed that Joe was beginning to drink more heavily. Not that he was ever unfit for work, but somehow you knew by the glitter in his eye or by the aroma that hung round him that he had taken a few pulls of gin to brace himself against the pain in his back. By the end of the day, he would be limping slightly, his face drawn and his temper chancy.

About this time, Simon Stafford began to look worried. At first he tried, not very successfully, to hide his anxiety, then one day confided in Jared that the lack of progress was draining his financial reserves, for the railway company handed out interim payments only for the amount of work done, not for the time taken to do it.

Jared became thoughtful. Should he offer to help? Working for a pound a week and a share of the profits was one thing; seeing those profits dwindling before his eyes was quite another. And yet, was it safe to risk his precious capital if things continued to go ill? He sat staring into the fire at night and made a great many calculations on scraps of paper. And he was often to be found in the thick of the work, estimating progress, examining the spoil the men took out.

He didn't discuss it with Jessie and although she knew that things were not going as well as expected, she thought it best to leave him be. Besides, she was still kept very busy in the shop, and was earning twenty or thirty shillings a week from it, even on this small site. She found this a continuing source of wonderment. She made more in two months nowadays than she had in a year as a chambermaid, and was saving most of what she earned, too, for it cost very little to feed the three of them from the stocks in the shop. They ate whatever was left over, or was not selling well. Jared scarcely noticed what he ate and Elisha had gone hungry for too long to be fussy.

With good food, the boy's face lost the sunken old man's look and he grew almost visibly. But while his body was recovering from years of hardship and abuse, his mind remained half-dormant, except for the tasks he had to learn. To work, to eat and to sleep was enough for him just then. And to be with Jessie. He followed her around like a puppy dog, striving to please her, enjoying talking to her.

The rocky outcrops continued to plague them and hold up the work, and there was no means of knowing whether the patches would peter out or not. Dynamite had to be used and men who knew how to handle explosives had to be found and paid at a higher rate than the others. Simon's expression grew more and more despondent.

'Who'd have thought that a simple cutting could turn out like this?' he said one evening when work had ceased for the day.

'It can be a bastard sometimes,' agreed Jared, keeping an eye on one gang, whose members had a tendency to be careless about their equipment. He wanted to make sure that they left no tools lying around for other people to fall over in the dark, or worse still for village lads to pinch, and that they observed all the precautions he had ordered on the slopes since Joe's accident.

'I might have to stop paying the men weekly,' Simon said abruptly. 'How do you think they'd take it?'

'Depends.'

'On what?'

'On what you change to.'

'Monthly?'

'Better not. They wouldn't take that without a fuss. It'd caus bad feeling. They'd have to manage while they waited and navvie aren't ones for savin' their money. There's not many of 'em got much put by.'

'Fortnightly, then?'

'That'd be better,' said Jared, nodding thoughtfully. 'I didn't realise you were cutting it quite so fine.'

'I didn't either,' confessed Simon, embarrassed. 'I didn't cost it out in enough detail, didn't leave myself with enough reserves. And now, with all the delays, well ...' He left the sentence unfinished, just sighing.

'You could always borrow a bit to tide you over,' suggested Jared, who had made his own investigations and come to a decision about the job. He had asked for and listened carefully to Joe's advice in this, because whatever faults he had, Clogger knew his stuff. He was rough and dirty, he strutted around like a cock on a dung heap and he boasted a lot, but he was a good railway man and understood the ways of the earth he had worked for years. Even when, as now, he was drinking too much, Jared would listen with respect to what he had to say about the work in hand.

'On what security?' asked Simon bitterly. 'I own no property. My sister has a small private income, of which the capital is untouchable, and a house she was left. I couldn't put those in jeopardy. They're all she has.' And although he knew Elinor had some money saved, he didn't think it was much and wouldn't touch it unless he was totally desperate. Which he wasn't yet. Not quite.

Besides, they had had another quarrel on his last visit, for she had had a second intruder who, although kept out of the house itself by the new locks, had trampled down her vegetable garden and left a dead rabbit dangling by the neck from the washing line. And this wasn't an isolated incident. Other people who lived outside the village had had similar incursions and tricks played on them. No one had been hurt, only a few things had been taken, and those more at whim than by value, but everyone was worried.

Simon had urged Elinor to move into a town, where she would be much safer, and she had refused point blank. They had quarrelled again. They seemed to quarrel every time they met lately. She was unhappy, he knew, but she hadn't mentioned going to live in Heptonstall again, thank goodness. He realised that Jared had said something and forced himself to pay more attention. 'Sorry. What was that?'

'Is that where you disappear to on Sundays? To your sister's?'

'Yes. She's living quite near here and she's the only family I have now. We Staffords were quite comfortably circumstanced once, but my father wasted the family money, just gambled it away. *All of it.* I can never forgive him for that. I should have inherited a house and land – not much, but more than adequate to live on. Instead, everything had to be sold when he died to pay off his debts, even the furniture. This cutting,' Simon laughed bitterly, 'was to have been the first step towards rebuilding my family fortunes. Like father, like son, they'll say, if I fail – like father, like son!'

'We're not sunk yet,' said Jared, eyes gleaming in the rays of the setting sun. Some men walked past them and he called, 'G'night, lads! See you tomorrow.' He watched the last of the gangs walk back to the camp, then turned to Simon again. 'I don't think this rock'll go on for ever. And even if it did, you should be able to make something from the job, if it's only a name as a reliable sub-contractor.'

'If my money lasts out.'

'Well – Jessie an' me, we've got a bit tucked away. For a bigger share of the profits, it might be worth our while to help you out.' He kept a careful watch on Stafford's reactions.

'*You?*'

'Aye. Me an' Jessie.'

'But you couldn't – I'm sorry, I don't mean to sound rude, but I wouldn't have thought that you would have – well, enough money to make the difference.'

'I might 'ave. How much would you need? I'd want to go over the figures carefully with you.'

Simon stared unseeingly into the sunset sky, face shining with the red reflected glow, then turned to face Jared. 'It's ridiculous, really. A mere couple of hundred would make all the difference and still leave us with some profit.' He looked at Jared as he said this, saw that he didn't flinch from the figure and hope dawned in him. 'You mean – you don't mean – have you really got that much?

'Might have.' They actually had more than that in their black box now, but there was no need for Simon to know that.

'I wouldn't need it for a week or two yet. If that bloody rock hadn't been there, I'd not have needed it at all, though it'd still have been tighter than I expected. But if you did have the money and were willing . . .'

'We'd better talk it over.' With his back to the light, Jared allowed himself a brief, triumphant grin. This was it! This was his next chance! 'We'll go back to the hut,' he said, face expressionless again. 'We've a lot to discuss. An' some of it's Jessie's money, so she deserves to know what's happenin'.'

Once the last customer had been served and the shop closed they all three sat at the rough table and worked far into the night, going over Simon's figures right down to the last halfpenny. For Jared this was a fascinating exercise, to see on paper exactly how a sub-contract worked out.

When they'd finished, he sat back, brow furrowed in thought, and the other two waited patiently for him to speak.

'Well – I think we can do it,' he said at last. 'If we make a few changes.'

Simon sighed in relief.

'The question is,' said Jared, before the engineer could become too confident, 'what'd be a fair percentage of the profits for us to ask, in return for riskin' our money? In one sense, we could ask what we liked.'

Simon tensed, frowning, then relaxed again as Jared winked at him.

'But I don't think we want to hold you to ransom. How about thirty per cent of the profits, my ten per cent as overseer to be included in that?'

Simon could not hide his relief. 'Well, I think that'd be – yes, very fair.'

Jessie almost held her breath in excitement, and her eyes were fairly shining with it, but no feeling showed on Jared's face. 'Right then,' he said. 'That suit you, love?'

'Yes.' But she knew she wouldn't sleep easily until they'd proved they could manage a sub-contract successfully.

The two men gravely shook hands, then Jared turned and shook

Jessie's hand, so after a moment's hesitation, Simon did too, though it felt strange to be treating a woman as a business partner, and such a pretty young woman at that.

'Right then,' said Jared. 'Let's talk about cutting costs, so we get the best profits out of it.'

'I don't see how we could tighten up much more,' said Simon dubiously.

'Oh, I can see a few ways. For a start, how much do they charge you for that room and parlour at The Green Man?'

'A guinea a week. But I thought we'd agreed it'd be better if I stayed there?'

'The company knows you're havin' a bit of trouble down here, don't they?'

Simon flushed. 'Yes.'

'Then they won't be surprised if you move out of The Green Man. Tell 'em you have to be on the site now, seein' as it's a bit tricky.'

'But where shall I move to?'

'Here!' said Jared, with the air of a conjuror producing a rabbit from a hat. 'There's a pile of lumber lyin' around still. We can knock you up a sleepin' space an' put it on the other side of this hut. Have you ever done any carpentering?'

'Well, I can hammer a nail in and saw straight, but I'm not up to anything fancy.'

Jared chuckled. 'You won't be gettin' anythin' fancy. It doesn't have to be perfect, just waterproof. All right, Jessie love, to have another member of the family?'

'Of course,' she said instantly.

'Now,' said Jared, 'it's Sunday tomorrow. No workin' allowed on the diggings, but who's to complain about a man building a roof for his own head?'

So Jessie went to church without her husband the next day, enjoying the walk along the leafy lanes and taking young Elisha skipping along beside her as her escort. Though he, like Jared, could see no point in churchgoing, the boy loved being on his own with Jessie.

By tea-time, the annexe, as Simon insisted on calling it, was complete. It measured five feet by seven feet, the exact size and shape being decided in the end by the timber available from Jared's scrap pile and the wall to which it would be attached. It smelled strongly of sawdust and tar, which they had used to make the overlapping edges of the planks as weathertight as possible. The roof was made of pieces of battered tin sheeting. They had even managed to cobble together a crude bed, made of planks and canvas webbing, like Jared and Jessie's own. They'd not got a feather mattress, but Jessie could buy one from the village and Simon said cheerfully he would sleep as soundly as a prince.

'We haven't discussed my keep,' he said, when they'd moved his things in and were admiring their efforts. Another of Jessie's sheets had been sacrificed to curtain off his space and was ceremonially drawn into place when the work was finished.

'And we shan't discuss it, either,' she said. 'Unless you start wanting any special treatment. If you're content to eat as we do, live as we do, we'll forget that.'

Jared looked at her sharply as she spoke, for she'd not consulted him, but after a moment's thought, he smiled. Trust her to soften the blow and win old Bony Stafford's friendship with a simple, inexpensive gesture!

'But I can't do that!' Simon protested.

'It's my investment in the contract,' she insisted. 'I earn our keep, and more, in my shop.'

'An' it's no use arguing with her when she looks like that,' said Jared. 'Once she's made up her mind, she'll not change it!' He gave her a hug to show her that he approved of what she had done.

Simon looked at them in wonderment and with more than a twinge of envy. Never had he met a couple so united. 'Well, if the three of us are to be partners, I suggest we start using our given names. I can't stay "Mr Stafford" if I'm part of the family.'

'That's all right with us, Simon lad,' said Jared, seeing that Jessie had temporarily lost her tongue.

When they were in bed that night, she whispered to him, 'Fancy me being on first name terms with Lord Morrisham's cousin!'

He chuckled. 'Aye. I could see that got to you. We're on our way, love, aren't we?'

'Yes.'

'And this is only the beginning. You'll see!' He felt jubilant, energy running through him like liquid fire.

He was soon asleep, but Jessie lay wakeful for a long time, worrying about the risks they were taking. She wished sometimes that she had a woman friend to talk to about everything. And she'd been feeling a bit tired lately. Not like her, that, let alone she couldn't afford to be sick.

25

Atterby: June 1838

*T*he woman looked pleadingly at Jessie. 'Can't you put it on the slate, love?'

Jessie hardened her heart. 'No. I don't do that. Ever.'

'But with my man only getting paid every fortnight, I haven't enough money to buy his food.'

The other women in the small shop muttered and nodded. They, too, were feeling the pinch.

'I run this shop because I have my living to earn, like anyone else. I can't afford to offer credit, and that's a fact! If I don't get paid, how will I buy more goods?'

'Your man's got plenty of money. He's the overseer.' There were more nods from the other customers.

Jessie knew she daren't give way, not even once. She hated to see the desperation in their faces, but she couldn't feed them all – and if she did let them have things on tick, some would never pay her back. 'That's his money. This is my shop. No slate.'

'He'll go mad when I've no food for him,' the woman muttered as she turned away, then swung round to say fiercely, 'You'll eat well, though, Jessie Wilde.'

But the navvies and their women managed somehow. They always did. They bought less tobacco and ale, and a few borrowed money from Jared, but fortnightly payments were still considered good by railway standards and after the first surge of anger, things began to settle down again.

Joe grumbled to Jared that the profits from Bet's ale-house were down.

'They'll soon go up again after the next pay.' Jared hesitated, then said, 'You're drinking some of the profits yourself, Joe lad. You can't have it both ways.'

'A man needs a drink or two after a hard day's work.'

'You're havin' more than a couple.'

'That's my business. When I don't turn up for work, or Bet don't pay you for the ale, then it'll be your business. Not until.'

But not only was he drinking heavily and swallowing some of the profits, he was keeping customers away by his surliness, Jared knew. He watched Clogger walk away, thinking that since the accident, the other man had suddenly begun to show his age. And he was usually limping by the time he returned from his day's labours, however hard he tried to hide it.

When Simon commented on the change in Joe, Jared shrugged. 'Some of the old ones go like that, all of a sudden. It's sad. They've worked hard all their lives an' what have they to look forward to? Nowt. I'll make sure I'm out of it before then. Bloody sure.' But he bent over backwards to excuse Joe's pugnacity and ignored the smell of booze on his breath. As long as the ganger did his work, he could stay on.

Bet, who helped Jessie out sometimes in the shop, had started to grumble about 'folk as booze all night an' can't pleasure a woman no more'. Jessie said nothing, but she longed for Joe to do something that would push even Jared's patience too far, for she was finding the old navvy more of a problem than ever. Once again he had begun to hang around the shop when Jared wasn't there, staring at her, whispering lewd remarks when no one else was nearby. And unfortunately, Elisha was terrified of him and always slid away into the back when he came in. Jessie said nothing to Jared. What good had complaining to him ever done before? He was blind where Joe was concerned and was known to be a soft touch for any old navvy passing through.

With Simon and Jared working in close partnership, work on the cutting was speeding up. If they had worked hard before, they were relentless now. Simon's face became as brown as Jared's and his hands grew rougher as he took part in any job he could.

They worked on the site until the daylight failed and the darkness became too dense to see the man next to them, then they came back to the hut, rapidly ate a meal and worked on their books and costs and planning before falling into bed.

Joe watched all this sourly. He resented the way Big Jared had done so well for himself, resented the new intimacy with the engineer. His desire for Jessie tormented him so much that somehow he managed to persuade himself that if he once had her, she would turn to him as the better man, since her husband was neglecting her. He knew how to handle women. Jared was too soft with them. He studied Bet through narrowed eyes. Look at the way she jumped to do his bidding. But she was a poor thing in comparison. That was why he couldn't always pleasure her. It was *her* fault, not his. She was getting old. Old and ugly. A man needed someone younger to tempt his appetite. He'd get rid of Bet after this job was over.

As the days passed, however, Jessie found Joe's renewed attentions so upsetting that she had to ask Jared to do something about him. 'He's really annoying me, love. You should see – '

He let out a sigh. 'I know he stares at you. I've seen it, too. But looks can't kill and he wouldn't dare touch you. Joe's more than pulling his weight and we need men like him at the moment. Now, I have to get the pays ready.'

'But, Jared – '

'Let it drop, will you?'

As Simon and Jared started coming home later, Joe grew bolder, turning up at the shop every evening just before it closed. On the excuse of making some minor purchase or other, he would hang around, not saying anything to which Jessie could take exception, but making her nervous with his mere presence. Like Jared, he was a big man and no one dared upset him. Jessie asked Elisha never to leave her alone in the shop when Joe was there.

'All reet. He's a nasty bastard, though. If I were bigger, I'd bash 'im ovver th'ead for yo'. That's what Jared should do.'

'I know you would, love. As it is, don't leave me alone when he's around. And – if he gives me any – any bad trouble, don't try to help me yourself, just run for help.'

'All reet, Jessie.'

333

But Joe, obsessed by the desire to have Jessie, renew his manhood and get his own back on Jared – whom he blamed for all his recent troubles, though he couldn't have said why – was not yet so far gone in his madness as to risk attacking her in her own shop, or even in the camp with people within calling distance. He was content to bide his time.

And Jared, working himself to the limit even of his great endurance, was too tired most nights to talk or make love to his wife in more than a cursory manner, often falling asleep as soon as he rolled into bed. She accepted this as the price of success, and made sure that he ate well, for it was all she could do for him. Not long now, she kept telling herself. Only a few more weeks. Then she'd see the last of Clogger Joe. Because she'd decided to tell Jared straight once this contract was over: either Joe went or she did. Not that she expected to have to carry out her threat, but it'd show Jared how upset she was.

At the end of June there were celebrations in Atterby and throughout the land to mark the coronation of the young Queen. The men on the diggings had taken very little notice of national preparations for this event, though every detail was reported in the newspapers. They affected scorn at the local activities because the villagers had not included the railway folk in their plans.

However, when the great day came, the navvies did make the coronation their excuse for a celebration and nothing Jared said would sway them from this. Fuming, he and Simon worked at what they could and scowled as they watched the men lounging around, boozing, smoking and gambling with dice or greasy cards.

The day wore on uneasily, but there was no real trouble, though there would be a lot of thumping heads the following day from the amount being drunk.

That evening Simon produced a bottle of wine to go with their evening meal and even Elisha was allowed a little in his cup to drink the health of the newly crowned Queen. Jessie wasn't much impressed by the taste of the wine, which Simon said was French claret, but she drank hers out of politeness, washing the taste away with judicious sips of tea. Jared tasted his more carefully, because wine was one of the things the gentry drank, so he intended to learn about it one day.

'It's not a *good* claret,' Simon told them, wishing he had a glass to drink out of so that he could enjoy the colour properly, 'but it's not too bad. One day I'll teach you about wine, Jared. It's the prince of drinks. The French have a saying: "*Un repas sans vin, un jour sans soleil*." ' He felt suddenly worried that they'd think he was trying to show himself superior. 'That means, "*A meal without wine is a day without sun*." The French make the best wine in the world, you see.'

'Mmmm.' Jared rolled the claret round his mouth before swallowing it, as he had seen Simon do. Like Jessie, he didn't think much of the taste. 'Well, I'm not what you'd call a drinking man myself, but it's nice to try summat new,' he said eventually, seeing that Simon was waiting for a comment. 'It's stronger than ale, isn't it?'

Simon laughed. 'Definitely! Wine's not for swilling down. You drink a glass or two with a meal to enhance the taste of the food. I'll show you one day. And, Jessie, if you put the remains of this bottle into a stew, it'll improve the taste of that too.' He could see they didn't really appreciate the glories of good wine and laughed again, at himself this time. One day, he vowed to himself, he'd have a nice home once more, with a cellar full of carefully chosen wine. He and Elinor would live a more gracious life then. You could get sick of mud and rocks and dirty men pushing wheelbarrows up slopes. 'I'll show you how to choose good wine one day, Jared,' he repeated.

'Will there be a "one day"?' Jared kept his voice casual. 'What happens after this contract is finished?'

Simon stared at him. 'I'd assumed,' he began, then broke off to stare at them again. 'I thought we made a good team. I'd just assumed we'd stay together. Don't you want to?'

Jared stared back at him very seriously. 'Stay together how?' he asked. 'It needs spellin' out, maybe.'

Simon reached across in one of his quick, impulsive gestures, to clasp a hand of each of them. 'Of course! I should have said something, not just taken it for granted.' He inclined his head to each of them as he spoke. 'Jared – Jessie – I would like to continue our partnership, to take on other jobs together.'

Jessie smiled, but Jared waited.

'As *equal* partners. I have the contacts, something of a name as an engineer – you, Jared, have experience of every detail of site-working. Your calculations on costs are better than I could ever do, and your knowledge of the navvies goes far beyond mine. And, Jessie, we could not have managed this time without you and your shop – and the way you look after us all. So, what do you both say?'

'I say we pour out the rest of the wine,' said Jared, 'and we drink another toast. Not to some Queen we'll never see, but to us – to the three of us – and to our future!'

It took another week of hard work to dig their way out of the rocky patches, and then, almost overnight, work speeded up and the end of the cutting was in sight. The company inspector and surveyor were breathing down their necks and turning up every day or two to check on the final slopes. And now the rock which had held them up for so long became an ally and made their work easier, because you didn't need retaining walls of brick for solid rock. The contract turned out to be profitable after all, as Jared had calculated for himself, though not as profitable as it might have been if he'd been involved from the start.

Now they had to discuss seriously what they were to do next. Simon had been 'sniffing around', as he called it, for a while.

'Be done in a week – ten days at most,' said Jared, sipping a pot of ale that Elisha had just drawn him, fresh from the barrel.

'I'll be sorry in a way,' said Jessie. 'I've enjoyed living here.'

'I – er – I heard about something today,' said Simon. This casual remark obtained their immediate attention and even Elisha stopped in his tracks to listen. 'The inspector was telling me that one of their sub-contractors dropped down dead just up the line, with his contract half-finished. About the same size of cutting as this, but there's a problem with a stream. He wanted to know if I'd be interested in taking it over and finishing it for them. The work's nearly at a standstill, because there were no detailed plans set down on paper. The contractor had everything in his head and no one is sure exactly how he had planned to proceed. That's a damned unsound way to work! Half the men have drifted away and the company's trying to find someone to take over and get things going again. It could hold up the whole line if it isn't finished more or less on schedule.'

Jared drank another mouthful. 'Sounds interesting,' he said slowly. 'But we'd have to go and see it first. Streams can be tricky. What did you tell that inspector?'

'I told him I'd have to consult my partner and then we'd need to go and look it over.'

'Right. Not tomorrow, but the day after, eh?'

'Suits me.'

Jared turned to his wife. 'Will you be all right on your own, love? We'll only be gone overnight.'

'Of course I will!' Jessie said stoutly, though she had a few reservations about being left in the camp with Joe still around and no Jared to protect her.

But that problem was solved for her in an unexpected way.

The next day Clogger got into a fight. Jared, drawn to the scene by the noise, was in time to stop him from doing permanent injury to his opponent, but then Joe turned on him. He was roaring drunk, swaying on his feet as he hurled abuse at everyone within sight. When Jared refused to fight him, Joe lurched towards him and kicked out at him with an iron-shod clog.

Jared picked up a metal crowbar and brandished it. 'I'm not fighting you, you stupid bugger! Get back to your hut and sleep it off!'

'Bleedin' coward!' Joe tried to find himself a crowbar, too, but found it hard to focus. Suddenly he sat down, breathing heavily, but still cursing. 'I'll get you, you bastard!' he shouted. 'You wait! I'll get you! You *and* your bloody wife. I'll have her splayed out beneath me afore I'm done.'

There was a hiss of indrawn breath from the men around them and a rumble of anger from Jared's gang.

He wanted to smash Joe's face in for saying that about Jessie. And he wanted to bang his own head against the wall. She had been right. Joe was doing more than just looking – he was intending. But Jared held himself back. He was the overseer. He mustn't fight.

He needn't ignore the incident, though. 'If that's how you feel about us, Joe, you'd better pack your things and get out of the camp! I'm not one of the lads now, an' I'm not gettin' into a fight just because you're mad drunk. Nor I'm not havin' *anyone* threatening my wife. Ever.'

'Bleedin' sow! She's been leading me on.'

Another surge of anger made Jared freeze and fight for self-control, then he said curtly, 'I've leaned over backwards to help you, but there's a limit.'

'I don't *need* any bloody help from a soddin' jumped-up young bastard like you!'

There was utter silence in the group around them.

'Well, you won't get it from now on.' How Jared kept his voice steady, he didn't know. 'I don't need someone running my gang who goes fighting mad for no reason. Or who says things like that about my wife. Get off the camp, Joe! Before nightfall. You've had your chance and thrown it away. You're past this sort of work now!'

'I'll get off this twopenny camp and find another, an' a better one, tomorrow!' roared Joe. 'I was buildin' soddin' canals when you were a snotty-nosed kid an' I'll still be buildin' 'em when you find you've bitten off more than you can chew an' have t'run for your life. Call yourself a sub-contractor! Couldn't build a line on a flat mile, you couldn't!'

He peered round at the crowd which had gathered. 'Away, lads! Who's comin' wi' old Clogger? I'll show you how t'run a gang! I'll find you the best jobs. Ain't no one knows the railways like old Joe.' He began to roar out a bawdy song, but after a while it penetrated even his sodden brain that most of the men had wandered away again and that no one was paying any attention to him. He blinked round in surprise and found only one person looking at him, and that with a chill glare.

'Get off the camp, Joe,' repeated Jared. 'I'll give you two hours, then if you've not gone, I'll throw you off myself. I'll send Billy over to your hut with your wages.'

Billy scowled when given this thankless task, but he did as he was told. Big Jared in this mood was not to be argued with. The men laid bets with each other as to whether someone would have to throw Joe off the camp by force, and how many it would take to do that, but no force was needed. Joe left in his rickety cart, still roaring defiance, with Bet sitting snivelling miserably beside him. She knew, even if he didn't, that he had just thrown away the best chance he'd ever had in his life, maybe his last chance of providing for his old age – and hers, too. She'd have preferred to stay on at the camp without him, but didn't dare say that to Joe, who just assumed she would go with him.

Jessie was delighted when she saw Joe leave, for Elisha had come running to tell her what had happened. She couldn't believe she was free of him at last. 'You won't give him a second chance, will you, Jared?' she asked later.

'No, love. He's past it. I reckon he hurt his back more than he'd admit and that was why he started drinking again. But he wouldn't ask for another chance now. There's too much between us.'

'I believe you're still sorry for him?' she said accusingly.

'I am a bit, poor old bugger. He's given his life to the railways and now that he can't dig any more, what is there left for him? Aye, I do feel sorry for him. But I'm not going to end up like him. An', love – '

'Yes?'

'I'm sorry. I didn't realise how bad he'd become about you. I should have listened to you, done something before now.' Jared sighed and ran one hand through his hair. 'I've been so busy with this contract – but I still should have listened to you. Can you forgive me?'

He held out his arms in invitation and she ran into them. 'Of course I forgive you, love.' She kissed him hungrily. 'Anyway, he was only being a nuisance. He never actually *did* anything. And we won't have to see him again, so it's all forgotten.' She felt a wonderful lightness at the thought of that.

Jared and Simon arranged to drive over to the other cutting the next day and make a careful survey of the land and what had been achieved so far. Simon had already done a preliminary check, but they needed detailed estimates of costs and a proper contract before they agreed to take it on, and Jared could do that more accurately. Jessie was to clear up the shop and then go and spend the night at The Green Man. Jared didn't want her alone in an almost-empty camp without his protection.

'No!' he said firmly, when she protested about this unnecessary precaution and expense. 'I know you've got Elisha to keep you company, but he'd not be able to protect you if there was any trouble.' He didn't think Joe would come back, but he wasn't risking it.

'Who against?' For with Joe gone, Jessie saw nothing to fear. The few men who were left were members of Jared's old gang. She knew them all and couldn't see any of them attacking her.

'You'll do as I say, love! The men'll be drunk by nightfall an' I want you safe out of it.'

'Jared, that's silly! It's a waste of money my staying at the inn. I've got so much to do here that it's a waste of time, too.' She looked up at his face, but he was not to be moved. 'Oh, very well. But I still think it's stupid.'

'Then do it for me, love, to set my mind at rest.'

'All right. For you.' She went over and hugged him. 'I'm so proud of you, love.' They stood quietly for a while, savouring a rare moment of privacy.

'A lot of it's due to you,' he said, twisting a tendril of her hair round his finger.

'No, it's not.'

'It is!' he said seriously. 'Without you I'd never have learned how to read and write - or to talk better. I needed you to - to polish me up a bit. I'd still be running a gang if it wasn't for you, love.'

She nestled against the solid warmth of him, wondering whether to tell him now what she suspected. Then she decided to wait. He didn't need distracting when he had a contract to estimate and negotiate. Besides, she wasn't quite sure that he'd be pleased, though she was delighted.

'We've still got some hard work ahead of us,' he went on, 'but we've made the start now, do you see, and it's up to me - no, up to all of us - not to mess up this chance. Me and Simon make a good team. Even if he is a gentleman born, us two get on well. An' I trust him.'

'You'd have managed on your own, Jared. You're that sort of a person.'

'Aye, maybe, but I'd not have got this far so quickly. I've set my sights on the moon now. Will you come an' live on it with me, if I buy it for you?'

'Yes, Jared. I'll come anywhere with you.'

Elinor woke up to hear someone shuffling round in the garden. Like a flash she was out of bed and peering carefully out of the window, trying to see who it was. A man, obviously, but although the moon was full, the intruder was hugging the shadows under the trees and she could not make out any details of his appearance, except that he wasn't very tall.

She jumped in shock as Thirza spoke next to her. 'He's out there again, isn't he, miss?'

'Yes.'

'We can't go on like this, miss.'

Elinor continued to stare outside. 'I'm not going to be driven away from my home.'

'Maybe if we moved to Heptonstall?'

'You know we can't do that.'

Thirza let out an angry hiss of breath. 'We could if we wanted to.'

'I won't alienate Simon.'

After a while, the intruder went away and silence reigned again, but Elinor couldn't sleep. Thirza was right, really. They couldn't go on like this. But she couldn't think what else they could do. She desperately didn't want to go and live in a town again.

'Oh, Simon,' she sighed as dawn crept across the lawn and peered through her window. 'What am I to do about you?' Because, of course, there was only one place she really wanted to go. Perhaps when this contract was finished she could persuade him to think again about Heptonstall? On this hopeful thought she fell asleep.

So did her intruder, a few miles away. He'd seen the two

women at the window. He'd allus had sharp eyes. He chuckled to himself. It was fun stirring them up like this. He wasn't going to rush into anything though. You had to be careful.

26

༄ ༇

July 1838

The next day Jessie waved goodbye to Jared and Simon from the doorway of the shop, then turned to tackle the clearing up and packing. It seemed strange to see the shelves almost empty, with only a few dry goods like flour and tea and currants left. Most of the shelves had been dismantled into planks, so any noise she made echoed round the hut.

For some reason, as the morning passed, she began to feel jumpy and ill at ease. It was probably because the camp was so quiet, she told herself, or because Jared had gone away. They hadn't been apart even for one night since they were married. She'd best get her work done. The sooner she could leave for The Green Man, the better. Jared was right. An empty camp was no place for a woman on her own.

She worked on steadily, with Elisha trotting here and there at her behest. When she had almost finished, she sent him off for some more water to scrub down the last of the shelves before they were dismantled.

She didn't hear the door open and the man come in until he was standing right next to her.

'Workin' hard, missus?'

She jumped like a startled rabbit and her heart began to pound with terror as she saw Clogger Joe. There was something different about him today, something both triumphant and possessive.

'Frighten ye, did I, missus?' He laughed hoarsely.

She remained where she was, kneeling on the floor beside her bucket, feeling quite stupid with fright and not knowing what to do. Why had Joe come back? How had he dared to return?

'Big Jared around?'

'He – he's just gone into the village for something.'

Joe laughed loudly. 'Saw 'im leavin' Atterby three hours ago,' he said. 'I watched 'im drive out with 'is fancy gentleman friend.' He spat on the floor to show what he thought of gentlemen as a species.

'They're just going to see someone. They won't be long.' She couldn't seem to move.

He reached down and pulled her to her feet, keeping hold of an arm that trembled in his. He laughed again. 'No, 'e'll not! 'E'll not be back till tomorrow. They had bags with 'em. I'm not stupid, missus.'

She pulled away suddenly, trying to kick out at him, but her foot caught in her skirts and before she could regain her balance, he had twisted her round, pinning her to him.

'I've waited nigh on a year to 'ave you,' he said slowly, revelling in the fright in her eyes. She was a scornful piece, but now that he had her, he would teach her a bit of respect. 'A year,' he repeated. 'I've not done that for no woman afore. Ye're a bleedin' witch!'

'Jared'll kill you if you touch me!'

'He'll 'ave to find me first, won't he?' Joe jeered. 'An' you! He'll 'ave to find us both afore he can do anything.'

Panic fluttered at the edges of her mind, but she wouldn't give in to it. 'What do you mean?'

'I mean we're goin' away, just the two of us. He'll soon find out he can't treat me like that. Oh, yes, he will. An' so will you.'

She started to scream, but he put his hands round her throat and squeezed till she could only gurgle and choke.

'There's no one near enough to hear you, missus. I made sure o' that. They're all down t'other end of the camp. So you can scream as much as you like an' no one'll hear. But I'd rather you kep' quiet because I don't like screamin' women. An' from now on, you're goin' to learn to do what I like. I'm not soft like your bloody Jared is. No, I'm not soft at all.'

She gazed frantically up at him, unable to move in his bear-like grasp, her head still spinning from the pressure on her throat. His eyes were gleaming down at her with a wild light, but she couldn't smell the usual gin on his breath, just the rank odour of his body. He's gone mad, she thought, mad!

Footsteps outside the hut made them both freeze where they were and Joe reach for Jessie's throat again.

'Joe? Is that you?' Bet stood in the doorway, her smile fading as she took in the scene before her. 'Joe – what're you doing?'

He swore at her. 'You get out an' mind your own soddin' business, you daft bitch! I told you t'wait in the village.'

'Joe – what are you doin' with her?' wailed Bet. 'She don't want you! She's Big Jared's woman. She's his *wife*!'

He threw Jessie to the floor, slamming her head on a pile of planks as he did so. She lay there, half-stunned, groaning, unable to focus properly.

'You say one word to anyone about this,' Joe threatened, striding over to Bet and grabbing her by the hair, 'an' I'll kill you!'

'I won't say nothin'. What do you take me for?' She smiled at Joe, a travesty of a smile. 'But Joe, if I ain't goin' with you, I want some money. That's only fair. I've worked for it. You'll give me a share, won't you, Joe? I'll need something to tide me over.' She stood her ground, though expecting him to hit her at any moment.

He spat on the floor. 'Bleedin' bitch!' he said after a moment.

'I want ten pound.' Her voice was shrill with fear, but desperation made her persist. 'I've worked real hard, Joe. I got a right to somethin'!'

He shoved four gold sovereigns and some loose change into her hand and pushed her out of the door. 'That's all you're havin'. An' if you come back pesterin' me, I'll thump you senseless an' take that away from you.' When he turned round, Jessie was trying to sit up, feeling sick and dizzy.

'I was goin' to have you now,' he growled, pawing at her breasts, 'but that silly bitch might go an' tell someone I'm here.'

Jessie pulled away from him, whimpering, still feeling disoriented.

He laughed to see her so humbled. She was no different from

any other woman when it came down to it. You just had to show them who was the master. Still keeping an eye on her, he went over and opened the trunks she had packed so carefully, searching through the contents and scattering things all over the floor. Not finding what he sought, he went over and shook her hard. 'Where's he keep the money?'

She stared at him glassily, slow to answer, and he slapped her face. 'The money! *Where's – the – bloody – money?*'

She struggled to gather her wits together. 'He took it with him. He said it'd be safer with him than with me.'

'Yer lyin'!'

'I'm not! You won't find any money here apart from a little loose change under the counter.'

He slapped her again out of sheer disappointment, scrabbled through the mess on the floor once more, just to make sure, then stood up and fumbled under the counter, growling in disappointment at how little there was. By then she was trying to crawl towards the door, so he ripped one of her best linen tablecloths into strips, rolled her over and began to tie her hands behind her back and bind her feet together. He kept stroking her body as he did this, his eyes gleaming with that strange light that sent shivers through her. Then the fumbling ceased. 'Not now!' he muttered to himself. 'No time now. Silly bloody bitch might tell.'

He fixed a gag of material in Jessie's mouth, then swung her across his shoulders as if she were a sack of flour. The pain in her head was so great she was only half aware of what was happening. When he bumped her against the doorpost, she fainted and didn't see Elisha hurtle towards Joe, screeching, 'Let her go! Let her go!'

One great fist thumped the lad aside and Joe kicked him a couple of times for good measure with his iron-tipped clog. 'Teach you to be cheeky t'me, you little bastard!' he said with great satisfaction.

He didn't notice the other figure peering from behind the remains of a hut fifty yards away. Bet had progressed rapidly from disappointment to jealous rage and a seething desire to take her revenge on Joe. Thirty-five years of hard living, with more downs than ups, had taught her to think on her feet, even through the ruin of her hopes. She couldn't go across the field to summon the few remaining men without Joe seeing her. Besides, she didn't want them to have any credit for rescuing Jessie. There'd be no reward for her if someone else saved Jared's wife.

She decided she would follow Joe and report back to the camp later. 'An' I hope Big Jared kills the bastard,' she muttered to herself. 'I'll teach that Joe to drop me like that! I were the one as earned that money! It's me as should be with him now.'

Clogger Joe threw Jessie's unconscious body on the back of his dilapidated cart. He covered her with some sacks and without a backward glance heaved himself into the driving seat. Clicking to the elderly bone-bag of a horse, he sat behind it humming tunelessly as it began to amble down the small, half-overgrown lane between the camp and the village.

Bet followed at a distance. She had no need to run or even to walk quickly, because the old horse had no gallop left in it. She ignored the light rain that began falling half an hour later, just muttering to herself in annoyance as she walked along in the direction the cart had taken. She did not feel cold. Anger kept her warm.

Joe drove for nearly three hours, making no attempt to spur his animal into anything faster than a stumbling walk. Big Jared wouldn't be back until at least the next day and he'd paid off that bitch, Bet. The thought of the five pounds still rankled with him, as did the knowledge that he'd not found any of Big Jared's money. But he had the woman and that was the main thing. He didn't think of her as Jessie. He rarely bothered to learn women's names. It didn't matter what you called them when you lay with them.

Twice on the journey he stopped at inns for a quick wet, purchasing a bottle of gin at each and emptying the first within a couple of hours. He made no attempt to release Jessie or to care in any way for her needs, though from time to time he did check that she was still securely tied up. As he did so, his hands lingered on her body in anticipation of pleasures yet to come and he roared with laughter as she whimpered in her throat and tried to pull away from him.

For the first part of the journey Jessie was barely conscious, but by the end of the afternoon, she'd regained her wits, in spite of a throbbing headache and the stickiness of blood on her temple where she'd hit the floor. But none of her struggling had loosened the bonds at all and her arms were now numb.

When she kicked the sacks away, hoping that someone might see her, Joe stopped the cart with a curse, slapped her face and pinned her more securely into place. He also threatened to knock her out again if she gave him any more trouble. She knew he'd do it, too, and didn't dare try to kick the smelly sacks off again. It was better to keep her wits about her than to be unconscious.

Terror curdled into acid within her as they continued to jolt along for what seemed like hours. She couldn't see any hope of rescue, for Jared wouldn't be back until the next day and anyway, no one would know where she was, but she tried to keep the terror under control. Panic got you nowhere. She'd have to find a way to escape – somehow. She didn't dare dwell on what would happen if she didn't.

Bet plodded along after the cart, cursing mechanically at the rain and the mud and, like Joe, stopping a few times for refreshment. She considered giving up, but each time another surge of anger sustained her in her decision to follow him. She didn't feel so much sorry for Jessie, as angry with her for letting herself be caught by Joe. She reckoned it should be worth at least ten pounds to Big Jared to find out where his wife was. And Bet wouldn't tell him till she had the coins in her hand. No, she bloody wouldn't. You couldn't trust men. The rotten devils always lied to you and let you down.

In the late afternoon Joe pulled off the road up a rough track with a brokendown rail fence running alongside it and stopped in front of some ramshackle farm buildings. Bet didn't dare try to follow him up the track, because there was nowhere to hide. She watched from a distance as a dog came out and started barking furiously. Joe kicked it out of the way and said something to a man who came out of a shed. The man took the dog away and then came back to see to the horse. He and Joe seemed to be arguing about something, but Joe settled the matter by slamming the man against a wall and waving a fist in his face. After that he took the horse into the barn and didn't come out again.

Joe turned back to the cart, dragged the sacks aside, picked Jessie up and carried her into the house.

She groaned as he took the gag out of her mouth. 'Where are we?'

'What's that matter to you?' He untied her feet and arms, but she couldn't move, because they were numb. As she tried to sit up and fell over, he roared with laughter and left her lying on the ground while he got himself another drink. He ignored her gasps and smothered groans as the circulation was restored to her chilled limbs, just sipped and smiled and watched.

After a while, he picked her up and threw her into a chair. He forced some gin down her throat and gave his hoarse wheeze of laughter as she choked and spluttered and spat it out again. He held her head still and thrust his face near hers. 'There's no one here. It won't matter if you scream. There's no help to be got for you. So behave.'

She shrank back in the chair, face bruised and filthy, blood matted on her bruised forehead and her dress torn. 'Jared'll kill you.'

'He'll have t'find me first. An' you too. By that time, it'll be too late.' Joe felt a twitching in his loins, but he wasn't ready yet. No need to hurry, though. He had all night. And all the next day, too, if he chose. Though he'd move on after that. Take her with him, too. She'd have learned how to behave by then.

Jessie tried another tack. 'Joe, you'd be better asking a ransom for me. You could get fifty pounds for me from Jared, maybe more if you don't touch me.'

He grinned, enjoying the feeling of power. He could feel the urge rising slowly in him. I'm getting there, he decided. Getting there. 'I've enough money of me own for now.' He began to unfasten his trousers. 'It's you I want, not money.'

He stepped out of the trousers and reached out to take hold of her.

Bet, crouching damply beneath a clump of bushes, heard the screams coming from the cottage and muttered a curse. It wasn't fair on the poor bitch. No, it wasn't fair. She took a pull of gin to deaden the sound of the screams and tried to think what was the best thing to do now.

In the morning Joe, in a foul mood and with a mouth like last week's bread, went out to relieve himself behind the cottage, then came back and pawed at Jessie again. She lay like one dead beneath his touch, muttering her husband's name beneath her breath.

'I'm hungry,' he decided. 'That's what's wrong. Get up an' make me summat.'

She shook her head and he slapped her face, but no amount of threats or blows would make her cook breakfast for him.

The other man came in from the barn to eat and grinned at the battered woman.

'Give yer a bit of trouble, did she, Joe?'

He spat in the fire. 'Needs tamin'.'

'How about givin' me a turn with 'er?' The man played with a knife from the table. 'I could persuade her a bit.'

'No. She's mine!' Joe untied Jessie and tossed her torn dress at her. 'Cover y'rself up! An' not a word out of turn or I'll strangle you.'

She knew he meant exactly what he said by that and why he was saying it. Silently she put on the dress, wincing as it touched her cuts and bruises and swaying dizzily from lack of sleep and food. She accepted a cup of strong black tea from the other man, shivering at the lust in his eyes. No, it was more than lust, it was madness – she was with *two* madmen! – but she made no effort to eat any of the stale bread he produced from a cupboard, because she felt too sick with shame.

She ignored Joe's presence completely; if she'd had a weapon she wouldn't have hesitated to kill him. She was sure that somehow Jared would find her. Then he'd kill Joe for her. Until he came, she must survive as best she could.

'Where's the money, then?' the other man asked after a while.

'The sod had taken it all with 'im!'

The little man jerked upright. 'Here, I ain't doin' this for nothin'! You promised me there'd be somethin' in it for me!' He gave a high, hiccupping laugh. 'I need to get away from here before they catch me. They nearly did last week. An' you *promised* me some money.'

'What yer gonna do about it? Tell the nearest magistrate?' Joe gave a short bark which might have been a laugh. 'I've a few things I could tell him meself if you try that! I know what you're like. You were daft when you were a lad an' you've just got dafter.' For all that the other man was his cousin, he had nothing but contempt for Vin and had never intended to pay him anything.

'Y'know I'd not roz on you! But fair's fair, an' I ought to 'ave somethin' for me trouble. I give up me bed, didn't I? An' there's the food, too.'

'Call that muck food!' Joe spat into the fire, but after a while he pulled out some coins and tossed them at the man. 'That's all you're gettin', Vin. I can't spare any more.'

The man scrabbled on the floor for the money, but was plainly not satisfied with the amount, for he cast resentful glances at Joe's hunched figure. After a while he muttered something about seeing to the animals and slouched out of the house.

At the end of the lane, Bet woke up, realised it was getting light and groaned. She stared at the tumbledown buildings, watched the man go into the barn and tried to straighten her stiff limbs. She was getting too old to live rough. Anger surged up again. She shouldn't need to, either, after all that hard work. It wasn't *fair*!

In the end, she decided she could do no more here. As soon as it was fully light, she set off back towards Atterby, stopping at the first village inn that was open for a drink of gin to warm her up and a bottle to take with her. She didn't think to ask what the village she had left was called. By the time she had consumed the gin, the sun had warmed things up and she was feeling sleepy. She settled down with a sigh of pleasure to have a nap on a sunny patch of grass. Even if Joe had moved on by the time she brought Big Jared back, the fellow whose place it was would know where he had gone. No need to hurry. She yawned and snuggled down.

27

Atterby Camp

Jared didn't arrive back in Atterby until the afternoon of the day after Jessie's abduction. He went straight to The Green Man to return the gig and see his wife, but Mrs Malterby could give him no news of her.

'We had the room ready for Mrs Wilde, but she didn't turn up.'

'*What?*'

She shrugged. 'Perhaps something cropped up at the camp?'

'Tell Mr Stafford where I am when he gets back, will you? He's following later by horseback. I'll go and look for my wife.'

Vaguely uneasy, but more irritated than anything by Jessie's not keeping her promise to stay at the inn, Jared walked over to the diggings. When he got there, he found a couple of his men waiting for him and they didn't look at all happy.

'With you in a minute, lads,' he said crisply. 'I need to see Jessie first.'

Three Finger Billy moved to block his path, shuffled his feet and spat on the ground as a preliminary to speech. 'She ain't here, lad.'

'What?' Jared pushed him to one side and strode into the hut. The place was in chaos, with clothes scattered everywhere.

Billy followed and stood awkwardly in the empty shop. He didn't relish the task before him, but it had to be done. 'Clogger Joe's got 'er.'

Jared swung round to stare at him, but made no sound, just

stood there motionless as all the implications of this statement echoed round his brain like distant thunder before a storm.

A small figure with a blood-stained cloth round its head stumbled into the doorway of Simon's sleeping recess. 'He took 'er, Jared,' said Elisha, his voice shrill with pain. 'Ah tried t'stop 'im an' he knocked me out. When ah come to, they'd gone, or ah'd 'ave followed 'em.' He put his hand to his head and swayed dizzily.

Jared stepped forward to support him, though in truth he felt as if he needed support himself, for the world was spinning and lurching around him and he felt sick with horror. 'When was this, boy?'

'Yesterd'y.'

It seemed to Jared that there was a roaring sound in his ears a thousand times louder than the sea he'd once seen pounding on Blackpool beach. The other two men said nothing until he raised his head again and looked at them with eyes that had lost all warmth in a face turned suddenly chalk white. 'Why didn't you lot follow him?'

'We knew nowt about it till we found the lad lyin' on the floor near the door,' said Billy. 'When he come to an' told us what'd happened, me and Macky here had a bit of a look round, but there was no sign of 'em nearby. An' no one in the village had seen 'em, neither. By that time it were dark.'

Jared closed his eyes for a moment. He had to think. Think! He couldn't give in to the horror and despair that was pulsing through him. *Yesterday!* Joe had had Jessie since yesterday! The thought was sharper than any physical pain could ever be. He picked Elisha up and sat him on one of the stools, but when the boy clung to him, sobbing, he patted the thin back automatically and held him close.

The two men watched him uneasily. He didn't look like Big Jared today. No sign of friendliness in his eyes, just a cold, hard light. And his face wore an expression of hatred that made it look years older.

'I'm sorry, Jared!' Elisha sobbed.

'Nay, you did the best you could, lad,' the man told him gently. He remained where he was for a moment, suppressing an instinct to rage and smash something because he had to keep calm and find Jessie. He knew with a sick certainty that he would already be too late to save her from being raped. The mere thought of Joe touching her made bile rise in his throat.

Oh, hell! Clogger Joe had had her for over a day. Time enough for any obscenity, and Clogger was not noted for treating women kindly.

What he was most afraid of was Joe murdering her in a fit of rage, for she wouldn't give in easily, not his Jessie. He prayed Joe hadn't gone on the grog. Lately, Clogger didn't seem to know what he was doing once he'd started drinking.

Jared detached Elisha's clinging hands from his jacket and turned towards the door. 'I'll kill him with my own hands,' he promised savagely. 'I'll find him and I'll kill him.' But first he had to get Jessie safely away. 'Fetch the lads, Billy.'

'Right. We're with you, Jared. All of us.'

The few men left on the diggings were only too happy to help search for Jessie. Big Jared was well liked, even if he had become a boss now, and she was both liked and respected by the men, for she had never tried to cheat them in her shop and always had a pleasant word for everyone. They exchanged opinions as they waited for instructions.

'That sod must have run mad.'

'I wouldn't be in Joe's shoes, with Big Jared after him.'

'That poor lass!'

'It don't bear thinkin' on, do it?'

Jared split them up into pairs to quarter the area in a systematic way, telling them to knock on doors and ask if anyone had seen Joe and his cart. Elisha was to remain at the hut in case any news came in. Jared went out with one group because he couldn't bear, he just couldn't thole, sitting and doing nothing.

They did not seek help in the village, only information, because this was railway business and they would settle it in their own way.

By dusk they were all back at the camp again and the only news was of a strange cart seen hanging around two nights past. But no one knew which direction it had taken when it left.

'Are folk round here blind?' Jared raged, gulping down without tasting it the mug of tea Elisha had prepared for him.

'We'll mebbe find somethin' tomorrow,' Billy offered.

Simon Stafford walked into the hut late that night, to find a haggard Jared and a white-faced Elisha sitting together in silence in front of the fire.

'What's the matter? I thought to find you and Jessie at The Green Man.'

Jared looked up with a face so set in misery that Simon's heart went out to him even before he heard why. 'Clogger Joe's taken my Jessie. He's had her since yesterday morning, since soon after we left.'

'*No!*'

'And we can't find a trace of which direction the bastard went.' Jared shook his head despairingly, tears welling unheeded in his eyes.

Simon went across to lay a hand briefly on his friend's shoulder. 'Whatever I can do to help, you know I will.' He sat down by the fire and his presence brought a slight comfort to Jared, though nothing could dispel the hard lump of anguish in his chest. They discussed how best to conduct the search the next day.

'We'll call in the local magistrate and the village constable,' Simon said. 'Someone should have informed them today.'

'No.' Jared knew what people thought of railway folk and also how slowly officialdom moved. He couldn't wait for that. He'd go mad if he didn't find Jessie soon! She had to be alive. She just had to.

'But – '

'The lads are all ready to help. We'll go further afield tomorrow. An' besides, I want to strangle that bastard with my own hands! You'll not stop me, Simon. No one'll keep me from him.' Jared spoke quietly, with a spurious calmness. But the violence behind his words was all the more frightening for being suppressed, as if it were building up inside him, ready to erupt.

'You can't kill him!' Simon protested.

Jared looked him squarely in the eye. 'If he's,' his voice faltered for a moment, 'if he's done owt to my Jessie, there's no power on this earth'll stop me from killin' him!' And Joe had had her for two days. There was no chance he hadn't touched her. That thought was nearly driving Jared mad.

An hour later there was a scratching at the door and Bet staggered into the hut, blinking owlishly in the light of the fire and the brightly burning lamp.

'Aaah,' said Jared softly. He stood up and went across to the filthy woman who stood there swaying, obviously more than half drunk. He curbed his desire to shake her and demand to know where his wife was because he'd seen Bet drunk before and knew how mean and stubborn she could become. He must play her carefully to get the information he'd no doubt she carried.

'Come inside, Bet. Come an' warm yourself by the fire, lass.'

She sauntered over to the warmth, tossing back her bedraggled hair and swinging her scrawny hips, enjoying what was, for her, a rare feeling of power. 'I've come a long way today, I 'ave, Jared Wilde,' she said. 'Ain't you got nothin' to drink?'

'There's some tea brewin'. That's all we've got. But you're welcome to some of that. Elisha'll get you a mug.' He nodded to the boy and shook his head warningly at Simon to prevent him from interrupting.

Bet threw Simon a would-be-provocative glance. 'Keepin' high company tonight, ain't I?' She tittered.

'So you've come a long way, have you, Bet?' prompted Jared, turning the conversation back into the channels he wanted.

She laughed bitterly. 'Aye. I have that!' She snatched the proffered tin mug from the boy's hands and gulped down the contents noisily, sighing with pleasure as the scalding liquid slid down her throat. Still not speaking, enjoying holding her audience in suspense, she wiped her mouth on her sleeve and held out the mug for a refill. Only when she had more cradled in her hands did she come back to her point, by which time Simon was ready to shake her in fury.

But Jared showed no signs of impatience. Like a snake poised before its kill, he sat and waited for the drab to speak.

'Joe's got your Jessie, the rotten bugger!' she said suddenly. 'Just up an' left me, he did, after all I done for 'im! Took her what didn't want him an' left me what did! Took the bleedin' money I earned, too! That ain't right!'

'No, it's not,' agreed Jared. 'Not right for you an' not right for me or my lass.'

'Ah. Bleedin' sod!' She sucked down another mouthful of tea. With an abrupt change of mood, she grinned. 'But I followed him, I did, an' he never even seen me!' The grin faded. 'Lousy, rotten devil! I worked hard. It's *my* money too! If he didn't want to stay with me, he should've paid me my share, that's what!'

'An' didn't he give you anythin'?' asked Jared, feigning shock and sympathy.

'Five pound, that's all he give me, *five – lousy – pound!*' The smile returned to Bet's grimy face. 'So I sez to meself, Big Jared'll pay me for news of 'is wife.' She paused and looked across at him calculatingly. In her drunken rambles back to the diggings, she had dreamed of asking as much as fifty pounds. Now, faced with the man himself, she hastily revised her estimate. 'Twenty pound. That'd be fair, wouldn't it?'

'You'll get a reward,' said Jared, in tones that brooked no haggling. 'But not till *after* we find my wife.'

She hugged herself, thinking it over.

'Come on, Bet,' he said, his patience almost at an end, his voice cracking with anxiety. If he'd thought it'd help to thump her, so help him, he'd have done it. But it wouldn't. 'You know you can trust me, lass. I'll see you right.'

She looked across at him, noticing the strain on his face, her mood changing yet again. 'A'right, then, Jared lad.'

'Where is she?'

'She's at a farm, if you can call that place a farm. Fallin' down, it is. Near fifteen mile away, I reckon.'

'Tell me how to get there.'

She tried vainly to explain, growing more and more confused. In the end, he cut her short.

'You'll just have to *show* us the road, Bet.' He turned to Simon. 'Go and hire the gig from The Green Man, will you? Wake them up, if you have to. Tell them it's an emergency, but give no details. We'll pay whatever they ask. Drive it yourself. Don't bring that boy of theirs. We don't want any outsiders involved.'

Simon nodded and slipped out into the night. Jared turned back to Bet. 'We'll leave as soon as Mr Stafford gets back. Do you want some bread and cheese before we go?'

'Go? I ain't goin' nowhere! I've walked all bleedin' day. I'm buggered. Never got no sleep last night.'

He took hold of her arm and swung her round to face him. 'I'm not leaving my Jessie in Joe's hands for a minute longer than I have to. We leave as soon as Mr Stafford gets back with the gig. Whether you like it or not.'

Something in his face made Bet realise the futility of trying to protest or argue, so she subsided on to a chair and accepted the hunk of bread that Elisha, silently watching everything, had cut. Jared looked at her. She suddenly seemed older and more worn, a woman who was well past her best years and who had led a very hard life.

'I'm sorry to drag you out again, lass,' he said, more gently. 'But at least you won't have to walk this time. We'll be travellin' in the gig.'

She looked up at him, softened by the kindness in his face. 'Ye're a good man, Big Jared. I'm sorry 'e done that to 'er.'

He froze. 'Done what?'

She wriggled uncomfortably. 'Soon after they got there, she started screamin' – on an' on. She were callin' your name. I heard 'er. So he must've been,' she hesitated, searching for a kinder word, but finding none, 'forcin' her. I'm sorry, lad.'

Jared picked up the stool on which he had been sitting, stared at it blindly for a moment and then hurled it into a corner. It knocked down two shelves with a clatter and one leg snapped off it.

Bet shrank back at the sight of the fury on his face, though it was not directed at her. 'I couldn't do nothin' to help 'er,' she quavered.

After a moment or two he regained control of himself enough to speak, but his voice rasped harshly in his throat, not sounding like his usual deep tones. 'I know, Bet. You've done what you could, comin' to tell me. An' I'm grateful. If – *when* – we get Jessie back, you'll never go hungry again as long as I'm alive.'

She nodded and went back to the bread, dipping it in the tea to soften it, for she'd lost several of her teeth and the others gave her gyp if she chewed anything hard. When the gig drew up outside, she followed Jared without a protest and sat hunched up in a blanket in the back.

He said little on that journey across the moonlit countryside, except to ask Bet for directions. Simon kept silent, too. He was not only worried about Jessie, but also about what Jared would do when they reached her. Much as Simon sympathised with his friend, he did not think he could just stand by and let him kill a man.

Once only they lost their way, but found it again when Bet recognised an inn where she'd bought a drink.

They came at last to the little village near the farm and walked the horse quietly through it, so as not to awaken the sleeping inhabitants. A couple of dogs barked as they passed, but there was no sign of human life. An inn sign swung to and fro, creaking slightly, but the moon went behind some clouds as they passed it, so they couldn't read the name.

The moon came out again just after they left the village, shining coldly down on them as they drove in and out of the dark patches of shadow cast by the trees. Simon had to wake Bet up to get directions again and they soon found themselves at the foot of the lane that she said led up to the place where Joe had taken Jessie. She could tell them nothing about the farm itself, except that she'd seen another man around the place. 'A funny fellow. He kep' watchin' through t'window an' – y'know – touchin' hisself.' She shuddered.

Her words slid past Jared. His attention was all on the action to come. 'Stay here, Bet, and don't make any noise,' he warned, tying the horse to a tree.

'Aw right, lad.' She sighed and huddled down.

The two men began to make their way as quietly as they could towards the farm.

A dog started barking as they approached the outbuildings and Simon muttered in annoyance. Jared didn't seem to hear the animal. A light was burning dimly in one window and he moved towards it. He kicked the dog aside when it attacked them and it fled, yelping. He didn't even turn his head to watch it, but quickened his pace, for it was suddenly unbearable to be separated from Jessie for a moment longer. She had to be there still, she just had to!

When he tested the front door, ready to batter it down if

necessary, he found it unlocked and smiled grimly. Careless, Joe. Very careless! he thought.

He opened it quietly and paused for a moment to take his bearings by the dim light of a dying fire, before striding across to the bed and reaching for the throat of the unconscious figure lying there next to Jessie.

After one gasp when the door opened, she stared across at her husband in silence, not daring to move in case she woke Joe. But the tears of relief that welled in her eyes were mingled with shame at being found naked and helpless like this.

The first Joe knew of Jared's presence was when a pair of hands seized him by the throat and yanked him from the bed. He struggled through the mists of gin-sodden sleep, recognising Jared's face with a kind of disbelief, as if it were a nightmare come true.

'Are you all right, Jessie, love?' Jared asked, his voice faltering as he spoke, but his hands remaining firm at Joe's throat.

'I am now,' she managed to say. She must not break down, not yet, not till she had seen him kill Joe. Then she would let herself utter the sobs that were making her chest heave and her throat ache.

Jared turned his attention back to the man struggling vainly in his hands. 'I wanted you awake first,' he told him, speaking slowly and distinctly, his words as sharp as gun shots. 'I wanted you to know who was killing you and why.'

Joe said nothing, still striving to get his bearings. Then he lunged suddenly, hoping to take Jared off his guard.

Avoiding the struggling figures, Simon slipped across to the bed and began to untie Jessie, his heart wrung by the sight of her bruised body and the tears pouring silently down her cheeks. She allowed him to help her, but all her attention was on what her husband was doing. Part of her wanted him to kill Joe. Part of her relished every muffled thump as one blow after another landed on Joe's body. But the rest of her wanted Jared's arms around her, not Simon's, wanted to be held close and assured that her husband could still love her.

Simon wrapped a blanket round Jessie and pulled her into a corner to avoid the heaving, struggling figures. Although the two men fought silently, the crash of breaking furniture brought the owner of the farm running in. He realised almost at once that someone had caught up with Joe and, as Simon moved across the room towards him, quickly ducked back through the door and ran away across the farmyard with a speed generated by fear and a guilty conscience.

The engineer made no attempt to pursue him. He must be there to stop Jared from actually killing Joe.

The fight was vicious and Joe fought surprisingly well for one just dragged from the depths of drunken slumber and lacking his favourite weapon of iron-shod clogs. Jessie, huddled in the corner, couldn't take her eyes off the two men, wincing and gasping and groaning as they gave and exchanged blows, as fists smashed against flesh.

Both were bruised and bloody now, and Joe was staggering, struggling to keep upright. But he fought on when another man would have given in to the black mists sucking him down, because if he didn't win, he was lost . . . lost . . . lost . . .

It seemed a long time until Joe stiffened, his eyes rolling up blindly. He uttered one long groan and started to fall. Jared took a step back and watched as his opponent crumpled slowly to the ground like a great felled tree, to lie unconscious, breathing stertorously through a broken nose.

Only then did Jessie break her silence, sob aloud and stretch out one hand towards her husband.

Jared didn't hear her, for he hadn't yet realised that he had won. He kicked the figure on the floor. 'Get up!' he panted. '*Get - up!*'

But Joe just lay there, motionless, breath bubbling out in snorts and wheezes.

With calm deliberation Jared stepped forward and kicked him several times in the groin. 'You'll take no more pleasure in women!' he said viciously through clenched teeth. Again he waited, as if expecting some response.

The unconscious man moaned, but did not stir.

Jessie stumbled forward and fell against Jared, who was still standing over his opponent with a wild light in his eyes.

Simon waited quietly, ready to prevent a murder. But there

was no need. As Jessie collapsed into his arms, Jared sobbed and completely forgot the still figure on the floor. He gathered his wife close and rained kisses on her bruised face, growling angrily as the blanket slipped and revealed the dark stains of more bruises on her body.

Simon moved to the doorway of the cottage, to give them some semblance of privacy.

'Jared, oh, Jared! I knew you'd find me! I knew it!' Jessie was shivering, clinging to her husband, great sobs racking her body.

'I came as soon as I could – as soon as I found out where you were.' Tears were running down his face too.

'I couldn't stop him t-touching me, Jared. He kept touching me. I tried. I did t-try! He – he's gone mad, I think.' She sobbed wildly against him. 'He couldn't – couldn't – but he still wouldn't leave me alone.'

'Shh, love! I'm here now, and you're safe. I know you couldn't stop him! Oh, hell, I should've killed the bastard . . .' He half-turned, as if to carry out the threat, but she clung to him.

'Don't let go of me, Jared! I n-need you to hold me. Don't let go of me! When he t-touched me, it made me feel – ' Her voice broke again.

He hardly took in what she was saying, for all his attention was focused on holding her, showing her how much he loved her, on begging her to forgive him for failing to keep her safe. Guilt kept shuddering through him. He had taken her away from a safe life and brought her to this. Her mother would never forgive him. He would never forgive himself.

Gradually her sobs lessened and with Jared's help she began to make an effort to cover herself with the torn remnants of her clothes, and even to wash her face in the water Simon pumped for her.

'What are we going to do about him?' Simon gestured to the unconscious figure on the floor. Joe was breathing unevenly, thickly, with little snorting sounds, and had not stirred since he fell.

'I'm doin' nothin' about him! He can bloody well rot for all I care!'

'We can't just leave him there,' insisted Simon, holding Jared's arm to keep his attention. 'When he recovers, he'll try something like this again. He must be locked away to protect other women. I think I should go and find the local magistrate.'

Jared and Jessie drew together instinctively and he spoke for both of them. 'Nay, we don't want anyone else brought in on this.'

Simon shook the arm he was holding, but he might as well have shaken a piece of granite. 'We must! Joe can't be left free or decent women won't be safe. Nor can he be left lying there. You don't want his death on your conscience.'

'Decent!' Jessie had an edge of hysteria in her voice. 'I'm not decent after that! I'll never feel decent again! I feel filthy all over – and if I've still got a soul, then that's d-dirty too.'

Jared pulled her into his arms and hugged her convulsively. He could think of no words of comfort to offer to her, nothing to comfort himself with, either, but instinctively he kept his arms round her and she stayed nestled against him, shuddering and shivering from time to time. 'It'll be no use going to a magistrate,' he said to Simon. 'They won't want to help railway folk. You know what they think of navvies.'

'You aren't just a navvy now, Jared. You're a sub-contractor. And they will listen to me! It helps sometimes to be so obviously a gentleman.' He was mocking himself, because on the railways it hadn't helped much. He'd have gone under but for Jared and Jessie. 'Will you wait here a little longer and allow me to go for help?'

She began to weep. 'I don't want anyone to know. Please don't fetch anyone else!'

'I must!' Simon turned to Jared and said in a low voice, 'Can't you see that she needs the help of other women? She can't drive back like that. She needs those scratches tending. And we must get her some clean clothes and a bonnet to hide her face.' The bruises were so severe he was sickened to think of how Joe must have hurt her, and she had one puffy, half-closed eye.

Jared looked down at his wife. He hadn't thought beyond the fact that he had got her back. She clutched the blanket round herself and continued to sob quietly and hopelessly against him. 'I don't want anyone to see me,' she repeated.

'She should see a doctor too,' Simon whispered.

Jared sighed and a shudder ran through him. He hated to admit it and the words came out in an angry bark. 'He's right, love.'

She started to protest.

Jared kissed her cheek carefully. 'No, love, you'll see he's right if you think for a moment. He's right about you,' another angry growl was torn up from the depths of his belly, 'an' he's right about lockin' that sod away, too. Go an' fetch whoever's in charge round here, lad.'

Simon sighed in relief. 'You – you won't touch him again if I leave you for a while?'

Jared stared down at the huddled figure, clasped Jessie as close as he could and shook his head. 'No. I went mad for a bit – but no, I won't touch him again. Not unless he tries to escape.'

'I don't think he's in any state to do that.' For Joe was still breathing heavily and his face was a dirty white colour under the congealed blood and dirt.

Simon slipped outside and ran down the hill into the village, knocking up the innkeeper and demanding to be told where he could find the nearest magistrate. By the time he had finished getting the information, lights were on in half the houses. But no one went up the hill to the farm and Bet slumbered on uneasily in the gig, even when Simon climbed up and took the reins, clicking to the tired horse to move on as he went for the local squire and magistrate.

28

July 1838

*I*t was more than an hour before Simon returned, an hour in which Jared and Jessie said little, but during which she gradually regained some measure of calm. She would not, however, leave the shelter of his arms for long, coming back to him again and again for comfort, as well as the reassurance that he did not now find her loathsome.

In all that time neither of them made any effort to tend to Joe. Jessie didn't even look in his direction and when Jared's eyes fell on him, they darkened and rage filled him. Nothing he could do would wipe out what had happened. He had failed to protect his wife, failed miserably.

Simon had been directed to the Big House, which turned out to be Butterfield Priory, a place he had visited with his sister, who lived a few miles away to the north. He hadn't realised how close they had come to Mellersley and Yettley in their slow night drive. They must have come nearly twenty miles. The squire, roused from slumber, was amazed to recognise Simon Stafford standing on his doorstep and at first thought that Elinor must be having trouble with intruders again.

When he was told what had happened in the nearby hamlet of Little Mellersley, he became speechless with shock that such a thing could have happened on *his* land. He listened in growing horror to the details and then exploded into rage. 'The scoundrel should be taken out and hung!'

'I agree. But we must abide by the law, must we not?'

'Aye, I suppose so. But if he'd attacked *my* wife – two days he had this poor woman, you said? – I'd have certainly killed him!'

'Er – Mr Wilde did have a – a fight with him.'

'Don't blame the fellow! Don't blame him at all! Hope he pounded the daylights out of him.'

'He did. However, like myself, Mr Wilde is a law-abiding citizen, so once the man was bested, we thought we had better report the matter to the nearest magistrate, which is you, sir.'

'Quite right. Quite right. Hit him a few times, did he, eh? Good and hard?'

'Well, yes. Very hard. The fellow had Mrs Wilde tied up – er – in the bed when we found him. Um – naked. And he had beaten her. Her whole body is covered in bruises.' Simon hadn't been able to avoid noticing that.

Squire Butterfield's already ruddy complexion took on an even darker hue. 'Damme, hanging's too good for fellows like him!' He shook his head and heaved a great sigh. 'Hmm. Well, I suppose I'd better come out and arrest him. He won't have been able to escape, will he?'

'No.' Simon was very sure of that. 'Mr Wilde knocked him senseless.'

'That's the ticket! Just what he deserves! Er – the lady – poor thing. Is she – all right?'

'Considerably battered and bruised. She must have fought like a wildcat. I was hoping to beg the loan of some clothes for her from your wife and some help – a lady will know how to tend her better than we could. And – and there's the woman who led us here. She's a rough type, but we couldn't have managed without her help. Perhaps she could wait somewhere?' Bet had not stirred during the drive round the village and was still curled up in the back of the gig, as far as Simon knew.

Martha Butterfield was summoned and proved to be a great deal more practical than her husband, whom she sent off to dress. She handed Bet over to her housekeeper and urged Simon to bring poor Mr and Mrs Wilde back to the Priory. 'For they can't drive through the countryside after a dreadful experience like that and she won't want to stay at an inn.'

'When she's had a little time to – to recover, I'd thought to take Mrs Wilde to my sister's.'

'She won't want to jolt across the countryside in her condition. No, Yettley is six miles away – we're the closest place.' Martha made an angry little sound under her breath and muttered, 'To think of it!' Then she said firmly, 'I shall not take no for an answer, Mr Stafford. You must all come back here. I'll rouse the maids and have rooms prepared at once.' And she left him, muttering again, 'And hot water, too, I think, plenty of hot water. Not to mention a hearty breakfast. Ellen shall . . .'

The squire followed Simon's gig in an elderly, but comfortable carriage, with two yawning stable lads sitting on the back outside bench, as well as the coachman, in case of trouble from Joe. When they arrived, Charles Butterfield looked round him in disgust. 'Might have known it'd be this place! Been a disgrace to the village for years, but Vin Pinter's the last on a three lifetimes lease and I couldn't get him out. Land's been farmed by his family for years, but he's the black sheep of a decent family. Prime land, too! But if he was involved in this crime, we'll have him!' His eyes gleamed with satisfaction. 'I'll be rid of him at last. Can't run a farm from prison, can he?'

Then a thoughtful look came over his face. 'Maybe he's the one who's been breaking into houses, after all? Mmm, I had my suspicions, but we could never find any evidence and he had witnesses to prove he was elsewhere when two of the incidents happened. I'll tear this place apart now, though. He must have put the stuff he stole somewhere.'

Inside the farmhouse, the squire bowed to Jessie, his face pink with embarrassment, and lost himself in a tangle of 'deeply regret' and 'shameful' and 'at your service'. He faltered to a halt, then cleared his throat and with carefully averted eyes, offered her his wife's cloak as well as the shelter of his house. 'Mrs Butterfield is having a bath made ready for you now. Ahem – we told the servants that you'd had a carriage accident. No need to feed gossip, eh?'

Jared answered for her, because Jessie was in tears again. 'We're both very grateful to you, sir, for your kindness.' He looked at the figure still lying on the floor. 'What about him?'

'Damned villain! Should be hung!' said the squire, who seemed fixed on this idea. 'We'll lock him up in Tom Beeton's shed for the time being. Used it before. No jail round here, y'know, only a small village. But it's a strong shed. He'll not escape. And – er – ahem – there'll be no need to trouble Mrs Wilde about this. You can testify for her. I'll hold the hearing in private tomorrow. Don't want the tale made public, do we?'

He bowed again to Jessie, whose white face and trembling hands had touched his heart.

'I meant to kill him,' said Jared dazedly, for he was now suffering from shock and reaction as well as Jessie. 'I meant to kill him – but in the end, I couldn't.'

'Best not,' said Mr Butterfield. 'Leave it to the law – though hanging's too good for a scoundrel who attacks innocent women.' He peered down at Joe, nudged him with one foot and said regretfully, 'Suppose I'd better have the doctor to him. No one would grieve if he died, though.' He turned to a stable lad. 'Here, Sam, you stay with this fellow till I can send a cart to carry him over to Tom Beeton's shed. After that, you'd better fetch Doctor Shawley to him. And no talking about this, if you value your job.'

'No, sir.'

Duty done, the squire turned back to the Wildes and Simon. 'Come home with me now. Let my wife see to Mrs Wilde. Have some breakfast. Damme, it makes you hungry catching villains, doesn't it?'

It was a welcome anti-climax to return to the squire's comfortable house and the ministrations of his plump, elderly wife. She tutted in horror at the sight of Jessie's battered face and swept her off immediately to bathe her body and put salve on her wounds.

Jessie went with her quietly. She found Martha Butterfield reassuringly normal and the idea of a bath filled her with pleasure. There was nothing in the world she'd like more at this moment. She managed a wan half-smile and a whispered, 'Yes, please!' in response to her hostess's offer. She had hardly spoken a word since they had found her.

'Will you be all right, love?' Jared asked anxiously. He, too, liked the looks of the old lady, but if Jessie wanted him to stay with her, he'd brave any number of old ladies, squires' wives or not.

'Yes. I'd love a bath. I feel – dirty.'

'I'll look after her, Mr Wilde, don't you worry,' Mrs Butterfield assured him. She put her arm gently round Jessie. 'Come with me, my dear. Oh, and after that, Mr Wilde, I'll come back and see to your face.'

'My face?' He realised for the first time that it was swollen and aching, and that his lip was split. 'It's nothing.'

'Nevertheless, it needs bathing,' he was told firmly.

'Come and have a glass of brandy,' the squire urged the two men once his wife had left. 'Nothing like it for picking a person up after a shock. We'll send one up to your wife, too.'

He swept Jared and Simon off to his library, a room more given over to sporting prints and guns than to books. There he set the bell pealing to summon a rosy-cheeked maidservant. She goggled at the huge, battered figure of Jared towering over the squire and could not take her eyes off him as she listened to her master's orders. Still staring, she dropped them a curtsey before scurrying off to find the brandy and to report to the kitchen staff that Mr Wilde was a giant and had a scarred face and looked fierce as anything and *she* wouldn't like to be left alone with him, 'deed she wouldn't.

Mr Butterfield gestured to his guests to take seats in front of a fire that was roaring in the grate, as if to deny the mild July weather. 'Nothing like a good blaze for cheering things up,' he remarked, patting an old spaniel on the head and sinking into his favourite armchair. Now that the excitement was over, he was beginning to feel his age.

When the maid returned, the squire himself filled glasses for his guests. His sympathy for Jared took the form of fussing over a drink for him, a fire and the comfort of a chair, rather than words. It was the only sort of sympathy Jared could have borne and he found it vaguely soothing, though bitterness and guilt were still churning inside him.

He sipped the brandy, welcoming its fiery taste, and answered his host's remarks in monosyllables, leaving the burden of conversation to Simon.

He chatted to the squire, while covertly observing his friend, about whom he was still desperately concerned. 'We're grateful to you for your help today, Mr Butterfield, very grateful indeed.'

'Glad to be of service. The fellow was employed by you on the railway, you say?'

'Yes. My partner had known him for a long time.'

'Disgraceful!' said the squire, and tossed off the rest of his brandy in a reckless way that would have made his wife scold him. 'They say they're a lawless breed, these navigator fellows.' The squire shook his head and made a clucking noise with his tongue. 'I hope one of those damned companies doesn't take it into its head to put a branch line through to Mellersley. We're happy enough without.'

'It's a pretty village,' said Simon diplomatically.

'Well enough, well enough.' The squire saw that Jared had finished his brandy and picked up the decanter. 'Have another drop, Mr Wilde. Very good for the nerves. Think I'll have another one myself. Not as young as I used to be.'

The three men sat in silence for a few moments, staring into the fire. They were all feeling exhausted after the events of the night.

The door opened and Mrs Butterfield bustled in with a bowl of water on a tray. 'I've left your wife soaking in a bath in front of her bedroom fire, Mr Wilde. How are you feeling? A little better? You have more colour in your face. No, no, don't move! Just sit there and let me attend to your injuries. I don't think I could reach you if you stood up.' She began to bathe the dried blood off his cheek.

'How's Jessie?'

'Exhausted, poor dear! But I left her to soak in some nice hot water for a while.' She lowered her voice. 'I – er – don't think there's any permanent damage.'

Jared nodded, grateful for this information.

'I'll go back up to her when I've finished with you and help her get ready for bed. My, that's a nasty gash! I'm afraid you'll have a black eye tomorrow as well. And just look at your poor lip.'

'Can I see her?' asked Jared, who didn't care about himself only about Jessie.

'Presently.' Martha Butterfield continued her ministrations. She didn't know which was worse, the poor girl upstairs with the haunted look in her eyes or this stricken young giant. 'Turn your cheek to the light,' she commanded.

Jared did as he was told, wincing as she ruthlessly washed a cut.

'Don't pull away. It has to be done. I always washed my step-daughters' cuts most thoroughly when they were children,' she continued to fill the awkward silence, 'and they never went septic. I am a great believer in cleanliness. Mind what I say, Mr Wilde, you are to keep those cuts clean!'

He grunted and she took it for agreement.

When she had finished, she bustled out again and could be heard ordering the maid to take some food to the gentlemen, before they drank themselves into a stupor. Simon found himself smiling, something he had not thought to do so soon, but Jared didn't seem to notice.

When trays were brought in, the squire's concern for his guests took the form of coaxing them into eating a few fresh rolls, with some delicious home-cured ham and a morsel or two of cold chicken. To his surprise Jared found himself ravenously hungry, but when Mrs Butterfield came down again, he abandoned his food at once.

'Jessie? Can I go to her now?' He needed to see her, check that she was all right – just touch her.

'Certainly. But remember she's exhausted, poor dear. I've put her to bed. You may go and sit with her if you will promise to see she eats something. I'm sending up some nice hot milk and some of these fresh rolls. Mind, Mr Wilde, I'm relying on you to make her eat something! She needs to build up her strength. And when she has eaten, you are to give her a draught which I shall prepare myself, so that she can sleep. Is that clear?'

'Yes, ma'am.' He wished the old lady would stop jabbering on and let him go to Jessie.

'And,' her face turned pink, 'I don't think you should talk about – about what happened. It's over now. Best leave the matter be. Forgive and forget. Not that there's anything to forgive in your wife, of course. But you know what I mean.'

Jared nodded, feeling soul sick. It was the last thing he wanted to discuss.

'I'll take you upstairs myself, then give you half an hour, after which I'll be up to see that your wife has done as she's told and had something to eat. Half an hour.' Mrs Butterfield wagged her plump, beringed finger in his face to emphasise her point, because he seemed only half-aware of what she was telling him.

Jared, who had been fending for himself since the age of ten, was not used to loving bullying like this, but found it vaguely comforting. He could not seem to concentrate much on anything just now, though.

His hostess took him upstairs and showed him into a pretty bedroom. Jessie was lying back against the pillows of a huge bed, her battered face chalk white where it was not bruised, and her eyes dark-rimmed with fatigue and filled with shadows. She started up when she saw them and Jared hurried to clasp the hand she held out to him.

'How are you, love?'

'Better, but so tired,' she said in a thread of a voice. 'Mrs Butterfield has been very kind.'

'I'm happy to be able to help you, my dear. Now, you are to eat as much as you can! Mind what I say!' She marched out.

A minute or two later, the clinking of crockery heralded the arrival of Betsy with the tray. The maid set this on the bed in front of Jessie, cast a scared glance sideways at Jared and scurried out.

'I don't feel hungry, Jared.'

'When did you last have anythin' to eat, love?'

She shuddered. 'Not since he – he . . .'

He raised the hand he was holding to kiss it. 'Then I think you'd better eat something now. That's two days without food. Besides, the old lady will be angry with me if you don't eat and I'm scared of her.' He was trying to speak cheerfully, but felt more like weeping at the haunted expression on his wife's face. 'Here,' he said, letting go of her hand to take a roll and butter it. 'Try a bite of this.'

Crumbs fell everywhere on the bed and Jessie, laughing shakily at his ineptness, took it out of his hand. She found it difficult to swallow, but he continued his nonsense about being afraid of Mrs Butterfield's wrath if she didn't, so she made an effort.

'She doesn't half order folks around, the old lady.'

'She's been so kind. She makes it seem – over. She's like my mother. Her bark's worse than her bite.'

When Jessie had eaten as much as she could force down, Jared gave her the medicine and sat on the bed, holding her hand till she fell asleep.

Exactly half an hour later, Martha Butterfield crept into the room, to find him asleep as well, lying on top of the covers next to Jessie, still holding her hand. She smiled and covered him with a blanket, before tiptoeing out again, to inform her husband and Mr Stafford that they were *not* to disturb Mr and Mrs Wilde, who were both asleep. 'In fact, you had all better stay for a few days. Mr and Mrs Wilde have both had a dreadful time and they need a rest and a bit of fussing over. Have they no home or family, Mr Stafford? Is there someone we should inform?'

'There is Mrs Wilde's mother, but she lives near York with her husband and – well, I'm not sure Jessie would want her fetched. Agnes Marley is – '

'Agnes?' Martha said quickly. Mother and daughter called by those two names must surely be . . . 'Was she Agnes Burton before she was married? And is Mr Marley a parson?'

'Yes, I believe so.'

'Oh, I'm so happy for her, so very happy!'

The squire roused himself. 'I remember Agnes. Pretty little thing.'

Simon thought of what Jared had told him about his grim mother-in-law and nearly choked on stifled laughter. 'I'm amazed at the coincidence.'

'The longer you live, the less you'll be surprised by such things.'

'Perhaps I should tell you something about my friends?'

Mrs Butterfield nodded and plumped herself down in a chair, her eyes bright with interest, listening as he explained Jared's background and the Wildes' recent achievements, ending up, 'Jared's not an educated man, but he's intelligent and will, I think, one day make a place for himself in the wider world. Don't underestimate him because of the way he speaks.'

The squire nodded. 'It's hard for a fellow to rise from nothing.' He offered a confidence of his own. 'My grandfather was a shopkeeper, who made enough to retire to the country and build this house. I'm proud of his memory.'

'And I was the housekeeper here until I married Mr Butterfield,' his wife added, with a fond glance in his direction. 'I'm his second wife.'

'There are some county folk who still turn up their noses at us,' Charles chuckled. 'But we don't care, do we, my love? So don't worry about your friends, Mr Stafford. We shan't despise 'em.'

Simon nodded in relief. 'Thank you, sir.' He sighed and stretched. 'And now, I think I should get back to the camp. The men will be wondering what's happened to us. I'll relieve you of Bet's presence, too. She's not exactly - er - respectable.'

'She has been no trouble.' Mrs Butterfield smiled. 'Though she did object to washing herself. But I am used to dealing with the lower orders. She did as she was told and took a bath in the scullery, then we found her some clean clothes.'

Simon could imagine the confrontation. He wished he could have stayed on with Squire Butterfield and his wife, who made life seem normal and wholesome again. He wished he could have gone to visit Elinor, who lived so close to here. He wished - oh, he wished the world were a kinder place, where people like Jessie didn't get hurt.

Vin Pinter trudged north from Mellersley, cursing every now and then under his breath. That was what he'd got for trusting his Cousin Joe. You'd never been able to trust him, not even as a lad. He was a rat, and always had been, cousin or not. And now look where he'd landed Vin - in trouble, that was what, big trouble. Worse than ever before.

He heard a cart rumbling along the lane towards him and hurled himself over the drystone wall that bordered it, listening to the horse plod past and mumbling under his breath. Where the hell was he to go now? He hadn't even had a chance to bring anything with him. He fumbled in his pockets. All he had were the few coins Joe had tossed at him and they wouldn't last long

He'd have to get some more money, and some clothes, too.

A memory flashed into his mind of the comfortable house where the two spinster ladies lived. Lots of food in their pantry. Lots of blankets on their beds. Not even a dog to give them warning. He grinned and began plodding along the lane again. You could have a lot of fun with women if no one was around to stop you. Their bodies were so soft that a knife slid in easily. He'd never killed one so close to home before, but as he was leaving the district afterwards, it wouldn't matter what he did now.

When he got to the house, he settled down at the back of the vegetable garden to watch. The older female was a rare tartar. He'd seen her at market. The other was the quiet sort, but he bet she'd scream just the same as any other woman once he started playing with her.

The sun rose in the sky and it began to get warm. Within the hour, Vin could feel the sweat dripping down his face, and still the two women did not unlock their door. They must be late sleepers. It was not until an hour later, by which time he was twitching and muttering to himself, that the old one came out with a basket on her arm.

'I'll be back in half an hour, Miss Elinor,' she called.

Vin grinned. Half an hour would be more than enough time to catch the tall thin one and put her out of action till he needed her, then he'd be waiting for the other when she came back. Smiling, he began to creep towards the house.

29

❧

Mellersley

Jared didn't wake up until late in the afternoon. He opened his eyes, coming instantly awake, as usual, and sighing with relief to see Jessie sleeping peacefully next to him. It hadn't been a dream. He had rescued her. Then he scowled as he remembered Joe and what he had done to Jessie.

As Jared's eyes lingered on his wife's battered face, Mrs Butterfield's words came back to him. *I don't think you should talk about what happened. It's over now. Best leave the matter be.* Yes, she was right. He would make it plain to Jessie that he didn't blame her, then they need never talk about it again.

He looked at a clock, ticking quietly to itself on the mantelpiece, and decided to get up. A door at the side of the room had been left open, so he went through it to find a small dressing room, where he could attend to his needs and wash his hands and face. The mirror showed him that his face was as battered as his wife's and that his clothes were dirty and badly crumpled, but he could do nothing about that.

He peeped in to see Jessie still sleeping peacefully, then left the room quietly through another door which led on to a corridor. He was hoping to find his host and hostess and apologise for falling asleep on them earlier this morning. Whatever would they think of him?

As he turned to the right, he bumped into a maid, who

squeaked in shock and nearly dropped the pile of clean linen she was carrying.

'Ooh, sir! Ooh, you did make me jump!' She took an involuntary step backwards.

'I'm sorry.' Why was she gaping at him like an idiot? 'I'm looking for Mr Butterfield.'

'Squire's not here, sir. He had to go into the village. But madam said we was to take you to her as soon as you woke up.' She put the linen down on a large, old-fashioned oak chest and dropped him a slight curtsey. 'If you'd come this way, please, sir.'

It made him feel strange to have maids curtseying and calling him sir. This must have been how Jessie had to behave when she was in service. Well, she'd not have to do that again, at least! He followed the girl down the stairs, across the hallway and along another corridor, marvelling at the thickness and softness of the carpet under his feet and the shininess of the dark wooden doors they passed. How many rooms were there in this house, for heaven's sake? Dozens, and yet he couldn't even remember what it looked like from outside. He'd not been looking at anything but Jessie when he arrived.

Now that he had her safe again and had had a good sleep, his natural strength and resilience were reasserting themselves. He was ready to face the world and get back to business. As soon as Jessie woke up, they would go to Atterby and she could stay at The Green Man while he wound things up there. Then they would move on to the new contract, which was going to rack and ruin with no one in charge. That stream had to be diverted and lost time made up. But he'd make sure he found somewhere decent for Jessie to live. He wasn't having her staying on the diggings again.

The maid showed him into a comfortable parlour which looked out over a garden full of flowers and neatly cropped grass. The gentry certainly lived in style, he thought, pausing in the doorway to stare round. He'd have a house like this one day, not as big, but full of comfortable furniture and with flowers and lawns outside. He realised that Mrs Butterfield was standing by the window looking at him, so he strode across to her, coming to an abrupt halt as he tried to decide whether it was correct to shake her hand.

She offered a hand, clasping his in both hers while she studied his face, then shepherding him to a chair. 'You look a lot better for your sleep, Mr Wilde.'

'I am, ma'am. Thank you. And grateful for your help. But when Jessie wakes up, we'd better get back. There's still a lot to be done.'

She put an instant stop to such a foolish idea. 'Your wife, Mr Wilde, will be in no fit state to leave here for several days yet!'

'Nay, surely...'

She held up her hand. 'Pray do not tell me my business, Mr Wilde!'

'But I...'

'I have been looking after the health of my family, my servants and the poor of this parish for many years, and believe me, I know what I'm talking about. Your wife is suffering from the shock of such a dreadful experience, as well as being badly bruised. She will need a few days of quietness in which to recover her spirits. She will also need *you* beside her while she recovers!'

'But we have to ...'

Again the uplifted hand stopped him. 'Do you question my knowledge?'

'No, I suppose not.' He was beginning to feel a little annoyed by her assumption of authority over them, though.

Martha smiled, recognising the look on his face. Just so had her step-daughters scowled at her when they knew she was right, but didn't want to admit it. 'She will need the comfort of your presence and love more than anything else, Mr Wilde, believe me.' The smile faded and her eyes searched his face again. 'I presume this – occurrence – has made no difference to your feelings for your wife?'

'Of course not!' He was indignant that she should even think such a thing. Make a difference! The only difference it would make to him would be to teach him to look after Jessie better. Much better.

'Mr Stafford asked me to tell you that he would wind things up at Atterby and would go on from there to the next camp – Hellerton, isn't it? Have I the name correct?'

'Yes.' Jared acknowledged defeat by leaning back in his chair and waiting to see what else the old lady wanted of him.

'So we'll just let your wife have a little holiday. Time will be the best healer in this case, in my humble opinion.'

Humble! There was nothing humble about her! 'Aye. I suppose we'd better do as you say, Mrs Butterfield. It's hard to know what's best.' Jared sounded the 'h' carefully, trying not to speak too broadly. He felt on edge in such surroundings and wasn't looking forward to spending several days here, but if Jessie needed it, then he would do anything he had to.

Jared was rather proud of how he acquitted himself during the rest of the day and at two meals, where he imitated the way his hosts ate and drank. Jessie hardly stirred, so he couldn't tell her about it all, or about the interesting conversation he had with the squire, as decent an old fellow as you could meet anywhere. The old lady's potion seemed to keep Jessie asleep and perhaps it was for the best.

She woke once or twice, seemed not to know where she was and wanted only a drink or to relieve herself. But in the night, she began moaning and sobbing, and clutched Jared for comfort once she realised where she was. Her anguished sobs nearly tore his heart in two.

'I thought – I thought for a minute that I was – back there.'

'Nay, love, I've got you safe and that bastard's locked away for good.'

She shed tears, of relief this time, and he cradled her in his arms until she fell asleep again. He didn't find it quite as easy to get back to sleep and felt another surge of hatred for the man who had done this to his brave, lovely Jessie.

The following morning, she was still white-faced and weak, though Jared and Mrs Butterfield between them managed to persuade her to eat some breakfast. He was convinced by now that Mrs Butterfield had been right when she'd said it would take Jessie a few days to recover.

After breakfast, he expected her to be kept in bed, but their redoubtable hostess had other ideas. She didn't want to give Jessie any time to brood on what had happened. 'I've looked out some of my step-daughters' old things for you to wear, my dear,' she said, coming in to see Jessie after breakfast. 'The skirts may be a bit short, but we shall not mind that. If Mr Wilde,' she fixed Jared with a compelling gaze, 'will kindly wait for us in the little parlour downstairs, then Nell and I will help you dress. You'll enjoy sitting in the garden. If I say so myself, I rather pride myself on my displays of flowers. And we have a nice, sheltered arbour in the rose garden, which is just the thing when one is feeling a little out of sorts.'

A little out of sorts! thought Jessie. She felt as though she had been dragged along behind a runaway horse. She felt as though every bone in her body had turned soft, too soft to hold her up. And she felt like weeping every time she remembered.

Martha smiled at her, 'Did you know your mother was a maid here once?'

Jessie blinked in shock. 'No.'

'Such a good maid, Agnes. You look very like her, my dear.'

Jared scowled, but said nothing.

'Well, I must go and speak to cook. Try to rest, my dear.' Martha left them alone.

Jessie sighed and managed a half-smile at Jared. Mrs Butterfield said it was best to put everything behind you, forget what had happened. She didn't know what to think, but decided to follow her kind hostess's advice. She was glad, though, that she had told Jared what had really happened between her and Joe. She distinctly remembered telling him that. It must have relieved his mind, though the touching had been bad enough.

When she heard a noise in the kitchen, Elinor thought at first that Thirza had forgotten something. She tiptoed out of the parlour to investigate, stopping dead in the doorway of the kitchen at the sight of a man, a scruffy weasel of a fellow with wild eyes, who giggled at the sight of her.

This is the one who broke in, she thought, taking a step backwards, the one who tortured our cat.

Vin sidled round towards her and brandished the carving knife. 'If you don't do as you're told, lady, I'll slice you to pieces.' He might slice her to pieces anyway. Like the cat. That had been fun.

Elinor took another step backwards.

'Come here, pretty lady,' he said in a sing-song voice, and tittered at the fear on her face. He followed slowly, grinning. No need to hurry. Much more fun when you took your time.

Elinor was afraid and her heart was pounding in her chest. His eyes were quite wild, with no sign of reason or understanding in them. And he kept making little chuckling sounds, as if he were enjoying himself. But how could she defend herself against that knife? She tried not to panic and continued to back slowly along the hall.

When she bumped into the hallstand, she sobbed aloud in sheer relief and grabbed at the handle of the big black umbrella which they used to shelter people who'd arrived in carriages.

Vin tittered again, then gaped as she hefted it in her hand like a sword. He sliced at the air with the knife, enjoying the sensation and feeling stronger again. 'Put that down and come here!' he ordered, brandishing it again and admiring the way the sun glinted off the blade.

'No.'

'I'll chop your ear off if you don't. You won't look so pretty then.'

She didn't answer, just stared at him, lips tight, eyes watchful, hand firm on the umbrella.

Vin stopped slashing the air and glared at her. It was a big umbrella and she wasn't supposed to defy him, she was supposed to be afraid. Women usually wept and pleaded when he brandished a knife at them. He waved it again. 'I mean it.'

At that moment Thirza puffed into the kitchen. 'I forgot my pur—' She broke off to gape down the hallway in horror at Vin and then grabbed her frying-pan off the stove.

He flattened himself against the wall, looking from side to side for an escape route. Two ladies at once were too much for a small man like him, especially ladies who were glaring at him like these were and waving weapons.

Before he could move, an umbrella descended on his head and pain lanced through him. He yelped and then screamed loudly at another blow to the other side of his face. Still screaming, as much in panic as in pain, he dropped the knife and huddled down against the wall. He put up his hands to protect his face, then the cast-iron frying-pan smashed down on his skull, sending him into instant oblivion.

The two women stood over him, panting. Thirza had the frying pan raised for another blow if he so much as twitched a fingertip. But he didn't. He just lay there, very still. She hoped she hadn't killed him.

'He's not very big,' Elinor said, poking him with the umbrella. She wrinkled her nose. 'And he smells awful.'

'He's big enough to do you harm with a knife.'

'Thank goodness you came back.' Elinor's voice started shaking suddenly and her hands began to tremble.

Thirza could only nod. She, too, was feeling all wobbly. Then common sense reasserted itself. 'We'd best tie him up, hadn't we, before he wakes up? We don't want him escaping. I'll go and get the clothes line.'

When he was trussed like a fowl, Elinor managed a wobbly smile. 'Simon worries about me living away from the town. But I think you and I are quite capable of looking after ourselves, don't you, Thirza?'

The maid looked thoughtful. 'I think we'd do better in future if we had a large dog to warn us if anyone came near. It'd warn them off, too.'

'Why not? I'd like a dog. Now, if you'd go for the constable, we'll get rid of this dreadful, malodorous fellow.'

Thirza picked up the frying-pan again. 'You keep this by you, then, just in case.'

When the squire was informed that a second villain had been caught causing trouble in the district, he went bright red and spluttered like a firecracker about to explode. 'Damme! What's happening to the world?' When he drove over post-haste to Yettley and saw who the villain was, he said, 'Aah!' very softly and smiled. 'Now, what do you have to say for yourself, Pinter?'

But Vin didn't say anything, or even notice who was with him. He had retreated into his own world and was mumbling and muttering to himself, fingers twitching, eyes rolling.

'Fellow's mad as a hatter,' decided the squire, after trying in vain to question him. He sent for the doctor, who agreed that they should commit the fellow to the poor house, which had a wing especially for lunatics.

'And keep him chained up,' the squire said as he watched them bundle the villain into a cart. 'He's dangerous.'

He went back inside the house to see Elinor Stafford, and assure himself she was all right. Over a cup of tea, he told her about all the doings in the neighbourhood, including her brother's visit. 'We'd better fetch him back again,' he said when he'd finished his tale and drained a second cup of tea.

'Why?'

'Well, to – to comfort you.'

Elinor smiled. 'I've got Thirza to comfort me and my brother sounds to be rather busy with other things at the moment.' The smile faded as she asked, 'How is poor Mrs Wilde?'

'Oh, all right.' He blushed. 'She – er – wasn't hurt too badly. Resting at the moment. M'wife says it's the best medicine.'

'I'd like to come over and meet her properly. I've heard so much about the Wildes from Simon and I remember when she used to maid my Cousin Susannah.'

'I'll send you a message when she's ready to receive guests,' the squire said. 'M'wife will know. Now, if you're sure you're going to be all right . . .'

'We're fine. We're going to get ourselves a dog. Thirza knows of a puppy we can have, one which will grow into a very large dog.'

He nodded his comprehension. He knew his own little world. 'Benford's bitch. She produces big sturdy dogs. Good idea.'

Jessie and Jared spent four more days with the Butterfields, days which fretted Jared greatly, as he knew that Simon needed him and that there was work to be done at Hellerton. Jessie remained listless and did whatever she was told, which was so unlike her that he held his impatience in check.

She didn't tell him, but what helped her most to come to terms with her ordeal was Mrs Butterfield's common-sense attitude to it.

'Nasty experience,' said the squire's wife, catching her guest weeping one day, 'but it's over now. You've got to go on living,

not sit and brood on it. Keep yourself busy! Your husband needs
to go back to work and you do, too.'

'Yes. Yes, you're probably right.'

'Miss Stafford said she'd like to come over and see you.'

'Not - not at the moment, if you don't mind. Give her my
apologies, but I think I'd rather meet her when - when things
have settled down again.'

But Joe died in the night and they had to stay on for another
day so that Jared could give evidence at the inquest. This was a
very cursory affair, at the end of which the squire declared that
Joseph Smith (no one knew Joe's real surname so the squire had
invented one) had died of a seizure and could not therefore be
brought to trial. The parish undertook to bury him decently.

It was quickly over - too quickly, it seemed to Jared. Would
he, too, be so rapidly forgotten when his time came? For all his
sins, Joe had been a good canal and railway man for most of his
life.

He could not, of course, discuss this with Jessie, who
shuddered at the mere mention of Joe's name and who did not
even ask how the inquest had gone. But it made him think.

The Wildes left Mellersley the next day, nearly a week after
their arrival. They received a warm invitation to come and stay
again, and they were to let the squire and his wife know where
they got to. The last was an order, not a request.

As the squire's carriage took them away, Jessie sighed and laid
her head on Jared's shoulder. 'They were very kind, weren't they?'

'Aye.'

'But I'm glad to be going back to our own life now, aren't you?'

'I am that!' For there were railways to be built and money to be
earned and a whole future ahead of them. Forget the past - it was
the future that counted. He'd *make* it count. And he'd look after
Jessie properly from now on. No one would ever hurt her again
- not unless they killed him first.

30

⟨⟨⟨⟨⟨⟨⟨⟩⟩⟩⟩⟩⟩⟩

August–November 1838

*H*ellerton, whose sub-contractor had died so suddenly, was a slack camp, by Jared's standards. It was another small contract and it would only take a few weeks to divert the stream and finish the cutting, but the men there had got into bad habits and were working in a sloppy, careless way. There had been a few accidents already, unnecessary ones to his mind. Were folk mad? Did they want to damage themselves? Well, they weren't going to do it on his patch, not if he could help it.

Simon had made some effort to tighten discipline but it was Jared's arrival which made the real difference, for he knew how to handle the men as Simon never would and was relieved to have something upon which he could vent the anger which still consumed him, and which Joe's death had done little to assuage. He concentrated first on his old gang, and they, working under Three Finger Billy now, set a cracking pace with which the others had trouble keeping up.

There was already a shop of sorts at the camp and although Jessie turned her nose up at its offerings, they could not dispossess the incumbent. Jared found Elisha jobs around the camp, but there was nothing for her to do. Inactivity made her fret and boredom wore away at her good resolutions to put the past behind her and concentrate on the future. So when Simon said gloomily that the paperwork was in a mess and that he had just dismissed the site clerk for incompetence, Jessie brightened up.

'I'll act as your clerk, then,' she said, with a return of her old manner.

'You?' Simon looked dubious. 'But Jessie . . .'

'Why not? I write a clear hand. You and Jared always check the figures anyway, so you'll soon know whether I'm capable or not.'

'Well . . .'

'If a woman can be monarch of this country, then I'm sure a woman can manage to deal with a few papers!' There was a new sharpness in her voice.

Simon looked at Jared.

He was mindful of Mrs Butterfield's advice to keep Jessie busy. 'We could give her a week's trial. There's no one else suitable in the offing.'

Like Jessie, Jared spoke more curtly nowadays. Simon could not help noticing that. Still, it was none of his business, so he made no comment, just got on with his work. His friend might be short-tempered, but he was as efficient as ever and work on the cutting was beginning to accelerate.

Aware of the gulf still yawning between them, Jared tried hard to get closer to Jessie. He put his arms round her one evening in bed and said quietly, 'You're so lovely.'

She shuddered and tried to pull away.

'Jessie, love!'

'I don't – don't want to. Not yet.'

He tried, very gently, to change her mind, but she first went rigid, then fought him off in a near panic, all the more frantic because it had to be done silently, so that neither Elisha nor Simon would hear. He let her go and they lay beside one another in the bed for a minute or two, her breathing, in the darkness, sounding very close to sobs. His heart twisted with pity and he tried to heal the breach.

'Nay, love, I'll not do owt you don't want me to. I can wait till you're ready again.'

She drew in a deep, shuddering breath. 'I – I'm sorry, Jared. I just – *can't*. Not yet.' She couldn't even talk about her experience, but Jared seemed to understand that. Although Joe had pawed her in the most intimate and foul way, he had not been able to rape her, but what he had done was enough to make her feel dirty, enough to give her nightmares. That inability to perform had made Joe angrier and angrier, which was, she supposed, why he'd slapped her around so much. But now, she couldn't bear anyone to touch her, not in that way. Not even her husband.

Jared tried to make love a couple more times, approaching Jessie in the most loving manner possible, but to no avail. She turned rigid as soon as he began to caress her. And yet, she seemed to need to lie in his arms, especially after one of the nightmares she still had about those two terrible days. It was almost more than flesh and blood could stand, to hold her so closely and not dare to show his love for her, though she must have noticed his body's response.

As a consequence, he threw himself into his work like one possessed and the men on the camp, while respecting his superior knowledge, were very careful not to do anything that might provoke Mr Wilde's anger. Here, no one called him Big Jared, not even the gang he had brought with him. Nor did his old gang tell anyone what had happened to Jessie.

'Our business, what happened,' Billy had said firmly before they arrived. 'Keep it to oursen, eh, lads?'

And they'd all nodded.

Jessie proved to be a competent clerk, dealing easily with attempts to cheat on the supplies and equipment she had to issue, and at least when she was working, she wasn't thinking too much. But the work wasn't enough to keep her fully occupied. It was the sort of job given to an older man, one who couldn't keep up or had been injured.

The navvies gradually accepted the presence of a woman, but she didn't joke with them as she once would have, and when one or two of them tried a few verbal gallantries, she turned on them like a fury. Her husband, when he heard of it, threatened instant dismissal if anyone spoke one more word out of place. And so did the members of the gang he'd brought with him. So the other navvies soon learned to take no notice whatsoever of her femininity.

As the days passed, Simon noticed that Jessie was not looking as pretty as usual. Perhaps this was because of the new way she was doing her hair, in a tight bun, or perhaps it was the strained expression on her face and the dark circles under her eyes.

'Are you sure you're up to working, Jessie?' he asked her one day. 'You don't look your usual self.'

'Am I not doing the job efficiently? You've made no complaints about my work.'

'Well, yes, of course you're doing your job efficiently. You know you are.'

'Then leave me to be the best judge of how I feel.'

Simon was not satisfied, however, and spoke to Jared about it that same afternoon as they inspected progress on the cutting. 'Jessie isn't looking very well lately.'

'What do you expect after what happened?' He kicked a rock away with unnecessary violence.

'Is she ill?'

Jared stopped walking to stare at him in surprise. 'Of course she isn't.'

'She looks ill, or at least under the weather.'

'Well, if she's ill, she's got me to look after her, so you tend to your own business.' And he was gone, striding down the slope, pausing to harangue a man about wearing the safety harness he'd introduced and to curse another for leaving his shovel lying around where folk could trip over it.

But Jared began to watch Jessie covertly. Yes, she did look dreadful, strained and unhappy. She had lost all her glow.

That evening, after supper, they went for a stroll through the lanes near the camp, which was the only way they could get any privacy, and he asked tentatively, 'Are you feeling all right, love?'

'Of course I'm feeling all right! What makes you ask that?'

'It's just – you look a bit washed out.'

There was silence while they walked on, then she said, 'I'm all right, but I am a bit tired. I think I'll go to bed now.' She turned and led the way back to the hut, not saying anything else.

The only one not to receive the rough edge of her tongue was Elisha, who still shared their hut and did a lot of the dirty chores for Jessie, as well as running errands round the site and into the nearby village.

When Jared wondered aloud one day whether they really

needed the lad, Jessie turned on him like a vixen defending her young. 'He's not going back to that place!'

'No, but there are other . . .'

He was not allowed to finish. 'I *need* him.'

'All right! All right!'

'And I'm the best judge of what I need! I more than earn his keep, do I not?'

'All right, I said!' And he slammed out of the hut, leaving her standing there with one hand extended as if to call him back. But the words lay unuttered on her lips and eventually she shook her head and went back to her work.

Matters came to a crisis three weeks later when a quarrel blew up between Jared and Jessie over a minor error in the accounts. He pointed this out to her rather scornfully and she defended herself vigorously, complaining about his handwriting. The disagreement rapidly turned into a heated argument and she accused him of not wanting her to work for them, of not wanting her at all any more. Then she burst into tears.

Jared turned to Simon, sitting embarrassed in a corner. 'Will you go for a walk or something? You too, Elisha. I want to have a talk to Jessie. This can't go on.'

'Yes, of course. Come on, Elisha! We'll stroll down to the village and I'll buy you a bag of humbugs.' Simon put on his coat and left without looking at Jessie, who was standing with her back to the room, her shoulders shaking as she tried not to weep. The boy followed him out reluctantly, staring back over his shoulder at the woman he had come to love like a second mother.

Jared went over to poke the fire, not knowing how to start.

'Look what you've done now!' Jessie scolded, without turning round. 'Embarrassing me like that!'

He ignored this. 'What's really the matter, Jessie? I know there's something. Can't you tell me, love? Can't I help you?'

Tears filled her eyes, but she shook her head obstinately, keeping her back to him. 'It's nothing. I – I'm just a bit tired. I'm not sleeping properly.'

'It's more than that.' A new tone of command was in his voice. 'Come and sit down over here. We have to talk.'

She shook her head, but he could see that tears were rolling down her cheeks. He stood up and walked over to her, took her by the shoulders and led her back to the table. 'We can't go on like this and you know it. You're not movin' from that stool till you've told me what's up – if we've to stay here all night!'

She still could not speak, but started to sob. He put his arms round her and she hid her face against his shoulder, her voice coming out muffled as she said, 'I think – I think I'm having a baby. An' I wanted to have it in – in joy, not like this.'

'But we haven't ...' His arms slackened from around her shoulders and his voice trailed away as he realised the implications of this statement. 'Oh, no!' he said, the words choking in his throat. 'Oh, God, no! Not that!'

She stared at him. 'Not what?'

'Not Clogger Joe's baby.' He almost retched at the thought.

She looked at him in bewilderment. 'Of course it's not his. How could it be?'

He just stared at her. 'What do you mean, how could it be? That bugger raped you. We were careful. Always. It can only be his.'

'But I told you – '

He didn't allow her to finish. 'Can't you get rid of it? It's early days yet. Women get rid of babies all the time. I'll ask around the camp.'

'It's not Joe's baby.'

His face showed only disbelief.

She tried again. 'It isn't his, Jared. I suspected I was carrying a child before – before that happened.'

'You said nowt to me about it. An' we've been careful. Bloody careful. Every single time. So it can't be mine.'

'Ma *told* you it doesn't always work.'

'Well, it worked all right until now.'

'Don't you believe me?'

He avoided her eyes. 'I don't know what I believe.'

'*Jared!* I wouldn't lie to you about something like this.'

'Maybe you're wrong. Maybe your body is just – upset – with the shock and all.'

She laughed bitterly. 'But I'm seven weeks late now and I've never been more than a day or two out before. Besides, there are other signs. I feel queasy in the mornings and my breasts are sore. Jared, I know I'm having a baby. And I know that it's yours.'

'If you say so.' But he didn't believe her, couldn't believe it, and he saw by her expression that she realised that.

'I thought you understood,' she said as the silence lengthened. 'I told you – after it happened. Joe – he tried to – but he couldn't. He could only – t-touch me.' And that had been bad enough, heaven knew. 'This is *our* baby.'

He couldn't force any words to his lips. And he couldn't believe her. He knew how loyal she was. She'd do anything to protect her child. Only it wasn't *his* child, couldn't be. He tried to tell himself that they would *make* it his. If he were the only father the baby knew, he would *be* its father. He saw how upset Jessie was looking and went over to take her in his arms. 'Eh, love, what a tangle this all is! And what a way to tell me about your – the child.'

She leaned against him, not fooled by his efforts, trying to think how to persuade him that the baby really was his. As if she'd have lied to him about something like that!

There was a tap on the door of the hut just then and Jared called out, 'Come in!' before she could do anything, so she had to wait for another opportunity to speak to him.

Simon was relieved to find Jared and Jessie standing close together. But they didn't look happy. He began to wonder if the attack had had any consequences of which he didn't know. A baby, perhaps? It was the only thing he could think of to account for their new sombre mood.

And when they told him about the coming child a day or two later, his heart went out to Jared. Another man's bastard was a hard thing to face. But he felt sorry for Jessie, too, for she seemed to grow paler and more unhappy with every day that passed. Several times he caught them arguing in low voices and each time they broke off at the sight of him.

During the next few weeks he watched them both change and grow apart, and could do nothing to help. It seemed to him that all the lightheartedness and joy had gone out of their relationship.

Both of them filled every waking hour with work. And they avoided being left alone together. Jessie kept Elisha with her as much as possible. Jared waited for Simon in the evening before he went back to the hut.

In September the four of them celebrated Jessie's twenty-first birthday quietly, with Elisha treated as part of the family. Jared bought her a silver locket. She scolded him for such extravagance, but wore it every day, and Simon would see her fingering it and sighing when she thought no one was looking. He bought her some books, novels by Jane Austen, his sister's favourite author.

Jessie read them, enraptured, coming to him to have new words or incomprehensible actions explained and listening to him gravely. They were the only things which seemed to take her mind off her own problems – for a while, at least. But they didn't solve the main problem: Jared's inability to accept that the child was his. Jessie realised now that they should have talked about what had happened while they were at Mellersley. Mrs Butterfield had been wrong about that, quite wrong. But how to right that wrong now was beyond her.

They completed the cutting just in time and in October, the newly completed Sheffield to Rotherham line opened and the company supplied free ale to the navvies who'd worked on it, plus a whole ox to be roasted.

Jared looked at Jessie across the table the day before the feast. 'We'll get you out of the camp, I think. Would you like to pay a visit to the Butterfields?' At the end of the contract, the navvies would be ripe for mischief, flush with money and spending it like water, mostly on ale, gin and the camp women. Bet was strutting around in a garish new dress bought for her by her new fellow. She seemed to have completely forgotten Joe now.

'Or you could go and visit your mother, if you want?' Jared added when Jessie didn't reply.

'No. No, I don't think so. Not yet.' For her mother would realise something was wrong and would not rest until she knew what it was. 'And I don't really want to visit the Butterfields, either. It'll remind me of – of what happened.'

'Then we'll find an inn somewhere and book you in.'

'Won't you be coming with me, Jared?'

'No. I'll need to keep an eye on things here.'

'Then I'll be all right here, too.'

'No!' He wasn't risking anything where she was concerned.

They glared at one another across the table.

Simon decided to intervene. 'Perhaps you'd like to pay a visit to my sister, then, Jessie? She was sorry not to meet you when you were at Mellersley.'

'Oh. Well, I wouldn't want to impose.'

'Elinor would be glad to have you. She's mentioned you several times and would enjoy some company.' And he was not much use to his sister at the moment, for they had quarrelled again last time he visited. She seemed very brittle and edgy lately. Surely it wasn't that old business about the house in Heptonstall? She hadn't mentioned it for a long time. No, it couldn't be that. Maybe she was still upset by her experience with that lunatic, even though she denied it.

Jessie looked at Jared, who shrugged. 'One way or another, you need to get out of the camp.'

She turned to Simon. 'Then I'd love to visit your sister.' Actually, she realised with a shock, it would be a relief to get away from Jared for a while.

31

November–December 1838

*I*t was Simon who escorted Jessie to Elinor's, driving her across country. Somehow it was easier with just him and she began to relax a little. 'Tell me about your sister, what she's doing now? I used to see her sometimes at the Hall, when she was visiting Miss Susannah. She looks very like you.'

'Yes. Tall and thin. *Bony*. I know the nickname the men have for me on the diggings.'

She laughed. 'Go on.'

'Well, Elinor lives with her maid, Thirza, who has been with our family all her life. They're both very fond of gardening and my sister likes to read and embroider and go for long walks. I'd rather she lived in a town, if truth be told, but she refuses.' He hesitated, but knew he had to tell her. 'When you had the trouble with Joe, the man whose farm it was ran away and broke into my sister's house.'

Jessie turned pale. 'He was a – a strange man.'

'Very.'

'He didn't hurt her, did he?'

'No. He tried to, but my sister and her maid captured him and handed him over to the constable. He was quite mad and they've had to shut him away in the lunatic house.'

'And is she – all right?'

'Oh, yes. She wrote to tell me she's bought herself a watchdog.' His voice grew soft. 'We used to have dogs at home. I miss them.'

'I've never had a dog. I don't know anything about them.'

'Um – I wonder if I might ask a favour of you, Jessie?'

'Of course.'

'While you're there, you'll see how Elinor is. I feel – well, that she's not really happy. No need for you to betray any of her confidences, but perhaps you could give me your opinion when you get back? And if you think I'm right, that there is something wrong, then I'll speak to her, make her tell me why.' And if it was still about the house in Heptonstall, they'd have to find some way round it, sell that one and buy another house in a similar location perhaps, not so close to Blackholm.

'Of course.' They rumbled along in silence for a while, then she had to ask, 'Did you tell her what happened? To me, I mean?'

'A little. Not the details, of course.'

When they arrived, Jessie envied the warmth with which Elinor and Simon greeted one another, then they both turned to her and drew her into their conversation, making her feel that they really did want her with them.

Suddenly a shaggy puppy came bounding across the lawn and through the open front door, barking furiously. Jessie stiffened, but relaxed when Elinor chuckled. 'Oh, dear. I thought I had Rags safely tied up. He keeps chewing through the rope.'

Simon looked at her. '*This* is your dog? But, Elinor, he's going to be huge.' He bent to stroke the dog, which was investigating his feet with great interest, and it promptly lay down and wiggled its belly at him. Simon obliged by tickling him and grinned at his sister. 'You must feel really safe with him to guard you.'

She laughed and snapped her fingers. The dog came to her instantly, nuzzling the hand that was stretched out and pressing against her skirts. 'You're not used to dogs, Jessie?'

'No. But I think I could get used to this one.' There was something so very reassuring about the happy, frolicking puppy.

After Simon had left, she turned to her hostess. 'Miss Stafford, I'm so grateful to you for having me.'

'Do call me Elinor.'

'Elinor, then.'

'And don't stand on ceremony about anything. Thirza and I

don't.' She saw Jessie's eyes go to the maid in surprise, and added, 'She's more like a friend than a servant.'

Thirza, who had come out to say farewell to Simon, gave her mistress a loving glance.

The evening passed peacefully enough, with a simple but delicious meal and careful conversation between two strangers. But in the night, Jessie woke up sobbing after a nightmare. She found a figure beside her, patting her shoulder, and when the tears came, Elinor held her close and told her to cry it out. Afterwards her new friend brought her a glass of milk and sat down on the edge of the bed while she drank it.

'You need to talk about it,' she said quietly. 'It won't go away until you do. I know that. I've had – similar problems myself.'

Jessie stared at her dark outline by the light of a half-moon. '*You* have? But – does Simon know?'

'He knows nothing. I – managed by myself.' But she'd had Thirza, always there, always ready to listen; Thirza who had seen what was happening and knew it was not her young mistress's fault. Who had Jessie had to comfort her? 'Can you not talk to your husband about it?'

'No.' Jessie struggled to hold back more sobs, but couldn't.

Elinor took her in her arms and just held her close as she wept again. 'Tell me, then. I'm happy to listen and help if I can.'

And it all came out in a rush of words, punctuated by sobs and agonised searching for understanding. And afterwards, lying spent on her pillows, Jessie did feel better in a strange sort of way. 'You're very kind. No wonder Miss Susannah loved you and wept when you went away.'

'You knew her?'

'I was being trained as her maid.'

'Then you knew what Lord Morrisham was like? Poor Susannah had a lot to put up with.'

'He was very – determined to get his way sometimes. He locked me up in the attic when I wanted to marry Jared. It was Miss Susannah who let me out.'

'He gave me the choice of staying in his house in Great Sutton and never seeing my brother again, or leaving. So I left.' Elinor looked sad for a moment. 'I was fond of Susannah and missed her greatly. We write to one another now, but her mother can't manage without her and I don't feel like going back to Great Sutton, somehow.'

'You can never really go back,' Jessie said, her eyes filled with tears.

'No, but you can go on and make a new life for yourself. Never doubt that. When I was acting as companion to Miss Butterfield, even for such a short time, I was happy again.' She had been needed and had grown fond of the frail old lady. 'We used to talk. She seemed to have made sense of this strange world of ours. But I seem to have lost my way since and I feel so useless here.'

Jessie could not be less than honest. 'Simon's worried about you. He's guessed that you're unhappy.'

'Yes, I know. But he won't admit to himself why.'

It wasn't until the following evening, as the two women were sitting quietly by the fire, that Elinor said abruptly, 'I'd like to tell you about my problem, so that you'll understand. Do you mind?'

'Not at all.'

'Miss Butterfield left me a house in Heptonstall. I thought of going to live there, but Simon doesn't want to go back. He said I should sell it and buy a house elsewhere.'

'Go back?'

'It's very near our old home. We had to sell everything when my father died. Simon took that very hard and vowed never to return to Blackholm.'

'But you still miss it?'

'Yes. Very much. I didn't realise how much I loved it all until we left. Not the house itself, that holds only bad memories for me, but the countryside.' Elinor gave a dry, bitter laugh. 'But I don't want to upset Simon – this is the only thing we've ever quarrelled about, the only major thing, anyway – so I can't seem to make up my mind what I should do. He says he won't come to visit me if I move there, keeps insisting we couldn't be happy. But I think we could. Well, I know I could.'

Jessie stared down at the folds of her skirt. Men were always telling women what to do or not to do. 'You should please yourself, I think. Simon has the railways. You can't see very much of him. If you think you'll be happier in Heptonstall, then you should go there.'

'You make it sound so simple.'

Jessie shook her head. 'I don't think anything to do with men is simple. But you're free, at least. You can do as you please.'

'And you can't? Don't you love your husband any more? Simon used to say how happy you were together, how much he envied Jared.'

'I loved the man I married. He's changed since – since it happened. And I don't understand him any more. He won't believe me when I say the child is his.' Jessie's voice grew fierce. 'I want the child, *our* child, but I don't want it to be brought up in an unhappy home.' The anger faded, to be replaced by despair. 'I try to make him understand. But if he won't – after the child is born – then I'm not sure what I'll do.'

They sat there together very quietly, then Elinor said, 'We both need something to cheer us up. Let's drive over to Heptonstall tomorrow and I'll show you my house. We'll take a little holiday. I've been over to see it a few times now the tenants have left. It's lovely. Reminds me of Miss Butterfield: stark and upright and at peace with itself.'

The village of Heptonstall was perched on a steep ridge, with open moorland behind it and the Rochdale Canal below. Elinor's house was built of dark stone and stood near an old church. She waved a hand towards the latter as they walked along. 'I still like to go and sit there. Parts of it date back to the thirteenth century. I like to think of what it must have been like then.'

They went to look round the house, which was a tall, narrow building of stone, rather plain in appearance. And yet, once you got inside, the rooms seemed to welcome you.

'It feels friendly,' Jessie said. 'And there's so much to see out of the windows. I don't like to feel shut away.'

'I love the place,' Elinor admitted. 'I don't know why, I just do. This house is where I want to live. No other would be quite the same.'

Jessie's voice was quite definite. 'Then you should come and live here.'

Afterwards they explored the village together, before walking up to the moors and standing in the wind, staring out across the rolling tops. Elinor threw back her head and drew in a few deep breaths. 'I just love it here.'

'Then come and live in your house,' Jessie said again.

'You know, I think I will.' Elinor beamed at her suddenly. 'Yes, you're right. I will do what I want. Simon has the railways. I'll have my house.'

Letters were waiting for them when they got back to Yettley. One for Jessie from Jared, in his round careful handwriting, saying he and Simon had a new sub-contract and would come to collect her in two days' time. One for Elinor from Simon, giving the same information.

On the day of departure, when they were waiting for the men to arrive, Elinor turned to Jessie. 'If you ever need help, or a refuge, for whatever reason, don't hesitate to turn to me.'

'Thank you.' But the few days' rest had filled Jessie with renewed determination. She was going to *make* things right between her and Jared. Somehow. She had to.

Early on a cold November day, with their breath hanging in the air like white mist as they got into the coach, the Wildes and Simon went south to begin work on the Great Western Line, at a small cutting near Slough. Here Jessie ran another shop, for Billy and the gang had ridden down with the drays which transported everything, including their hut.

Even though it was only a two-month job, she had the satisfaction of making a respectable amount of money as well as feeding the three of them and the work filled her days at least, until she was too tired to do anything but sleep at night. But for all her resolutions to solve her own problems, she felt no closer to Jared. He seemed to be living behind a wall and she couldn't penetrate it, couldn't make him see the truth.

'You're working too hard,' he said abruptly one evening.

'So are you.'

'I'm not pregnant.'

'You're not here, either, so leave me alone to work as I choose.

With you out all day and most of the evening, I have to do something to fill my days.'

Guilt pierced him. For he didn't need to be away so much, of course he didn't Only somehow, he couldn't bear to see any sign of the child she was carrying. It made him feel angry.

Jessie knew he was avoiding her. She had tried to get him to spend more time with her, but he just insisted that he had work to do. So she wanted no time in which to think. It did no good. She had thought and thought until her mind became a blur. She could only hope now that the child would resemble Jared so closely when it was born that he would have to believe her. And that was a very faint hope.

One thing she was resolved on, though. She would not bring up a child with a father who didn't want it. She had longed for a family of her own since she was a small child and now, when that dream was about to come true, it had been spoiled by one wicked man. And although Joe had paid for that with his life, she was still paying and would continue to pay if Jared could not be made to believe the truth.

Christmas passed quietly. The Wildes were invited to Butterfield Priory and were also invited to spend the festive season with the Marleys.

'Do you want to go to your mother's?' Jared asked when the letter arrived and Jessie passed it to him to read.

'We can if you want?'

'I can't go. But you could.'

'On my own?'

'You know I can't leave the camp for so long.'

She shook her head. 'No. Not without you.'

'Well, how about going to the Butterfields? Or to Simon's sister's? You got on well with her.' Jared sometimes felt jealous of the warmth in her voice when she spoke of Elinor.

'I'm not going anywhere without you.' She wasn't going to parade her unhappiness. It was bad enough having Simon watching them with his gravely sympathetic expression; bad enough that Elisha knew and hugged her sometimes suddenly for no reason – except that they both knew the reason, really. No, she wasn't going anywhere. No one else needed to know how things stood.

Jared sighed loudly and ran one hand through his hair. 'I don't want you round the camp if the lads go on a randy.'

'If you're here, I'll be fine.'

He breathed in deeply, then let the air out again in a sigh. 'Very well. But if I say you're to stay inside the hut, you're to do that. And if I say you're to go and stay at an inn, you're to do that, too.'

'All right. *All right!*'

Simon decided to spend the festive season with his sister, as he usually did. He was not entirely looking forward to being with her. She'd be bound to talk about Heptonstall, and he wasn't changing his mind about that. Still, it would be a relief to get away from the tension that filled their hut, with Jessie and Jared hardly saying a word to one another, and both of them looking so grim and sad.

Jared sat brooding over his meal that night and then said abruptly, 'The lads are all set to make a feast of it. They'll stop work for two days, one to get roaring drunk and one to recover from their celebrations.'

'Yes. You said so before.'

'I've been thinking about it an' I'm not having you in the camp while that's going on, so I've booked us some rooms at the inn in the village. Elisha can stay here an' fetch me if there's trouble.'

'I'd rather he came with us.' She didn't want to be alone with Jared. They'd only quarrel, as they did every time she tried to convince him of the truth.

'It's added expense an' he has a bed here.'

'If it's not safe for me, it's not safe for a lad his age. You know how they torment folk sometimes when they're drunk.'

He closed his eyes and wished she'd just do as he said sometimes. But she wouldn't, so he shrugged and said, 'Oh, very well.' And at least it seemed to be giving Jessie some pleasure to make the boy happy. What about her own needs, though? And those of her husband? He'd accepted her baby, would do his best for it. Hadn't he said so several times? So why did she persist with this charade of it being his, which infuriated him, absolutely bloody infuriated him?

Everything had gone wrong since Joe – everything! It was

agony to lie next to her and not be able to touch her, love her, hold her. But her swelling belly reminded him that another's child lay between them and that stopped him trying to make love to her. And if the need for release kept him awake at night, well, she didn't know, for she was sleeping more lately.

Jessie shed tears when a parcel arrived from her mother just before Christmas, containing a beautifully worked infant's christening gown and a letter full of instructions to her daughter as to what she should and should not do in her condition. Mrs Marley sounded very happy at the prospect of becoming a grandmother and had 'the parson' (for she always referred to her husband in the old way) not been suffering from a severe dose of the influenza, she would have come to spend a day or two with Jessie and Jared before Christmas.

They were both glad not to have to face her.

Simon arrived at Yettley to find the house in chaos, with packing cases everywhere. Elinor, who had been watching for him through the window, turned to grimace at Thirza. 'Keep your fingers crossed for me.'

He came in smiling, bringing a whirl of frosty air with him. After hugs all round, he asked, inevitably, 'What's happening? Are you moving, after all?' To a town, he hoped, somewhere safer.

'I'll tell you when you've unpacked. Your room's ready.'

Elinor watched him go upstairs two at a time and was sitting in the parlour on her own when he came down.

'There, not much to unpack.' He sprawled in a chair opposite her. 'Why didn't you tell me you were moving? Where are you going?'

She took a deep breath. 'Where else but to my own house?'

He jerked upright. 'Heptonstall?'

'Yes.'

'How could you, Elinor?'

'How could I not? I need a home, Simon, a real home. Please – don't get angry.'

But he *was* angry. Furious. 'I shan't come to visit you there. I'm *not* going back.' He came to clasp her hand in his. 'I can understand your needing your own home. But you could sell that house and buy one somewhere else, somewhere without all the sad memories.'

'There are happy memories, too. It's not in Blackholm itself, after all.'

'It's very close.'

There was silence then she said firmly, 'I love that house, Simon. I want to live there and nowhere else. And I love the moors, too. I can't tell you how much I've missed them.'

He looked at her, anger written all over his face and in the stiffness of his body, then he walked towards the door.

She stood up. 'Where are you going?'

'I'm going out for a walk.'

When he had gone, Thirza came in. 'So he took it badly, eh?'

'Yes.' She wiped away another tear.

'Well, don't you give in to him, love. He's being unfair to you.'

Elinor looked down at her lap and then up at her friend and maid. 'He is upsetting me.'

'He'll come round.'

'I'm not so sure.' But she wasn't going to change her mind. She needed a permanent home, had done for a while now.

32

January–February 1839

*I*n February they were to move to another cutting in Yorkshire. It would be the biggest sub-contract they'd ever undertaken, but Jared and Simon had costed it carefully and were sure they could manage. They had better reserves now and were beginning to be known by the railway companies for the efficiency and safety of their work. Injuries were inevitable on any railway job, but Stafford and Wilde had had no fatalities, and (of much more importance to the companies) they had met all their deadlines. They could still not be classed as big contractors, but they had a solid reputation in the making.

The baby was due in April and fortunately this would be in the middle of the contract which should last until July, or even later. There was another cutting only a mile or two down the line and the company had promised that one as well to Stafford and Wilde, if they finished the present one on schedule.

'I'll run a shop again,' Jessie said, as they discussed the arrangements.

'No!' Jared's response was immediate.

'What do you mean by that?'

'I mean, you're not running a shop. You're looking tired.' He wanted no harm to come to his wife, though he wouldn't care if the baby failed to survive, as so many did. 'An' you're getting bigger now. You need to rest, not work.' He saw the protest in her eyes and added, 'An' I know you. You work yourself till you drop if you get a shop going. You always do.'

'I'll go mad with nothing to do.'

'We'll rent a proper house near the diggings. You'll have that to look after.' He would feel better having her living in safety and comfort.

'A small house won't take much looking after, then what will I do with myself all day?'

'How should I know what women do with themselves?' he demanded, taking refuge in anger. 'Other women don't seem to have any difficulty keeping themselves occupied.'

'Well, I'm not other women! I'll go out of my mind staying at home all day. An' what's more, I won't do it! I like to earn money!' Jessie was putting some aside secretly now, just in case. She tried not to think how she might have to use it, and had wept over the necessity when he wasn't there, but she felt a burning need to have something behind her. A little here and a little there. It soon mounted up, tucked into a felt bag in the bottom of her trunk. Jared suspected nothing and she hoped desperately that she wouldn't have to use it.

A battle royal raged for two days. Simon and Elisha kept out of the way as much as possible. Jared was so unshakeable in his resolve that in the end Jessie wondered in despair if he'd force idleness upon her.

'Ah could run t'shop for you, Jessie,' said Elisha one day after Jared had stormed out yet again. 'Ah know what to do an' ah can do me sums better'n most. Ah won't let no one cheat me.'

She smiled absently at him and thanked him for his offer, but he was still only a lad, however much he'd grown lately. No one would take notice of him.

Then Bet turned up, thin and weak after an attack of the influenza that had been going round the country all winter, killing rich and poor alike. She had aged considerably since they last saw her and hadn't eaten for two days. She had lost any feminine charms to which she could once have laid claim, along with several more teeth and her never ample bosom. Now she looked like a younger version of Ma.

Unsure of her welcome, she approached Jared first, for he had once said she need never go hungry again as long as he was alive and she had treasured that thought. Too busy to bother with her, he passed her on to Jessie, who welcomed her with open arms in the realisation that here was the solution to her problem.

Bet found herself being ruthlessly taken over. Protesting loudly and squealing like a stuck pig, she was given a bath in Jessie's battered tin tub in front of the hut fire. Her lousy ragged clothes were burnt and her hair doused in an evil-smelling concoction that would kill the lice.

She sat by the fire afterwards, wrapped in a sheet. Watery-eyed from the strong soap, she sniffled miserably over a pot of tea and wondered if it was all worth it for a meal or two. But by the time Jessie had clad her in one of her old dresses and given her a nice piece of steak for her tea, Bet began to come round to the idea of working in the shop. She was not overfond of hard work and had a suspicion that Jessie would prove a hard taskmistress, but there might be compensations. Like this food.

She wouldn't have admitted it for the world, but she also enjoyed the light, tingling feeling of clean skin. She stroked the dress furtively. It was not only warm but pretty, and had a petticoat and matching shawl, too. She lifted the tacked up hem again to admire the lace on the bottom of the petticoat, then let it drop and stared into the flames. There was good solid food in her belly and the tea was hot and strong. No need to let a fellow use her to get it, either. What more could she ask of life?

There remained only Jared to convince and Jessie approached him a day or two after Bet's arrival. 'I've been thinking about the shop . . .'

'Not that again. Let it go, Jessie. I'm not having you working those long days.'

'I've got a plan.' She barred the doorway. '*Listen* to me, will you! You're always rushing off somewhere lately.' Avoiding her. They both knew it.

'I'm trying to make a future for you and your child.'

She looked at him sadly. 'Your child, too.'

He just stared at her, lips tight, a frown on his brow, annoyed with himself for this slip. 'Well, go on. I'm listening.'

'I've got it all worked out how I can run a shop without working long hours. Elisha can handle the money and Bet can handle the serving. You said we'd look after her, so we'll have to find her some sort of work.'

He pursed his lips, considering this. 'You're absolutely determined, aren't you?'

'Yes. I *need* something to keep me busy. And anyway, I like earning my own money.'

'Oh, hell, all right! But you're not working in the shop all day, and that's flat.'

So they moved to Mernham in grand style, with two heavy drays taking the hut and their possessions. Jared drove Jessie in a gig that Simon had picked up cheaply for twenty pounds, drawn by a horse, also purchased at a knock-down price. It looked a sorry beast, but Simon assured them that it would fatten out with good feeding and give them years of hard work, so they bowed to his superior knowledge. He rode behind them on his sturdy mare.

Jared had rented a house while he was surveying the lie of the land, and this was the first time Jessie had seen Ash Cottage. Simon went off tactfully with Elisha to stable the horse at the inn, so that she and Jared could go inside together. He had offered to find himself separate lodgings, feeling that they might draw closer together again without his presence, but Jared had nipped this idea in the bud.

'Nay, it's more convenient living together. There isn't a night we don't have something to decide or discuss.'

And Jessie had added, 'Please stay with us, Simon. We both enjoy your company.' It was such a help to have a third person around when Jared got in one of his moods.

So there was nothing Simon could do but accept graciously. And having a proper house would also mean that his sister could come to visit. She and Jessie got on so well. And he was not going to visit her, oh no!

Standing outside the front door on that first morning, staring at the house, Jessie clutched Jared's arm and for once he didn't move away from her. 'This place is far too big for a cottage! It's why, it's fit for a gentleman! You should have found us something smaller!'

'Time to show a bit of prosperity and impress folk. We're gettin' on in the world now, just like I promised you.'

Once he'd have added, 'Jessie, love', and given her a quick hug, she thought sadly, but didn't comment on this. 'We'd get on a sight quicker if you hadn't wasted our money on this big place,' she said sharply, to hide her pain.

'No. You're wrong. As soon as the baby's born, we're going to splash out a bit in other ways. I'm buying you some new clothes, for a start. You're the wife of a railway contractor now and you'll have to live up to that. You'll not be serving in a shop again, if I have my way, even if you run one.' He opened the gate and bowed to her. 'This way, madam.' And suddenly, his smile was genuine. Suddenly, he seemed like the old Jared again.

For the first time in months Jessie felt almost light-hearted as she smiled back and took the arm he offered her. They walked together along the path to the neat villa which stood in a walled garden, not a big one, but enough to give it dignity and separate it from the neighbours. He opened the front door with a brass key and led her into a pleasant hallway. From there they did a tour of the parlour and the dining-room, the kitchen, scullery and washroom, then mounted the stairs, laughing over the hideous wallpaper, to inspect the four bedrooms and the two attic rooms.

'Whatever do we want with all this space?' she asked, but gently, her eyes on the view from the bedroom window.

'What does anyone want with it? Room to breathe. Room to be private.'

Yes, she thought, room to quarrel privately, too.

When they came back down again, Jessie returned to the kitchen, to cast a proprietorial eye over its dull range and dusty shelves. 'This room must be scrubbed out properly.'

'Not by you.'

'But I . . .'

'I've hired a woman from the village to come in and do the scrubbing. She'll be here tomorrow morning at six. Till then it stays dirty.'

'You didn't think to ask me about that, I suppose?'

'I knew what you'd say.'

'Oh, did you?'

'Near enough. But it's time you started acting more the lady, and ladies *don't* scrub floors and blacklead kitchen ranges! Besides, you've been looking exhausted lately. A rest'll do you good. I'll be glad when you're rid of that bloody baby!'

She looked at her stomach and blinked tears from her eyes. *Bloody baby*, he'd said. That showed how he really felt. What would he be like after the poor little thing was born? She rested one hand protectively across the swelling. Well, she wouldn't let anyone ill treat it. Or even remain indifferent to it. If Jared didn't grow to love it, she would have to think about her future. She'd seen women stay with husbands just because they couldn't manage on their own. Most women were like that. Her own mother had been unhappy in her marriage, but had not thought of leaving Frank. Even Lady Morrisham had been trapped with a man she feared. Oh, Jared, she mourned to herself, what have we come to?

For Jessie, the next two months were bittersweet, a lull after the trials, tribulations and sheer hard work of the past year. She set up the shop and Elisha lived there with Bet. She missed his cheerful face, but didn't trust Bet on her own not to turn to drinking again. And as the unlikely pair worked in the shop, they gradually forged a kind of friendship, for each understood how hard life could get and each appreciated this haven they'd been offered.

To her own surprise, as well as Jessie's, Bet really took to working in the shop. 'I don't miss the fellers, but I do like talkin' to folk,' she confided in Jessie. 'An' it's nice havin' proper clothes.' She stroked her second dress, another of Jessie's cast-offs, for Jared had insisted on two new dresses being made to accommodate his wife's expanding figure. 'I've never had so many clothes afore. Or petticoats.' Bet poked out a toe. 'An' these boots don't leak at all.' She beamed down at them.

Jared had hired Sally Dawson to come in and do the rough work at Ash Cottage. Sally had a tiny house full of children and a shiftless husband who was only employed on a casual basis. She was a hard-working woman, not fat but stocky and muscular with arms like sides of ham and work-worn fists that could knock

414

a man sideways – and did on the rare occasions her husband dared to waste more than a few pence on booze.

With Sally working at the house, Jared felt Jessie would be safe enough. He could never forget, not even for an hour, that he had not protected her before, and felt he would never, ever stop blaming himself for what had happened. But he would make sure she was well protected from now on.

With Sally's help, Jessie made the cottage as comfortable as possible. Simon picked up some pieces of furniture at an auction in Slough and she bought some more crockery and other bits and pieces herself. Jared was too busy to drive her into the nearest town, but Simon found the time. Living in the house, he was all too aware of the strained relations between the two of them and did his best to cheer up Jessie when he could. But he refused to discuss his sister with her and had not been to Heptonstall to visit.

Once or twice he tried to discuss the present situation with Jared, but was told in no uncertain terms to mind his own business.

'It'll pass,' said Jared harshly. 'Once she's had that damned baby, things'll come right again.'

'But the baby will still be there,' protested Simon. 'You can't wish it away. And have you thought – it might really be yours?' He believed Jessie now. She might lie in a fit of panic, but she wouldn't go on lying like this. No, he definitely believed her.

Jared made a scornful noise. 'An' I might never know for sure whose it is.'

It took a few days for Jessie to grow used to being addressed as 'ma'am' by Sally Dawson. She developed little routines, going to the camp shop in the mornings and, if it wasn't raining, again in the afternoons, otherwise sewing for the child. Somehow she was managing to fill all the hours of each day. She looked forward to Sundays, on which Elisha came to church with them and then stayed for a meal, for this was another place where the local magistrates would not allow Sunday working at the camp.

The shop wasn't making as much money as it would have done with her in charge, but it was still making a steady profit and she had got all her suppliers of fresh produce sorted out now. It was, she thought, something to do. But her heart wasn't in it as it had been before, and she experienced no joy in her success.

Shy at first in her new role, Jessie made the acquaintance of the vicar's, doctor's and shopkeepers' wives, who were the society of the little village. Had it not been for her condition, she and Jared would have been welcomed into their small circle and invited to dinner – though Jessie was glad not to associate with the doctor, to whom she'd taken an instant dislike, for he treated her like a childish fool. But a pregnant woman was not expected to go out socially after the baby began to show, so of course they weren't invited.

The ladies visited her at home, however, or asked her to take tea with them. They would stop to talk to her in the street and prattle on happily about their own pregnancies and the infancies of their children. The real gentry, who lived up on the hill at Mernham Manor, were still far out of the sphere of a mere railway contractor and did not even accord her a nod as they drove past in their glossy new carriage. Well, Jessie didn't care about that.

There were two falls of snow during the next few weeks, but luckily none deep enough to prevent the gig from getting through to the diggings. The frozen earth made progress slow down and Jared became even more irascible as he worried over the mounting costs. Then, suddenly it seemed, there was a feeling of spring in the air. The last traces of frost vanished, and the early flowers and watery sunshine began to cheer everyone up. Even Jared was not immune to it all and found himself smiling occasionally.

Jessie grew very ponderous in her movements as April drew to a close, short of breath at the slightest exertion and puffy about the ankles and hands. The doctor suggested that she keep to her bed, but she refused, though she did consent to spend part of the day with her feet up on the sofa in her parlour.

Mrs Dawson's eldest, Jane, aged twelve, was hired to live in and wait on Jessie at three shillings a week all found. The Dawson family entered on a brief period of unprecedented prosperity with meat or bacon to eat two or three times a week. Jane went round nearly bursting with pride at her new print dress, apron and mobcap which her mistress had made for her.

Towards the end of the month, Jared and Simon were summoned to a meeting with the railway company officials about the second contract. Jared was reluctant to leave Jessie on her own, but the doctor assured him that the baby would not be born yet, so he agreed to spend one, and only one night away.

Jessie waved them off cheerfully, feeling better than she had for days. The fine weather made her decide to change the sheets on their bed and she summoned Jane to help her. After that, still feeling well, she began to clear out the drawers in the bedroom. They were all in a mess and must be set to rights before another hour had passed.

This burst of energy was so unlike her recent behaviour that Jane began to eye her strangely, but Jessie did not notice her young handmaiden's covert looks. She ate a hearty midday meal and began to plan a rearrangement of the furniture in the parlour. In the middle of this she clutched her stomach and looked puzzled.

'I think I must have indigestion.'

'Oh, ma'am,' Jane clasped her hands together, 'you 'aven't started, 'ave you?'

'Of course not! You heard what the doctor said. At least a week yet.'

But the indigestion grew worse and soon Jessie was forced to concede that the girl might be right.

'I knew it!' said Jane triumphantly. 'Soon as you started clearin' them drawers out, I knew what was up. My mam was just like that with our Mary an' our Willie.'

These knowledgeable words from a scrawny twelve year old made Jessie laugh, then she stopped with a gasp as a stronger contraction took her by surprise.

'Are you 'avin' another pain already?' demanded Jane.

'Yes,' said Jessie faintly. 'And that one hurt, too!'

'I'd better run for my mam, then,' said Jane, ever practical. 'It's comin' on quick, it is.'

'Yes, you do that,' agreed Jessie, feeling suddenly alone and helpless. If only Jared were there! But he wasn't. She gritted her teeth and tried to speak cheerfully. 'Go on, then! What are you waiting for? And get the doctor too. I'll go up to bed.'

As the door banged behind Jane, Jessie started up the stairs, leaning on the banister, but had to sit down halfway, as another bout of pain caught her by surprise. She got to the bedroom and sat gasping on the bed, but pulled herself together and managed to change into the old shortened nightgown she had ready to wear for the birth.

She had meant not to cry out, despising such weakness, but now she found herself moaning as the pains grew stronger. She was afraid that the baby would be born with no one there to help, and cried out in relief as the door banged again and Mrs Dawson and Jane rushed into the room.

'Doctor's over Twylford way,' announced Mrs Dawson. 'Looks like he'll be too late to help. But don't worry thysen, Mrs Wilde. Me an' Jane know what to do. Men aren't much use at times like this, anyway, doctors or not.'

Jessie opened her eyes after another set of pains to see Mrs Dawson's grubby hands coming closer. 'Well, you can just wash your hands before you touch me!' she said, faintly but firmly.

'What? That's only a bit of chicken blood!'

Jessie struggled into a sitting position. 'I mean it! Wash your hands! And you too, Jane.'

Humouring her whim, Mrs Dawson splashed about on the washstand, enjoying the nice smell of the lavender soap that Simon had bought for Jessie in the apothecary's shop in the nearby town. Jane followed suit.

Within the hour Jessie was bearing down and only half an hour after that, the baby was born.

'Eh, who's a fine little lad?' cooed Mrs Dawson, wrapping him expertly in a cloth and waiting for the afterbirth. When she had cut the cord, she placed the infant in his mother's arms, mistaking Jessie's tears of dismay for tears of joy.

'I mind 'ow I cried over my first,' she said, hugging Jane, who had been the baby in question. 'Though she wasn't a boy, which 'er father 'ad set his mind on. An' now look at 'er, do! Nearly woman hersen, she is!'

Jane wriggled uncomfortably in the unaccustomed maternal embrace. She was more used to slaps than kisses from her parent.

Jessie lay on the bed, her son in her arms, and let the tw

women clear up. She gazed down searchingly at his features, looking for a resemblance to his father. Her heart sank as she found none. He looked more like her mother than anyone else. He stopped wailing and stared up at her blindly, opening his pink mouth and nuzzling her with his cheek. A wave of tenderness flooded through her and she stroked the dark down on his skull with one fingertip. Only now did she realise that they'd planned no names at all for a boy. They'd both been willing it to be a girl. Well, this was no girl, and Jared would just have to get used to that!

'What are you goin' to call him?' asked Mrs Dawson.

Jessie looked at her blankly for a moment. It would be no use waiting for Jared. 'Richard,' she said suddenly. She had always liked that name. 'Richard Wilde.'

'That's nice,' said Mrs Dawson. 'Richard's a fine name. I might call my next Richard, if it's a boy.'

'Are you . . . ?'

'Oh, yes,' said Mrs Dawson cheerfully. 'I mostly am. This is the longest there's been between 'em. Well, it's as the Lord wills, ain't it? That's what the vicar says, anyway. But I say it's my old man as wills it. He's a bit lively! In bed at least.' She laughed heartily at her own joke.

By the time Jared arrived home the next evening, the doctor had been, stood at the foot of the bed and pronounced mother and child to be in excellent health. By that time, too, a strong bond had been forged between Jessie and her son. How could you help loving a little creature who was dependent upon you for everything and who nestled against you so trustingly?

When Jared appeared unannounced in the doorway of the bedroom, she looked up, smiling, but her smile faded as she saw the tight, aloof expression on his face.

'So it's a boy, after all?'

'Yes. Oh, Jared, he's lovely! I didn't expect him to be such a dear! Come and meet your son.'

Ignoring the cot and its contents, he came over to the bed. 'How are *you*?'

'I'm fine. It was very quick – and easy, they tell me. But it hurt. I wanted you with me!'

He clasped her hand, his face still shadowed. 'I'm glad you're all right, anyway.'

'You haven't looked at the baby. He looks just like my mother!'

He gave a snort and stood by the cradle, staring down. 'That's all I needed!'

'I've called him Richard. Is that all right?'

'Whatever you want.'

'He *is* your son,' she insisted. She could not keep the tears from her eyes. He saw and wished desperately that he could feel differently about the child, but something inside him seemed to freeze at the mere thought that it might be his. He just could not believe it.

'Well, if you'll excuse me, I'll go an' get washed an' then see if Jane can find me somethin' to eat. I'm starving.' And he walked out of the room, not looking at the cradle again and leaving her in tears.

A cautious knock on the door heralded the arrival of Simon and without realising it, he rubbed salt in Jessie's wound. 'May I? Oh, my dear, he looks just like you! Isn't he handsome?'

The baby woke up and began to cry lustily. She reached out to take him and held him fiercely close, as if to protect him from the world.

'Jared can't accept him, can he?' Simon asked softly, seeing the pain on her face and the tears in her eyes.

Jessie shook her head wordlessly and then laughed shakily as she had to wipe away a tear that had fallen on the baby's face. 'He *is* Jared's, though.'

How could Jared not believe her when she looked like that?

'He'll come round, Jessie. Give him time.'

'Will he?' she asked. And would she feel the same about him if this went on much longer? Jared was tacitly accusing her of being a liar. And that was eroding their relationship day by day.

'Of course he will!' Simon said, more confidently than he felt.

'I wish I could believe that.'

When Simon went downstairs to eat, he had a row with Jared over the baby, and the men's angry voices reached Jessie in the bedroom above. Jane, sitting shivering with fright in the kitchen, couldn't understand what they were going on about and only hoped the stew was all right.

In the end, Jared stormed out of the house and went down to the village inn, where he sat morosely in a corner and tried to get drunk. The well-meaning congratulations of the men around him soon drove him away, denying him even this solace. And he could not stop wondering if Jessie really were telling the truth. She had said it so many times, even now, weakened by childbirth. Why would she continue to lie to him?

Well, the answer to that was easy. To protect the child. She was a fierce defender of those she loved, his Jessie was. And yet . . . Oh, hell, he didn't know what to think, didn't know anything any more, not about himself, not about Jessie, and most of all not about that damned child.

33

May 1839

*D*uring the following weeks, Jared slept in a separate bedroom, pretending he was doing it because of the child's disturbed nights. The only one to be convinced by his charade was Mrs Dawson, who congratulated Jessie on having such a thoughtful husband.

Even young Jane asked hesitantly what was wrong with the master.

'He wanted a daughter,' said Jessie lamely. 'He – er – had his heart set on a daughter.' It was the best she could think of.

'He isn't like other men, then.' Jane was patently unconvinced by this explanation. 'They usually want a son first off. And Master Richard's a fine little lad, aren't you, my little duck?' She had developed quite an attachment to the child and would rush to pick him up if he cried.

Jessie changed the subject firmly and began to discuss the day's meals and what needed to be bought in the village.

She stayed in bed only a day or two after the birth, scandalising the vicar's lady by going out for a walk around the garden on the third day, and ignoring the doctor's disapproval. She couldn't stay in bed and just brood on the gulf that was steadily widening between her and Jared. Things had been bad before, but they were far worse now. She was beyond tears by this time, though she had wept bitterly at first over his refusal to have anything to do with the child.

He left the house every day as soon as it was light, and didn't return until it was dark. If he could, he even avoided being in the same room as the baby. He seemed more like a stranger than the husband she had loved and still loved so dearly. She knew Simon was upset by their estrangement and that the two men had had words more than once, but there seemed to be no way anyone could penetrate the wall Jared had built around himself.

Three weeks after the baby's birth, Jared himself brought matters to a head. He asked Simon to leave them alone and took Jessie into the parlour. 'It's no use,' he said, without preamble. 'I can't accept him.'

She looked at him in icy horror. 'What do you mean, "can't accept him"?' she whispered. 'He's your *son*. I've told you and told you. Yours! Not Joe's.'

He shook his head, feeling numb and disoriented with unhappiness.

'You haven't tried, Jared. You haven't even gone near him!'

'I can't and that's that.' He avoided her eyes as he added, 'I've been making inquiries. There's a woman over near Sheffield. She fosters children. She's well thought of, looks after them really carefully. She'll have him for five shillings a week – and she knows a good wet-nurse for another five.'

The room spun around Jessie and there was a roaring sound in her ears. Jared's voice seemed to be coming from a great distance. She thought for a moment that she was going to faint, then pulled herself together to fight for her son. 'What are you saying, Jared? That's my son you're talking about. *My* son, as well as yours. Part of me! Part of us! Why won't you *believe* me?'

'Because I know you. You'll fight like a tigress for anyone you love. Look at what you've done for Elisha. Would you do less for your own child? No!' He walked over to the window and said in a muffled voice, 'If it had been a girl, perhaps . . . maybe not even then . . . but I can't face the child every day. I thought I could, but I can't!'

'I won't give him up. And you can't make me!'

'It's all arranged. I'm to take him over there tomorrow night.

She sat in numb disbelief.

He looked at her as if she were a stranger. 'It's all arranged,' h repeated. 'And if you make me, I'll take him away by force, Jessie. Once he's gone, you'll forget him. We'll have other children, children of our own.' He stretched out his hand to her and she slapped it out of the way. Angrily he caught her in his arms and kissed her savagely on the lips. 'You'll forget him,' he said. 'I'll *make* you forget!'

She opened her mouth to scream and he covered it with his hand. 'This is between you and me, Jessie. You'll not call Simon in!'

She sagged against him. 'Jared, please listen to me.' But she didn't know where to find the words to convince him.

'Not if you're going to ask me to change my mind. I've been thinking of this for months. It's hard, but it's the only way. And it's best done quickly before you grow attached to the child.'

'I already love him. He's born of my body.'

'Then you'll have to choose between him and me,' he said, still in that same harsh voice. He caught her in his arms and tried to kiss her again. 'Jessie, you'll surely not give up everything we've built together for that – that creature?' It was as near as he could come to begging.

Still she fought against him and suddenly he let her go. 'It's the only way,' he said wearily. The baby began to cry in the kitchen and he turned on his heel and walked out of the house.

She swayed dizzily and had to lean against the wall. She couldn't believe that Jared, her Jared, had planned such a dreadful thing. But he meant what he said. He hadn't even pretended to listen to her. The baby's crying penetrated her daze and she stumbled into the kitchen.

Simon, sitting by the fire, jumped up at the sight of her face. 'What is it?'

She stared at him blankly.

'Jessie. Are you all right? What's happened?'

She must not bring him into their quarrel. This was between Jared and herself. 'We – quarrelled again,' she said jerkily. 'He – I'm upset. I think I'll go to bed.'

'Can I do anything to help?'

'No.' She picked up the baby and left the room.

* * *

In the morning Jared came into her bedroom just after dawn, before he left for the diggings. 'I'll come home early to take him.' He could not bear to look at her white face and guilt made him add, 'He'll be all right. She's a good woman. I checked everything. You'll be best staying here.'

She looked at his hard expression and the plea she had been going to make died on her lips. How could Jared, who had lost his mother so young and never really known a family life since he was ten, understand her feelings? He seemed to be waiting for her to say something, but she remained silent, just looking at him reproachfully. But his expression didn't soften.

When he and Simon had left, she went downstairs and sat by the kitchen table to feed her son. Her mind was at first a blank, but gradually she pulled herself together and began to set the plans she had made in motion. She felt that she was being torn in two, but knew quite definitely that she was not going to let anyone part her from her son. Jared's son, too.

It was quite simple, really. If he could not believe her, then she'd have to leave him and take little Richard with her.

'Run over to Mr Sherbin at the inn,' she told Jane, 'and tell him that I want to hire his gig and a boy to drive me. My mother's ill. We heard yesterday. Mr Wilde doesn't want me to go to her, but I must. She's very ill. I have to go! Tell Mr Sherbin that I'll be ready in an hour and I'll pay in advance. I'll get a coach for York in Sheffield.'

She pushed the goggling Jane out of the door and flew upstairs, pulling her tin trunk out from under the bed and then pushing it back as she realised how strange it would look to take something so big. She remembered that Simon had a valise and darted into his bedroom to find it, tipping its contents on to the bed and muttering, 'I'm sorry, Simon,' as she did so.

She packed as much as she could, mostly things for the baby, then went into Jared's room and opened the black tin box, to which they both had keys. Swallowing hard to keep the tears back, she counted out a hundred pounds, which she thought ought to be enough, together with her own savings, to set her up in a little shop somewhere. There would be enough left behind for Jared to manage on, too. She had helped earn the money been happy to count it into the box every week, but now her mood was bleak as she took it out. It felt like stealing. She left a note on his bed, saying how much she had taken and why.

She was ready before the gig arrived, pacing up and down impatiently in the kitchen with Richard in her arms, terrified that Jared might return home early.

Jane was bewildered. 'But when are you comin' back?' she asked, for her mistress had given her no instructions.

'I don't know! It – it depends on my mother. There's a note for Mr Wilde on his bed. You'll be able to manage, look after them. I'm relying on you. Keep the place clean. Get your mother in to help you, if necessary.'

Jane opened her mouth to ask something else and Jessie's patience snapped. 'Leave me alone, can't you! Go and – and scrub the scullery floor or something!' Snivelling, the girl went away.

Ten minutes later, Jessie was sitting in the gig, bowling down the lane and asking the driver to go faster. She was terrified that Jared would come after her and drag Richard from her arms. She intended to travel partway to London, not York, and then take a stage coach to some town chosen at random. There, she would settle down and pretend to be a widow, setting herself up in some sort of business. What else could she do? Maybe, after some time had passed, she would write to Elinor, invite her to stay. She was sure Elinor wouldn't betray her whereabouts. But for now, she wasn't going to involve her friends.

At the diggings, Jared couldn't settle to anything. He kept seeing Jessie's face, hearing her anguished plea to be allowed to keep her son. He felt worse than he had before he took his decision. The men kept away from him as he paced up and down the top of the slope like a caged bear.

By midday he gave up any attempt to work and acknowledged to himself that he was being unfair, that he could not do it. And – what if she were right? What if Richard really were his son? He felt in such a muddle inside that he could not think straight. Maybe – just maybe – he'd not been thinking straight since it happened. He no longer knew.

He went to find Simon. 'I've got to go home and see Jessie,' he said. 'I've hurt her – hurt her badly. Can you manage without me?'

'Gladly!' said Simon, who had heard Jessie's muffled sobs the night before. 'And don't come back today.' He hesitated, then added awkwardly, 'Be kind to her, Jared. She's been very unhappy. And – I really don't think she'd lie to you about something like that. Not Jessie.'

Jared looked at him with haunted eyes, but said nothing, not trusting his voice.

But when he burst into the kitchen at Ash Cottage, calling for her, it was empty. Hearing footsteps upstairs, he ran to find his wife.

'Jessie!' He came to an abrupt halt in the bedroom doorway. 'Oh – it's only you, Jane! Where's your mistress?'

She gaped at him. 'Gone, sir.'

A leaden weight seemed to settle in his guts. 'Gone? What do you mean, gone? Where has she gone?'

'To her mother's, sir,' said Jane unhappily, fearing he would be angry with her. 'She said her mother was bad and you didn't want her to go to Mrs Marley, because of the baby, but she went anyway. An' you're to have the rest of the pie for tea.'

'Gone!' he echoed stupidly. 'She's gone?'

'Yes, sir. And little Richard with her.'

He stared at her uncomprehendingly for a moment, then pushed her to one side as if she were a doll and rushed into Jessie's bedroom, flinging open the drawers. Most of her things were still there, but all the baby's things were gone. He stood for one endless moment in the centre of the room, ignoring Jane's frantic demands to know if he was all right.

Everything was suddenly very clear to him. He couldn't live without Jessie. The mere thought of a future without her made him want to fall on the bed and weep like the child he'd never had time to be. But he must not do that. It would serve no purpose. He'd been wrong. He couldn't ignore the fact of the baby. It was born; it was there.

Suddenly he remembered Jessie's face; how she had looked last night as she swore that the baby was his. No one could look as harrowed as that and still be lying, surely? Not someone who

428

loved him as he knew she did. A thread of hope began to grow inside him. If she really was telling the truth . . .

He began to pace up and down. And even if she wasn't, how could he ever have believed that a person as loyal as Jessie would give up her child or continue to love the man who had stolen it from her? He must find her, tell her he couldn't live without her, persuade her to come back. He must accept the child as his. Hell, it *was* his!

Suddenly it seemed dreadful that he couldn't even remember what it looked like, except that it had dark hair, darker than Jessie's. He sucked in air as the realisation struck home – more like his in colour. He hadn't even tried to see a resemblance after that first day.

He took a deep breath and turned to Jane. 'How did Mrs Wilde travel?'

'In Mr Sherbin's gig, sir.'

'Do you know where she was going?'

Jane stared at him in puzzlement. Surely that was obvious? 'Yes, sir. She was going to York, to her mother's. She said she'd get a coach in Sheffield.'

'What? Oh. Well, um, I had word brought to me at the diggings that Mrs Marley is getting better, not in danger any more.' He wished to hell the girl would shut up. 'I'll go and fetch Mrs Wilde back,' he said abruptly, and was gone, leaving Jane gawping out of the window, watching him stride down the lane as if the devil was after him.

He hired the inn's second best gig, because Simon had their own vehicle and he didn't want to tell his friend what had happened. By dint of bribing the young stable lad, Jared got him to drive as fast as he could. He was sure that Jessie would not be going to her mother's. She was one to hold her griefs to herself. And if he didn't catch her quickly, she might vanish entirely; he might never see her again. 'Faster!' he said, in a strangled, throaty voice. 'Go faster, damn you!'

They met the other gig from the inn when they were nearly in Sheffield. It was empty. 'Stop!' Jared yelled at the top of his voice.

Both vehicles were reined in so quickly that the horses stood shivering in bewilderment.

'Where's Mrs Wilde?' he called to the other driver.

'Took the London stage,' answered the lad, staring in amazement at this wild-eyed man. 'She'll be setting off just about now.'

Jared offered him no explanations, just left him goggling as he told his own driver to urge the tired beast on again. He had guessed right. She wasn't going to her mother's. But where the hell was she going?

He hired a chaise and driver in Sheffield, having missed Jessie by only ten minutes, and had to pay dearly for the privilege. Jared handed over what the landlord asked without arguing and urged this driver also to spring the horses, promising him a sovereign for himself if he overtook the London stage coach. The man was only too happy to oblige.

Only an hour later they came upon the slow-moving coach on a hill and Jared ordered the driver to pull up the chaise in front of it and stop it.

'What are you doin', you blamin' idiot?' shouted the driver, flourishing his whip at them. 'Get that bleddy thing out o' my way!'

Jared leaped down. 'I'm sorry!' he said, forcing himself to be civil. 'I think you have my wife and son inside. She was going to see her sick mother. But her mother's better. So it'd be a wasted journey, do you see?'

The driver blinked and looked at him suspiciously, but Jared tossed him a half sovereign, so he shrugged and nodded to his assistant. It was no business of his whether the man was telling the truth or not. 'Lady with the baby. Get 'er baggage down, Tommy lad!'

Jared hadn't waited to see what the driver would do. He went and opened the door of the coach. Jessie, who had heard his voice, shrank back into the corner, clutching Richard to her.

Jared held his hand out to her. 'Come on, love,' he said gently, ignoring the stares of the other passengers. When she didn't move, he felt compelled to add, 'Your mother's better. There's no need for you to go anywhere – no need for *anyone* to go away at all.'

She looked at him beseechingly. 'Richard?'

The other passengers continued to watch them with uncon-cealed interest.

'We'll take him home with us,' said Jared, holding out his hand to help her from the coach. 'He's too young to travel.'

She still hung back. 'Do you really mean that, Jared? I can take him home?'

He nodded. 'Yes, love. I promise you no one's going to do anything you don't want.'

She could see in his face all the love that had been missing over the past few months and gave a sob of relief as a great burden seemed to slip from her shoulders. Tears welled in her eyes, but she smiled through them and began to fumble for her things.

He held out his arms. 'Give him to me and get your stuff together quickly. We've held these good people up for long enough.'

He threw Jessie's valise into their carriage and turned back to help her. He could feel her trembling and when she stumbled, took the baby from her again and carried it. Neither of them noticed the stage coach drive off.

He helped Jessie into his carriage and got in after her, still holding the baby.

The driver looked at him for instructions, but Jared had forgotten his very existence. He closed the carriage door and sat down beside his wife. 'I'm sorry, love,' he said huskily. 'I think I must have been – a bit mad.'

She looked at him, her eyes red-rimmed from weeping. 'I won't give up my baby,' she said, a catch in her voice. 'And he *is* your son.'

'No, love, I know you won't give him up. I was wrong to ask you. And – I believe you. So I'd better get used to him, hadn't I?'

It was the way he had called her 'love' again that convinced her that he meant it. 'Oh, Jared,' she said brokenly, 'I was torn in two!'

At that he pulled her closer, kissing her passionately, as he had not kissed her for months. The baby, crushed between them, howled in protest and they drew apart, both smiling down at the tiny creature.

'He looks like you!' said Jared in surprise.

She nodded, almost beyond words. 'And like you, too.'

He looked at her over the baby's head. 'I couldn't live without you, Jessie.'

She tried to smile, but her lips were trembling.

'Come on, love,' he said gently. 'Let's take our lad home!' He rapped on the carriage roof and as it began to move, took her and the child in his arms again.

34

❦

July 1839

*W*hen the cutting was finished, the navvies moved down the track to the next site, which was a very similar job. Jared hired extra carts and drays and the men moved the shanty town themselves, joking as they dismantled the huts, enjoying the change from digging and hauling muck.

He took a few days off while this was going on, taking Jessie and the child to visit her mother. Simon's sister came to stay at Ash Cottage while they were away, arriving a day early, so that she and Jessie could catch up with one another's news.

'How are things now?' Elinor asked, when the men were outside.

'Better. And yet,' Jessie hesitated, 'there's still a sense of – of awkwardness with the child. Though Jared does try, he really does.'

'Give him time.'

'Mmm.' Jessie decided it was better to change the subject. 'How's Simon feeling now about your move?' She knew he had gone over to Heptonstall a few weeks previously, but she hadn't asked him about it, because he had been very touchy on the subject.

'He's coming round, as Thirza said he would. But he was very grumpy the first time he visited us.' Elinor gave Jessie an impulsive hug. 'I'm so glad I listened to you about that. I've not been as happy as this for years. Last time Simon visited me we met some people we used to know and they seemed really pleased to see us. That helped. But he still finds it painful to go back, I know.'

When the Wildes left the next day, Jessie wished she and Elinor had had longer together. She felt she had found a real friend, someone she could confide in as she never could a man, even her husband, and she wished they lived closer. But you couldn't have everything, and at least Simon was reconciled now to his sister's living in Heptonstall, so they would all see one another from time to time.

In Shilwick it was immediately obvious that marriage suited Agnes, who looked much less severe and fussed over her first grandchild as if there had never been a baby like him in the world. Jessie could not help wondering if her mother had ever cuddled her like that.

Jared watched, managing to smile now and then. He had grown used to young Richard and had to admit that the child was a nice enough little creature, but he still didn't feel connected to him as Jessie was. When Bet told him, in an unguarded moment, that Joe hadn't been much of a man towards the end, he just nodded. He hadn't needed that confirmation. He had accepted fully that Jessie hadn't lied to him and that Richard was his son. Yet, however hard he tried, he didn't feel like a real father. He just didn't.

By the time the visits were over, the new shanty town was set up and work could really begin on the cutting.

At first it went well, then suddenly things slowed down.

'It's a bugger, this one is,' Billy told Jessie one day, when she was visiting the camp shop, 'a real bugger.'

'You watch your language in front of my wife,' Jared snapped.

Billy shuffled his feet and grinned at Jessie. 'Sorry, love. Didn't mean to offend.'

'That's all right. What's wrong with this place, though? I thought it'd be like the last one. It's only just down the road, after all.'

He shook his head. 'Some of 'em – well, you can't put a finger on it, but they're bug— bad 'uns. An' this has got that feel to it.'

'Are you going to stand here nattering all day?' Jared demanded.

'Just getting summat to eat,' Billy replied, exchanging glances with Bet. Big Jared was in a fratchy mood lately, by hell he was!

And that mood didn't lighten. In fact, Jared and Simon would sit there in the evenings, worrying over how long it was taking, how everything was going wrong here and why accidents were happening, whatever precautions they took.

'At least nothing serious has happened,' Simon said one evening, leaning back in his chair to stretch his arms and yawn.

'Don't say that!' Jared exclaimed.

'You don't believe in those old navvies' superstitions, surely?'

'I don't believe in tempting providence, that's for sure.'

As Jessie lay in his arms that night, she asked, 'You're really worried, aren't you?'

'Mmm.'

'Why?'

'I don't know. Just a feeling you get. An' I've never been wrong before. Joe – ' He broke off as she stiffened, then finished. 'For all his faults, Joe had the same sort of feeling for working the earth. I've known him walk away from a job because of it – and save his life by doin' it. Trouble is, me and Simon can't walk away from this one.'

'Would you if you were just a navvy?'

He nodded. 'Aye, I think I would.'

After that, she began to worry, too. Jared was not usually a fanciful man.

A week later, while she was in the shop, there was a rumbling sound, followed by a confused babble of shouts and cries and curses.

Bet abandoned her customers to rush outside, shouting, 'There's trouble.'

Jessie put Richard down in the cradle they kept at the shop for him and followed her outside. Men were pounding along from all directions towards the far end of the nearer slope. Jessie followed them, gathering up her skirts and running as she had not done for years.

As she reached the top of little hill, Bull came to bar her way. 'Better not go any further, missus.'

'Why not?'

He couldn't think how to soften the news. 'Big Jared's trapped under that cart down there.'

She looked at the half-buried vehicle and tried to shake him off, to push past him, but he kept hold of her arm. 'I have to go to him,' she insisted.

'You'll get in the way. They're still tryin' to dig him out.'

She froze. 'You mean he's *buried*?'

'Aye.'

'But you said he was under a cart.'

'If he's lucky, he is.'

Bet came to stand next to Jessie. 'Eh, they were right – it's a bad 'un, this place is.'

Bull glared at her. 'Shut up, you stupid trollop!'

Billy came striding up the slope towards them, looking grim. 'You stay here an' keep folk back, Jessie. We need Bull to help us dig.'

Her voice was shrill with suppressed panic. 'Jared?'

'We'll get him out.'

'Are there any others trapped?'

'Aye. A couple.' He was clearly anxious to get back to the scene of the accident, so she just nodded and stayed where she was.

A small group of women gathered round her to wait. They didn't say much, simply stood there. Two of them, those whose men were also trapped, had their arms around one another. Jessie felt very alone, then Elisha came up, carrying Richard. She took the baby and cuddled his warm little body to her, but that didn't drive away the fear, the dreadful saw-toothed worry about Jared that was nearly tearing her apart.

Beside her, Bet stood fidgeting, then reached out to put an arm round Jessie's shoulders, giving her a quick hug when no protest was made. 'He'll be all right, love. Big Jared's tough.'

'Shall I go an' fetch the doctor?' Elisha asked suddenly.

'Yes. Tell him the company will pay.'

I'm not thinking straight, Jessie decided as she watched the lad run away towards the village. She should have thought of that before. She hadn't realised that anxiety could make you so stupid. She didn't like the doctor, who had treated her so scornfully while she was expecting Richard, but if there were broken limbs, they'd need him.

'Your Jared will be all right, love,' Bet repeated as the minutes crawled past, with another hug. 'He's a big strong fellow.'

Jessie hardly heard her.

A few minutes later there were cries from the place where the earth had slipped into a huge mound. Jessie thrust Richard into Bet's arms and took a step forward. The men had stopped digging. The end of the cart was half uncovered now, and the front was balanced precariously on a pile of timber, where the earth had pushed it. Billy was lying on his belly in the mouth of a short tunnel which had been dug along the side of the cart and from which he had been scooping earth with his bare hands, shoving it backwards into other willing hands and propping up things as he went with planks.

Then he shouted and the men behind him moved away. He began to wriggle backwards slowly, tugging something with him. The others stepped forward as soon as there was room and took the burden from him, while he stood there, panting and wiping the muck from his face.

Jessie could hardly breathe and her chest seemed to be squeezed tight by a solid lump of fear. Someone bent over the still, mud-covered figure, then stood up, shaking his head, and someone else offered his jacket to cover the dead man's face. When the men moved back a little and the figure was revealed, she let out a soft moan of relief. She couldn't see who it was, but it wasn't big enough to be her Jared.

She jumped in shock as a voice beside her asked, 'What happened here?'

'Simon! I thought you were seeing the company man today.'

'I was. I'm back.' He peered around. 'Where's Jared?'

She had to force the words out. 'Under that pile of muck.'

He let out his breath in a raw sound. 'Oh, hell!' Then he tore off his coat and slithered down the muddy slope, immediately joining the relays of men, who were relieving one another every few minutes as they dug with their bare hands, afraid of using spades in case they injured anyone buried there.

Jessie didn't even hear Bet repeating her litany of: 'He'll be all right. He will.' All her attention was focused on the small group of diggers. Voices drifted up to the top of the slope.

Billy: 'There's two more to find.'

Simon: 'Big Jared?'

'Aye. An' Fat Freddy.'

Bull shouted suddenly, 'They've got another.'

A man indistinguishable beneath a coating of mud, cried from inside the excavated space, 'It's Big Jared. He's trapped by the back wheel, but still breathing.' The wagon rocked dangerously above him and he yelled, 'Can't you brace that bloody wagon better nor that? Do you want the rest of us killed, too?' Men moved forward.

'We'll lift it off,' said one.

'No.' Simon took charge, sending men running for bigger timbers and bracing them carefully around and under the heavy wagon, so that it was raised slightly but could not roll back on to the two men trapped beneath it, whatever happened.

'Is that high enough?' he called.

'Aye,' came a voice from the tunnel.

'Hold on a minute.' He made a final check and only when he was absolutely certain everything was secure did he nod to the man standing by the hoist. 'Right. Take it slowly.'

It seemed to Jessie that everything was moving in a dream. Men who normally heaved dirt out of the ground with cheerful disregard for those around them were behaving as if they were shifting eggs. Only Billy's legs were showing now, for he had wriggled into the space beneath the wagon. His voice sounded muffled. 'Ease it up just a bit more! *Careful!*'

Simon beckoned another man to help him and bent over the timbers.

Jessie wanted to scream at them to hurry, hurry up and free her Jared, but she bit back the words. Behind her, Bet was rocking Richard and crooning to him. The woman whose man had been killed had been taken away by her friends.

Another voice spoke from behind her. 'What's happening here? The lad said there were injured men.'

Jessie turned to see the doctor from Mernham. 'They're only just getting them out. The first one they found was dead.' She took a deep sobbing breath. 'They're just freeing my Jared. He was trapped by the wheel. It caught his leg.'

'Might be an amputation, then.'

She gasped, then glared at him, amazed by this callousness. 'No, it won't!'

'If his leg is badly smashed, it's often best to – '

'You haven't even seen him! Don't you dare – ' She broke off at another shout from below.

Billy was edging backwards again, pulling another body. As soon as there was room, other hands were there to take the still figure from him. This was a large man.

Blood, thought Jessie. That's blood. It was so red against the mud – bright, vivid scarlet. But she wouldn't let herself give way and sob. Jared would need her to stand between him and the doctor. That man wasn't going to chop his leg off if there was the slightest chance of saving it.

They were carrying him up the slope now, four men, all members of his old gang. She turned to the doctor. 'Do you want to examine him here, or shall we carry him to the shop?'

'Is there a table there?'

She nodded.

'Might as well take him into the shop, then. It'll be easier to examine him.'

'Elisha, run ahead and clear everything off the table,' she ordered.

He was gone, twisting in and out of the spectators who fell back as Jared's unconscious body was carried through the crowd.

Jessie walked next to him. He was breathing. She could see his chest rising and falling. But his leg was a mess of mud and blood, with the bone showing through where the wheel had trapped him. It made her feel sick to see it, but she couldn't, wouldn't, give way to that. She needed to be strong.

Inside the hut, Elisha was waiting. He had the table cleared and had swung the kettle over the fire to heat some water.

'Good boy!' Jessie approved.

The doctor ignored the lad. 'You'd better wait outside now, Mrs Wilde.'

'I'd rather stay and help.'

'No. This is not for a woman's eyes.' He was already pulling the torn trousers away from the big gouge, jerking the leg about as he did so.

She went to get him a pair of scissors, saying, 'I'm staying!' as she slapped them into his hand and said, 'It'll be easier if you cut it.'

As long as Jared was still breathing, she wasn't moving from his side. She kept watching his chest, reassured by its rise and fall. He hadn't moved, though, showed no sign of returning to consciousness, and there was a huge bump on his forehead, with the torn skin around it oozing blood. Perhaps that was for the best.

Simon came into the shop to stand beside her and wait, his arm warmly comforting round her shoulders.

The doctor muttered something about 'stupid woman', then looked round. 'I need some water. And some clean cloths.'

Jessie found a bowl and held it out to Elisha. 'Rinse it out first, and make sure the water's not too hot.' Then she looked round almost in panic for some clean material. Finding nothing, she lifted her skirt and untied her top petticoat, slipping it off without thought of embarrassment, because Jared needed it and nothing else counted.

The doctor flushed and looked away, but Simon braced her so that she didn't fall, taking the petticoat from her as she let go of her other skirts.

Without hesitation, she tore down the side seam and used her teeth to start another tear going, holding out the first strip. 'Here. It was clean on today.'

As the doctor worked carefully to expose the wound, Jessie passed him pieces of dampened material and Elisha brought more water.

When all the muck and blood were cleaned away from the leg, Jessie gulped and had to swallow down a feeling of nausea. It was bad. She could see that. She looked up at the doctor and he shook his head.

'We'll need to remove the lower leg.'

'What if you didn't remove it?'

'Then we'd risk gangrene and him losing the whole leg – if not his life. It's safer this way. You, boy, go and bring that other bag from my gig. Madam, it's time for you to leave.' He appealed to Simon. 'Can you not take her out?'

Jessie looked down at the leg, thought of her Jared turned into only half a man, knew how he would hate that and felt determination rise in her. 'I think we should try to save it.'

'Madam!' The doctor tried to shepherd her away from the table, but she shook him off. He glared at her. 'I've given you my professional opinion. Now leave me to do what is necessary.'

She hesitated for a moment, then shook her head again. 'No. He's not – not the sort of man to cope with that.'

'He'll cope if he has to. They always do.'

'But if he finds out there was a chance of saving the leg, that we didn't take that chance – ' She stared down at her unconscious husband. 'No. I know what he'd want.'

The doctor looked at Simon. 'Sir, could you please take her away? She's hysterical and doesn't understand the imperatives.'

Simon looked down at Jared. Like Jessie, he thought of Big Jared without his leg, and like Jessie, he shook his head. 'I agree with her. If there's even the slightest chance of saving the leg, he'd want to take it.'

'Even if we do save it, he'll be horribly scarred.'

'That doesn't matter,' said Jessie impatiently. 'As long as he can walk on it.'

The doctor looked from one to the other, his lips tight and anger clearly visible. These railway folk were too damned independent. 'On your own heads be it then, but I tell you frankly, you are probably signing his death warrant.'

There were footsteps by the door and two men carried in the final victim, lying him on the floor. He, too, was bloody but breathing. The doctor looked at Simon. 'Can you start to clean away the mud from that fellow? I must finish here. There's a bone to be set and skin to be sewn up. Mrs Wilde can help me. Maybe that will show her what we're up against.' He scowled at Jessie again. 'I hope you've a strong stomach, madam?'

She stared him in the eye. 'I've a stomach for anything that will help my husband.'

An hour later, the doctor finished with the second man, who was not as badly hurt as Jared and was now conscious and groaning. 'I can do no more at the moment.' He pulled out a watch and flicked open its case. 'Yes, as I thought. It's nearly time for tea.' He studied the two injured men again. 'You can move them if you go carefully. They'll be better in the comfort of a bed in a proper house.' He had not attempted to conceal his disapproval of the camp and its facilities. 'Keep that wound as clean as you can. I shall come and inspect it tomorrow.'

'I'll arrange for a carriage to take Jared home,' Simon offered.

The doctor turned at the door, his voice indifferent, thoughts already elsewhere. 'A cart would be better. And drive it slowly.'

Simon nodded and left the hut.

'You can bring the other man back to our cottage as well,' Jessie offered to his friends.

Billy exchanged glances with Bull and they both shook their heads. 'I think he'd feel better here, Jessie lass. Can he stay with you in the back of the shop, Bet? It's the warmest place, I reckon, an' the driest, too. His wife'll come an' help.'

She nodded. 'Aye. But I've the shop to manage, mind on. An' he's a big sod, Freddy is. His wife an' me can't move him about by oursen.'

Another woman stepped forward. 'I'll stay, as well.'

Jessie stayed next to Jared while they waited for the cart. Bet brought a howling, hungry Richard in to her from the front of the shop and she fed him there and then, covering herself as best she could with Bet's shawl.

When the cart arrived, Jessie sat in the back next to her husband, holding Richard tight, her expression grimly determined. Jared was alive, and he was going to stay alive – and he was *not* going to lose his leg.

Jane came rushing out of the house as the cart drew up and gasped when she realised that her master was lying on the back of it, injured.

Again, Jessie took charge. 'Calm down, Jane, and don't you dare cry. I need you to help me with Richard. Here, you take him.'

Simon, like the others, did her bidding, his admiration for her deepening as they worked together to get Jared inside and a bed brought down to the parlour for him, since the stairs were narrow, with a bend, and the doctor had said to keep the leg straight in its makeshift splint and to bump it as little as possible.

Only now did Jared show signs of returning to consciousness. 'I'll need someone to help me here in case he struggles,' Jessie decided. 'You'll be needed at the camp, Simon, I know.' She stared at Jane, who was too small to be of use, then her face cleared. 'Is your dad working today?'

'No, ma'am.'

'Then check that Richard's all right in his cot and run for your dad. And tell him to put clean clothes on and wash his hands. The doctor said Mr Wilde's leg must be kept still and also clean, so we're not having any dirty people near him. Tell your dad I'll pay him day rates.'

Only when everyone had gone rushing off to do her bidding did she sag for a moment against the bed. But Jared stirred, so she straightened her shoulders and went to sit by him. She held his hand in hers and kept a damp cloth on his forehead to cover the graze and keep him cool. 'You're not losing that leg,' she promised him. 'I'll make sure of that.'

When he regained consciousness, half an hour later, they had to hold him down for a few moments until he had gathered his wits together. Then Jessie told him what had happened, for he could remember nothing at all about the accident.

'My leg!' he said harshly, terror in his face. 'Is my leg going to be all right?'

Jessie summoned up a smile. 'If we take care, yes, though it'll be badly scarred. So for once, you'll do as you're told, Jared Wilde.' She nodded to Mr Dawson to leave them alone. 'Thank you for your help. You can wait in the kitchen now, ready for when I need you again to help me lift him.'

'Are you sure you're telling me everything?' Jared demanded, keeping hold of her hand.

She weighed things up, but knew he would not be put off with smooth phrases.

'The doctor wanted to take your lower leg off, in case of gangrene. But I said you'd risk gangrene to keep it. So we've got to keep it clean and still so it can heal.'

He looked at her and managed a smile. 'I bet you had to face him out over that. He's an arrogant old fart.'

'I did. And I'm going to prove him wrong.'

'That's my girl.' He closed his eyes and said in a bewildered voice, 'I feel tired.' As his breathing deepened, he squeezed her hand and mumbled, 'Don't leave me, love. I can face anythin' if you're there.'

'I won't leave you.'

It took over a week to be sure that Jared had a good chance of keeping his leg, a week of anxiety every time Jessie dressed it. Mr Dawson helped her move the patient as needed and thought himself in clover with such an easy job and wages paid every day.

Jared, who had never spent so much time lying idle, was fretting to be up and doing, but Jessie scolded him sharply when he tried to get out of bed one day.

The doctor radiated disapproval every time he came on his daily visit and still foretold disaster each day. Jessie wasn't sure he was really pleased that the leg had remained healthy.

The baby seemed to know that something was wrong and fretted, chewing his fingers and wailing for his mother as he never had before. In the end, she brought him into the parlour-cum-sick room and let him roll about on a rug beside the bed.

Jared didn't seem to mind. He was quite easy with Richard now, but she knew, she couldn't help knowing, that he still kept a mental distance from his son. It was the only blot on her horizon, or it would be, once Jared had recovered.

Simon came back every day from the diggings, exhausted. It was as if the accident had been a catharsis for some deep-buried elemental spite in the ground, for once the spill had been cleaned up, things went well again. More than well.

Billy and an older man called Frank were doing a better job than had been expected filling in for Jared. 'It takes two of them to do what you did, and they're not quite as good as you, even so, but you'll be pleased with how they're coping, I think,' Simon told Jared, who was well enough now to insist on hearing all the details of what was happening every night after dinner.

'We've been lucky this time,' Jessie said one evening when the two of them were alone together, 'but I'll tell you frankly, I don't like the idea of you going back to work on those slopes.'

Jared looked at her, his face serious. 'A person can drop dead any time, or catch a fever, or be knocked down by a carriage. No one is ever safe, love.'

'No. But a shop would be a lot safer than this life.'

'An' I'd go mad working indoors.'

She nodded and picked up the baby. She had known he wouldn't even consider anything else, not till he'd had his fill of the railways anyway, and perhaps that day would never come, but she'd had to try. 'Here, you take him. He's restless today and I have a lot to do. You can have him on the bed with you while I get on with things a bit.'

She was doing this regularly now, forcing him to look after the baby, hoping to forge a bond between the two of them, but it didn't seem to be working. She would find a way, though. She had come so far that she would surely manage the rest. She wasn't having her son brought up with a father who paid him no attention. Even as a child, she had always vowed that her children would be loved, openly loved, not like she had been.

She rolled up her sleeves and began to change the sheets on Simon's bed upstairs, thumping the pillows and the feather overlay that covered the mattress to fluff them up, venting her worries on them. She *would* find a way.

35

August 1839

*I*t was a warm August day. In the garden, Mr Dawson was clearing the beds at the front, ready to plant some flowers. Next door, someone had lit a bonfire and the smell of smoke drifted across the fence.

In the parlour, Jared was sitting on the sofa with his injured leg stretched out along it, trying to hide his irritation at this long convalescence. Three weeks already, and more to wait before he could start doing things again. He felt as if he would go mad, lying around all day like this.

Jessie smiled at him, not fooled at all. 'It's a good sign.'

'What is?'

'You getting so restless.'

He pulled her closer for a quick kiss. 'Woman, half my frustration is because I can't bed you as you deserve.'

She sat on the edge of the sofa, her hand in his. 'I love you, Jared Wilde.'

'An' I love you.' His voice was husky. Every day, it struck him anew how close he had come to losing her. Every day, he breathed a prayer of thanks that she had stayed with him. And every single day, he told her how much he cared for her.

A little later, she carried Richard in and laid him on the sofa next to Jared. 'Here, you can help me by looking after your son. I have to go into the village. It's market day.'

'Open that window before you go, will you? It's too warm to be shut away from the fresh air.'

She pulled a face. 'Everything will smell of smoke. I don't know where Mr Thomas next door finds all that stuff to burn.'

Jared grinned. 'Perhaps he just likes making bonfires? He's getting too old to do much else but potter round the garden.'

She did as he'd asked, then walked briskly out.

A little later Jared began to feel sleepy – he had never slept so much in his whole life – and took the baby into his lap. Richard, who had just been kicking and waving his arms about wildly, amusing his father with his panting efforts at exercise, settled there and soon his head began to nod, so Jared allowed himself to sink into a nap, as well.

He woke a little while later to find the room filled with smoke and Richard struggling and coughing in his arms. The curtains were well ablaze and an armchair near them had also caught fire. Jared pushed himself awkwardly to his feet, yelling, 'Jane! Jane!' but no one came.

Clutching the baby to him, he grabbed at the furniture and gasped as pain shot through his injured leg. Like Richard he could not help coughing, for smoke was billowing round them. Even as he watched, the flames leaped from one piece of furniture to another and Jared exclaimed in shock. He had not realised fire could spread so fast.

Grunting with the effort, he managed to hobble slowly towards the door, clutching Richard to his chest. As he fumbled to open it, he felt a wave of dizziness and realised that the baby had stopped struggling and was coughing more weakly now. He had to concentrate, concentrate. He must not let the smoke overpower him. He could hardly see what he was doing, so thick was the smoke, and grunted in relief as his fumbling fingers found the handle.

He yanked so hard that the door banged open and he nearly fell over. The flames inside the room roared even more hungrily in the sudden draught of air. Jared cursed and concentrated on putting one foot in front of the other, tediously, slowly and painfully, holding on to the door frame. When he was in the hall, he hesitated, then turned and risked another painful step backwards to pull the door closed. It might hold the flames in a little longer.

'*Jane! Jane!*' Where the hell was that girl?

She appeared at the back of the hall and screamed at the sight of him.

As she opened her mouth to scream again, he cut in, his voice hoarse with the smoke, 'The parlour's on fire. Go and get help. I'll carry Richard out.'

She clapped one hand to her mouth, then turned and rushed off.

Jared concentrated on limping down the hallway, the pain a living presence that dragged at him with every step. When he got to the kitchen doorway, he bumped into Mr Dawson, who was rushing in with a bucket that slopped water everywhere.

Jared grabbed at the man to stop him rushing towards the parlour. 'Never mind that. The fire's caught hold. You go up to the bedroom and fetch down the tin box from under the bed.'

Mr Dawson looked at him numbly, mouth open as if he didn't understand what was being said.

'Go an' get that bloody box! Black. It's under the bed,' Jared roared. All their savings were in it, banknotes as well as coins. Without the money, they'd be in serious trouble with the contract. He breathed a sigh of relief as Mr Dawson dropped the bucket and began to run up the stairs. 'Nearly there now, lad,' he told his son. 'Nearly there.'

His foot slipped in the puddle of water and he groaned aloud. For a minute he could only stand in the doorway and wait for the pain to subside.

The kitchen seemed almost normal, except for the strong smell of smoke. But behind him he could hear the flames roaring as they hungrily consumed the front of the house. He had not realised how loud a fire could be. Or how the smoke hurt your throat.

As he reached the outer door of the kitchen, Mr Dawson stumbled into it from the hall, holding something out to show him. 'Is this it? 'Cos if it isn't, I'm not going up them bloody stairs again! The fire's in the hall now.'

It was an effort to focus his tear-filled smoke-stung eyes on what the other man was holding out and Jared had to blink several times. As the object came into focus, he sighed in relief. 'Yes, that's it. Now help me outside, then see if you can save anything from in here.'

Even as he was speaking, two other men rushed inside, men he knew by sight. 'We'll get you out!' they yelled, and made a chair of their hands to carry him. Jared clung to the baby and let them stagger outside with him, then take him in a wheelbarrow to a bench across the other side of the back garden and dump him unceremoniously on it. He had never felt so helpless in his life.

'You'll not stop the fire. See if you can save owt,' he ordered. 'An' you put that box down next to me, Dawson, then go an' help.' In spite of the pain, relief coursed through him. They had the money. That was the most important thing – after the boy.

After the boy!

He sat there frozen with that realisation, staring down at his son, who had stopped coughing and was staring solemnly back at him. My son's safe, he thought. My son. For several long moments, they held one another's gaze and the world seemed to narrow down to just the two of them.

Jared suddenly remembered a day from his own childhood when he'd been carrying his little brother Sean down a country lane. The baby had been laughing up at him and his mother had been walking beside him, holding the hands of his two little sisters. Before she fell ill, they'd been happy, hungry sometimes, but happy. How had he forgotten so much about his family?

He bent to plant a kiss on his son's smoke-stained cheek. The resemblance between Richard and little Sean was very marked. Why had he not seen that before? He studied his son's face. Yes, the lad was very much a Wilde. Big already. And you couldn't mistake those eyes, or the shape of the ears. Even the colour of the hair, which was thick for a baby.

A sob forced itself up his throat, then another. How could he have denied the child? *His son!* How could he? Near the house, men were shouting, carrying things outside, then rushing back for more, but Jared just sat there, tears rolling down his cheeks, hugging his lad to his chest.

It was there that Jessie found them. She panted across the

garden to fling herself down on the bench and try to hug the two of them at once. 'You're safe! Oh, Jared, Jared, you're both safe! When they said the house was on fire, I dropped everything and ran.'

'I got him out,' Jared said. 'Oh, hell, Jessie, I thought for a minute we were going to be killed, those flames spread so quickly. But I got him out.' He hugged the child to him. 'I got our lad out.'

She looked at him incredulously, joy coursing through her. That was love in his voice, love in every action – love for his son.

He looked at her and blinked, then said in a quiet, shaking voice: 'Me an' the lad are fine, we're fine. I've only just realised – he looks like my brother Sean did when he was a baby.'

'Does he?' She could hardly speak for the joy and tears were mingled, clogging her throat as well as making her feel light-headed.

Jared continued, the words pouring out of him and a half-smile on his face, 'Yes. An' I daresay he'll grow up to be just as much trouble as our Sean was, into everything.' He shifted the weight of the child and put one arm round her. 'But we'll sort him out, eh? We'll keep him in order.'

She could not mistake the fondness in his face and stretched up to kiss him, her tears joining with his. 'Oh, Jared, you're a lovely, lovely man.'

And although they had lost nearly everything in the fire, they both looked so happy that folk stopped to stare at them.

When Mrs Dawson came pushing through the crowd with Jessie's shopping bag, followed by Jane, who kept staring back over her shoulder in horror at the blazing house, Jessie gave them a beaming welcome.

'I don't know how you can sit there smiling at a time like this, I really don't.' Like her daughter, Mrs Dawson kept turning to gape at the house, which was ablaze now from top to bottom.

'We're alive,' Jessie told her. Then sharing another loving glance with Jared, she added, 'That's the most important thing in the world. The three of us are alive and well.'

Jane and her mother exchanged glances, but did not say anything.

* * *

Four weeks later, Jared was well enough for them to make the trip to Shilwick to stay with Agnes and John Marley for a few days.

'You look happier than last time I saw you,' Agnes said abruptly, as she and her daughter were bathing the gurgling, splashing baby.

'I am.'

'What were wrong before?'

'Jared couldn't settle to being a father. I want – I want my children to have a good father, not like mine.'

Agnes fiddled with the edge of the soft towel. 'I – have something to tell you myself.'

'Oh, yes?' Jessie grabbed her wet, slippery son, who had nearly wriggled out of her hands.

'I'm – you're going to have a brother or sister.' Agnes went bright red.

Utter silence, then Jessie hugged her mother, the wet child squashed between them. 'Oh, what wonderful news.' Richard roared his indignation at this treatment and she took a step backwards.

Agnes was still pink. 'It's been a bit of a shock. I thought – thought I was past all that.'

'How does John feel about it?'

'He was so shocked at first that he couldn't speak.' Agnes giggled suddenly. 'Then he was so pleased he couldn't stop smiling for days.'

Jessie hugged her again for good measure. 'That means Richard will be older than his uncle.'

'John's asking your Jared at the moment if he'll be godfather.'

'I'm sure he'll say yes. Oh, I'm so happy for you!'

'I'm happy myself.' For John was a wonderful husband and their life together was more than she had ever hoped for in her wildest dreams.

When Jared came back, looking pleased with himself, Jessie went to put her arms round him. 'Did John tell you the news?'

'He did.' He chuckled and bent closer to whisper, 'I never saw anyone so set up with himself. You'd think there'd never been a baby made before.'

'He'd given up hope of a family, I think.'

'An' your mother's looking years younger. But she was never as beautiful as you, love.'

'Never mind "beautiful". I don't think I've ever been so happy in all my life,' Jessie said softly, leaning into his arms.

He kissed her soft cheek, then her lips, then looked very solemnly into her eyes. 'And I'll do my best to see that you stay happy, love. You and our Richard.' He grinned. 'And another half dozen like him.'

'Cheek!' She pretended to thump him, then they lost themselves in a kiss. If they went on like this, it wouldn't be long before Richard had a little brother, she thought dreamily. Or sister.

Salem Street

ANNA JACOBS

In 1820 Salam Street is sparkling and new: eight small terraced houses built by a Lancashire mill owner for his best workers. Annie Gibson's family is one of the first to move in – a step up in the world for them. But when her mother dies, Annie's happy childhood ends and she is left to bring up her brother and sister.

Red-haired, intelligent and startlingly pretty, Annie soon finds herself banished from home by a jealous stepmother. She finds work in the local doctor's household where she learns about the fascinating world outside Salam Street. And when her adored childhood friend, Matt, asks her to marry him Annie thinks her dreams are coming true.

But suddenly everything turns upside-down. Abandoned and pregnant, Annie returns to Salem Street, where an unexpected offer gives her independence. One day, she vows, she will move into the wider world again. One day . . .

SALAM STREET is a heartwarming saga in the great tradition of Catherine Cookson and Josephine Cox.

HODDER AND STOUGHTON PAPERBACKS

High Street

ANNA JACOBS

In 1845 Annie Gibson can finally leave Salem Street. Her dreams of being able to open an elegant dress-making salon in the High Street of Bilsden, a Lancashire mill town, have come true. And she is going to take her father and his second family with her, away from poverty, away from the Rows.

But Annie has not left trouble behind. Someone is trying to undermine her business. Her family have their own ideas about what to do with their lives. And several men are persistently trying to win favour with the beautiful young widow – including Frederick Hallam, the mill owner, and Daniel O'Connor, her childhood friend.

As Annie gets better acquainted with both, she becomes increasingly confused about her feelings. Can she really be in love? And can she risk trusting any man again?

Don't miss the first volume in the Gibson family saga, *SALEM STREET*, also available from Coronet Books.

HODDER AND STOUGHTON PAPERBACKS

Ridge Hill

ANNA JACOBS

It's 1848 and preparations are underway for Annie Gibson's wedding to Bilsden's wealthy mill owner, Frederick Hallam. But not everyone is as pleased as they are.

Frederick's daughter, Beatrice, is horrified at the prospect of a new attractive stepmother arriving at the house on Ridge Hill and decides to make life as difficult as possible for her. Even Annie's own family feels threatened – because she now expects them to mingle with the rich folk of the town. Only Tom, Annie's brother, is thrilled and determines to enjoy the fact that the richest man in town has become his brother-in-law.

But after a while, real troubles begin to pile up for the Gibsons. Tom's happiness is jeopardised by the news that he is the father to a child he never knew about. Annie's son, William, is devastated to find out that his real father is not the man who brought him up. And even Annie's joy cannot last. Because someone has uncovered secrets which she has fought so hard to keep hidden.

HODDER AND STOUGHTON PAPERBACKS